I0766928

K. A. KNIGHT
WRITING THE MONSTERS YOU LOVE TO HATE.

The Cities

Their Champion Book Three

K.A. Knight

N
WORSHIPPERS
OF THE SUN
THE FORGOTTEN
THE
LOST
PARADIS
TOWN OF
SPRING
DEAD
SEA
THE
WASTELAND
THEIR CHAMPION SERIES

BERSERKERS
THE RING
THE SEEKERS
REEVES
THE RIM
DEAD SEA
THE CITIES

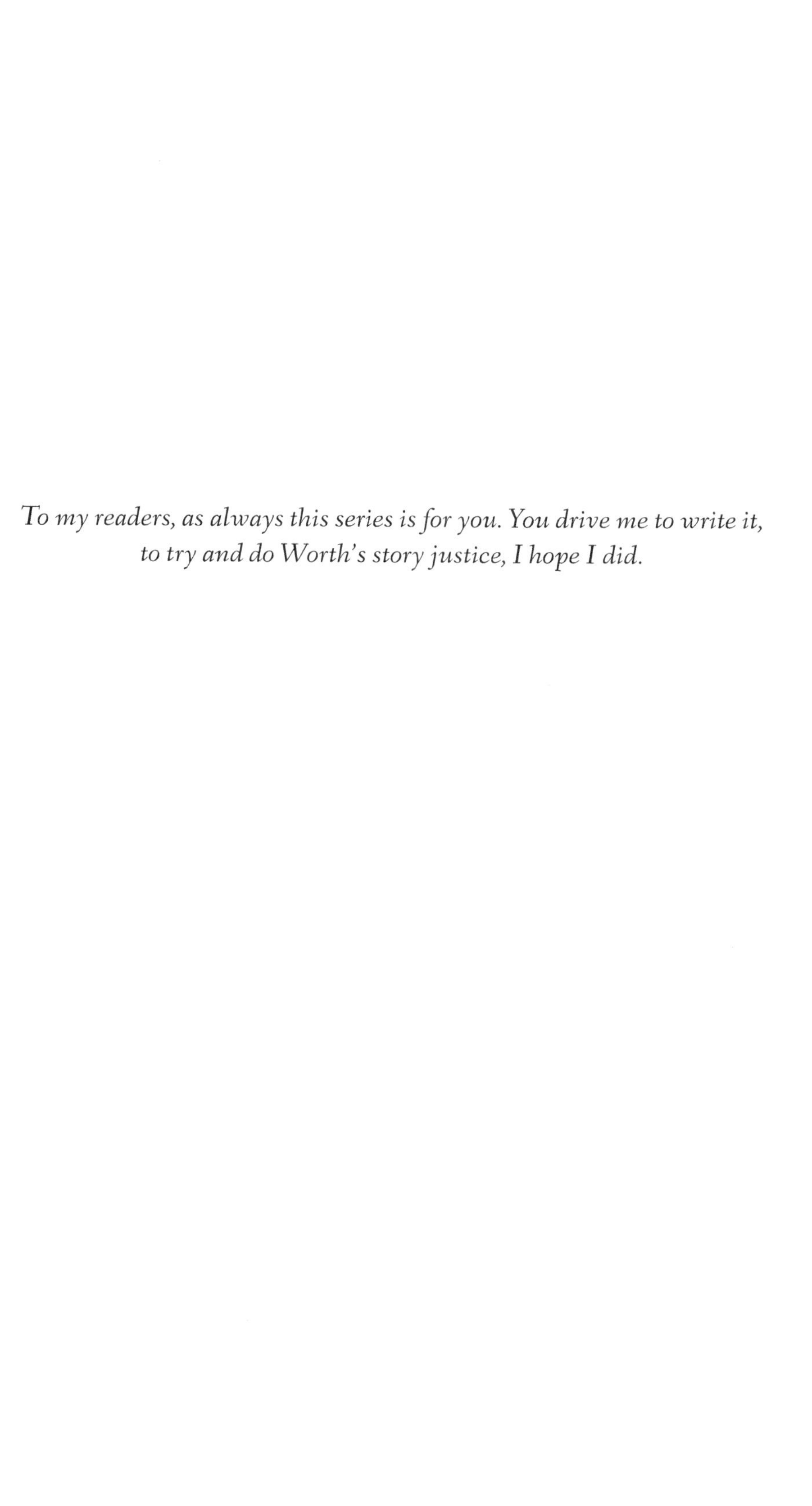

To my readers, as always this series is for you. You drive me to write it, to try and do Worth's story justice, I hope I did.

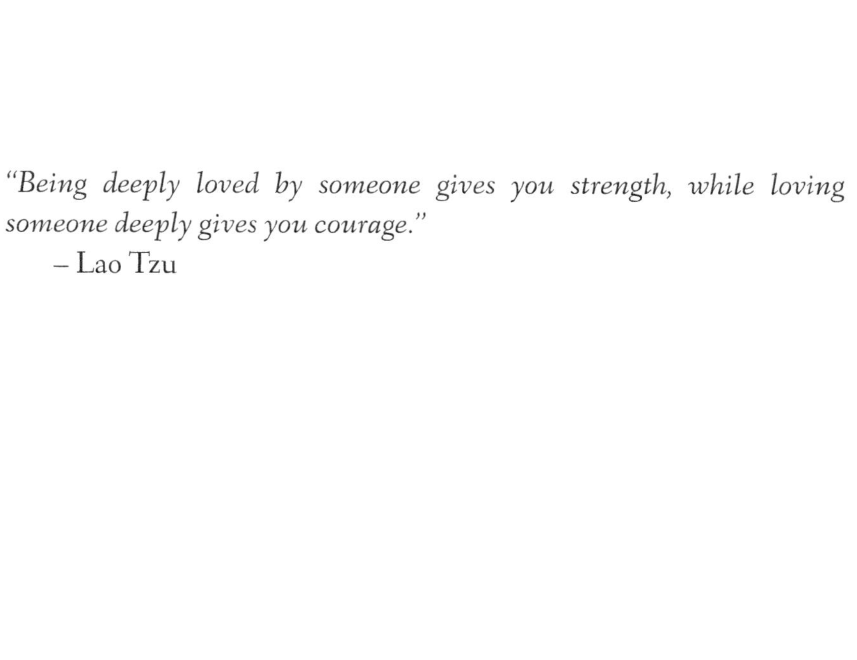

"Being deeply loved by someone gives you strength, while loving someone deeply gives you courage."
– Lao Tzu

Chapter One

BLOODBATH

Blood splatters across my face, dripping into my parted mouth, and I quickly spit it onto the dying man, not wanting any part of him in me. He groans loudly, the sword protruding from his back as his hands scramble to get a grip on the stone floor of the throne room before he attempts to crawl away. I look over at Dray next to me with an arched eyebrow to see him grinning madly, watching the man.

"How far do you think he will get?" I ask calmly, glancing back at the man who is making painfully slow progress as he drags his limp body over the floor. I scoff when I notice he's heading toward the door to the throne room. Really? Does he think he will get away? What a fucking idiot.

"I say a quarter of the way before you get bored and kill him," Dray replies with a shrug, grinning at me as he strokes his blades across his chest, those ice-blue eyes heating as he watches me.

"I say halfway before you kill him so you can fuck me," I retort, with a smile curving my lips.

"What's the winner get, soulmate?" he purrs, his eyes heating as they flicker over my body.

"A king or a queen." I grin and he laughs, the sound loud in the stone room.

All of the gathered Berserkers and Seekers are now leaning against the walls or filling the tables, enjoying the show. Bloodthirsty lot, they are... I guess I am too. Ivar's body is still to the side of the throne, a reminder of what happens to those who hurt me and mine.

A slice of panic cuts through me at the thought of what The Cities are doing to my men right now, but I push it away. I'm a queen now and I can't afford to be weak. Besides, they have survived there before, so they can survive there again. I know it. At least until I get them free—and I fucking will—and kill anyone who dared hurt them. But first, I have some cleaning up to do. We are heading for war, I can feel it in the air. A line has been drawn in the sand and I need to make sure I can trust the men on either side of me. Some of these Berserkers helped and enjoyed torturing, raping, and killing people. They will die for their past crimes, here and now. I won't give them a chance to betray me or stab me in the back. No fucking way.

I look back down at the man, who hasn't made much progress towards the door, seeing the trail of blood behind him.

Sands below, he is taking a long time. Can't he just die already?

He's a tough fucker, I'll give him that. He sort of looks like a tortoise... with a sword protruding from its back.

He had tried to run at me, thinking he could do what? I don't fucking know, but I swatted him away like a fly and then stabbed him. The gathered warriors know who I am, know what I can do, and they don't bother to help. For fuck's sake, I just killed Ivar the Destroyer while he sat with his limp dick on the throne. This simple man thought he could take me? What an idiot.

"Fuck this," I grumble, already bored and filled with an urgency to race to The Cities, even though I can't.

As I cover the short distance between us, I hear him crying. With no fanfare, I place my booted foot on the sword and press down until he's skewered to the floor. He stops moving and blood pools around him.

"Guess I get a queen, soulmate," Dray calls, and I flip him off without looking.

"Anybody else want to challenge me?" I shout, my voice echoing around the room. I really hope someone does, I could use a way to burn some of this worry and energy off, if not in a fight then at least I can take it out on Dray. The sick bastard would love it.

"You're no queen, ya a fuckin' slave whore!" a rumbling voice yells, as a mountain of a man steps forward. Instantly, all the men surrounding him step away, creating an empty gap around him like they don't want to be associated with him. Smart move.

"You're big." I nod, and he starts to grin, his wide, sweaty, meaty face breaking into a crooked, yellow-toothed smile until my next words stop him. "I've fought and fucked bigger." I chuckle and laughter echoes from the men gathered around the room.

With a roar he charges at me, and I watch him move, analysing for weak spots. He's big, a fucking solid hitter. One smack from him and I'll be out cold, but he is slow, really fucking slow, so slow I have time to reach down, pull the sword out of the dead man, and sprint forward. He falters for a moment before heading towards me, and at the last possible second, I drop to my knees, sliding through his legs and lifting the sword at the same time, gutting him.

I roll when I'm through and flip to my feet to watch him as he stumbles, letting out a low whistle when he looks down at his guts spilling out onto the floor.

"Fucking—" He doesn't finish his sentence as he topples over, his head landing just before my feet. Looking up at the crowd, I see some grinning, some appearing terrified, and others appearing downright angry.

"Cunt!" someone calls, and I whip around but Dray is already in motion.

He moves like silk to the wall where everyone is backing away from the man who must have shouted. As the enraged Seeker King faces him, the man looks like he's going to piss his pants…oh wait, he just did. In one smooth move, Dray slides around the man and slits his throat, letting him fall to the floor as blood splatters across his chest. This man wears blood the same way others would wear jewellery. My crazy ass soulmate.

"Does anyone else want to insult my queen?" he growls menacingly, stepping out with a blade in each hand and narrowing his eyes on the gathered crowd. "If I hear one fucking whisper, I will skin you alive and make a coat for her!" he yells.

No one speaks up, in fact, I think a few people physically can't because they're so fucking scared. Dray does make an intimidating sight standing there covered in blood, blades in each hand, and his face carved in cold fury. Me? I'm turned the fuck on.

I never said I wasn't crazy…

Dray nods with a smirk and slides back over to me. Tilting my face up with his blade, he presses the cold, bloody tip of his sword against my chin. "I was promised a queen, unless you want me to get on my knees right here and taste you, I suggest you finish up here quickly."

I resist for a moment, but I know he will do as he says, he doesn't give a fuck. Crazy bastard would probably kill anyone who was unlucky enough not to escape in time and see it happen.

"Where are the slaves?" I ask, needing to free them before Dray has his wicked way with me.

A throat clears, and I look away from Dray and focus on a familiar man—it's the rebel guard I'd met in the hallway. He drops to his knees instantly, tilting his head down as I step closer to him. "Don't kneel for me. I lived my life on my knees, and I won't let anyone else do the same," I say softly. I hear the men closest to us suck in a shocked breath, but the rebel at my feet simply stands with a knowing smile.

"My name is Roan, My Queen."

"The slaves?" I repeat, growing bored. "He killed them," he growls.

My body turns ice-cold and I step closer, fury racing through my body. "What did you say?" I query quietly, deadly.

"Ivar had them all killed last night... He was going to take you to the room and show them all off. I'm sorry, My Queen," he whispers, with fear in his eyes. We are on the same side, but he stood there and did nothing as innocents were slaughtered? Obviously reading the question in my eyes, he hurries to explain, "None of the rebels were in the castle, we were out meeting with others to figure out a way to get you free. When we got back we found out—" He stops, swallowing hard, sweat breaking out across his brow.

I step back and flicker a look over the uneasy crowd. "Who?" I call loudly, and they share looks.

"Who?" someone repeats in confusion.

"Who killed the slaves? I want them before me...*now!*" I scream, gripping my sword in my hand as I prowl down the lengths. "Who killed the innocents? *Who*?" My fury echoes around the walls.

"We were ordered to," someone fires back.

"So? You could have said no. You could have not done it. The guards who followed those orders made a *choice* to. They killed women and children on a mad man's whim just to keep themselves alive," I growl.

"She's right," a big man calls. "We neva hurt tha kiddies or tha women, we didnee stop it, but we never did it by our hands, Ma Queen. I kna a few of them," he offers hesitantly, treading forward.

"Bring them to me," I order, before stepping back. I feel Dray behind me, his warmth centering me as guilt and hate roll through me.

I know Ivar killed the slaves to get a reaction out of me. Their blood is on my hands. Just another of Ivar's games. Even when he's dead, he still manages to deal a crippling blow.

"What are you going to do, soulmate?" Dray rumbles.

"Kill anyone who touched the slaves. Then, I will find that room and lay them to rest. I need to see their faces. They died because of me, because of Ivar's game. I need to do this. I can't change what happened, but I will not fucking let their deaths go unavenged," I vow.

"That's my girl," he whispers.

Chapter Two

FINAL GAME

"Ma Queen," the big man calls, and I focus back on him to see him dragging two men kicking and fighting over to me. He drops them on the floor at my feet, and I look at the big man with an arched eyebrow. He is huge. He reminds me of those giants my dad used to tell me about in stories—all muscle and so massive, I have to tilt my head back to meet his gaze.

"Can anyone confirm these men killed the slaves?" I yell, and three men step forward, all with grim expressions.

"Yes," one says.

"I heard Ivar give them the order," the other replies, and when I look at the third, I can see the pain in his eyes.

"I saw them," he offers softly. "I couldn't—" He looks away, swallowing hard before steeling himself and facing me once again. "I saw them. I was ordered to watch."

"Why?" I find myself asking.

His eyes spit fire, and they're filled with so much pain and hate.

"One of them...I loved her," he rasps, his lips thinning as he bites on them.

"I'm sorry," I whisper. He nods and steps back, staring at the men at my feet.

"Were there any others?" I question him. "No, just those two," he confirms.

Crouching down to the level of the men who are on their knees in front of me, I grin. The one on the left spits at me and it hits my cheek. Keeping my eyes on him, I reach up and wipe it away. "For that, you will not die quickly." He just glares at me.

"Now, do you admit you killed the slaves?" I inquire almost pleasantly. My body is itching to kill them, calling for their blood, to make them pay.

I look between them. The one on the left who spat on me is a skinny man, almost too skinny, but it's clear he was born like that. He has long, ratty hair, which I'm pretty sure has never seen water or a brush, and his nose is crooked from being broken one too many times. His eyes are dirt brown and dead looking.

The man on the right almost appears normal, classically handsome even. He has bright blue eyes, filled with warmth and life, pink plush lips, and high cheekbones. That beauty alone makes me falter. I never trust anyone that beautiful. He doesn't even have a mark or scar on him. If he has made it through this life with no scars, he's a fucking monster. It tells me he will do whatever it takes to stay alive, to protect himself above all others. He has no allegiances and he can't be trusted. Just by looking at him, his eyes, his body language... I can tell he enjoyed torturing and killing the slaves. And I know he'd do it again. I also know, as his mouth opens, he's going to spout nothing but charming lies.

"Of course not! He must have me mixed up, My Queen. I know it's hard to believe that they confused me with someone else, seeing how I am so much better looking than all these barbarians. But, then again, they aren't the smartest." He winks at me, a smirk curling up at his lips like he thinks he has me. Oh, how very wrong he is. I would prefer a monster with horns and blood covering him, because at least

I'd know where I stand. This...this man is nothing but a very good liar.

"You forget one thing," I whisper seductively, leaning closer to him, and I see his eyes flare in satisfaction.

"What's that, My Queen?" he purrs.

"I'm the fucking barbarian queen," I murmur in a velvety voice, before I snap his head to the side and bite down on his flesh. Ripping my mouth away, I take a hunk of skin with me, hearing a 'pop' as I go. Blood fills my mouth, and I spit his skin and gore onto the floor in front of him as he screams and falls back, clutching his bleeding neck and looking at me in pale horror. All that charm falls away and shows me the frightened little boy he'd kept buried deep. He is used to his charm working...but he can't fool this monster.

"You-you fucking bitch!" he screams, as blood drips steadily down his throat.

I grin then, knowing my chin and teeth are coated in his blood, and I turn my gaze to the other man who holds it defiantly.

"You don't scare me, little girl. I lived with Ivar for years. I have seen things that would scare you shitless," he snaps.

"Oh, I don't doubt it. Ivar always was creative," I murmur. "Do you admit to killing the slaves?" I ask again.

"Yes," he spits again. "I had my fun first too. Those fucking bitches screamed until the end, thinking someone would save them." He laughs then and I nod, before standing up. I look at the man from before, the one who was made to watch his love be tortured and killed.

"Take your pick." I gesture at the men and his eyes go wide before filling with satisfaction and bloodlust.

"Him." He nods at the sobbing man still holding his neck. "He killed her."

"He's yours."

The man still bleeding on the floor freezes at that, and glances back at the encroaching guard. All that sadness for his lost love has been wiped away and in its place is hate. He looks every bit the Berserker warrior as he prowls to the injured man on the floor.

"Stand up, I won't kill a man on his knees, not even a worm like you," he growls.

The other man, still on his knees, starts laughing, so I whip out my fist, knocking him sideways to the floor. He groans as he cups his cheek, and I wave my hand at the avenging guard to proceed. The beautiful man, the worm, gets to his feet, still clutching his bleeding neck, and faces the Berserker.

"She loved it," he gargles with a smirk.

I don't even know where the Berserker produced the blade from, but the next thing I know, there's one sticking out of the worm's chest and his mouth is opening and closing as blood bubbles there. The worm looks down at his chest in shock before slowly falling to his knees, his eyes unfocused and draining of life until he tips sideways and sprawls across the stone floor. We all watch him die. Not a single man steps forward to try and stop us. They knew what would happen. You don't hurt a Berserker, you kill them or they will only come back stronger than before, fighting through the pain and fire until they get their revenge. They are warriors, fighters, and I am honoured to be one of them right now.

Turning to the other man, I grab his shoulder and haul him to his feet, making him meet my gaze. I will use him to send a message—anyone who followed Ivar or who wants to live the way Ivar did will die by my hand. There's been enough blood and suffering, it's time we become the clan we're meant to be.

"Anyone wanting to kill, rape, or torture better leave now, because I will find you. That is not the way this clan will be. We are warriors, we are bred to fight, we survived the scorch and this dead world, and we will be reborn in the flames once again. Mark my words, Berserkers, break my rules and face my blade," I yell, before I cut the man's throat—not a nice way to die. I don't cut too deep, that would be too quick, no, he will suffer. I might not be able to torture people like Ivar did, but I won't let this man's death be quick, not for his crimes.

I watch him die, we all do. As he chokes on his own blood, he tries to hold it in but it seeps through his fingers until he falls at my feet... dead. Then, I meet every eye in here, letting them see how serious I am. I'm giving them a choice. We can be better, we can be part of this world again, join the other clans, stop this fighting, and heed the outcome of the Summit and the lives lost for this.

"Take me to the room, take me to their bodies," I order the Berserker who is still watching the man he killed. I point at the giant man as well. "You, come with us," I say, then I turn to the rebels. "You are in charge while I'm gone. Let who wants to leave do so. Contact the rebels and The Ring, and tell them I am coming." I turn away then, striding from the room, but at the doorway I stop to look back at the rebels. "Oh, and throw his body to the ferals." I grin, flicking a look back at Ivar's corpse. With that, I storm from the room with the Berserkers and Dray on my heels, trepidation worming through me. What I am going to see now is bad, Ivar's parting gift to me, but I know I can face it. I have survived most of my life at his hands, and I can survive their deaths at it.

The room is actually Ivar's torture room above the cells. As soon as I see it, I turn away. "I need to release my friend first," I mutter, having completely forgot about Evan for a moment. They follow after me and I find Evan standing at the bars with a furious expression on his face.

"Worth, what the fuck! I thought you were dead!" he screams, rattling the bars. "Get me out of here."

I nod at the giant Berserker, and he unlocks the cell door and swings it open. Evan pours out and stops behind me with a nervous look at the others, but he seems to relax when he spots Dray. "Ah, so you killed him?" he questions, and then and there he earns more of my respect. He didn't ask Dray, he asked me.

"Course I did. I've got to go bury Ivar's final gift, then we rest here tonight. Tomorrow, we are heading out," I inform him.

"Where to?" he grumbles.

"Paradise, I need my father's help with something. I will fill you in there, go get some rest. There are rebels upstairs, tell them I sent you," I demand, turning away as I head back up the stone steps to the room with the closed red door. I stop outside, hesitating.

"No, I'll stay with you," Evan growls, and I shrug, not warning him about what lies on the other side of this door. He will have seen worse by now...right? Or maybe I am too jaded.

Reaching for the handle, I quickly push it open before I change my mind. The smell hits me first. It might have been less than a day, but that many bodies and blood...yeah. It punches me square in the face and I have to quickly swallow. It doesn't smell like fucking daisies out in the Wastes, but I will never get used to the smell of rotting corpses. Anyone that says they can is a psychopath.

Not wanting to look weak in front of the Berserkers, I hold my chin up and step into the room. The lights are burning in each corner, illuminating the horrifying sight as I stop just inside the door and stare. My gaze swings from side to side, taking it all in.

There is so much blood.

I can almost feel the pain in the room, and every time my eyes land on glassy dead eyes in one of the slaves' skulls I cringe. There has to be twenty of them in here, all women ranging in age from young children to adults. Every single one dead, naked, and covered in blood. They weren't killed quickly, they suffered, and now I know why Ivar would have brought me here. He would have made me walk around each body, telling me what they did to her as he forced me to kneel and watch, and after? He would have done those things to me, not killed me of course, but everything else. It's the exact same thing he did the last time I was in the castle with him, before I won my freedom.

The Cities

I hear someone gagging, and I glance over my shoulder to see Evan. He's as pale as a ghost and looking like he might faint, yet his eyes can't seem to move from the bodies. "What the fuck?" he yells and turns away, gagging again.

"Ivar," I whisper, looking back over the room. "Once he realised that whatever he did to my body wouldn't break me anymore, he got good at using others. He liked to play with his slaves, he liked to hurt them," I admit, my words sending me tumbling back into my own memories.

"This can all stop, pet, you just need to scream for me," Ivar taunts and laughs.

I clamp my lips shut, my eyes locked on the girl hanging from the ceiling. Her hands are shackled together and tied to the chain dangling from above, her feet dusting the floor slightly. Her head is lowered, her long brown hair covering her face and the blood I know that's there. We have been here for three hours. Ivar killed the first girl in the first hour. Her name was Kit. I don't know this slave's name, she is new.

"Scream for me," he whispers gravely in my ear.

My head is locked into a wheelchair one of the warriors found on a raid. It has a clamp, which goes around my head so I can't move, preventing me from looking away from the horrors before me. My hands are nailed to the chair arms, my blood running down the side. My ankles are bound by barbed wire, meaning every time I move it tightens and cuts into my skin more. My pain here isn't the main focus, no, that was an afterthought. Today is all about my mind. Again and again he keeps trying to break me, it has become a game now. One I will win, but today...today is testing that resolve.

"No?" Ivar sighs, standing back up from where he was crouching next to me.

He wanders back over to the girl, turning sideways so he can see me as he grabs her hair and yanks her head back. Her eyes are dazed and set in pain, and blood is smeared across her cheeks and lips. Her eyes lock on me. "What shall I do to you?" he murmurs, and the girl starts to struggle. Wincing, I try to look away, but I can't.

Ivar leans over, letting go of the girl's hair, and rips away her tattered bloodstained shirt. My breathing picks up as her breasts are exposed to the cold air. No, no, no, please not again. She starts to sob then, her whole body shaking.

"Please! Please, leave me alone!" she begs.

"What do you think, pet? It's your choice," he calls, mocking laughter leaving his lips as she struggles.

"Fuck you!" she cries desperately, and I freeze. Oh, shit.

I know before he moves it's going to be bad, but even I'm shocked when he darts forward and bites her nipple. My eyes fly wide as she screams and he jerks back, ripping her nipple away with him before spitting it out on to the floor. Her screaming cuts off as she slumps forward, blood pouring down her chest.

"Still no scream? Guess I need to get creative, pet." He laughs, blood flying from his ruby red lips.

Sands below, please no.

"Soulmate?" Dray calls, and I shake away the memories, all of them fighting for the spotlight in my mind from merely being in this room, but I won't let them. I lived them once, I won't do it again. He's dead, but it doesn't mean his ghost and haunting memories can't hurt me if I let them.

"We need to bury them, there is space on the cliff edge out back." My voice is surprisingly even despite the pain still lingering in my mind.

"I will grab some more men," the big man informs me, and I nod, stepping farther into the room.

My eyes catch on the little girl in the corner. Her light red hair is stained with blood, and although I can't see any wounds, that only makes it worse. A noise catches my attention, and I watch the Berserker drop to his knees next to a pretty blonde-haired woman who is lying on her back with a stab wound above her heart. He grabs her and pulls her to his chest, whispering to her as he rocks her dead body. I look away then, offering him the privacy he deserves as I move through the room, stepping over bodies.

I memorize each face and burn it into my mind. They are my burden to carry and I will do so each and every day. By the time I have circled the room, men are gathered at the doorway. "One body each, cover them and carry them to the cliff. We need shovels. We're going to bury them and give them the respect they deserve!" I yell. They move into the room then and Dray stops next to me.

I grab the little girl, holding her to my chest, her body cold and stiff, but I concentrate on Dray as he grabs a woman and holds her to his chest like a doll. Swallowing hard at the questions in his eyes, I turn away, needing to get away from this room. I barely stop myself from running, and with each step away, I feel a weight lifting. I wish I could burn that room to the fucking ground, but I will settle for their peace in death. The rest of the Berserkers see us as we go and they follow after us. The trek out to the cliff is hard, but each pull and pain in my muscles just reminds me I am alive.

I lay her little body gently on the ground and look over at the crosses already buried here—our graveyard. "Let's get digging!" I shout.

Two hours later, all the bodies are buried, and we had a moment of silence for their deaths. With it, I vowed that they would be the last to suffer in this castle. The walls are filled with echoes of screams and ghosts, and we can never change that, but maybe we can add some good memories here too.

We file back into the castle and the drinking starts early. I notice Ivar's body is gone—good. I slip from the room with Dray on my heels. I might be queen, but I'm used to being by myself and right now I need some space. I feel like I'm about to explode with everything that has happened these last few days. I need a moment to just stop, to think. I freeze in the hallway, unsure where to go. I have no bedroom here, no escape. Most rooms hold pain and suffering for me, so where do I go?

I spot Evan heading downstairs and he stops at the top. "I'm going to sleep in the cells, at least they're familiar. I'll see you in the morning," he tells me and I nod, understanding that. "Oh, and Worth? Glad you didn't die," he shouts, before he turns and leaves Dray and me alone.

Me too. As hard and painful as my life has been, for once I realise I'm glad to be alive. I never feared death before I met my guys, never even thought about it, but facing down Ivar, I had a niggling thought in the back of my mind. If I died, it would hurt them. I have people who care about me now, people who depend on me, and that is

weighing me down. Each word or action I take has to be thought through before I make it. For tonight, I just need to be me.

The Champion.

Not a Berserker Queen, not a slave or a drunk. The Champion.

And tonight, I will have the Seeker I always wanted.

Chapter Three

PAIN IS PLEASURE

No fucking way was I sleeping in Ivar's room. Instead, I find myself outside of the east tower. The west one was destroyed a long time ago, but the east tower still stands strong, the spire reaching into the sky. It's blocked off, the door locked and unused. I snuck up here once and found a forgotten bedroom. Ivar didn't want his men to be that far away from him, and no way was a slave getting a room. One of his men found me and dragged me to Ivar, then he locked the tower after punishing me, but I still remember the glimpse of the room and freedom I found up there.

I can't find the key so I turn to leave, but I blink in shock when Dray rams his shoulder into the door and it breaks open, the old lock clattering to the ground. "You wanted in?" He grins.

"You are a man of many talents, you crazy bastard," I tease. I push the door farther open and head inside, with Dray on my heels. I look over my shoulder to see him moving the door back in place before he turns to follow me.

Stone steps, at least fifty of them, spiral upwards, leading to the tower room. I start to head up the stairs before I hear a grunt and I receive a slap on my arse. "Hurry up, soulmate, before I throw you over my shoulder," Dray growls.

Men.

I roll my eyes but speed up, my legs cramping after being stuck in a cell without much exercise. When we make it to the top, the brown wooden door is standing open so I slip inside and my shoulders relax. Finally. I'm finally away from people and their prying eyes, and I can just take a minute to relax. It's exactly like I remember it, a forgotten gem in the midst of a medieval castle. A large, four-poster canopy bed sits opposite the doorway, pressed against the stone wall with steps leading up to it. The bed is covered in a dusty white sheet, protecting the bedding underneath. This has to be the only room in the whole fucking castle that doesn't have some type of bloodstain somewhere. It also holds no ghosts for me.

Two large, arched windows sit on either side of the bed, looking out across the Wastes. A balcony lies to the left, with wooden shutters covering it, darkening the room. To the right of where I am standing is another doorway, presumably to a bathroom. I glance to the left, spotting an old-fashioned dressing table and mirror, which is the only furniture in the room apart from the low-hanging, useless chandelier.

"I'll go get some torches," Dray murmurs, and before I know it, he's gone.

Stepping farther into the room, I kick off my boots and lay them gently at the bottom of the bed, before heading straight for the balcony shutters. They are a bit stiff from years of disuse, but I manage to pry them open enough so I can step out onto the terrace. A crumbling wall surrounds it, with dead brown vines wrapped around the grey stone. It looks like a piece of the world long forgotten, a place away from the bloodshed and pain. It's just here, existing in the center of it.

Being careful not to rest too heavily on the crumbling wall, I lean out and look upon the wasteland spread out below us. I can see far past the courtyard and ramp into the castle, and the huts for the other warriors, and out into the dust-covered land we call home. It has a dangerous beauty about it, the sun beating down on a world that just won't die. Our people are strong. You have to be to survive here.

What are my men looking at right now? I wonder. Do they see the Waste and think of me like I do them? Or are they prisoners looking at nothing but four walls?

I hear footsteps and without moving too much to give it away, I palm a knife and wait for them to draw closer. When they're near, I spin, pressing my blade against their crotch, and when I see who it is, a smirk crosses my face. Dray grins down at me, moving closer and digging the blade in more.

"We have been in this position before, soulmate. Do you remember what I told you?" he growls.

"That my knife turned you on," I reply with a laugh. He grins then presses closer. "Still does."

"Crazy bastard."

He licks his lips then. "So fucking beautiful." "The view?" I ask, confused.

"No, you in a crown. I told you, you're a fucking queen. I knew it the first moment I saw you. I told Archel you would be mine. But, Taz? I was wrong—I am yours."

"You won a queen," I remind him. "But I'm no queen." I may have played that role earlier, but I am and always will be a warrior, the champion.

He steps closer, obviously sensing that the title makes me uneasy. "I don't give a fuck what you go by—Taz, Queen, Champion, Slave... To me you are just my soulmate."

My heart softens, but a strong mix of desire, urgency, and pain overwhelms me, needing to be let out. A wild lust he can take. I know he can.

"That's sweet, but right now I don't need sweet. I need the man who rips out people's throats with his bare hands. I need you feral. I need to feel alive, to feel pain and your touch. I need to be reminded that everything that happened here is in the past. Please, Dray, remind me," I beg almost urgently. Every time we are together it seems to get violent, but maybe that's exactly what I need from him. I don't turn to Dray for sweet words and love, I turn to him for claiming, ownership, and pain mixed with pleasure.

"Every day, for the rest of our lives," he growls.

He grabs the blade then, wrapping his hands around it, and I stare deep into his eyes. His cold gaze burns through me, and he doesn't even wince as he throws the blade behind him, but I know it had to have cut his palm. He brings his hand up and I sigh, seeing I was right. His palm is slashed and bleeding, dripping down his arm. He laughs then, the sound moving through me, stirring my fight. "This won't be the last drop of blood spilled tonight, soulmate."

We both snap then, bored with words. I want to feel his actions. I want his mouth, cock, and blood like he said. I want him to feel the pain ripping me in half, I want to carve it into his body, I want it all...

I push him back, smashing into his chest until we land heavily on the stone floor. I drop my mouth onto his, biting at his lips, and he growls. He grabs my hips and throws me over his head, and I roll at the last minute, ending up crouched as he flips and stands, prowling towards me. I jump to my feet and back away, farther into the room. He follows after me, looking like a feral animal, his ice-blue eyes locked on my every move. Blood trails behind him from his hand and he still has his blades strapped over his chest.

"Are you running from me, soulmate?" he growls.

"Never. Just getting you exactly where I want you," I taunt, as I spin slightly to the side and he follows, until his back is to the dressing table.

I run at him then and he catches me mid-leap, falling back against the old, wooden table. It creaks under our weight and he smashes back into the mirror with a grunt. The glass shatters and drops around us, no doubt cutting into his back, but it only makes him wilder. He grips my hips and spins us, throwing me into the mirror.

The air is knocked from my lungs and he's on me in an instant. His hand grips my throat, pinning me there as he kicks open my legs and steps between them. "I love it when you fight me," he whispers seductively, licking his lip as he squeezes harder, cutting off my air supply.

I scramble my hands on either side of the dressing table and a shard of glass cuts my finger. I feel along the rough edge and grip it in my palm, cutting it slightly as I bring it up and press the jagged edge to Dray's neck, drawing a drop of blood. He smirks and presses closer, causing a line of blood to drip down his chest. "You want to fight, soulmate? You want to feel that knife's edge of pain and pleasure?"

If I could pant, I would be. Instead, dots dance in my vision and my arm starts to weaken, but I hold the glass there. He is waiting for me to fight. To prove to myself that I'm alive. To fight for it. To fight him. "Do it, soulmate, you are stronger than this. I can take it all, fucking fight."

I start to struggle then as anger burns through me, but it's not enough to get free. He growls, slamming me back harder, my lungs screaming for air. "Fight! Fight like a fucking Berserker. Let me see why you are still alive, why you are a Champion."

With all the effort I have left in my air-starved body, I slice the glass downwards on his chest, and when blood wells instantly, I realise I cut harder than I intended to, but he just laughs.

"Yes, like that!" he growls.

My fingers spasm and I drop the glass to the floor, reaching out to grip his arm and dig my nails in as I wrap my legs around his waist. I drop forward, dislodging us from the dressing table, and he stumbles back, having to let go of my neck to stop us from falling to the floor. I suck in air, coughing from the sudden inhale of oxygen, and spin away from him. He turns with me, watching me as I steady my breathing. He tilts his head, his eyes wild and his chest heaving as blood pools in his belly button. He's wild right now, I know it, and I'm going to fucking *tame* him. He wanted the Champion, he wanted a fight, so he's going to get one.

Maybe I had forgotten who I was, scared of the way people would look at me. But I now know I am a Berserker. A fighter. A woman. I'm powerful, deadly, and I am a fucking queen. He will be mine—my king and my man. His blood, pain, and heart—all mine. But the most important thing he's giving me is myself. He's giving me back my fight, reminding me who I was the day we met. I was a slave with nothing but the will to not fucking die.

My eyes flicker to the bed and a smile turns up the corners of my lips. Still watching him, I step closer and grab the sheet off of it, and rip it down the middle. He watches me as I tie one end around the top left poster of the bed. Crawling across it, I tie the other to the top right before sliding from the bottom of the bed, waiting. Obviously impatient, he prowls towards me, speeding up, and at the last moment I slide to the side, pushing him in the middle of his back. He sprawls onto the bed and I jump onto his back, pinning him. Grabbing his hair, I tilt his head to the side and lean down to whisper in his ear. "You are fucking *mine*."

He growls and bucks until I slide to the side and then he flips. I jump back on him, pressing my knees on either side of his hips as I lean down and kiss him, distracting him. He groans into my mouth, sucking at my tongue, before pulling back and biting down on my lower lip. I reach up as he bites my mouth, bucking beneath me to try and dislodge me again. I drop lower, pressing myself over his groin and we both groan into each other's mouths. My hand touches the edge of the cloth and I grab it, pulling it farther down before tracing down his shoulder to his hand. Gripping both hands, I thrust them upwards, and that's when he starts to struggle, growling into my mouth. I have to let go of one of his hands to tie the other with the cloth, and he takes the opportunity to grip my hip while I quickly finish tying the knot around his wrist, binding it. Pulling back, I bite down on his lower lip and he moans, thrusting upwards. I press his free hand to the bed next to him and quickly tie that one as well before sitting back on top of him.

He snarls, twisting and bucking, tugging at his restraints to try and free himself. The wood of the posts creak but holds firm, and he lies back, panting, his eyes narrowed on me.

"Soulmate," he growls, tugging on his bindings again.

Leaning down, I lick at his mouth. "You want me? You'll get me on *my* terms. I'm going to ride you as you buck and fight helplessly beneath me. I'm a fucking queen and I take what I want, and what I want is you," I whisper into his mouth.

Leaning back, I lift up and reach between us, flicking open his pants. He tugs on the bindings again. "I want to touch you!" he rumbles.

Yanking at his trousers, I work them down his thick thighs until I can pull them to his ankles. Unbuckling his boots, he helps me kick them off before he lifts up, so I can pull his trousers fully off and throw them to the floor. I glance up to see him watching me with need so strong I almost falter. His cock is hard and standing at attention, waiting for me.

"Soulmate, you better fucking get up here," he demands, leaning back onto the bed, finally giving in to me.

Crawling up his body, I stop to lick the tip of his cock, tasting his precum, and he growls again, his hands straining as he tries to reach me. Relenting, I climb up his body and leave my knees on either side of his hips, rubbing my wet pussy along his straining cock. I almost whimper. "I forgot how big you are," I admit.

He gnashes his teeth then, straining to reach me like a caged animal. Groaning at the sight, I sit up and grab his cock, lining him up with my entrance before sinking down onto his length. He groans, stilling beneath me as I seat myself to his balls. Splaying my hands on his chest, I start to rock myself on him, riding him, using him for my own pleasure. I lift and drop myself faster and faster, chasing the bliss and ignorance that comes with pleasure. Rocking harder, I drop my head back as sweat drips between my breasts.

"Soulmate," he rasps.

Leaning down, still rubbing myself on him, I let him suck one of my nipples into his mouth, making me moan as he bites down hard. I reach between us and finger my clit, my pussy fluttering, my release building. Ripping from his mouth, needing to move, I ride him faster, spreading my knees for better control. Each slide of his thick shaft inside of me, hitting those nerves, makes me wilder until I'm almost feral too.

My release hits me out of nowhere, and I cry out and still above him, my pussy clamping down on him as I shake from the force of it, my vision almost blackening.

I gasp, my eyes springing open as I look down to see his hands now resting on my bare breasts from where he just ripped off my shirt.

"H-How—" I sputter in my pleasure-fuzzy brain.

He leans up then, so our faces are inches apart. "Dislocated my thumb, slipped out a hand out, and untied the other," he confesses.

"Dray...what—that's fucking crazy!" I gasp.

He shrugs then with an evil smirk quirking his lips. "I wanted to touch you, and it's my turn now," he purrs darkly, before he spins us and I'm lying on my back with him hovering above me. He grabs the crown twisted in my hair and flings it away. "Hold on, soulmate," he warns, before pulling out and ramming back inside of me.

I scream from the force, my hands scrambling on the bed, ripping at the sheets. He groans, grabs them, and then places them on his wounded chest. Instead, I slip them around and dig my nails into his back as he starts to hammer into me with no finesse or rhythm, just fucking me hard and fast like he wants to split me in two. Reaching down, he grabs my leg and throws it over his hip and hits deeper inside me, bumping my cervix. My eyes close as I scratch down his back, painting his skin with my pleasure.

He growls, his hips stuttering before he pummels into me, harder and faster than before. No restraint, no worries, no past or future. Just two animals fucking. Screw being king and queen, this is what I want. My eyes open in shock when he bites down on the soft spot between my shoulder and neck, the pain shooting through me and mixing with my pleasure, making me scream for him.

He yanks back and I see the blood coating his lips, and I can feel it dripping slowly down my skin. "Yours," he snarls.

My nails rip down his spine, urging him on as he hammers into me, my release building again from his rough treatment. One more thrust is all it takes before I explode once more, the force of my orgasm making me fight against him, scream his name, and rip at his back. He pins my writhing body down and fucks me harder until he stills with a howl, his come spurting inside me.

Panting, he collapses on me, his weight heavy and reassuring. I wrap my arms around him, still feeling his softening cock inside of me. Dray lifts his head, his hair plastered to his forehead from sweat, his blue eyes icy and looking right into my soul. His plump lips quirk up as he softly moves a strand of tangled hair from my face. "There's my fucking champion," he whispers.

I grin then too, and his thumb sweeps across my bottom lip. "I love you, soulmate," he admits.

"Dray," I gasp, my eyes flying wide.

"I do, I love you. I won't say forever because that isn't enough. I don't want just one lifetime with you, I want them all. So, I won't say I'll love you forever, I will say I'll love you always."

I blink back tears and swallow hard. "I love you too," I croak. He grins then, flashing white teeth with a crazed smile.

"I couldn't imagine my life without you, you make it whole. I love you," I repeat.

I feel his cock hardening again inside of me. "Say it again," he demands, thrusting shallowly.

"I love you," I gasp.

He grips my chin, forcing me to look at him. "Better not forget it, because you're never getting away from me," he snarls, picking up speed.

We fuck hard and soft nearly all night long, neither of us able to get enough of each other. He's wild but so am I. We paint each other's skin in our pleasure with the moon shining in through the balcony. This might be a castle and I might be a queen in a tower, but this is no fairy tale. Dray isn't prince charming, no, he's the beast, a monster, and he doesn't save me. I save my fucking self. This woman doesn't need a prince for that, just a sword and air in my lungs.

Chapter Four

What Next?

"Wake your ass up," comes an annoyed voice from above me. My eyes snap open instantly and lock onto a grinning Archel, who is crouched by the side of the bed. I glance down at his neck to see a blade at his throat, and I follow the arm to Dray who is lying under me with his eyes still closed, but they slit open and meet my gaze. He speaks without even looking at his assassin.

"If you see any of her, I will rip your eyes out," he threatens casually, and Archel snorts.

"Don't worry, she's not my type. Plus, my girl would kill me," he mutters and we both blink before looking over at the assassin. Girl? He has a girlfriend...someone can put up with him?

"Later you are spilling, for now, get the fuck out," Dray grumbles, dropping the blade and closing his eyes.

"Those pesky rebels and Berserkers are calling for their queen, and so is a doctor who is a real fucking killjoy. Better get up and down there before they all kill each other." He sounds way too happy about that, and I groan as he starts to whistle as he leaves the room. "Oh, and the ray of sunshine sent up some clothes for you."

I hear the door shut and grumble as I lay my head back on Dray's chest. "We better get up."

"Nope," he argues.

"They will just come up here eventually," I tell him with a laugh, propping my chin on his chest.

He slits his eyes open again, his hands moving from the bottom of my back to cup my arse, pulling me up until I can feel his hard length pressed against me. "Then I will kill them." He shrugs, like it's simple.

"You can't kill everyone," I point out helpfully.

"Sure I can. It's that simple, soulmate. I don't give a fuck about anyone but you," he growls, and my heart softens.

"Liar, you care about your people," I reply.

"I do," he agrees, his eyes blinking fully open. "But I love you, I would give up everything, kill anyone, for you."

"Crazy bastard." I grin before dropping a kiss on his lips. "We are still getting up, then you are going to let Doc look at your wounds," I order as I slide from the bed.

"Like fuck I am, they are fucking cuts," he grouses, getting up and prowling after me as I head to the bathroom to try and get cleaned up with a horny, pissed off Seeker on my heels.

"Yes you are," I tease.

The bathroom doesn't have much, just a sink and a toilet, and the best bit? A huge iron tub. I almost groan at the thought of getting a bath, and hurry over and turn on the taps, praying Ivar's indoor plumbing works this far up. It's one of the few luxuries of the castle. I guess his royal dickness couldn't live without running hot water. I wonder how he did it, but that soon disappears when water spurts from the tap with a rattle. It's dirty at first, but it soon runs clear and I let it go for a bit to wash away the grime and dirt from the unused tub before I add the plug and let it fill, steam rising from the hot water. Sands below, that is going to feel amazing.

A noise has me turning to see Dray placing our swords and knives within reaching distance before he hops into the bath and slides down in the tub, parting his legs with a pointed look at me. Why do we always end up in the tub? Can't say I'm complaining though. I slip in after him, leaning my back against his chest as I watch the tub slowly fill. The only sound in the room is the water running.

"Do you want to talk about what happened?" Dray asks softly, his arms wrapping around my middle and hoisting me back so not an inch of room is left between our bodies.

"Honestly? Not really. Physically, he has hurt me worse before…" I trail off, Vasilisy's face flashing in my mind.

"But?" he prompts. "Vasilisy," I whisper.

"I'm sorry, soulmate, I know you liked him." He squeezes me then and drops a gentle kiss on my shoulder.

"I did, he was a good man, an even better warrior. Death is never pretty, but he deserved a better one," I mutter.

"I'm betting he was fine with it, everything he did was for you," he offers.

"That's the point. I am sick of people dying for me. I would rather they live. I want them to fight, I want them to rage, and I want them to live. Is that too much to ask for?" I snap.

"No. I won't die for you, soulmate. I am far too self-serving for that, plus that would mean a world for you without me in it. Not happening. I know my limits, I know how to survive, and I plan on staying by your side until the day we both die. I promise you that," he whispers against my wet shoulder.

I settle back then, flicking off the tap with my toe. "Good, you die on me and I swear to God, Dray, I will bring you back and kill you myself," I growl.

He nips at my skin. "Always so feisty," he mumbles against my skin.

"You fucking bet, I'm a queen now, and queens get what they want."

"And what do you want, soulmate?" he inquires seriously.

"You, my men. I want to live until we're old, I want to stop having to fight every day, but first I want to stop this war," I admit honestly.

"Then let's do just that," he states.

"You make it sound so easy." I sigh and lean my head back against his shoulder.

"Nothing worth doing is ever easy, nor is anything worth loving, but that doesn't mean it's not possible. Let's get washed and go talk to your new generals. I know how to build up men you trust and we don't have a lot of time. I suggest you pick three generals, and leave them and some rebels here in case of any leftover Ivar supporters, then bring some with you. Send the rest to The Ring, because, soulmate? There will be a war, and we are going to be on the winning side."

"I suppose you better wash me then, my king," I murmur. "Yes, my queen." He grins, licking at my shoulder.

We washed quickly, with Archel's warning running through my mind, and I find the clothes he was talking about waiting near the door for us on the broken dressing table. The jeans are a washed out black and have a few holes, but they are better than the ones I had before, and they even have a belt to tighten them so they fit properly. I grin at the socks and slip them on. I'm not even going to ask where he found socks, but this being queen thing might be good. The shirt is white and I groan when I realise it has sleeves—it is way too fucking hot out there for sleeves. Grabbing one of Dray's knives he left on the side table while he dresses, I make quick work of cutting off the sleeves and grin at the tank top I created. I pull it on before adding my holster around my thigh for my knife, and then I slip another into my boot. I almost well up when I see Archel has managed to find my holster for my swords, and I slide it over my shoulders and sheathe both of the blades into their rightful places. Gripping my damp hair, I quickly plait it before curling it into a bun on top of my head. It is getting long for sure, so I need to remember to cut it again soon.

The Cities

When I turn around to grab my boots, my eyes drop to Dray's hands where he is quickly sheathing all his knives across his chest with expertise that has my new panties wet and my mouth dry. He catches me staring and smirks, so I grab my boots and slip into then, lacing them up tight so sand doesn't get inside.

I don't bother putting on the leather jacket, since I want them see all of my tattoos and brands. I'm not ashamed anymore. They are each a reminder of another horror I have survived, another warrior mark, and I will wear them with pride.

I wait for Dray as he grabs his own boots and laces them, and then he pushes back his hair and look at me. "Ready?" I ask.

"Not quite," he replies, and I frown, but it turns into a gasp as he prowls towards me and grabs the back of my head hard, kissing me.

His tongue sweeps in and he tangles it with mine as we both groan. Eventually he pulls back, leaving both of us panting and watching each other.

"Now I'm ready." He smirks.

Rolling my eyes but secretly pleased, I grab my jacket and stroll from the room with Dray on my heels as we head downstairs and back to reality. I push open the door at the bottom and spot Evan leaning against the opposite wall with a scowl.

"Bout fucking time," he snaps. "Come on, they are all waiting." "Who?" I ask, as I join him as he starts to walk quickly.

"Your rebel buddies got here early this morning. They must have ridden all night and there's a message from The Rim for you. The Berserkers are also waiting on you, being a queen sucks," he adds with a grin at me.

"Shut up, Doc, and lead the way," I warn.

He laughs but leads us through the castle. I'm glad we don't go to the throne room, but instead stop at a big brown door just down the corridor from it. Evan swings it open and I spot a large round table in the middle of the room with paintings, torches, and other shit on the walls around. It reminds me of the room from The Summit, which has me wincing, but I cover it when every eye turns to me.

Berserkers, Seekers, and rebels alike stand on our entry, all watching me. That's when I realise they are waiting for me. Fuck, this queen shit really is hard.

"Sit," I bark.

I spot the heartbroken man and the giant from yesterday leaning against the walls. Ignoring everyone else, I go straight up to them. "I never learned your names."

The giant smiles ruefully. "Bern, Ma Queen," he offers.

"Henry, My Queen," the smaller man answers, with that fire still in his eyes, one I know too well.

"Thank you, sit, please," I add as an afterthought. I see their eyes widen but they rush to do as I ask. Dray is right, I need generals I can trust.

I turn to the others, but a man blocks my path. I suck in a breath but straighten my spine, waiting.

"Tazana," he greets, watching me carefully.

Noah's father stands in front of me, looking the same as he did the last time I saw him, just with more wrinkles. He looks just like an older version Noah, and my heart clenches from seeing what my first love might have looked like if he had survived. "Erik." I nod.

He opens his arms then and pulls me to him. I stiffen and he squeezes before letting go. "You look good." He nods to himself.

"Thank you for coming so quickly," I reply, unsure what else to say.

I move around him before it can get more awkward, but I stop cold and turn to stare at him. "I'm sorry about Vasilisy, he was a good man."

He winces. "He was, but he has never been the same since he lost his wife, so maybe it was for the best. Some men can't live on without their love. He died willingly for his family, for you, and the cause he believed in, and that means he died happy," he states, looking at me so seriously I glance away, focusing on the table again.

One chair is left with its back to the door, so I frown. Dray steps forward then, grabs a Seeker by the scruff of his neck, and yanks him from the seat that faces the door then offers it to me. I can't help but smile as I round the table and slip into it. Henry, Bern, Erik, Archel, and the rebel from yesterday are sitting there, waiting. I spot Evan lingering near the door and look at Dray.

"Let him look at your wounds," I order. He grins at me. "No."

I hear Archel snigger, so I twist a blade from my side and without looking, throw it at him. I hear a yelp and glance over with a smirk to see him on the ground, having rolled from his chair, and the blade sticking from the wood where his head was. He laughs, gets to his feet, and yanks out the dagger, throwing it back to me. I catch it mid-air and sheathe it before looking back at Dray. More laughter booms around the room, but I concentrate on my Seeker King.

"I cut you and fucked up your back, let him look," I snap.

"No," he teases, leaning closer. "Just some more scars from my soulmate."

I groan. "They might get infected, let him look. Please," I add almost painfully.

His eyes narrow, the icy blue taking up my entire vision as the rest of the room fades away in our staring contest. He finally groans. "Fine, but they better still scar. I want them as a badge of honour," he grumbles.

I must be getting used to his brand of crazy, because I just nod and look around him to Evan. "Doc, check out his wounds, will you?"

Evan eyes Dray worriedly, but grabs a bag on the floor I didn't notice before, and steps closer. Dray does nothing to help him, just sits there, waiting. I can sense Evan's nerves and I don't blame him. He places the bag on the table and opens it, before grabbing a bottle and some cloth, and then turning to Dray. He mumbles something before stepping up and trying to get to the still weeping cut down his chest. Dray growls and steps back, Evan throws his hands up and looks to me for help.

Men.

Sighing, I stand up and kick out my seat, pointing from Dray to it. "Sit, now," I command.

He grins and slumps into the chair, stretching his legs out and watching me. "Anything else, soulmate?" he asks.

"Lean forward," I demand, smiling now.

He does as he is told, and I move to the side so he can wrap his arm around my waist and lean into me. I nod at Evan then and he approaches, able to get to the scratches on Dray's back with him leaning forward like this. I turn back to the table. "Okay, so let's start at the beginning. As you all know, Ivar is dead."

Erik and a few others cheer, and I smirk and let them calm down before I open my mouth to carry on, but a growl and a scream has me looking back at Dray and Evan with an arched eyebrow. Dray has a blade pointed at Evan, who is frozen with the now wet cloth touching Dray's many scratches crisscrossing along his back. I take a good look. Most are bleeding, red, and raw, but some are just scratches. Fuck, I really did let go last night.

"If you kill him, I will be really mad," I warn.

"What about maiming?" Dray inquires, and looks up at me, blinking innocently.

"No killing, torturing, or maiming. Let him look at your wounds or I will never play with you again," I grind out.

He growls but sheathes his knife. "Carry on, ignore him," I tell Evan, and look back at the table where everyone is watching Dray and me curiously, all apart from a laughing Archel.

"Aww, has Dray got a boo-boo?" he taunts.

"I'll gut you, then you'll have to go crying to your woman about a boo-boo," Dray fires back.

Rolling my eyes to the ceiling, I try to find my patience. Sands below, sometimes I want to kill everyone just to get some peace and quiet.

"Enough!" I yell and everyone falls silent.

"So, oh great Berserker Queen...what next?" Archel calls with a grin.

"We do not have time for this. This is what is going to happen. We are going to gather our best, I will appoint generals, and then head to The Ring. We will leave men behind to defend the castle. Before heading to The Ring, we will stop at Paradise to get some information. Once there, we are meeting up with Seekers, Worshippers, Reeves, and anyone else. We are preparing."

"Preparing for what?" Erik questions, leaning into the table with a frown.

"War."

The room erupts into chaos, so grabbing my knife, I smash it into the middle of the table and the room goes silent again. "The Cities came here and they took what is mine, but they wont stop there. They want the North, they just don't realise they can't have it. It's ours and we need to defend it. We will make peace once and for all, and we will drive them south until they never forget who it belongs to."

"Okay, so we are making a stand at The Ring?" Archel asks, confused.

"No, you are going to wait there while I go to The Cities and bring them north. We fight where we know, in the Wastes, not on their turf."

"You're headin' to The Cities?" Bern inquires.

"Yes, but first I need to get back what they have taken from me. Then, I will lead them north right to our awaiting armies." I look at Erik then. "Gather your rebels, send word across the sands, we need every fighter." I look at Dray then who nods. "Bern, Henry, you are my new generals. Decide who is staying and who is coming. Archel, get your Seekers ready to leave, and send word to the others." He looks to Dray for confirmation and then nods at me. "We leave in two hours, go," I order. Bern looks at Henry before he focuses on me.

"Some Berserkers left in the night, I just thought you should know," he informs me. I nod, my face calm, I expected that. There are still monsters in these walls and after the message I sent yesterday, I expected some deserters, that's their choice.

They get up slowly, but then Evan steps forward. "What are you getting from Paradise?"

"The key to winning this war," I answer, and then turn to Dray, dismissing them all.

I hear them leave as I plant my hand on his shoulders and push him back so Evan can get to the wound on his chest. "Anything else?" I ask.

"Not that I can think of. You need to convince the others though, but I have a feeling they will follow you." He shrugs, ignoring the man who is cleaning the bleeding wound. "We need to go shopping though."

I tilt my head in confusion. "Shopping?"

He grins then. "Weapons, we need more weapons."

I rack my brain and then smirk. "Let's go shopping then."

Chapter Five

SHOPPING SPREE

Dray eventually gets tired of Evan and I have to step in when he pins him to the wall, and I give up trying to let Evan treat him after that. Instead, I distract him with the idea of new weapons and he follows after me as I find my way through the castle. It is bustling with activity as everyone prepares to leave and head out. You can taste the excitement in the air and everyone grins and greets me as I walk past. We walk silently down the halls, heading to the front of the castle where the weapons store is. Men are filling in and out, packing up weapons to take as they get ready to fight. I head past them all, slipping to the back where I remember the hidden door is. Ivar showed me more than once, and loved telling me where he got each and every one from. It should be untouched.

I depress the stone next to it and the door swings open, letting out a gust of stale air. Wrinkling my nose, I step in with Dray following on my heels with a torch. He slips it into the metal holder on the wall and I turn back with a grin. "This enough for you?" I wave my hand around to encompass the walls and shelves covered in every weapon imaginable. It's even bigger than the collection he has in his bedroom. "I think I just came in my pants," he mutters and I laugh, looking back at the walls.

My eyes catch on a bow and I falter for a moment, wishing Drax was here. In fact, I wish all of them were here, but I shake it off though, not wanting to linger on thoughts of them when I don't have time to be weak. "Let's shop," I offer instead.

I head to one of the walls, noting the small daggers there. I grab a handful and after placing some in my boots, I grab another holder and wrap it around my hips and add them there also. I step back and look over the other weapons, I take another whip, since I enjoyed the last one, and coil it and add it to my belt. I still have my two swords and other daggers. I spot Dray sliding his hand across some smaller curved daggers and grin. He looks over his shoulder, obviously feeling my gaze, and winks at me.

"You have the best toys, soulmate," he purrs.

Shaking my head, I look over the others, trying to think if I need any more, you can never have too many weapons, but I don't want to weigh myself down too much, it will only slow me down and I'm betting I can't sneak a lot of these into The Cities. "Here, soulmate," Dray calls.

I head over and place my head on his shoulder to see what has caught his attention. I whistle when I do, ridiculously attracted to the weapon he is palming and testing the weight of. There is something so hot about a man who knows how to handle his weapons. "This should fit you well," he states, bringing my mind out of the gutter.

The axe in his hand is small, a lot smaller than normal axes, almost like it was made for a woman. The edges are blackened to stop the shine in the light and I spot runes running down the sharp edge. The handle has similar symbols engraved in the black leather. It's beautiful. Dray turns and offers it to me. I take it and give it a few swings, spinning as I go to test the heaviness. It feels good, smooth, and easy to use without throwing me off balance or weighing me down.

I give it a few throws in the air before looking over at Dray to see him advancing on me, his eyes icy, and his lips thin and hard. I don't back away like everyone else would, I meet him halfway. He grabs the back of my head and yanks me to him, our lips smashing together desperately as we battle with our tongues.

I groan into his mouth and he yanks me closer, the weapons forgotten between us. I trace my hand down his chest before twisting one of his nipples roughly. He groans into my mouth and bites down on my bottom lip, making me gasp at the pain flowing through me. "We need to get ready," I remind him, but even to me it sounds lame.

"Don't worry, this won't take a minute," he whispers, before spinning me to the wall and pinning me there.

He kicks open my legs and slips his hand around me to flick open my jeans. I jerk against him, starting to struggle, but he keeps me pinned there as he yanks down my jeans until they are tight at my ankles, keeping me there so I don't fall over. He cups my pussy, leaning closer. "Always so wet for me, soulmate, especially when there are weapons involved. Are you sure you're not the crazy one?"

I push back, trying to get free, but he smashes me into the wall again and pushes my panties to the side, running his fingers down my wet center, making me freeze. Biting my lip to stop from crying out, I pant into the wall, trying not to push against his fingers for more. He dips one inside of me before rubbing my clit, with no rhyme or reason as he attacks my pussy with one hand and keeps me pinned here effortlessly with the other.

I groan when he pushes two fingers inside of me and curls them, and I can practically feel the smirk on his face, the bastard. "Dray," I warn.

He slams me harder into the wall and starts fucking me with his fingers. I have no choice but to stand there and take it as he yanks a release from me. I gasp and sputter with how quickly I came apart on his fingers. He lets me go so I spin, stumbling over my jeans before he presses me back to the wall, and as I watch, he sucks my cream from his fingers and closes his eyes in bliss before they lock on me again.

He runs his eyes over me, but seems to stop at the brand on my shoulder and I frown. He's never been bothered by them before.

His hand grabs at my belt and I watch in confusion as he winds the whip around his hand. "Hands up."

I arch my brow so he grabs my throat and squeezes. "Now, soulmate."

Grinding my teeth, I do it, curious what he has in mind. He loops the whip around them and ties me to the wall behind me before stepping back and staring at me. "I saw their tattoos. Tell me, soulmate, did they get it for you?"

"Huh?" I ask, confused.

"Did you not think I knew about your other boys getting your brand on their skin?" he inquires, almost purring.

"Well, no?" I ask, beyond confused now.

"I have been waiting for you to ask me to get it done, I'm tired of waiting," he explains as he palms a knife, I lick my lips at the flash of steel and he grins as he releases his chest holster and spins it so his bare chest faces me. My eyes dart from his eyes to his hands and back again.

"Dray, what?" I gasp.

He grins at me and places the tip of the knife on his chest, right above his heart. He starts to drag the blade so I pull on the whip, trying to get to him and he frowns, stilling. "Stop moving, I need to see the brand as I do it, we don't want to have to burn this off and start again, do we?" he says casually, and I just gape at him. He can't be serious?

"What the fuck?" I yell.

"I don't see a tattoo artist here and I'm not going one more second without your symbol on my body, so I suggest you help me or we will have to keep going until we get this right," he points out calmly, while smiling at me, all crazy and sexy as hell.

I still only because I really don't know what else to do. He looks back down and concentrates on the knife in his skin. I watch as he carves the brand from my skin onto his, right above his heart. They have all taken something that I see as a reminder of the hell I went through, a symbol of pain, and made it one of love. He winks at me every now and again and checks his progress. It's slow going, but he doesn't utter a peep, even as blood pools down his chest and drips to the floor. Fuck, I'm going to have to get Evan to check him over again. When the last line is complete, he looks up at me, smiling widely and happy as hell with his crazy self. "What do you think?" he

queries, and he looks so hopeful.

I clear my throat and lick my dry lips, unable to stop the sappy smile curling my lips. "I love you, you crazy fucking bastard."

He smirks at me and steps closer. I tilt my head back and he kisses me softly, his bleeding chest pressing to my white shirt, but I don't give a fuck. "Good thing you're pretty," I tease.

He drops his forehead to mine and watches me with those icy eyes. "Let's go get your other men."

I nod, my smile disappearing. I had forgotten, for just a moment. "Then I can show this off to them," he adds, and a laugh snorts

out of me.

He unties me and I wind my whip again, adding it to my belt before hovering my fingers over his carved symbol. "We should get Evan to check this though."

"No," he argues straight away.

"But, if it gets infected it will mess with the design and no one will know what it is," I cajole, matching his crazy with mine. It works.

"Fuck, you're right, okay."

He turns and heads away, muttering about doctors and killing people. I shake my head but follow after him, almost floating, his love is filling me up that much. For someone whose own father forgot about them, who didn't love them enough to have someone like

Dray...someone whose love might be twisted and a bit mad but so big and consuming, it's a bloody miracle.

Sands below, I'm one lucky bitch. Maybe karma is finally paying off from all the shit I've been through, but they make it all worth it. Each fight, each horror and loss, I would do it all again to have my men.

42

Chapter Six

A War Party

The next hour or so goes quickly as I help everyone pack and get ready to go. I check over the selection of Berserkers to be left behind, before grabbing my weapons and supplies, and heading down to the bay where Bern has found me a ride. Near the wall of the castle, there's a type of roughly constructed garage where they store bikes to keep the sand from getting in and ruining them. Bern leads me down to the end where a tarp covers something.

"Found this, thought it might suit ya, Ma Queen." He grins, wiggling his massive eyebrows at me as he tugs on the tarp to reveal the bike underneath.

My mouth drops open. Now I know what people mean when they say love at first sight. She is a beauty—smooth, sleek, a crotch rocket for sure. It has low, silver handlebars with spikes facing outwards, looking sharp enough to skewer someone if they got too close. The detail on the bodywork is what has me drooling though. A skull with a crown on it is painted on the bottom side, surrounded by flames that trail off around the body. She's lean, mean, fast, and lethal.

"What's that?" I tilt my head, pointing at the black straps across the handle.

"For ya to strap in ya sword or gun or even a bow, makes it easier to draw or kill some bastards while ye ride," Bern rumbles, and then laughs when my face lights up.

"Sands below, I'm so turned on right now. Who's a pretty one," I coo, and I hear a laugh boom out of him again before he slaps me on the shoulder.

"Aye, long live our fucking queen!" he calls, making me grin and shake my head as I step closer to check out my new ride.

"I'm not riding bitch." Dray grins, leaning against the post of the covering.

"A found ya Seeker man one too, not as fancy, but it'll do," Bern offers, jerking his head at a silver bike next to mine. Where mine is a speed rocket, this one is clearly not. It's bulkier, with flames painted down the sides. Scratches, blood, and even a bullet hole also decorate it. It's perfect for the crazy bastard of mine.

"Aww, we should get matching bikes," Dray coos, and I shake my head as I climb on my bike.

"You checked it out?" Dray asks, nodding at the bike. Bern nods. "Aye, it's safe."

"It better be. If she dies on it, I will hunt you across the Wastes and wear you for a coat—" Dray's threat cuts off, his eyes lighting up as he checks out his new ride. "Ooh, look, a bullet hole!" he exclaims, squatting down to run his hand over the body of the bike.

I roll my eyes, but I can't fight the smile that turns up the corner of my lips. Glancing back at Bern, I reluctantly climb off my bike and say, "Let's sound the horn, it's time we ride out."

"Aye, let me gather the war party for ya, Ma Queen." He salutes me by fisting his hand over his chest and smacking three times before hurrying away.

"Are you ready for this?" Dray inquires, leaning back on his new bike.

I once found an old porn magazine that had a half-naked girl sprawled on a bike, it was hot, but not as hot as my crazy Seeker King on his, looking like sex and sin incarnate. I find myself licking my lips to try and quench the fire burning inside of me. He leans farther back, his legs thrown over the bike as he tilts his head and smiles at me, like he knows exactly what I'm thinking. His blades flash in the sunlight, his chest tanned, and his new scar brand standing out proudly between his holster straps.

"Keep that thought for later, soulmate," he purrs.

Grinning, I stride over and grab his hair, yanking his head back harshly and angling his face until I can kiss him. He groans into my mouth as we eat at each other before pulling away, both of us breathless. "I intend to, but yes, I'm ready."

And I am. I can feel it coming, like a storm waiting on the horizon. My whole life has been leading up to this fight and it's finally here. My every cell calls for blood. We share a dark look, both of us speaking without words about love, madness, and our need to make our enemies pay. "Let's head out, the king and queen ride front and center," I whisper hoarsely.

I let go then and step back before I do something stupid like have sex with him right then and there on the bike. I swing onto my ride, sliding one of my swords into the handy leather strap, and secure my bag to the back. Then I slip into my leather jacket to protect my skin from the sand and unbearable sun. We're going to be riding fast without many stops, so I need to make sure I don't burn on the way.

A Berserker walks past, heading to another bike, and I almost pout when I spot the black goggles on his head. Fuck, I could have used those. Sand in the face is a bitch and you can barely see without shades or goggles, not to mention how the sand dries out your eyes.

Sighing, I glance away, but then do a double take when Dray hops up, grabs the goggles off the stunned Berserker, and saunters over to me. He offers them to me. "A present, for you." He grins.

"Aww, did you steal them just for me? Such a romantic," I tease.

I grab them and put them on, grinning at the now pissed off Berserker. When he continues to glare at me, I narrow my gaze and he jumps, hurrying away, obviously realising it's not worth the fight.

Dray hops back on his bike and revs the engine. I get mine going as well and we pull away from the shielding with my new goggles in place, letting me see easily. Once we reach the edge of the camp where the others are slowly gathering, I'm glad I have them. The wind is picking up, blowing sand everywhere, and I can already feel it coating my hands and exposed face. Turning in my seat as we wait for the others, I grab my bandana from my bag and tie it around my neck before covering my nose and mouth. There, that's better.

I look over at Dray to see he has done the same, and he winks at me before covering his eyes with silver shades, looking hot as hell. Think post-apocalyptic GQ, he would definitely make the cover.

We only have to wait a couple more minutes before our war party is ready. Dray nods at me and I pull out, gunning it when I reach flat terrain. He rides next to me, with Bern and Henry behind us, and the rest spread around. I spot Archel speeding around my people only to fall back and then do it again, obviously getting a kick out of annoying people.

I lean closer to the bike and go faster, testing my new ride. Each mile we cover gets me closer to getting my men back.

Sands below, please let them be okay.

For hours and hours we ride, and ride hard, not stopping once. I know the vague location of Paradise from when we left, but I keep double-checking the sun and locations we pass on the way. It seems as though we are coming from an opposite direction than I'd travelled before. I know the people of Paradise might not be happy when I ride up with a war party, but I only need to run in and get the maps from my father and then we'll leave. My people can wait outside for all I care, I need those maps.

I watch as our messengers break off from the party, speeding across the Wastes to carry out my orders. I suck in a breath through the clingy black material covering the lower half of my face. It's happening, we are getting them back.

Archel pulls up alongside me and signals for us to pull over. I resist, but his eyes narrow and he points again, so with a growl I slow down and follow him, veering from the sand covered, cracked motorway to the side of the road. We move around the broken and burnt out cars until there's a big enough space for all of us to stop. I hear the others following as I kick out the stand on my bike and pull down my bandana with an annoyed glare.

"What?" I snap, now that we are on the road, I don't want to stop.

I want my men and each minute away from them is too long.

"We need to break. It won't do any good if they're half dead when we get there," he points out gently. His soft tone makes me take a breath and look over the gathered warriors. He's right, they need to at least drink and have something to eat.

I nod and he calls out, "Break time! Ten minutes, then we're back on the road!"

I slide from my bike and stride off to stretch my legs, needing to keep moving with all this tension racing through me. I hear Dray following quietly behind me, but not even he can calm me at the moment. I will only be calm when I see them for myself, so until then, I will just keep moving. I spot a dip in the sand in the distance and head that way, crouching at the top of the hill when I reach it. It leads down to railway tracks and a turned over train. Dried blood covers some of the old yellow vehicle and glass litters the ground. I spot what looks like a campfire, so I slide down the hill and walk over. Bending down to touch the charred wood, I frown when I realise it's still warm. Who would be camping here?

Something glints in the sunlight, causing me to tilt my head and palm my sword as I stand up and walk over, then pick up the object. I brush off the dust to reveal a broken knife. The handle is intact and well worn on the small knife, but the actual blade has broken halfway down, and is jagged and coated in blood. I swipe my fingertip along the blade and raise it.

The blood is fresh.

I quickly scan my surroundings for the source and spot a couple of splatters, so I follow them. Since they lead around the train, I glance up the hill, and seeing Dray's silhouette, I beckon to him. He immediately sides down, silently moving to my side. I jerk my head at the blood, and he nods, grabbing two big ass lethal knives from his sheaths.

Crouching down when we reach the corner of the turned over train, I peek around the edge before pulling my head back. Moving slowly, so we do not announce ourselves, I look again, noting the body of a man leaning up against the train not too far away. He's covered in blood, so I can't tell if he is dead or alive. A woman is on her side farther up, but I can't make out much else. There doesn't seem to be anyone around though. Could they have been attacked by a scav? Hunting party? Rogues?

Fuck it.

Standing, I stride around the corner, keeping my eye out for any movements in case it's a trap. I stop in front of the man and Dray turns his back to me, spreading his arms to keep watch so I can check the man over. His eyes are shut, and one is swollen and purple. He has a split lip, his cheekbone is cut, and his face is dotted with blood steadily dripping from an unseen wound in his brown hair. The previously white shirt he's wearing is torn and stained red, clinging to his stocky build. His trousers are cargo pants and dark, bunched up strangely. When I look closer, I realise why they look so wrong.

Fucking hell.

Holding in my gag, I reach out and push up the loose ends to check and... yes, I'm right. His legs from the knees down are missing, ripped away, it looks like, and blood is pooling underneath him. It's been hours, maybe not even that, since they were taken from him. When he doesn't move, I lean closer to check his pulse.

Fuck, I kind of hope he's dead. This must have been unimaginable agony for him. When my fingers touch his cold, clammy neck, his eyes fly open and a whine leaves his lips. I freeze.

"I'm not here to hurt you," I murmur softly.

He darts a look around and tries to move, but a scream erupts from his cracked lips, cutting off as he chokes on his own blood. I wince and wait for it to pass, not having any water to offer him, plus, it wouldn't make any difference, he's dying.

"Rosalina," he croaks when he can finally speak, his voice weak and weedy.

"Rosalina?" I echo, scrunching my nose.

He looks to the side with heartbreak written in his eyes, and I follow his gaze to the woman close by. I can see from here that her chest isn't rising and falling, so I know she's dead, but I stand up anyway and go to check her. She's naked from the waist up, and her trousers are intact, but her shirt is nowhere to be seen. Long, thick cuts mar her back, layered over older scars. She was a fighter, a survivor. I lean down and press my fingers to her pulse, but feel nothing. I turn her slightly and gasp, closing my eyes for a moment before I find the courage to open them again.

Half of her face is ripped away, her eye socket bare and lips half chewed. No blade did this, teeth did.

Cannibals.

I lay her gently back down and rush over to the man. Tears well in his eyes and his gaze seems glued to the woman. "What happened?" I ask gently.

"They—" He coughs again, blood rattling wetly. "They attacked us. I thought we were safe for a few hours of sleep, but I was wrong. They came in the night... must be their territory." He closes his eyes for a moment before looking back at me. "She's gone, isn't she?"

"Yes," I answer bluntly.

He nods, leaning his head back against the metal of the train. "She's my sister," he whispers, sounding pained. He blows out a breath and looks over at me, his eyes pleading. "Kill me, please."

I thin my lips and he smiles sadly at me, showing me missing teeth and a mouth caked in blood. "I don't want to be sitting here waiting for them to come back and eat the rest of me. I'm going to die anyway, let it be on my terms. Kill me," he urges, his voice stronger this time.

"Soulmate?" Dray murmurs from behind me. "Are you sure?" I query, needing to know.

"Yes, I don't have a weapon to do it myself, broke mine in one of the bastards. Kill me, please, kill me," he begs, sobs racking his body.

He's right, he's going to die. It's his choice to decide how—wait to be eaten alive, die from blood loss, or let me kill him. I won't let him suffer any longer. I slip a knife from my belt while he isn't watching and quickly stab it into his neck and pull it out. Blood spurts straight away, letting me know I struck true. It takes a minute for the light in his eyes to dim and then wink from existence. At least he'll be with his sister now.

I stand up and sheathe my blade. Fury, worry, and tension run through me, a volatile mix I need to get out.

"I need to kill something," I spit.

"The cannibals can't be far. They wouldn't have left fresh kills and meat. Let's go hunting," he suggests, and I nod eagerly.

I throw the two corpses another look before stepping up behind Dray, my sword in hand as I follow him.

There's a bloody handprint on the door farther down the train. I tap Dray's shoulder and he follows my gaze, a grin lighting up his face as he heads over. We each take a different side of the door, looking at each other. I nod and he rips it open as we spin to stare inside. I don't bother crouching, they don't have weapons apart from their teeth, but they're fast and we need to be ready to strike.

The light streams in from the sun behind us as an awful, rotting stench hits me, making my eyes water and my nose burn. Fuck. I squint into the darkness and then freeze, spotting the shifting bodies and shadows in the deep recess of the carriage. I step back and Dray copies my movement.

"You ready?" I ask.

He grins, holding his knives. "Fuck yes."

I hit the side of the train with my sword, the clang loud on the metal. "Feeding time, you creeps!" I scream as loud as I can, before Dray and I step back again, rearranging ourselves side by side. I hear them first, sniffing and panting, their feet and hands dragging on the metal lining the inside of the train.

I wait with bated breath as excitement courses through me from the imminent fight. One of them sticks their head out, its eyes unfocused and nostrils flaring, catching the scent of us before it growls. I part my legs farther, giving myself a more stable stance, and wait as he snarls and jumps, aiming for us. More stream from the train, drawn by the first and our scent, heading straight towards us.

I start swinging, losing myself in the feel of my blade cutting through the monsters, their howls of pain and screeches of anger driving me on. Dray and I dance side by side, moving like we have been fighting together all of our lives. I throw a knife into a cannibal's skull when it sneaks too close to him, and he yanks me around to avoid the teeth of another. We move, we kill, and we fight, and before I know it, we're standing in the middle of a pile of dead cannibals.

I scan the ground and train, looking for any that escaped, but it looks like we got them all. My eyes catch on Dray's to see him watching at me. We're both covered in blood with our chests heaving, sweat dripping down our faces and, suddenly, we are racing towards each other. Colliding with our need, our lips crash together. We let each other know we are alive with our kiss, riding the exhaustion and lust that comes from surviving and killing. We only pull back when we have to breathe.

"Dray, Worth? You down there? Time to go!" comes Archel's yell.

We share a grin as we sheathe our weapons. "Come on, soulmate, time to ride."

"Filthy bastard," I mutter, and a startled laugh bursts out of him as he helps me over the dead corpses and around the train. Twining our fingers together, he swings our arms between us as he whistles.

Crazy motherfucker.

Chapter Seven

Sand Bath

The warriors are waiting for us when we get back to the top of the hill. I clean my hands with someone's rag and a bottle of water, the clear liquid turning red as it runs into the sand below, darkening it. I chug the rest before donning my goggles and bandana, and swinging back on my bike.

I scan my gaze over the group, and my eyes catch on Bern as he hits Evan in the shoulder, laughing his ass off. Evan grumbles with a reluctant smile on his face as he holds a blade tightly in his hand, looking awkward. I blink, watching as he hesitates with it, obviously unsure what to do with the new blade. I wonder if he has ever swung one or used one before? By the look on his face, I would say no. Slipping from my bike, I stop before a random Berserker warrior with two sheaths on each thigh.

"Give me one of those," I order.

He eyes me for a second before stripping it off and handing it over without complaint. I head over to Bern, Henry, and Evan. "Here." I hand it over to Evan.

He looks it over in confusion, his eyebrows drawing together. "I ain't putting it on for you, Doc, you don't get my motor running. Strap it on and add some blades, you are going to need them."

He takes it, and we watch as he struggles to strap it on. "Thanks, Worth," he says softly, after finally figuring out the sheath.

"Can't have you getting killed," I grumble. "Dray stabs himself way too often for no doctor to be around."

An arm drops around my shoulder and I'm pulled into a side. "Don't let her fool you, Doc. It turns her on when I bleed."

Evan groans, looking disgusted while Henry laughs. "It's true," I admit, grinning at an uncomfortable looking Evan. "You know how to handle them?" I nod at the blades he has strapped on.

"Yes," he grunts, glancing away. "Sort of...I'm better with a scalpel."

"When we stop tonight, I'll give you some lessons," I offer and sigh. He perks up then, but looks suspicious. "Why?"

"Don't worry, Doc, I just don't want you getting killed. You look heavy and I don't want to have to carry you to a grave. Too much effort," I tease, laughing at Evan. I wrap my arm around Dray's waist and pull him away, as Henry and Barn's laughter follows us.

"Do I need to kill him?" Dray asks casually, his arm still slung around my shoulders.

I stumble at his words and gape at him. "Evan? No, why?" I question, confused.

"Just making sure he wasn't a threat. You have enough men, soulmate," he quips.

I sputter before narrowing my eyes. Grabbing a blade, I have it pressed to his throat in a second. Everyone freezes, the whole war party going silent. Dray's icy eyes gleam with excitement and heat as he presses into the blade, with that crazy smile curving his lips. "If you wanted to fuck, soulmate, all you had to do was ask," he growls.

I lean in close, almost touching his lips. "You don't get to tell me whom to fuck. If I wanted to have a massive orgy right here right now, you still wouldn't get a say in it. You can be jealous, you can be crazy, but you can*not* control me," I warn, my voice low and sensual, deadly serious. I have been controlled most of my life, and I won't let that happen again, not even for love.

"I don't want to control you. I just want to be yours," he replies almost sweetly, his eyes softening. "Doesn't mean I won't kill someone for looking at you wrong." He grins.

I roll my eyes, but pull the blade away. "I wouldn't expect anything else." I look around at all the Berserkers and Seekers gathered. "Are we having a fucking play? No, get the fuck on your rides! We are rolling out!" I scream, before heading to my bike.

"She's as crazy as he is," one of them mutters.

"Too right, crazy fucking slut leading others," someone scoffs.

I turn just in time to see a blade sticking out of the eye of the man who had spoken.

I look to Dray, watching him scowl at the now dead man. Sands below. A thump sounds, and I turn back to see the dead Berserker tumbling off of his bike and to the ground. Archel steps over the dead man, grabs his bag, and then pulls the knife from his eye. He tosses it at Dray who catches it and sheaths it without looking.

"Man, next time, kill someone who has some good stuff to steal," Archel complains, rifling through the bag before dropping it to the ground with a disgusted huff.

I decide to just ignore it all and climb back on my bike. Maybe I'm learning which battles to fight.

We ride hard again, travelling under a large, broken bridge, down motorways, and swerving around crumbling buildings and rusting cars. A pack of ferals chases us for a while, but they can't keep up so they soon stop trying. The sun is scorching down on me, heating me in my leather to an uncomfortable degree. I can feel the grit of the sand on my skin, the tiny granules even making it under my bandana. By the time the sun starts to dip below the horizon, I know we only have around two more hours to travel, so I decide to stop us for the night. We'll head towards Paradise bright and early in the morning—if we approach in daylight, they won't think we're attacking them.

I scan the horizon before seeing the shadow of a small building. It won't fit us all, but it gives us something to have our backs to. Usually, with a party this big, we just sleep on the ground, so it doesn't bother me. I change direction and head that way, slowing my bike and parking on the side of the building when I get there. I hop off, stretching my sore legs, and whistle while winding my finger in a circle. The Berserkers know what that means, so they search the building checking for threats before making a circle with the bikes, a first line of protection against anything or anyone. Not that anyone would be that stupid to attack a party this size, but you never know.

Dray and Archel pull up next to me as I round the building and check it out. It's made of red brick, and covered in graffiti and warning signs. An old bathroom symbol hangs crooked near a horrible, peeling blue door, which has blood and bullet holes in it. Gripping my new axe, wanting to test it out, I kick the door. It swings open with a thud and I peek inside. Stalls, most without doors, stand to the right with sinks to the left, and another closed door stands at the back of the room. The white tile of the floor is cracked and covered in sand, dirt, blood, and grime that will never be washed away. The lights hanging from the ceiling have stopped working long ago. A small, once frosted window hangs in shards at the back of the room, letting in the last rays of the day. Mirrors above the sink are either broken or covered in so much grime and filth, that they are opaque. I step inside, my boots clomping on the floor.

The sinks are filthy as well, the taps missing in some cases, and the once white basins lined with black grime, dried red blood, and sand. I turn my back to the sinks and take a look in each stall, only one has a non-broken toilet, the others are cracked, chipped, or even missing in one case, its porcelain smashed all over the floor. I head to the door next, twisting the handle, and it swings open, showing me a shower cubicle with no windows. It's not as bad in here, it's still filthy, but there's no blood. The floor is like a wet room and I shut the door before turning back.

At least there are no bodies, cannibals, or ferals hiding in here. I sigh, staring down at my axe and whispering to it that I will get to use it soon, before I sheathe it and turn to see Archel and Dray waiting at the door. Bern peeks in behind them and I spot Henry lounging near the doorway when I step closer.

"Get fires going to ward off ferals. I want patrols swapping every four hours and one of you always awake. Tomorrow, we'll head out at first light to Paradise. Get them prepared," I instruct the others, before turning my attention to Dray. "Bring in some water, we need to wash off the blood and cannibal stink."

"Ya, Ma Queen," Bern calls.

"I'll take first watch." Henry nods, walking out of the bathroom. "What, I don't get invited for a shower?" Archel teases.

I saunter over until I'm almost chest to chest with him. "You couldn't handle me," I say in a sultry tone, before a mischievous grin tugs at my lips. "Plus, wouldn't your girl kill you?" I inquire, digging for information.

He laughs then and steps back. "She would try." He sounds wistful, his eyes far away. "Wouldn't that be great?"

Dray gives him a wicked smile, nodding in agreement. "You are both nuts," I comment with a laugh.

"And we picked crazier women, what does that tell you?" he counters, with a barely there smile before slinking out of the room.

Dray abruptly pushes away from the doorframe he was leaning against and smacks the wall. I blink but shake my head when I see he just smashed a huge spider that was crawling towards me. "So, if I'm invited to stay, does that mean I get to wash your back?" He wiggles his eyebrows, his eyes dropping to my breasts.

"If you're a good boy," I purr.

"Soulmate," he whispers, stalking over to me and gripping my hips in his calloused hands. "Where's the fun in that?" he finishes, pulling me close.

"Here, Ma Queen, ya water," Bern calls with a huff, dropping what must be a couple of gallons at our feet before winking and closing the door behind us.

I arch my eyebrow at Dray. "Bring that," I order, before twisting out of his hold.

I start to strip as I walk, losing my leather jacket and placing it on the least disgusting sink, before unlacing my boots and placing them just outside the shower cube door. I remove all my sheaths and hang them on the back of the shower door, keeping them in reach just in case, before I unbutton my jeans and wiggle out of them. I fold my jeans and then quickly remove my ruined t-shirt and fold it too, crinkling my nose as I lay them on top of my leather jacket. Dray watches me the entire time I strip until I'm completely naked.

I frown down at my skin, taking in the sand clinging to my tanned legs and arms, and I know it's going to be a bastard to get off. There's also blood still staining my hands and arms, as well as my chest. I must look like a mess, but from the tent in Dray's pants and the way he's licking his lips, I would say he doesn't care. Fuck, he probably likes it.

I give him a slow, knowing grin, and step into the cubicle. He lugs the water into the tiny room and drops it at my feet before getting undressed in record time, but leaves his chest holsters on. I eye them before looking at him.

"You like it when I wear them," he says in explanation, then shrugs before uncapping a jug of water. "At least we aren't having a sand bath like the men," he grunts, lifting the water, his arms bulging with the movements. "Turn around, soulmate, let me get your back first."

I do as I am told for once and the warmish water trickles down my back. I watch it drain away, the colour slightly pink as it leaves my body. I wrinkle my nose when I can feel the wet sand sliding from me, and Dray drops the jug to the floor and scrubs my back to get rid of it.

"Front," he demands, his voice gravelly.

I turn and he does the same to my front, not letting me lift a hand to help as he meticulously cleans the blood and sand from my body until I'm wet and clean in front of him. "Your turn." My voice is husky from having his hands trace every inch of my skin. I really don't think my nipples needed cleaning, but I'm not going to complain.

"I'm not done," he growls.

I frown, but my expression changes, my lips parting, as he drops to his knees. Cupping some water in his hand, he slides it between my thighs, and covers my pussy with it. He looks up at me, smirking. "Missed a spot."

He pushes my thighs open and I widen my stance, expecting him to use his hands. This is strangely intimate, not that we haven't been closer and done dirtier stuff to each other, but this is soft and caring and...fuck—

His tongue licks a long line up my pussy and my eyes widen as I look down at his icy gaze. "Dray," I warn, but he ignores me and buries his face between my thighs, licking me and nipping at my folds. He moves his head just far enough away to speak.

"We are heading for the Cities, for war. I'm going to have you as many times as I can just in case we don't come back. I've had nothing but fantasies of you for the last couple of years, and I plan to fulfil every one."

When you put it that way...

I reach down and grip his hair, winding the short locks through my fingers to hold on as he goes back to devouring my pussy. He eats me the way he fights, the way he fucks—hard, fast, and brutal. His tongue strokes me as he pushes two fingers inside, stretching me. I gasp and hold on tighter, grinding against his mouth, begging him for more. I reach up with my other hand and cup my breast, tweaking my nipple as he lashes my clit again and again with his tongue, his fingers curling inside of me. I'm on the edge, I can feel it, as I dance across the edge of exploding, but when something cold touches my pussy my eyes fly open, my hips stilling as I peer down at a grinning Dray.

His lips and chin are covered in my juices, and I follow his hand to see he has the side of one of his blades pressed to my clit. Before I can protest, he goes back in, licking around the blade and my hole, lapping at my juices as he presses harder with the blade, the steel edge biting but not cutting, and suddenly, I'm rocking harder into his mouth and hands, exploding. He groans, licking my pussy like I'm his favourite treat, lashing me even as I shiver from aftershocks, my clit oversensitive. I yank on his hair, pulling him away.

He takes the blade with him, and I see my wetness spread across the silver surface. Eyes still on me, he licks it clean, his tongue dragging over the weapon until there's nothing left. I tighten my grip in his hair and tug him to his feet. He stumbles up, the only time I have ever seen him ungraceful, and I push hard at his chest until he falls back against the tiled wall. He growls, pushing away and stalking towards me to grab me, but I jump at him. He catches me mid-air and spins me, smashing my back into the wall. I wrap my legs around his waist and slam my lips onto his.

I groan into his mouth, tasting my salty tang mixing with his natural taste. He tangles his tongue with mine, sucking it into his mouth as his hands span my waist and pin me to the wall, his fingers digging into my side hard enough to bruise. I love it when he treats me roughly, like I'm not made of glass but a warrior, who's woman enough to take it all. Jerking his head to the side, I bite down on his neck, grinding my teeth into his skin. He growls before reaching his hands down and cupping my arse, digging into my globes.

"Mark me, soulmate," he demands, rocking his hard cock against me, resting against my aching center.

"Fuck me," I order.

Reaching between us, I grab his cock, stroking him a few times before lining him up. "Now," I snarl.

He thrusts into me, stretching me around his hard length. I groan and rock my head back into the wall, closing my eyes in bliss. The bite of pain from him plunging in so quickly dissolves as he rocks his hips before pulling out and hammering back in. Dray doesn't do soft, but that's fine, I love it hard and rough. He lowers his head, biting and licking at my nipples. I hold him to me as he fucks me hard and fast against the dirty wall.

He hammers into me relentlessly, forcing my body to accept him, his hips smashing into mine. With each thrust he twists at the end so he presses against my still sensitive clit.

"Dray," I beg.

His eyes are wild, his lips thin with need, and his face a mask of desire as he stares intensely at me. I trace my hand down his shoulders and onto his chest, stopping at the raised edge of the brand he cut into himself. As I trace it, his hips stutter and he groans, his eyes hooded in pleasure. He's such a pain whore. I can't help but grin as I dig my finger into the cut harder and he yells, slamming into me. I hear a tile crack behind us as he fucks me brutally, my hand gouging into the cut as moans leave my mouth unchecked.

He smacks his hand into the wall next to us as he holds me up with the other, tilting my hips back to hit deeper until, with every thrust, my eyes are nearly rolling back into my head. He hits my clit on the next plunge, his cock dragging over the bundle of nerves, and I come with a silent scream, clenching around his cock as he explodes too, filling me with his come. He groans and buries his face into my shoulder, biting down on my skin to muffle the noise. We slump against the wall with his softening cock still inside me as I try to catch my breath.

"Sands below," I gasp out, my eyes closing as I lean my head back, wrapping my arms around his shoulders to hold him to me.

"Fuck their bunker. Paradise... Paradise is here between your thighs," he groans, kissing my skin where he bit softly before pulling back and looking at me with a smug, satisfied smile.

I laugh, slapping his shoulder. "Come on, let's get cleaned up before someone barges in here and you kill them for seeing me naked."

We washed up again after that, taking our time learning each other's bodies. No sex, just exploring. It was sweet. Afterwards, I got dressed, grimacing at the horribly stained shirt I had to put back on. He helped me into my jeans and weapons, and I helped him sort his before we braced ourselves to face the warriors gathered outside.

When we open the door, the smell of roasting meat and the sound of laughter hits us. I stand at the doorway watching with a small smile on my lips. Is this what it feels like to be part of something? Part of a family, maybe? The only thing missing are my men.

Five fires are set up within the ring of the bikes, each filled with Berserkers and Seekers talking and eating as they regale each other with stories. I spot men patrolling around the circle and Bern's giant frame at the front of the group. It makes me relax a bit, so I head to the nearest fire that's not as busy as the others where I spot Evan and Erik. Slipping through a gap in the circle, I find a spot and sit down with my legs stretched out towards the flames. Dray comes up behind me and sits down, his warmth blanketing my back, letting me relax further knowing it's not an open target. I lean back into him as he stretches his long legs out on either side of me. I feel the hard weight of his weapons against my skin and almost grin.

Erik nods at me from across the fire, while concentrating on ripping some meat from the stick in his hand. Evan passes me some he's cooked, and I take half and give the rest to Dray behind me. I eat quickly, realising how starved I am, and once I've finished, I snuggle back against Dray's chest and concentrate on the dancing fire, the voices of the others talking, and the flames twisting and curling in front of me, lulling me into a peaceful trance.

"You will never escape me, pet, wherever you go. Nowhere in the Wastes is safe from me, not even your own mind."

Blinking hard, I swallow and ignore the memories twirling

through my head as fear claws at my throat. I feel like I'm trapped, my heart banging against my chest.

"I'm always with you, pet, don't you see that?"

No, no. I close my eyes and breathe slowly, concentrating on that as I try to block his taunting. *It's just memories*, I tell myself, *just a ghost of your past, he can't hurt you.*

He can't hurt you, He can't—

"Want to play with me, pet? You know how much I enjoy our games."

Grinding my teeth, I force the memories back, focusing on anything but him, and trying not to stiffen against Dray.

"This Paradise, what is it?" Erik asks, his voice bringing me back from the brink. "I've heard the rumours, every babe out here has, any of it true?"

I focus on it, letting the harsh, rough quality of his voice bring me back to the here and now, and finally break my gaze away from the fire and swing it to him. He's leaning forward, watching me and waiting for an answer. The reflection of the flames sparkles in his eyes, reminding me so much of Noah. It sends a pang through me, but I ignore it and cuddle into Dray. He wraps his arms around me, holding me against him like he will never let me go. Erik's eyes flicker down to Dray's arms, but he says nothing.

"Some of the rumours are true," I start, pulling his gaze back to mine. "They have grass, they have safety—medicine. It's not like the Wastes. In Paradise, it's like the world never ended, like nothing ever changed. They have structures, government, an army, women, and children. They also have no sense of the real danger out here, they're...unprepared," I finish, looking at Evan. Erik follows my gaze and his eyes widen with understanding.

Evan ducks his head. "It's true. We know hardships, probably not the same ones you had out here, but life wasn't easy...Paradise isn't perfect. I learned that the hard way," he mutters, and I remember his story about the woman he lost.

Archel drops down in the circle, leaning back and watching the stars. "Full of dead men," he offers. I look at him in confusion, but he doesn't meet my gaze. "Monsters just the same, but they cover it up better. Out here, what you see is usually what you get with people. There, they are all liars, covering their evil and desires with a pleasant smile."

We all stare, but he doesn't elaborate further, and I catch Evan giving him a strange, considering look. "It's also run by my father," I add, my voice calm.

Everyone turns to look at me, as Erik blinked in astonishment. "Your father? I thought he was dead," he growls.

"So did I. Seems he escaped Ivar's wrath and hid down there, made a new life," I mutter bitterly.

"He's a fucking idiot," Dray snarls, his voice cutting through my nasty thoughts.

I shrug, not wanting to admit how much it still hurts that he didn't love me enough to look for me.

"He's an idiot if he didn't care enough to risk everything, to never stop looking, to burn the whole world to find you. You don't need him. Look at me, soulmate." He turns me so I'm facing him, his icy blue eyes staring deeply into mine. "I mean it. Family is a choice, the ones we are born into aren't forever, and just because you share blood doesn't mean you should love them. I chose Archel rather than my family and now you. Nothing, I mean nothing, would stop me from coming for you. Not a scorch, not a war, not fucking anything. You are too important. You are my everything. If he isn't willing to risk it all for his daughter, he doesn't deserve you. The weak don't survive in this world, you know that, and he's weak," he growls, gripping my face to make me look at him.

"Dray," I whisper.

"No, he might have been your father once, but this world changes everyone, not always for the better. I know what and who I am, Worth, and so do you. Don't you ever let him make you feel less for doing what you had to in order to survive. I'm so fucking proud of you, so fucking honoured that you chose me time and time again.

You're a warrior, a fucking Champion, and now a queen, and you're starting to act like it. Let him see that, let him see your scars, your story. Don't ever feel bad for not loving him, he has to earn that, and he hasn't yet. Sometimes, soulmate, family become strangers and strangers become family."

What can I say to that? He's right after all. He shows me it's okay to be angry, it's okay to hate the man who raised me and love a man who did not. Major... sands, I miss him. I could use his presence right about now, but I can't dwell on all I have lost or I will never surface again. I have lost too much, yet looking into Dray's eyes, I know I've gained just as much.

A family.

We're fucked up, brutal, blood loving psychopaths, but we are a family...scars and all.

CHAPTER EIGHT

AIN'T NO PARTY LIKE A SCAV PARTY

We'll reach the bunker in under two hours tomorrow if I'm right about where we are," I explain. After we had finished eating, I'd gathered Archel, Bern, Henry, Dray, Erik, and Evan to discuss our plans.

Archel looks around with a smirk. "Wait, does this make me a general?" he taunts.

"I don't know, assassin, do you want to be one?" I counter, genuinely curious. It seems like the only person he cares about is Dray and this mystery woman. If something more exciting came up, I don't doubt he would leave, since he's only here because of the upcoming deaths he gets to wield.

He shrugs, grinning at me. "Such a sweet offer, how could I refuse? I'll be your general, Worth, until I'm dead or I get bored."

Well, fuck, I guess that's the closest to a confirmation and a 'thank you' that I'm going to get.

"You're right about where we are. I remember this place from patrols," Evan interjects, ignoring the assassin's interruption alto-gether. "Around two hours' drive," he confirms.

"Good, I will only take Evan and Dray with me—"

"Ma Queen!" Bern protests, making me blink in surprise.

Henry leans forward. "Please take one of our generals. I know you can look after yourself, better than any man here, but what kind of general would I be if I left you to walk in there unprotected?"

Dray leans closer, whispering in my ear, "Let them prove themselves to you, that's what they're craving."

I nod, looking between their eager faces, and then a smirk crosses mine. "Bern, you come with us as well, let's show them what Berserkers are about."

He booms a laugh, slapping Henry on the back. "Tough look, lad."

Henry smiles, but nods to let me know he approves.

"The rest will stay outside as a show of force without making them think we mean harm. We are not staying. We will be on our way straight to The Ring after, where we will meet with everyone else. No one kills any Paradise guards, we can't afford a war on both fronts," I finish with a sigh, weariness flowing through my body.

"Okay, it's ma watch. Henry, ya rest." Bern clambers to his feet and nods at me before ambling away.

"I'll take early morning," I volunteer, but Henry laughs.

"You are queen now, let us do the watch, you need to save your strength."

I frown but he continues, "Without you, we are leaderless. We all know you don't mind getting your hands dirty, but we need you strong. We need you confident, so get some sleep." He stands then and wanders away.

Archel yawns and stretches.

"Let me guess, going to find a nice shadow to crawl into?" I joke. He laughs, grinning at me. "Shh, don't give away all my secrets."

He disappears then, like he was never here to begin with. I shake my head, not knowing how he does that, but I guess that's why he's such a good assassin. I'm more a punch first ask questions later sort of person.

Deciding there is nowhere better to sleep, I slip from Dray's grasp and curl up near the flames. Dray lays down next to me, pillowing his shoulder under my head, and pulls me back into his arms.

"Sleep well, soulmate, dream of only me and yours," he whispers, kissing my head gently.

How does he always know?

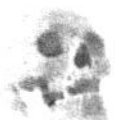

Something pulls me out of my slumber. I keep my eyes closed and my breathing even as I listen for whatever it was. Dray is warm at my front. Obviously, I flipped over in my sleep, and now he is curled around me with the flames still heating my back. I feel him tense slightly and know he's awake too. Slowly, so I do not alert whoever it is, I slip my hand up from his stomach where it was resting, and ever so slowly slide one of his blades from his chest holster. I feel him doing the same, pulling a blade from my thigh sheath. I tap his chest three times, then two, then one, and we both spring into action.

Turning, our blades aiming for our new prey, we stop only a hair's breadth away from a wide-eyed, guilty looking Archel, before his expression transforms into a grin. "Thought I was going to have to jump on you," he says cheekily, straightening from his crouch. "Get up," he orders, before striding away.

"I'll kill him," Dray mutters, and I snigger as I roll over and climb to my feet, stretching out my back. It can't be urgent, so I saunter over instead of rushing.

I can just see his silhouette on the edge of the camp with someone else, possibly Erik, standing beside him. I move through the camp as silently as I can and join them, looking out into the Wastes. I instantly spot what they're looking at and crouch lower into the sands to sit and observe. We are all silent, watching them.

Lights from cars shine out onto the sand as they speed past where we are. They don't seem to know we are here, and the flames from the fire are low, so unless they are specifically looking for us, they won't notice. *Patrols?* I wonder, watching them. They appear to be sweeping the area and are familiar with where they're going. This isn't the first time they've been out here.

"Patrols," I offer.

"Looks like. From your Paradise?" Archel guesses.

I nod. "Probably. They are the only people around here with trucks like that."

When the lights start to fade into the distance, I stand. "Keep an eye out, if they get too close, we'll move," I order. "I don't want to look like we're running, and I'm not killing a patrol, that wouldn't go over well."

"Understood," Erik rumbles, speaking for the first time.

I stand and nod at Archel before heading back to camp with Dray on my heels. Now that I'm awake, I'll head over to check in with other watchers. I find Bern over on the other side of our camp, behind the toilet building. He's leaning back against the wall, sharpening a sword in his lap as he looks out into the Waste. I quieten my steps, sinking slightly into the sand.

"I know ya there, Ma Queen," he calls and I grin.

Sliding down the building next to him, I see Dray talking to Henry a bit farther out, so I relax and let the peacefulness of the night wash over me. "Any problems?"

"Nah, just some scrapping Berserkers and Seekers. I sorted it," he rumbles, his gaze flickering down to his blade and then back to the sands around us.

I nod. I expected some infighting, especially since we added Seekers to an already volatile mix of people, so it doesn't surprise me.

"You're an odd one, ya know that?" he says, and I flick him a glance to see him smiling at me.

"How so?"

"Ye haven't asked me story, or anything, yet ye trust me to be ye general. Plus, I ain't ever seen a woman fight like you." He shrugs.

"Did you want me to ask you your story?" He shrugs again and I sigh.

"I don't ask because I have enough of my own skeletons and nightmares without adding others, and to have survived this long, you must have a boatload of both. I trusted you because you didn't lie to me, you helped me bury those women, you were gentle and respectful, and you were disgusted by the fact they had been hurt and killed. I don't judge someone by their past, I judge them by their actions now, and yours showed me everything I needed to know," I tell him, looking down at the sands.

"Good. But in case ye wanted to know, I was born Bernie Jennifer Waltx, I lived ma whole life up north. I was nineteen when the scorch struck, lived in a tiny village. We survived well for a while, off grid, until the food ran out. Then we simply started scavenging, hunting, to survive. My mother passed away peacefully, my father has been gone since I was a babe, and I had no siblings. I got tired of being alone, so I started to explore. I ran into a Berserker. He was a mean motherfucker, but he could fight. He taught me everything I know, how to hold a blade, how to wield one, and I helped him hunt down the rapist who'd killed his wife. Afterwards, we went back to the castle and the rest...is history." He shrugs, recollecting it all like you would read a storybook.

"Then ye came alone, Ma Queen, so fierce. You reminded me of him, a true warrior. Ivar was a bastard, and I hated what he turned us into, but it was all I knew. I have to live with tha regret every day, knowing that I dinnie do anything to protect the people he hurt, but I will make up for that now. I will balance my sins and earn my place at those pearly gates, even if it takes the rest of my life. You trust me... well, I'll trust you. I'm putting my soul in ye hands, Ma Queen. Use me, make me a better man...us better men, then Ivar ever did. That's the weight on your shoulders and I know you can do it."

I stare at the side of his face as he continues to sharpen the edge of his sword. "What makes you so certain?" He looks up from his blade now, meeting my gaze, pride shining in his eyes.

"You might not have known me, but I knew you. Saw you fight before, saw you win. No matter what odds you faced, you always won, you never stopped. The kindness you showed those girls, those slaves, tells me everything I need to know as well," he explains.

"Yeah, well, we're facing much worse odds now. Honestly, I might not make it back from the Cities," I admit.

"Then you die trying to save the ones you love. There are much worse ways to die." He grins and I laugh. He's crazy just like us, must be a Berserker thing. "You'll come back, Ma Queen, you have too many people depending on you not te. Plus, ye a stubborn bitch, ye wouldn't give them the satisfaction of dying."

"Very fucking true," I reply, laughing and settling back against the wall as I watch Dray head our way.

"I'm going to sort some Seekers out. Seems they need a reminder of who's in charge." He grins, excited at the prospect.

"Don't kill them all, we need some alive to fight with us."

He winks and slips away to deal with his people, and I lean my head back against the wall, rolling it to the side to look at Bern. "Mind if I spend the watch with you? There's no way I'm going back to sleep now."

"Don't want to watch the bloodbath?" he jokes.

Looking out at the landscape of sand before us, I grimace. "No, sometimes you just need a little peace."

"Then find your peace, Ma Queen. I'll find it with ye."

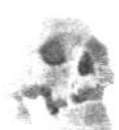

The sun rises over the sands, instantly heating the world and making us all sweat. I climb to my feet and stretch. After spending the last couple of hours with Bern, my body feels stiff. I nod at him and slip back into camp to see everyone still sleeping. Archel was right...they do need their rest, and with the sun's rays only just stretching across the sky, I can let them sleep for a little bit longer. Unable to sit still, though, I head over to Evan and nudge his shoulder with my boot. He has his hand stretched out in front of him, like he's seeking someone even in his sleep, and his face is scrunched up as if he's in pain.

I nudge him again and he springs awake, his eyes wide and confused, his hair sticking up on one side and his face coated in sand. I smirk at him. "Come on, sleeping beauty, time for your lesson."

I wander a few steps away then, letting him wake up as I eye a flat, empty space just beyond the bikes to show him some moves to help protect himself. My life would be easier if I wasn't worried about him dying all the time...that's what I'm telling myself anyway. Not that I care what happens to him...at all. Even my own mind calls me a liar on that one. Somehow, that grumpy bastard has become my friend.

"It's fucking early," he grumbles behind me.

"Sorry, princess, want me to let you get some more beauty sleep? Maybe just watch as you fumble with that dagger of yours and get yourself killed?" I taunt, turning to him and crossing my arms.

"Fuck you, Worth," he mutters, before sighing and sitting up. He strips off his jacket and throws it to the side as he glares up at me. "Fine, what do I do?"

I lead him past the bikes to the flat area before taking off my jacket too, and leaving my sword sheathed within it, I hold my arms out to the side. "Stab me."

He recoils a bit in shock. "What?"

"*Stab* me," I repeat, rolling my eyes. "Fuck, you're slow."

He narrows his eyes in anger and pulls out his dagger, but hesitates again.

"What's wrong, princess? Scared of breaking a nail?" I gibe.

He growls low and hard before jumping to his feet and slashing at me. I dodge him easily and smack the side of his head. "Too slow, again."

He lunges at me again. "You're transmitting your moves before you even make them, which will get you killed, and you're too slow. Stop worrying about hurting people. When it comes to a fight, either you fight with everything you got or you die. Your opponent won't care if they hurt you, so don't worry about hurting them," I instruct in a firm tone, smacking his hand this time when he tries to upper cut me with the blade. "Again."

We do this time and time again, dancing across the sand. Sweat pours down his face, his arm weak as he continues to signal his moves. I can see some of the others watching us, gathering, but I ignore them. "No, too fucking slow and you're still signalling! Your eyes and feet are giving you away," I growl, and this time when he goes to attack, I grab his blade, spinning to dislodge it from his arm, and have it across his neck from behind in a second.

"You're dead. Again!" I yell, giving him the blade and moving back.

When he extends his sword, I kick his legs and he yelps as he falls to his ass in the sand. With a wordless scream, he gets to his feet and comes at me in a whirlwind, his anger taking over. I block and dodge each hit. "Good, you're getting faster. That's it, stop worrying about hurting me. Don't think too much, just *move*," I order, slipping past as he strikes out randomly.

"That's it!" I yell, moving around him as he slashes again and again before stopping, and panting as he watches me, his eyes wide and dagger held close. I grin then. "Getting better, but you're still slow, and I could see you moving a mile away. Let's go again."

He groans but nods, which is good. I can teach him everything I know, but he has to want to learn, and he has to want to survive, or what's the point? We parry for a while until I call stop. By now, people have gathered to watch. I scan the crowd and then beckon Archel.

"Two blades, no deep hits," I instruct.

I pull my own from my leg sheaths, holding the handles with the blades pointed out as I widen my stance and look at Evan. "Watch what we do, Archel, slow it down," I command.

He grins as he saunters over, pulling two blades out and flipping them in his hands. One minute he's standing, relaxed, facing me, and the next he's moving. He's fucking fast and I have to move at the last minute. I let everything else go, just concentrating on the fight. We spin and turn, landing hit after hit on each other, but it's an even fight. Where I'm fast, he's smoother...stealthier. Stinging cuts line my body, but I also land multiple cuts on him, although we're making sure to pull the hits so we don't kill each other.

He laughs as he spins and I join in, loving being able to just let go during an even fight for once. He's good, I'll give him that. He feigns right and then spins left, his blade lands at my throat and he grins at me. "I win."

"Do you?" I whisper, glancing down. He follows my gaze and sees my blade pointed at his cock.

He howls with laughter and steps back, respect in his eyes. "Always the cock, huh?"

I shrug then and sheathe my blades, looking at a gobsmacked Evan. "When I get through with you, I want you to move like that. Again," I call.

He groans but grips his blade, and instead of just blocking, I actively move with him this time with one blade until we are parrying blows. His footsteps are unsure and stumbling, but he soon catches up, and what he lacks in finesse and technique, he makes up for in attitude. He doesn't quit, not once, and every blow he comes back swinging.

"Again," I demand after I disarm him.

"How did you learn to fight?" Evan asks as he rips into his meat. The fire is blazing between us, and the others are packing up while we eat a quick breakfast before getting on the road. A small cut lines his cheek, but he doesn't seem to care. I barely notice the ones on my arms and chest from Archel.

"The hard way—from doing it. I took the strengths and styles of others and made them my own, learned from each clan's weakness, and then used those against them." I shrug, sipping my water.

"Weakness?" he echoes, focused.

"Yep, Berserkers are hard hitters. They come at you strong, but get inside that protection and you can take them down easily, and they don't do well on far attacks or against speed. Scavs and Roadies are mostly stupid, they rely on weapons and can't think a few steps ahead, so confusing them is easy. Worshippers are more reserved, get them angry."

"Seekers?" he inquires, stumbling over the name.

"Harder. They're controlled, smooth killing machines who are fast and good thinkers. It's a hard fight." I shrug. "Advice for you? Run, run as fast as you can," I tease.

"That's right, pretty boy, run," Archel jokes.

"Got it, run." Evan rolls his eyes. "So, you're an assassin?" he questions Archel.

"The best." Archel winks.

"Boys, please, if you're going to measure dicks, at least let me finish eating first," I grumble, making them all laugh.

"We all know mine is the biggest." Dray shrugs and stands up, flicking open the button on his jeans.

"Sands below, I swear, if you pull your cock out, I'm going to cut it off and feed it to you," I warn, narrowing my eyes on him.

He winks down at me and looks at the others who are cupping their junk protectively. "Don't worry boys, she wouldn't—she likes it too much," he teases, but sits back down.

I roll my eyes again. *Men.* "And on that note, it's time to go."

I finish my water and climb to my feet, slipping into my jacket and grabbing my bandana from my pack before throwing it over my shoulder. Everyone else packs up, and I slip onto my bike and rev the engine. "Let's ride!" I yell, hearing some people whoop as more engines roar. I grin as I cover the lower half of my face and set off through the Wastes.

The Cities

About thirty minutes into our trip, I'm gunning it hard, wanting to get to Paradise as soon as possible. Only the sun glinting off metal in the road alerts me to a problem, and I quickly slow down, turning my bike sideways and almost tipping it. The others follow me, diverging from the broken, cracked road into the sand.

It's a fucking ambush.

I slip from my bike as fast as I can, grabbing my swords and turning just as a war cry goes up. I was out in front, so only Dray and Archel are by my side, the others speeding closer as I race towards the charging scavs. I notice some Berserkers in their midst and frown. Fucking deserters who are obviously not happy with the change of leadership.

The clanging metal is drowned out by engines revving as the others race towards us. There must be at least forty scavs and Berserkers altogether, just waiting for us to pass them. They knew we were coming and laid a trap. Raising my blade, I block the downward stroke of a sword heading towards my face wielded by a Berserker. He spits at me, his nostrils flaring and eyes wide. "Fucking dead bitch walking!" he shouts.

"Not today, motherfucker," I fire back, and break our weapons' lock and stab downwards, impaling him. I sweep away, my back meeting Dray's and Archel's sides as we move together, protecting each other's backs.

I rip open a Berserker's cheek and he roars as he falls back, but a scav quickly takes his place. I manage to kill four and wound even more by the time I hear engines cut off and the war cry of my people. I peer through the gaps of fighting bodies to see Bern tossing people away like they're toothpicks with Henry by his side as they fight to get to us. I scream back, pushing into the scavs and deserters.

I spin and slash, gutting men and cutting their throats, and even in the red haze of bloodlust, I remind myself who my men are so I don't hurt them. My body is tiring, but I keep fighting, never giving up. Some of them land hits, but the blood they spill only infuriates me more. Dray stays by my side the whole time, moving with me as we decimate their ranks. I stop for a moment, panting as I hold my sword in front of me, and some of the scavs who ambushed us look around, obviously realising they're outnumbered, and start to back away.

We chase them onto the road, but they jump into their cars and onto their bikes and peel away. Gasping, my blood-covered swords hanging at my sides, I watch as they race away into the sands.

"They will come back, they obviously want you dead," Erik growls.

"They do, but next time we will be ready," I snap.

I slice through the tripwire they had set up across the road and turn to face my warriors. "They thought they could kill us! They know better now!" I scream and raise my sword. They cheer and Archel grins at me, looking way too pleased. Dray is cleaning his blades, his eyes smouldering as he stares me. Evan is panting hard, his knife clutched in his hand and his eyes wide. I sheathe my swords and step closer, taking his knife and sheathing it for him.

"You did well," I praise in a low voice.

He blinks before swallowing hard as he nods. Bern claps him on his back, sending him stumbling forward. "We will make a Berserker out of you yet!" he yells, and cheers go up again, making me smirk. Evan looks bewildered.

"The first kill is the hardest, after that it gets easier," I offer, just as arms wrap around me and drag me back into a hard chest.

"You are a fucking masterpiece when fighting, do you know that?" Dray murmurs into my ear, making my grin grow.

I turn in his arm and kiss him hard before pulling back to gaze up at him. "We need to get to Paradise."

"Lead the way, soulmate, we'll follow you."

CHAPTER NINE

CALL ME DADDY

I spot the towering warehouses in the distance and know we're getting close. I stop us outside of the fence to give orders. "Okay, listen up! Bern, Archel, Dray, and Evan are with me, the rest of you stay out here. Do not attack anyone, or I will kill you myself," I say seriously, scanning my eyes over the gathered group. "Watch out for rogue Berserkers or scavs!" With that final instruction, I sling my bag over my shoulder.

I hear some grumbles, but they climb off their bikes, and stretch before settling in. "Let's go," I call, and Bern, Dray, Archel, and Evan all head my way as I slip through the fence, and try to remember the way in without asking Evan for directions. My father gave me a map last time I was here, but it must have been lost somewhere at The Ring when Ivar took me. This place is like a maze, no wonder no one has ever found Paradise. It's in the middle of nowhere, so unless you were really looking for it, you wouldn't notice it. By pure luck alone I stumble upon the hidden entrance to the bunker. But now we have another problem—how the fuck do we get in?

"I'm betting they have cameras," I murmur.

"You should flash them, that'll get their attention," Archel teases. I arch an eyebrow. "Why don't you?"

He cups his junk protectively and sighs dramatically. "Alas, I can't, my woman would kill me."

"She's definitely made up, no one could put up with him," I tell Dray loudly, just as a siren comes from the bunker doors and I hear the mechanisms of it moving. "Huh, well that was easy."

I keep my hands away from my weapons, not wanting them to shoot first and ask questions later. But it's especially hard when guards pour out from the partially opened door and immediately point their guns at us. Reluctantly, I hold up my hands. "I'm here to see my father!" I shout to be heard over their yelling.

"Don't move!" a few of them shout, and I roll my eyes.

"Do we look like we're moving? No. Now lower your fucking weapons, I'm starting to get annoyed."

"Stand down!" comes a stern order from inside the bunker. I smirk as I watch my father hurry outside, pushing through the men to get to me. He stops just before them, staring at me in confusion.

"Taza—Worth, what are you doing here?" He frowns, looking at the men behind me before his eyes once again focus on me. I feel nothing...my real father is dead, and this man is still just a stranger.

"I need your help." It pains me to say it, but I swallow my fucking pride. I would do anything for my men.

"Why would we help you, savage?" A man pushes through the crowd to stand shoulder to shoulder with my father. He's more muscle than skin, his face is all hard lines, and he has short grey hair, and clothing pressed within an inch of its life with the nametag "Captain" proudly embroidered on the pocket.

"Because if you don't help me, I have an army of pissed off savages outside your gates just waiting for a fight. It would be a shame if we had to take what I need by force. And I will if I have to, that's not a threat, just the truth. You're in my way of getting to my men, so I suggest you let us in and give me what I fucking need before I lose my temper. And for the last fucking time, lower your guns before I get really annoyed."

Dray and Archel snigger, and I hear Evan sigh as he steps up next to me. "She speaks the truth, Captain."

"You're with them now, the savages?" the captain scoffs.

Evan stands straighter. "She saved my life. If that makes me a savage lover, I guess that's what I am." He shrugs and I grin over at him before replacing it with a glare, aiming it at my father and his men. I take a step closer and their weapons, which they were starting to lower, rise up and focus back on me.

"I have lost people I love, I have faced down a fucking mad king, and I have been tortured, raped, and almost killed. Yet I'm still standing, I'm the fucking Queen of the Berserkers, and those savages as you call them? We *rule* the fucking Wastes. I suggest you choose your next words very carefully, because I'm losing my patience."

"Worth, that won't be necessary, will it, Captain?" my father asks. I look into the captain's eyes and see nothing but spite, hate, and death there. This man is one to watch, he doesn't give a fuck about Paradise, he only likes the power. I step closer to him, ignoring the guns that follow my movement. "I've killed men like you for less, so I suggest you show some fucking respect. I know you, and I know your type. I can see it in your eyes. You call us savages, but I'm betting you have crossed lines that we never would just to keep your power. Push me, Captain, I dare you. I'll teach you why they call me the

Champion."

He scowls, his face reddening, and I grin. "Oh, that hurt, didn't it? You don't like women, especially strong ones. I wonder..." I take another step closer, almost touching him now. "If I started looking into it, how many women have you hurt inside these walls that were made to protect them?"

"Too many," Archel says darkly. I don't look away from the captain, sensing he's about to explode. "I know that for a fact. I've seen the aftermath of what his men do to women. I won't kill you here and now, that honour rests with my woman for what you all did to her." I blink in surprise and glance over at Archel to see his face cold and so full of fury that even I wouldn't mess with him. What did they do to his woman? I debate killing the captain, but I can read between the lines. Whatever he did to her, Archel is right, she deserves to be the one doing the killing. So, I step back and wink at the man.

"Don't worry, I'm not your death, she will be." His eyes widen then, flashing with fear, and I know he hurt that woman. Archel's woman. Shit. Blood is going to rain from the fucking sky. I wouldn't mess with the assassin and especially not someone he so clearly loves. He will gut this place for revenge, and I'm betting his woman will be at his side, because he would only love a strong fighter. I turn, giving the captain my back and nod at Archel.

"After we're done, get your woman, get your revenge."

A genuine smile forms on his face. "You'll like her, Worth. She's a stubborn bitch, hell of a fighter too."

"What's her name?" I inquire, purposely ignoring the angry captain, his unsure men, and my father, showing them how little respect and worry I put into them. Instead, I trust Dray to watch my back. He's staring at the captain with death in his eyes.

"Piper," Archel answers, and Evan's head swivels his way, his eyes widening in shock.

"What the fuck did you just say?" he yells, frozen to his spot. I look between them. That name seems familiar...*oh shit.*

Well, this should be fun.

"What's it to you, Doc?" Archel teases.

"*Piper*, my fucking Pip? You know where she is?" Evan screams, pulling out his dagger and advancing on Archel.

Sighing, I slip between them, pressing my hands on each of their chests. "No killing, not yet. Plus, there's enough love to go around." I grin then and I hear Dray laugh.

"You know her?" Archel queries, his voice deadly. "You let her get hurt? Attacked?"

"Attacked? They told me she was dead! I didn't believe them..."

His voice trails off, and his face goes pale as he realises what Archel said. "They-they hurt her?"

Archel watches Evan in sympathy, some of his anger dissipating. "They did more than that. When I found her, she was nearly dead, yet she still tried to fight me off. I saved her, took her somewhere safe where they would never find her."

"Is she—" Evan starts and then swallows, tears gathering in his eyes.

"She's alive, stronger than ever. She can shoot a mean bow. When I left, she was on her way to leading her own Clan. She protected them from an eater attack. Has nightmares, though, real bad ones."

Evan growls, grinding his teeth. "She always did, she would only ever sleep if I was there. Fuck!" he screams, clutching his head. "She alive, she's alive, Pip—" Hearing the panic in his voice, I reach out and grip his shoulders, forcing him to look at me. When he finally meets my gaze, I see a broken man. His eyes are distraught and filled with tears, his face wild.

"Do not do anything stupid. We'll get what we need, and then and only then do we get revenge," I growl.

Evan looks over my shoulder. "You're sure it was people from here who attacked her?"

I feel Archel's front hit my back. "Yes, I saw their bodies as they were being eaten. They were guards."

Fuck.

I look over at my father, who's frowning and trying to listen to the conversation.

"I need to see her. Worth, I have to—" "No," Archel snaps, his tone sombre.

"What did you fucking say?" Evan rumbles lowly. I sigh at the look in his eyes, he's hoping for a fight.

"I won't compromise her safety. That place is her home, her fucking sanctuary. How do I know you didn't hurt her too? I will kill you and all of them before I let anyone near her again," Archel warns coolly, his tone so calm that even I question if I want to be in the middle of them.

I look to Dray for some help, but he just grins maniacally at me as he tosses his blade up and down, before catching it and throwing it again.

"Fuck, okay. We don't have time for this. Wait…" I narrow my eyes on Archel. "Is that why you agreed to come so quickly?"

He winks at me. "Don't worry, queenie, I wasn't going to kill them…just hurt them, kidnap them, and offer them to her as a gift."

"How romantic," I retort with a snort.

"You—agggh!" Evan throws his hands in the air and I slip from between them. They'll have to deal with their love triangle another time. Right now? I need to get serious so I can get my men back.

"Both of you stay out here and get your shit sorted. We have a fucking war coming, so we don't have time for this crap. Oh, and no killing each other. If we don't come out in two hours, get our warriors and storm this fucking place," I order, then glance at Dray. "Come on."

I throw Evan and Archel one last narrow-eyed look to see them staring each other down, before I turn back to the Paradise people. "Let us in."

My father nods, stepping aside and gesturing towards the door. As I stride past him, the captain leans down and hisses in my ear, "Your daddy won't always be here to protect you."

"But I will be," Dray snarls from behind me. He darts an arm out and grips the collar of the captain's shirt, pulling him close and getting in his face. "If you so much as breathe on her again, I'll skin you alive." Dray's icy eyes penetrate the captain's stare for a long moment before he abruptly pushes him away, making the older man stumble back.

I laugh and look up at my savage man.

"You can call me daddy if you want." He wiggles his eyebrows and I snort as I turn away.

We're marched straight to my father's office where men are stationed outside and the captain follows us in. It looks exactly the same in here. Dray glances around, laughs, and then sprawls in the chair in front of the desk. Grinning, I perch on his lap and he wraps his arms around me. He looks calm, even half asleep, but I know he sees everything, his body tense under mine. The captain glares at us as my father sits heavily in his chair. His eyes flicker to Dray and he frowns before he looks back at me.

"What happened?"

He looks tired, really tired, and not as put together as he was when we last spoke. *Is that blood on his arm?*

I tilt my head. "I could ask you the same thing."

He frowns, rubbing at his head and looks at the captain. "There has been unrest here."

"Enough, we tell her nothing, daughter or not. You shouldn't have brought her here in the first place, and now she has led a whole army here. You have been stripped of your leadership. Now, savage, why are here you?" the captain snaps.

I freeze, my father isn't the leader anymore? What the fuck has happened since I have been gone?

Dray stiffens even further, and I lean back on him to stop him from ripping the man apart. "You are really going to have to stop insulting me," I point out casually.

"What are you going to do, little girl?" he sneers.

"Not me, him." I jerk my head back at Dray. "He's more... savage, as you call us. Doesn't take well to me being insulted."

"What happened to your other...erm, boyfriends?" my dad stumbles over his words.

"The Cities," is all I say, and they both straighten. "That's why I'm here, not to invade you, so you can keep your little fucking bunker for all I care. I only need one thing."

"And what's that?" the captain says sarcastically.

"I need the maps I saw on your desk the last time I was here, the ones of the Cities."

The captain swears and looks at my father in disgust. "Why?" is all my dad simply asks.

"Because they are starting a war, and I plan to stop them before it escalates, get my men back, and lead the people who took them into a trap. You can either help or hide down here."

"Your war has nothing to do with us," the captain snaps, crossing his arms over his chest with a scowl turning up his thin lips.

"You really think once they're done with us 'savages,' as you call us, they will stop? They want Paradise, they always have. If we don't stop them, they will storm this place and take it for their own. You've been separated from the rest of the Wastes, from the world, for too long. It's time you joined us, because without our help, you will burn."

"How do you know?" my dad queries, ignoring the muttering captain.

"My men, they were originally sent to the Wastes to find Paradise for the Cities, they never planned to go back though. I'm guessing the Cities took them to find out what they know. My question is—why are they curious about a bunker in the middle of nowhere?" I lean forward on Dray's lap, my expression speculative and my tone suspicious as I press, "What are you hiding?"

The captain and my father share a glance then and I know whatever they say next will be a lie.

"A safe place, that is all," the captain deadpans.

"Bullshit," I snarl. "But keep your secrets, I just need your maps. I won't ask how you got them, just give them to me and I will take my army away and stop the threat before they kill you all for whatever you're hiding."

The door opens then, and we all glance over at the soldier looking in. "Captain, we have a problem."

He nods and turns to glare at Dray and me, before turning a stern expression on my dad. "Give them nothing," he demands, his jaw clenching. "Don't even fucking speak until I'm back, you're on thin ice."

He strides away then and slams the door behind him. I blink as I turn to see my father scrambling across the desk to stand in front of me, grabbing some papers as he goes, watching the door before looking at me. His eyes are wide and filled with panic.

"We don't have much time," he says urgently. "I'm not in charge anymore, Tazanna. You need to get out of here and fast. Here." He hands the maps over, his hands shaking. "Unrest was an excuse, it's a fucking uprising with the army in charge and they're taking no prisoners. I'm so sorry. I thought what we were doing here was to save people, but apparently I was so wrong, forgive me," he rushes out, with tears in his eyes.

"Come with us," I beg. There is no love lost between us, but it seemed like last time maybe, just maybe, we could work through those feelings in time, but when faced with the idea of leaving him here with a clear fucking psychopath, all of that love comes flooding back.

He smiles sadly then. "I can't, these people need me. He'll kill them all if they step out of line. I wasn't brave enough to save you, but I will save them or die trying. I'm trying to be a better man, one you would be proud of. Let me have that. Now, you must go," he urges, shooting nervous glances at the door.

"We can fight this," I argue, standing. "Please, let me help," I implore.

He smiles at me then and cups my cheeks. "I'm so proud of you, you're so strong, just like your mother. But your family, your real family, needs you. Go. I will keep him from following you."

"He won't be happy. What if he tries to kill you?" I ask, worried. "Then I die protecting you, something I should have done a long time ago."

"Soulmate, it's his choice, we have to go," Dray rumbles as he stands, wrapping his arm around my shoulders.

My dad looks at Dray, his eyes widening as he takes in the weapons, scars, and everything that is just Dray. "I love him," I whisper, and my dad sighs, peering at the Seeker King.

"Keep her safe."

Dray looks at my father, his eyes cold and deadly. "Always, though it tends to be her keeping everyone else safe." My father and Dray exchange a nod before Dray strides to the door, peering out and scanning the hall, before stepping out to keep watch.

I smile to myself as he leaves. My 'savage' man is giving me a few private moments with my dad.

Holding the maps close to my chest, I turn my attention away from the door and fix my gaze on my father. He's so much smaller now, weak, but I see a fire, a fight in his eyes that I didn't see before. "You'll always be my father," I admit quietly, earning me a smile.

Reaching out, he gently squeezes my shoulders and then releases them. "Go."

I search his watery gaze for a moment longer before nodding and turning to leave. My heart clenches in my chest, knowing that this will probably be the last time I'll see the man who raised me, the last member of my real family. But sometimes, you have to let someone make their own paths, their own decisions. To stop that would be to take away their free will, their freedom, and I will never do that. He has made his choice, chosen to take a stand, and he's found the thing he is willing to fight for. I can respect him for that.

"Tazzie," my dad grates out, his rough voice full of unspoken emotions, making me freeze in the doorway and glance over my shoulder. "Stay alive. I don't know what the Cities want from Paradise. All I know is the captain will kill anyone or anything to stop that secret from getting out. It's bad, really bad."

I stare at my father, surrounded by his books, office, and luxuries, and for once all I feel is love and regret. Maybe in another life I could have forgiven him and we could have been a family. But maybes are for dreamers, people who wish on stars. That isn't me. All we have is one life, one chance to make a difference, to love, live, and laugh as big and as much as you can. He made mistakes, he wasn't perfect, he was human. But all I see when I look back into his bright blue eyes is the man who read me bedtime stories.

Yes, he made mistakes, but he was my father, and the world will be a little bit darker without him in it. All that we can hope is for is that our loved ones remember us, still love us, and pass on our memories. I can ensure that.

I will never forget him. Even when he forgot me.

"Goodbye, Daddy," I whisper, and then rush after Dray. My father made his stand, now it's time I made mine.

CHAPTER TEN

KILL COUNT

We get lucky as we run through the corridors of the underground bunker. All the guards seem to be distracted by something, so we manage to slip through without being noticed. We head straight for the door, intent on getting outside, but as we head to the hangar, a guard turns the corner, his eyes widening in alarm. Before he can sound the alarm or ask what we're doing, I sprint forward, leap into the air, and tackle him to the ground. I smash his head into the white floor below, and he's knocked out instantly. Climbing to my feet, I grin back at Dray who's staring at me like he wants to tackle *me* to the floor.

"Later, big boy." I tap his chest as I glide by him, and he quickly follows as I sneak back through the hangar door. I frown when I notice the blast door is slightly open, but it works in my favour, so I roll underneath it with Dray close behind and instantly sit into a crouch.

"Where are Evan and Archel?" I hiss, climbing to my feet and looking around at the empty ramp leading to the blast doors.

What's going on? Where is everyone?

An alarm blares then, coming from Paradise, and I spin, looking at the blast doors. I can hear gunshots, the siren almost covering them and...screams? Fuck! Looking down at the map, I debate my options for only a moment before I fold it up and stick it in the back of my trousers, then pull out my swords. I look at Dray to see he has his blades in his hands as well. We nod at each other, but a noise behind us has us whirling.

A blood covered Archel strides towards us with a pissed off looking Evan, who's clutching a knife. I check them over, but it doesn't look like the blood is theirs, so I roll back under the blast door and move away quickly. Ducking behind a truck just in case anyone is waiting to shoot us, Dray, Evan, and Archel join me.

"What happened?" I question, as I look around the corner of the truck.

"Fucking traitors," Archel spits.

"The rogue Berserkers?" I growl, looking over at Archel.

He nods. "Attacked when they were changing guards, got under the door. I couldn't stop them all, they left twenty outside and some slipped past while we were fighting."

I grin then, unable to help myself. "Only twenty? You're getting slow if it took you that long to get through them." I tease.

"You want to wager that?" he challenges, smiling back. "Most kills?" I offer.

"You're on!" He stands up then and I follow him.

"You are all fucking crazy," Evan groans while Dray laughs.

Archel heads around the right side of the truck and I go around the left, with Dray and Evan on our heels. I look back at Dray and motion to Evan. He understands and moves closer, protecting the doc. The hangar is filled with trucks, weapons, and supplies, but it's deadly silent apart from the blaring alarm as the lights flash across the white utilitarian walls, creating a creepy effect.

We move silently across the wide open space, our eyes scanning everything until we get to the door. I press my back against the wall next to it, and Archel copies me on the other side. Excitement courses through me, my body moving smoothly, my adrenaline pumping. I grin at Archel and he returns it. I hold up a finger then drop it and we move at the exact same time. Rushing through the door, I spin left and he spins right, but no one is in sight. I press my back to his, and look down the empty corridor. Even the guard I knocked out is gone, leaving behind just a blood smear to show where I took him down.

"It's too fucking quiet. They must be fighting elsewhere," I mutter softly.

Just then I hear gunshots and I point down my hallway, going silent. Archel moves up next to me while Dray protects our back as we press up against the walls, stilling. Even though we haven't really worked together, we're comfortable with one another, but the most important thing is that we trust each other. I trust his skills and he trusts mine. I know Dray is looking after Evan, so I can concentrate on hunting down the rogue Berserkers who have laid siege to Paradise. I shouldn't help, not after the captain's rude behaviour, but there are innocents down here. They don't deserve to die, not even the assholes, especially since the rogues are here because of me.

We move around the corners, ducking low in case anyone shoots at us. The gunfire is getting louder, so we slow down slightly, and I stop at the next corner, ducking low as I peek around the bend and spot the flashing of guns at the other end of the corridor, moving the other way. A line of soldiers are firing into what looks like a never-ending horde of rogues, who are ripping, slashing, and tearing these prissy guards apart.

I glance back at Archel. "Get ready to lose, assassin," I taunt, before slipping around the corner.

I move to the back of the guards, hearing them shouting and swearing at each other as they continuously shoot at the Berserkers, the bullets just barely slowing them down. I hear a guard's gun click empty and he looks up just in time to see a Berserker leap at him with a war cry. His screams start instantly, his blood spurting as he's ripped apart. The line breaks as guards start to fight hand-to-hand.

I jump into the melee, my swords flashing as I arc one down and hack through the neck of the Berserker on top of the guard. He howls and falls to the side, bleeding out, and I spin with the movement and grab the back of another's head. When he snarls into a guard's face, I slit his throat and let him drop the floor.

"Two!" I call to Archel, and hear him swear as he appears behind me and takes down a Berserker who was trying to sneak up on me.

"One," he replies with a wink, not sweating or even out of breath. I move farther into the hall, and the Berserkers start to notice I'm here and yell as they all head towards me. "That's it, you motherfuck- ers, come and get it!" I shout, swinging my swords in an arc as I walk towards them. A big bastard with a scarred face rushes me, his long sword coming down to cleave my head off.

I duck under his arm and stab forward, impaling him on my swords, and keep moving as I spin to the right. Pulling my blades free, I hear the thud as he falls behind me. I duck under an arrow and slide across the floor, thrusting my swords upwards, and cutting the femoral artery of a Berserker as I move through his open legs.

Jumping to my feet behind him, I grin at another Berserker as he narrows his eyes and waits for me to make a move. Playing it smart, I see. "Four," I yell for Archel's benefit.

I hear the sounds of his blades and the death gurgles following, and know he won't be far behind me. I flick my eyes next to the Berserker, and like I predicted, he turns slightly to look, so I jump at him. He doesn't even have time to raise his sword to stop me as I hack through his arm holding it. He howls, his blood spraying me in the face as his arm hangs half cut off from his shoulder. He blinks in shock as I spin and slash his throat, making blood arc behind me as I move on again.

A guard is firing at a Berserker who just keeps coming, so I wait for him to run out of bullets before I throw one of my knives, and it embeds in the Berserker's chest. He freezes, looks down at it, and as the guard falls to the floor, crouching and protecting his head, I leapfrog from his back and throw two more blades before landing behind the Berserker and turning to find my next opponent. Only a few are still remaining, and I glance behind me to see Archel laughing and fighting two. I sweep my gaze and spot an open door at the end of the hall coated in blood.

"You clean up, I'm heading deeper!" I call, before rushing to the doorway.

Slipping in and crouching to the floor, I peek around the door, noting the occupants before forming a plan. There are at least fifteen Berserkers, with multiple dead guards on the floor, and what looks like a few innocent Paradise dwellers cornered while the Berserkers taunt them. Standing up, I swing my blades as excitement courses through me. I can fight some of my tension and anxiety over my men away. Let's show both the Berserkers and Paradise who they are messing with.

Kicking open the door, I press my fingers to my mouth and whistle. Every head turns my way. "Alright, bastards, why don't you pick on someone who can fight back? Unless you are all scared." I grin then, my swords held loosely at my sides.

They are half turned towards me, forming a barrier between the Paradise dwellers and me. I see pale, fear-filled faces peeking between legs, silently begging me. Their sobs fill the air, and the familiar scent of blood hangs heavily in the room from the guards left gutted and ripped apart along the floor. I'm guessing this used to be some kind of canteen, since tables fill the big room, some turned over and covered in half eaten food, with some still standing.

"Fucking slave!" one of the men shouts, and it seems to wind the others up. Four men step forward.

I grin, walking farther into the room. "Only four? Damn, you should have brought more," I sneer.

The other Berserkers stop and watch, still blocking the dwellers as the four rogues circle me. I note everything about them I can in under a minute, looking for weakness to use against them. One holds an axe, but seems to hold himself stiffly, maybe an old wound? One is faster, holding two daggers in each hand, which are covered in blood. But he has a patch over his left eye and seems to overestimate each step—he's struggling to see, so the wound must be fresh. Another man is slow and lumbering, favouring his left leg. The last one I spot has no visible weakness, so I know he'll be the hardest since he holds his sword with ease from years of use.

He dies first.

We all move at the same time and I head straight for the last man. He raises his sword and one of mine clashes with his, blocking his downward swing while my other buries deep in his stomach. He gags, his eyes widening in shock as I spin, pulling it with me and letting him drop to his knees. A dagger flies past me, the air whistling next to my ear, and I feel it cut as it passes followed by blood dripping from the wound.

I duck as the axe soars above my head, so I turn behind the Berserker and, like I predicted, he struggles to turn, giving me enough time to slit his throat. Using him as I shield, I spin and hear the thud of dagger embedding in his chest before I drop him and leap over his body, heading to the one favouring his left leg. I slide to the floor, avoiding more daggers, and slice at his leg as he howls and stumbles before falling to the floor. I'm on him in a second, crouching on his chest as I drive one of my swords into his heart. It sticks into the floor beneath him and I growl in frustration as I struggle to pull it out, but I leave it there, having to jump to my feet to face the last man.

"Tazzie!" I hear my father shout, and I stumble for a second. I didn't even know he was here with the dwellers, but I didn't really look. That stumble costs me precious seconds and a cut opens up across my shoulder from a dagger I only just manage to slightly evade. I look at the cut and then at the last of the four Berserkers who's palming another dagger.

"Now you've pissed me off," I snarl. Holding my remaining sword, I dodge flying daggers as he rapidly throws them at me while I advance on him.

"Boo," I whisper when I get to him. He stabs at my arm, the blade implanting in my free arm, and I hack at his side with my sword.

He stumbles to the side, clutching the wound gushing blood, and

I slash again and again until he falls as nothing but a blood covered rogue. Breathing heavily, I look down at the knife sticking out of my arm. Eyeing the remaining rogues, I pluck it out and throw. It hits one the Berserkers and he goes down hard. The others seem to hesitate, and I use that to rip off the bottom of my shirt and bind the wound on my arm to staunch the blood flow. My fingers are tingling, but I can still feel my arm, which is good because it means he didn't hit any nerves or arteries.

"Who's next, you murdering pricks?" I call before eyeing them. "Or are you all scared a little slave girl is going to kill you?"

"You're the only one dying here, and when you're dead, we'll all have our fun with Ivar's whore."

I roll my eyes. "Sure thing. Those are some big words for a man hiding in a corner."

I hear the door open and I know it's Archel, Evan, and Dray. "These are mine," I growl in warning, not looking away from the Berserker.

"Awww, soulmate, at least let me get one or two?" Dray implores, sidling up next to me. He looks at my arm and his face flashes ice-cold. "Which one hurt you?"

"I already killed him," I reply with a satisfied smile. When he doesn't lose that look of death from his eyes, I sigh then concede, "*Fine,* you can have four, I'll take the other seven."

"Hey! That's cheating," Archel complains, coming up on my other side, and I grumble.

"Fuck, fine, you can have three! That leaves me with four, sound fair?" I look at both of them and they nod. "Good, that ugly bastard with the blue hair is mine though."

"Got it," they both say and move apart so we have room to fight. "If you would so kindly line up in front of your chosen target," I tease, with mirth dancing in my eyes as I stare down the Berserkers. They finally snap, bored with our talking. How rude.

The big, blue-haired bastard heads straight for me. A sword is too good for him, so I sheathe it and grab two small daggers, holding the hilts towards my body and wait. He yells as he swings his sword and I duck, moving under his grip. I stab at his side before spinning away. Two big cuts have opened on his side, dripping blood.

I grin at him as he lets out an outraged roar, before swinging and charging with no finesse. I duck and weave, moving around him and opening cut after cut until blood is dripping from so many wounds his face pales. Only then do I jump onto his back. He falls to the floor and I wrap myself around him as his knees absorb the impact. He tries to pull me off, but I duck my head into his shoulder and laugh. "Say hi to Ivar for me," I whisper into his ear, before stabbing both blades into either side of his neck and yanking them out before flipping off his back.

He falls to the floor, his eyes wide and unseeing, and I sheathe the daggers and grab my swords again, before turning to the next man. One has gotten smart and grabs my father, holding him like a shield with a knife at his throat. I swagger towards them, leaving Evan, Dray, and Archel to deal with the rest. "Not a smart move," I tell him and shrug.

"I'll kill 'im!" he shouts, and I spot a drop of blood from a cut on my father's neck. I meet his eyes to see he's scared but resigned. He thinks he will die here.

Slipping my bad arm closer to my body, I slowly pluck a blade from my thigh, shielding my movements as I turn slightly to the slide. "Do it, I don't even know him," I answer calmly

He freezes for a second, thinking through my answer, and that's when I move. I snap my bad arm back, clenching my teeth as the wound opens again, and let the dagger fly. It hits him square in the eye and he drops the blade from my father's neck. I rush him, grabbing my dad and pushing him to the side before pulling the blade from the screaming berserker and slitting his throat.

He gurgles, his one good eye wide and filled with fear—the look you get when you realise you're going to die. I watch him, my face cold and deadly, until he falls backwards to the floor. Turning my back on him, I spot the blood-soaked dwellers, all pale and clearly in shock. Dray is hacking at a Berserker, Archel kills the last one standing, and I even spot Evan with a body or two at his feet. My father stumbles towards me, his face ashen as he looks at my bleeding arm then back to my face. In his eyes, it's clear—I'm nothing but a stranger to him.

"How...are you okay?" he asks, keeping a clear distance between us, which shouldn't hurt, but it does.

Evan rushes to my side, tugs away my makeshift bandage, and mumbles about idiot warriors as he pokes and prods at the edge of the wound. "Grab me a kit, now!" he yells, and my father jumps but rushes away to get it, using any excuse to get away from me.

Gritting my teeth, I look at Dray who follows my father's hasty steps with a glare of his own, but Archel steps in front of me with a grin. "I win," he taunts.

"Fuck," I mumble, then bite my tongue to hold in a scream as Evan digs his finger into the wound. I taste my own blood as I glare down at the doc who's ignoring me while he fishes around in the wound. I open my mouth to shout at him, but he pulls the tip of a blade from the injury and tosses it aside before pressing his hands against the still bleeding wound.

Well shit.

"Thanks, Doc," I say instead, and my father hurries to our side, passing over what looks like a medical kit with shaking hands.

"You okay?" I ask him, but he refuses to look at me, just stares at my arm as Evan treats it. "Where's your captain?" I snap, and he looks at me then, blinking to clear his foggy brain.

"I don't know...I came out when the siren sounded to see the guards already fighting, they were trying to get us all to fall back farther into the bunker, but we got cut off and I heard over the radios they were leaving us to die," he mutters, finally straightening into the leader I remember from the first time I came to Paradise. "Goddamn army men, do they really think we would stand for this? They will never lead after this!"

The door opens then and guards rush in, the captain at the back of them. I roll my eyes. Of course he's hiding behind his men. He looks around the room before his eyes lock on me. Dray and Archel move to my side, standing with me while Evan keeps tending to my arm. The way he keeps pulling on the wound makes me want to wince, but I refuse to show any weakness in front of this man.

"What the fuck are you doing here? We didn't need your help, I had it under control!" he yells, marching up and going toe to toe with me. I have to crane my neck back to meet his eyes, and I know he did it on purpose to try and intimidate me. Idiot doesn't realise I've been fighting men bigger and stronger than me for years. My size and gender make arrogant men underestimate me, but I use that to my advantage.

"Let me guess? Let the grunts do the work while you hide behind them shouting orders? A real fucking leader fights alongside them, and you don't tell your people to do anything you wouldn't be willing to do! I would face an army for my people, what would you do for yours?" I say it loudly, hearing the shuffling of his men as they realise I'm right.

"If it wasn't for you, we wouldn't be in this situation. No one knew where we were! You led them here. Who's to say you aren't behind this attack and then killed your own people to try and get on our good side?" he questions.

I hear them murmur then, obviously thinking through his logic and he steps back, sweeping his arm across the dead Berserkers. "They bear the same marks as you and your army, so tell me, savage, why we shouldn't kill you here and now?"

At that, the guards point their weapons at us. This whole situation is so ridiculous, I start laughing, I can't help it. They shift nervously, looking at their captain for direction. I wheeze, I'm laughing that hard, before I manage to get some words out. "You think I would kill my own people? To what? Make friends with you? Bitch, please, I don't need you. *You* need *us*. We rule the fucking Wastelands. You might have guns and a bunker, but we have the whole fucking north and our armies to back it up. So, I suggest you reconsider aiming those guns before I get annoyed and decide to go to war with you."

I take a step forward, forcing Evan to let go of my arm. "Think carefully about your next move. Do you really want a war? You've seen what us so called savages can do. Do you think you can survive that?" I look around at the groups of people huddling in the corner, and the dead guards and Berserkers. "Because I don't think you can, without us here, you would have died, and your people know it. So, go on, insult us one more time and you'll be the reason why your people are wiped from existence."

I'm done playing. I refuse to cater to this man. I've bowed and scraped as a slave until I won my freedom, and I won't go back to that. No man, captain or not, owns me, and it's about time he realises that because I'm smarter, stronger, and hell of a lot more likely to survive.

That's what I always do—survive.

My father steps between us then, holding his arms out to either side, but I don't take my eyes away from the captain. He looks like he's trying to think of a way to frame us, make us appear as if we're the bad guys, so he can shoot us.

"I was a witness," my father starts, meeting the captain's incensed stare and holding it before scanning his gaze across the crowd. "Without these people, without Worth and her savages, we would have been slaughtered." He returns his gaze to the captain with a fire in his eyes. "After all, *you* made no move to come and save us! We need to work together, not separately. I'm taking back leadership. You no longer run this bunker, Captain. You and your guards might think you protect us, but it is clear you can't do that well enough. Our people deserve better, you will not sully that by destroying the bonds with the people who just saved us from certain death." He tilts his head back and I hear the dwellers we saved mumble before they stand one by one, and step next to my father, blocking us from the guns.

"We would have died." "Where were you?"

"They might be savages, but they saved us."

One after another they throw in their support. I know it's not for us, but more so for my father, which doesn't matter.

"Stand down," the captain calls, and the guns instantly drop. He looks at me then, realising he's not going to get what he wants. "We owe you thanks," he says stiffly, his face red and his jaw clenching, "but do not overstay your welcome. I will escort you outside." He flashes me his white teeth. "After all, out there you rule, down here you do not."

As the last word leaves his lips an explosion rocks the ground and I stumble, but Dray catches my arm, keeping me upright.

"What the hell was that?" the captain shouts, looking at his men. "Report!"

"Sir, it looks like the barbarians got into the armoury and set charges around Paradise!"

The captain swears and my father steps forward. "We need to evacuate. Until you can search the bunker to ensure there are no more surprise charges, we will not be losing any more lives today." He looks at me then. "Lead the way, Worth, let our people be safe in your Wasteland until we can ensure it is safe down here to come back home."

Well, fuck.

Anxiety tightens my chest knowing I can't leave all these civilians alone outside while their guards sweep the place for bombs. That means more time away from my men, but how can I abandon these people and go to my men with more innocent blood on my hands?

The answer is I can't. Looks like we're setting up camp outside of Paradise until we know it's safe.

Sands below, this is going to suck.

Chapter Eleven

An Empty Paradise

We all move out of Paradise quickly. The bunker door is raised and then closed on us as soon as we are through, while the captain and his guards move back into the bunker to check for explosives and any living Berserkers. Turning around, I blow out my breath and take in the Paradise dwellers. They all look terrified and are gazing around in awe. I'm betting it's the first time a lot of them have been outside. My father grabbed some supplies on the way out and we helped drag them outside. Crossing my arms, my eyes run over the gathered people.

"I'll go get our people. They can help set you up. We won't do it too close to the bunker just in case, but you want to be shielded by the buildings. We will circle the camp with our army as a protection measure," I order loudly, and my father nods and turns away to talk to his people. I look at Dray. "Keep an eye out, I'll be back."

He nods, watching the dwellers with a smirk. I move swiftly, heading back to our army who are busy watching the road and fighting between themselves. "Alright, pack up people! There's a change of plans." I glance at Bern and Henry then who move closer. "Rogue Berserkers attacked the bunker, they set charges, and we are waiting outside with the dwellers to ensure they aren't slaughtered. None of them are to be killed, anyone who touches a Paradise dweller dies by my hand, make sure they know. Grab your shit, we are going to be camping for a day or two."

"Aye, Ma Queen." Bern moves off quickly for such a big guy. "You sure about this?" Henry asks.

"No, but if we leave them they will die, and I can't live with that. My men are fighters, they can survive a bit longer, I have to trust them with that. Plus, it will give the leaders more time to get to The Ring. Keep a close eye out though, I don't trust these people," I instruct, and Henry nods and moves away. I grab my bike and drive back to where Dray, Archel, Evan, and my father are setting up camp away from the blast doors, and to the side of the building where it is sheltered by another structure. It's a smart move, makes a tunnel of sorts, but with plenty of room to manoeuvre.

I wait for our people to roar to a stop behind me, all the dwellers look up in fear and cringe away. "No one will hurt you, they know the price, but do not betray my people while we are here protecting you, or you will suffer the same fate. Death by my hand. Berserkers camp this side, make a blockade, Seekers take the other side. I want three people on watch on either side at all times. Bern and Henry, organise someone," I look over at them then. "I want two men on top of that building on lookout at all hours, and two men stationed outside the blast doors. Understood?"

"Yas, Ma Queen."

"Yes, ma'am," comes the calls and I nod, moving my bike to the side and parking before heading towards my father.

"We will keep our people apart and hopefully we will survive the next day or two. Get them ready for the night. I saw you grab tents, didn't I?"

"Yes, there won't be enough for everyone," he muses, his hair out of place, and his shirt ripped and covered in blood.

"Don't worry about us, we have our own and we are used to sleeping outside," I reply with a shrug.

"Ma Queen, I have found you a tent, you should have one." Bern lumbers over with a tent over his shoulder.

"Who did you steal it from?" I see a frustrated looking dweller glaring at Bern's back and snicker. "Thanks, put it near the entrance, will you?"

He nods. "We are putting the bikes across as a first defence as well." He trudges away again.

"Your people respect you," my father murmurs, and I look over at him as Dray appears at my side.

"She earned that through blood, sweat, and years of torture. How did you get your leadership?" he snaps.

"I was, er, voted in," my father replies, not looking Dray in the face, and that's when I realise he is scared of him. "I'll go help my people."

"Wait, you have water going down there somehow. Is there anyway to access it up here?"

"Erm, I'm not sure, let me grab someone who will know." He rushes away then and we watch him go.

"How can he not know about his own people? Do they really think that little of water when the rest of the North constantly battles dehydration?" Archel spits. "Fuck, I want to kill them all. Spoiled bastards."

"How the other half live," I scoff.

A man comes running up with sweat dripping down his head and his shirt removed. He's well-built with short, styled blond hair and green, loose trousers. "Hi, erm, your father said you needed to see me about water irrigation?"

I look at Dray with a raised eyebrow and he smirks. "He's too pretty for your harem, soulmate."

My mouth drops open. "Not what I was thinking." I look back at the man who is staring between us, confused. "But you're right. God, he looks like a puppy."

The man blinks at me, his cheeks heating though he doesn't know what we are talking about. "I'm Jason, I work on maintaining the water supply for Paradise. I've been up here before when the pumping system broke down, so I know how to access it, which he said you needed—"

"Wow, okay, stop talking," I tell him with a grin.

He snaps his mouth shut and winces. "Sorry, I get nervous and ramble and you're scary. I mean, you're covered in blood and with all these swords and okay shutting up now."

Dray laughs. "Yeah, soulmate, you look scary." I eye him again and he grins. "I lied, you look fucking hot. I'm turned the hell on by all the blood."

Jason gulps, his eyes flying wide, and I take pity on him. "Okay, show us how it pumps down there, and is there a way to access it to get water up here without stopping the flow to the bunker?"

He nods emphatically and turns, rushing away before stopping and looking back. "Sure, I'll show you." He waits, almost bouncing on his feet.

"Come on." I grab Dray and drag him with me, avoiding Evan who is clearly looking for me, his face curled into a scowl.

The dwellers move aside as we stomp through their midst, stopping what they are doing to stare. Most seem scared, but some nod in greeting which is an improvement I guess. Jason leads us around the Seekers who are setting up camp at the other end of the tunnel between the buildings, and then around the corner of the large white building. A wall of sand is backed into the buildings here, obviously creating a barrier, with a wired electric fence at the back to stop intruders, I even spot cameras. That explains how they keep this place so secure and private. Behind the building is a smaller one, the sides silver and the top made of brick. It's tucked away, hidden almost, so if you were coming from the road you wouldn't see it. He heads straight there and we stop behind him as he runs his finger down the brick at the side, a scanner pops out and I raise my eyebrows. He scans his palm and eye, and the light turns green just before I hear the click of the door. He looks back with a nervous smile.

"We had to upgrade it, it got broken into a couple of years ago and wrecked by a couple. They nearly killed us all, we were without water." He shakes his head.

"I'm betting they just wanted a safe place to lay low and something to drink," I defend, crossing my arms. "What happened to them?" I demand.

He looks away nervously. "The guards got here first. I didn't see, I was just called in to fix it."

"But?" I press.

"I saw them dragging the bodies away for burning," he admits and steps into the building, effectively ending that conversation.

Anger flares within me. These people have no clue how to survive out here and they killed someone for wanting water? It's true we kill for less, but when we do it, it's because you have stolen or pissed us off. You know what to expect out there, but in Paradise it should be civilized, yet they just hide that bloodlust under a veil of civilisation.

I step in behind him, with Dray on my heels, and then I look around in shock. Even their water station is high tech. No wonder they don't understand how to function outside of Paradise. The room is split in two, and there is a wall and a door hiding the other half. Metal stairs lead up to platforms hanging over what I can only assume is the water pump. Other than the fact it takes up a lot of room and goes into the floor, I couldn't begin to explain what it is, but Jason seems comfortable.

He moves around it as we linger near the doorway, but when he doesn't come back or speak, I get bored and decide to investigate. Walking over to the other door, I open it and stick my head in. I blink at what I see and step into the room, whistling as I look around. It looks like a changing room for workers with lockers on the back wall, benches running down the middle, mirrors on the closet wall, and a toilet stall and shower stall in the corner. I head that way, sticking my head around the curtain to see a wide, white shower stall. I wonder if it works? Maybe I'm becoming pampered, because I would love to shower off all this blood, sweat, and grime.

"It still works," Jason calls happily, and I look back to see Dray with his arms crossed waiting in the corner of the room, and Jason at the doorway.

"Good, my people can shower here if they wish." Jason fidgets and I sigh. "What?"

"There might not be enough water for that." He shrugs.

"They won't all shower anyway, most believe the blood from battle should stay on their skin as a warning, and being too clean would make them seem like pale faces." I grin and Dray barks out a laugh.

"Oh, erm, okay. Anyway, we have some containers for storing water in emergencies here. I will fill them and we can take them back to camp," he suggests, looking between Dray and me, waiting for instructions. "Do it." I look at Dray then. "Stay with him, I will go get some people to carry them back."

Jason nods and rushes away to do as he was told. I move to the door, but a grinning Dray blocks it as he looks down at me. In the harsh, white lighting, the cut brand on his chest stands out, and I find myself leaning forward and idly tracing it with my fingers. "Guess we can have another shower party, soulmate," he growls, and I shiver at the need in his voice.

"You'll have to wait until we get the water to camp," I counter, wishing I could just shut the door and jump him. I still have the excitement from battle coursing through me and I need to take it out on him.

"Be fast," he purrs, leaning towards me.

I move past him, purposely brushing my breasts against his arm, making him growl as I saunter away. I move to camp quickly, and grab Bern and Erik and a few other Berserkers. They follow me back, whistling at the water pump. Erik and a Berserker grab one of the huge containers of water, hefting it between them as they take it back. Jason takes the other with another Berserker, while Bern grabs one by himself and doesn't even seem to strain as he leaves.

"Bern, distract Doc for me, will you?" I call from the doorway.

He looks back at me with a grin, his eyes darting behind me before he nods. "Have fun, Ma Queen," he yells, trudging away.

I shut the main door to the pump room and look back to see Dray lingering, his eyes locked on me like I'm his prey. Grinning, I wander past him, stripping as I go. My clothes drop to the floor before I step into the cubicle, then I throw my sword holsters over the curtain rail and flick on the water. It spurts from the showerhead, cold at first, but by the time the curtain draws back it is heating up. Ducking my head under, I slick back my hair and turn to face Dray.

The water washing down the white shower drain is pink as blood flakes fall from my body. Dray seems to take up the whole entrance, his muscles bulging as he watches me, his clothes having been lost on the way here apart from his blades that he always keeps across his chest. "You were magnificent down there, soulmate," he growls, his eyes ice-cold and wild. "I wanted to throw you into the wall and fuck you in front of everyone, just to let them know you are mine."

I arch my eyebrow at him. "Don't you mean that you're mine?"

"That too." He smirks, stepping into the stall and backing me against the wall.

"You could now," I offer, my pussy already wet from him getting rough with me. He growls as the leash he has on his control snaps.

He leans down, grabs my thigh, and throws me into the shower wall. I grunt at the impact and he uses that to push his tongue into my mouth, battling it with mine. He pins me there, pressing his thigh against my bare pussy as he grips my face and devours my mouth. I moan and he swallows it down as I move against his leg, needing the pressure. He bites my lower lip in punishment, so hard that I taste blood, which only seems to drive him wild.

He pushes me back against the wall again, making me grunt as he moves his leg and his hand replaces it. Moaning into his mouth again, the pain from my bruised lip mixing with my pleasure, I push into his hand as he cups me. He pulls back slightly, panting as he stares at me. "So fucking wet, soulmate, you drive me crazy."

"Fuck me already," I demand, making him smirk.

He pushes my head to the side and kisses down my neck as he strokes my pussy, his fingers running along my wet heat before he pushes two thick fingers inside of me, making me gasp again. The bite of pain only has me trying to ride his fingers harder. He knows exactly how to play my body. Slowly, Dray pulls them out, curling and dragging them along my nerves inside before pushing them back in, fucking me quickly with his fingers as he bites down on my neck. Throwing my head back, I reach out and grip his hair, holding him to me.

"Dray," I warn.

He doesn't reply, but his thumb starts to rub circles on my clit before pressing down hard. My eyes close in bliss and I raise my hips to meet his fingers, riding them shamelessly as I chase my orgasm, which I can feel building. My stomach tightens, my pussy pulses, and before I know it I'm coming so hard my eyes actually blacken for a moment. Before I even recover, he pulls away, grabs my weak thighs, lines up, and slams inside of me.

I almost scream, my pussy still clenching hard around his cock from aftershocks as he forces me to take his length. He doesn't give me time to adjust before he pulls out and slams back in. He reaches around me, placing his hand between the back of my head and the wall, and continues to drive into me. Lifting my hips to meet his thrusts, I cross my ankles and kick at his ass to make him fuck me faster, harder.

The slap of our bodies meeting, and our grunts and pants fill the air over the sound of the running water, the spray hitting Dray's back.

"Harder," I demand, kicking him with my heels again.

He growls at me, his teeth flashing as he grips my hip with his other hand, his fingers digging in painfully, and starts to hammer into me for real. Fucking me ruthlessly.

"Yes, yes, yes," I chant, the edge of pain and pleasure already building back up for another orgasm.

"Soulmate," he snarls, and I snap my eyes open, locking my gaze with his, and he bends his head down and sucks my nipple into his mouth.

Groaning, I tighten my pussy around him and he grumbles against my nipple, only making me gasp again. He twists his hip at the end of every thrust, catching those nerves inside of me, and when he bites down hard on my nipple, I come apart around him, my pussy milking his cock as he explodes with a growl.

We sag against the wall, both of us breathing hard and covered in sweat, but satisfied. "Fuck, I'm going to be sore tomorrow," I admit.

"Yes, but it was worth it," he replies, with that smirk tipping up his lips that drives me crazy.

I grin back, cupping his cheeks, and he leans into the touch, closing his eyes. "Who knew this is where we would be? So much has changed, it feels like so long ago when I saw you in The Ring, or even when we fought under the stars before I left."

He opens his eyes, peering at me intently. "I was always yours, even then, I was just letting you come to terms with it."

I laugh. I can't help it as I trace the scar on his face, proof of the warrior he is. "Well, I guess I did."

"'Bout time too." He winks.

"Come on, we better get washed up before Jason comes back and scolds us for wasting water." I wiggle in his grip and he slides out of me, making both of us groan before he drops me to the floor. My legs are weak and I nearly collapse, but he wraps his arm around my waist and brings me to his chest, before turning us so the water is washing over us both. "I love how you are so strong in front of everyone else, but with me you show weakness," he whispers, before leaning down and kissing me gently. He sucks my damaged lip into his mouth before pulling back and kissing it better.

I peer up at him, unable to help myself. "You tell anyone and I'll slit your throat."

He laughs and turns me in his arms, whispering into my ear, "I wouldn't expect anything less, soulmate."

I grumble but let him wash my body, his fingers insistent and methodical as he wipes away all traces of battle and sex before I turn and do the same to him. There is even some soap left in the shower and we luxuriate in it, never taking anything for granted—just one of the things I learned out here. I flick off the water, not wanting to waste too much, and step out. Dray finds two towels and we dry off quickly before dressing, ready to return to our people and whatever problems are waiting.

I head to the main doorway, but he catches me around my waist and spins me. I stumble into his chest and he presses his lips to mine, devouring my mouth again before pulling away. "I love you. I gotta keep saying it, never know when it might be the last."

"I love you too, crazy," I reply, and he kisses me again before letting me go.

Luckily the door doesn't require scanning to get out, so I swing it open.

Feeling more relaxed as I step out, I stop when I see a pissed looking Evan waiting on the other side. His eyes drop to my arm and I follow his gaze to see it bleeding again. He throws his hands in the air. "Fucking idiot, you ripped the cut again! Back in, we have to wash it and dress it," he orders, pushing past a smirking Dray and me.

"Yes, soulmate, you ripped it again," he teases.

I groan and head back inside. *Sands below, can't a girl catch a break?*

"And I'm not even going to ask what happened to your lip!" Evan shouts, making Dray and me snigger.

Chapter Twelve

Savages and Dwellers

After Evan patches me up, again, we head back to the camp, which is set up nicely. Tents in an array of colours block the middle and some of the ends of the tunnel, and you have to pass through the bike barricade on either side to get through. It's as safe as we are going to get.

I leave Dray talking to the Seekers as Evan and I weave through the camp. I don't bother stopping in the middle with the pale faces or dwellers, as I have started to call them. They throw us looks of unease and it's clear they are hoping we will leave them alone. I understand. In the space of a day, they have been attacked, herded, forced from their homes, and are now setting up camp with 'savages,' so I leave them be.

You can see the obvious difference as you pass through the camps. The Seekers are almost silent, working diligently, their eyes sharp. The dwellers are cringing and huddling together, struggling to even get a tent up, and then you pass into the Berserker camp.

Laughter and loud voices rings out, and you can smell blood and cooking meat. They might not have tents, but they don't care. Packs, weapons, and more are spread out with some men already asleep. Two men are fighting in the middle of a circle of cheering men, who are watching and calling encouragements. They are half naked, with blood running from cuts and bust lips, and sweat shining on their bodies.

Long honour braids fly in the wind as men tangle and tease, and they laugh and joke...it feels like home and it feels right. A smile curls up at my lips as I take it all in. They have firepits ready to light at dark, and the bikes are positioned with spears on top with men waiting there as patrols. A tent is pressed to the wall of the building and tucked away to the side, surrounded by men, obviously for me. They've found crates, pressed them together, turned them upside down, and made tables where some men are drinking and gambling.

A thump and a cheer goes up, and I turn to see one of the fighters on the ground and he isn't getting back up, the other fighter leans down, cuts off his braid, and throws it away, cheering as he faces the crowd. He stops when he sees me, his chest heaving, blood pouring from his split lip, and his brown eyes dark and excited. His long braid is thrown over one shoulder, his thick thighs are encased in leather pants laced at the side, and big ass boots cover his feet.

"What says you, Champion?" he calls, daring me, challenging me.

The crowd stirs, looking from him to me, as excitement and nerves courses through their midst. I can hear the unspoken question

—will I fight? This is who we are, we measure ourselves up, keep each other sharp, and move up the pecking order by fighting. We solve our issues that way, and through this challenge, they are asking me if I am really still a Berserker. I unbuckle my holsters with a smirk and pass them to Evan before moving forward.

A cheer goes up as I step over the crudely drawn circle in the sand, and the fighter grins, nodding at me in respect before marching to the other side. We size each other up as I crack my neck from side to side and widen my stance. Adrenaline pumps through me. Once, I was forced to fight for my life, but I'm choosing to now. I won the crown, but I need to prove to them that I deserve it. That I am one of them. Even when I hated it, I couldn't deny I was. I have always been a Berserker through and through.

He jerks his head, throwing his braid over his shoulder, and crouches slightly, his hands held in front of him. "No weapons, first blood," I call.

He nods. "Your blood, unless you get ya hands dirty, Ya Majesty," he taunts. Laughter goes through the crowd.

"You talk too much," I counter, as I push off and sprint at him, giving him no warning. I leap off the ground and jump him. My legs wrap around his neck and I fall backwards, bringing him with me before I let go and roll away, grinning at him as dust and dirt covers my back and side. My breathing picks up and bloodlust surges through me. He flips to the side, licking his bust lip, and returns the grin.

We circle each other, moving in and out looking for openings, each scanning for weaknesses. He's a hard hitter, so I can't let him get a hold of me or it's over. I need to be fast and smart. He feigns left, testing me, before darting right, his fist coming at my side. I move out of the way into a roll, shifting into him instead of away, and before he can block, I uppercut his family jewels and dance away. He groans, dropping to his knees with a wheeze before getting to his feet, his eyes pained and strained. I don't bother taking a cheap shot while he is down and end it, because I want this to be fair. I want them to see what I'm made of, what Ivar created—his downfall.

"Ya fight dirty," he comments and laughs, spitting blood to the sand and watching me.

"Always." I nod.

The Berserkers gathered tighten their circle, cheering and shouting at us to get on with it. He rushes me again, both fists moving through the air towards my face. I duck and weave as he pummels at me again and again. I keep my eyes between his fists and his feet, noting he moves them to the side when he is about to hit. I let him tire himself out as I dance and spin, and his fists eventually slow enough for me to duck between them and upper cut his chin before dancing away. He grunts, stumbling back, and I kick out at his side. He grunts again, falling sideways, and the crowd starts to chant my name.

"Worth, Worth, Worth, Worth!"

Laughing, I go on the offensive now, seeing the strain in his eyes and knowing he is winded. I sweep my leg and he stumbles over it, then I grab his swinging braid and smash my fist into his face again and again. I feel my knuckles split, catching on his teeth, but I keep going until I see red covering his face, then I let go and step back. I look at my knuckles and see the damage isn't that bad, it's reopened one of the old scars, but other than that it's not my blood. His nose is smashed and gushing blood, his lip is busted even more, and his eye is going to be sealed shut tomorrow. He wobbles, but stays upright.

"First blood," he concedes, and then spits blood on the ground again, grinning at me, and showing a missing tooth and blood covering his mouth. He starts to laugh and I do as well as the crowd goes wild, cheering for me.

I look up, panting, and spot Dray, Erik, and Archel standing at the edge of the circle. Archel winks at me and disappears. Dray runs his eyes down my body, the ice seeming to melt so I quickly look away before he jumps me or the other way around. Erik nods at me with respect in his eyes, and I know he is finally realising I'm not the same girl who loved his son. I'm a queen who got revenge for his death. I couldn't protect my loved ones then, but I can now, and I will stop at nothing to save them. Not ever again.

"Who's next?" the fighter roars, slamming his fists into his chests.

I step up and he looks at me before offering me his braid.

I lean close. "Keep it, warrior, it was close, but don't let them know I said that or you're dead," I joke and step away. Evan pops up and hands over my holsters, which I slip into, but he spots the blood on my knuckles and groans.

"Fucking hell, I've started carrying a bag around just for you, do you know that? Why are you always covered in blood?" he grumbles, prodding my split knuckle.

"It's not always mine." I shrug.

"It's not always mine," he mocks. "Fucking brilliant. Do you have a death wish?" he grumbles, but I let him as he seals the wound and Erik walks up.

"I remember when you could barely swing your own fist," he comments, his eyes sad.

"I learned fast," I admit, and he winces and looks away before glancing back at me.

"Not like my boy. I don't blame you, Worth. I want you to know that."

I nod, looking away.

"Done," Evan interrupts and I stride away, heading to my tent. I can't get close to Erik again, his family has a nasty habit of dying and I can't deal with that. Pushing aside the green flap, to what looks like an old army tent, I spot a rolled out sleeping bag with a crate and a lamp on the top. Other than that, it's bare, but it's better than nothing. I place the maps on the crate and throw my swords on top of them before looking around.

The tent flap moves behind me and I don't turn, expecting Dray, but it's Erik's face I spot when he circles me. "I didn't mean to upset you. I didn't want you to blame yourself if you were. Guilt is a hard thing to live with and you have enough horrors without that. My boy loved you and you loved him, you gave him happiness. His life might have been short, but he experienced so much, things others can only dream of. He had the loyalty and love of a good woman, and if he were here now, he would be so proud of you. Some things happen for a reason. He died so you could live, and now look at you. You are saving us all from a war. Life is full of choices, he made his, and you have made yours. Now, I'm making mine."

I turn to face him fully and he smiles at me. "I, Erik Cadmar, offer you my sword for as long as I shall live. My blade is your blood, my blood and life yours to do with as you wish. My shield shall be your shield and my war cry will echo yours. On this, I promise." He falls to his knees, his sword dug into the ground in front of him, and his bowed head resting against the handle. "Tazanna Worth, Queen of The Berserkers, I ask for you accept my warrior's oath."

"Erik," I snap, but he refuses to look at me. "Why?" is all I can ask. I saw warriors do this to Ivar a long time ago, but not much since he went all bat shit. His life would quite literally be in my hands, a warrior's oath is binding and forever, to break one would mean death. "Because it is the right thing to do, because we are family, because I spot a cause worth fighting for when I see it. I always did. Everyone else saw a little slave girl. I saw the woman you could be, and so did Noah."

Swallowing, I look away, blinking back wetness I won't let fall. "I accept your oath. Rise," I order, remembering Ivar's words from so long ago. Back then, it was amazing when it happened, to have people respect you that much. He had droves offering their swords and it slowly dwindled over the years. To do anything other than accept it would be a punishment, a way of saying I didn't trust him as a warrior. The flap opens then and Bern, Henry, Archel, Dray, and Evan all peek in.

"Ah, fuck this, I dinnie know she was accepting oaths," the big man booms, before dropping to his knees, his axe in front of him. Henry mirrors him silently, his blades in front of him.

Archel hesitates and then looks at me. "You always have my blades, but my oaths are for someone else."

Dray moves past them all, getting to his knees in front of me and I gasp, trying to stop him. "You can't," I hiss.

"Can and will. Soulmate, my swords, blood, and life have been yours since the first time I saw you. This just makes it official, I'm no king without my queen, and my life and heart are already yours. Do you accept my oath?"

I nod. "I accept," I whisper, and he gets to his feet, grinning.

Bern and Henry repeat Erik's oath, changing it slightly to match them, and I accept again, letting them rise. I look around at the gathered men and pride fills me. I must be doing okay. I must be a good enough person for so many to be willing to fight with me. I might have made it this far building myself back up, but my men helped me on the way, they showed me the path, and right now, I notice their absence most of all. I wish they were here to witness it. Drax would make some joke. Maxen would stare at me intently like he could see my soul. Thorn would smile, the one just for me, and Jax my silent Jax, would bare his soul in front of everyone if that is what I asked.

I have lived a hard life, but they made it worth it, and these men right here just gave me another reason to keep fighting, because now it's not just me that lives and dies by my choices, but them as well. The weight bows my shoulders, but I know I can survive it. After all, I have survived worse.

After I accepted their oaths, I let them gather around as I open the maps. "Is that...the Cities?" Erik asks, his eyes widening.

"Yes, I saw them the first time I visited Paradise. I don't know how they got them, but they are the most accurate maps we are going to get, and they will help us plan our battle strategy, and Dray's and my entrance and exit plans." I shrug, looking over the map. It's incredibly detailed, showing the three cities linked together and the wall separating them from the North.

"It seems the middle one is where we need to be. That's where they have holdings and where they will keep my men. We could sneak in, I'm not sure how high the walls are, but I can see a sewer pipe entrance right here we could get through," I theorize, but it doesn't feel right. How are we going to sneak through the Cities, find my men, and get them out without being detected? We even dress and look Northern. "They will notice us," I finally admit.

"So let them," Archel responds, and I blink up at him. "You are a queen, you're a fighter, and no offence, but you aren't a sneaky person

—more a knock the front door down and stab person. They will expect a sneak attack. They won't be expecting you to come through the front door. You're a queen, act like one."

A slow grin crawls across my face. "It could work. Go in there and demand my people back, show them who we are. They committed an act of war. We can show that we aren't just barbarians and we know what that means. We can hint we know what they want from Paradise, let them know not to mess with us. If they kill us, then so be it, because that means war and they will have to come north for you to slaughter them. We offer them a choice, they think we are weak, so let's show them how strong we are."

"You're going into their strong hold, they have the advantage," Erik reminds me.

"True, but who just walks right into an enemy lair? They are going to think we have backups in place. I will encourage them to think that as well of course. Kill us and they trigger a war, one they can't win."

"I don't like it, it's too risky," he grumbles, studying the maps.

"It's the only way," I reply, but then a thought hits me. "Chaos, we cause chaos."

Dray looks at me then. "You have a plan, don't you?"

I nod. "I'll tell you when it's time, but for now I need you to trust me to handle this. The rest of you will be waiting here." I point to a spot on the map in a stretch of the Wastes just before The Rim. "We will meet you there."

"I hope it's a fookin' good plan." Erik sighs, but nods. "I trust ya."

"Good." I roll up the maps and place them in my bag before

standing and stretching. "Now, let's eat. Hopefully the guards will clear Paradise tonight and we can be on our way tomorrow. I will meet up with the other leaders at The Ring and get them involved before heading to the Cities."

They nod and stand, all filing out, except for Dray. He steps close and I tilt my head back to look into his eyes. "We go in together, we come out together, or we die together. These are your options," he tells me.

"Don't worry, I don't plan on dying, but I need you to trust me. I'm relying on you for this plan to work. I will explain everything, I promise, but Dray, there is a chance we aren't getting out. I'm taking that chance for my men, for my family, you don't have to."

He growls before grabbing me and pinning me to his chest. "You forget, where you go, I go. We will take that chance together. If anyone can survive, it's us. The Champion and the killer. We fight together, we die together. There are no other futures for us. Whatever it takes, we face it."

Sighing, I lean up and kiss him, letting him know how much that means. I will feel better with him at my back. This plan is not great, it has its risks, but I can't do anything else. Even fighting a lost cause, I would do it for my men, facing the Cities and a threat I might not be able to win. They would do it for me. It's time I showed them I would do it for them. Dray's right. Whether we live or die together, at least I will be with them.

"Let's go eat," I murmur, pulling away. I twine my hand with his and head out through the tent. The sun is now lower in the sky and fires are already started, with Berserkers gathered around and cooking meat. I grin and head for the table where Evan and Archel are arm wrestling. I haven't asked them if they sorted their shit out, since they are adults, but they must have come to some sort of peace, even if they are still rubbing against each other, testing each other. I can't wait to meet the woman who has to put up with Evan's moods and Archel's crazy though. She must be a fucking better woman than most.

I sit next to Evan with Dray taking the seat next to me, and Bern and Henry join us. I spot Erik with his rebels, speaking in low tones, obviously telling them the plan, but I ignore them. It's a problem for tomorrow. "I bet a dagger on Evan," I remark.

Archel throws me a glare and Evan grins. "I'll take that," Henry offers.

"Don't fucking lose now, Doc," I demand, watching them both.

I never noticed all of Evan's muscles before, but he's quite strong, and within a minute he smacks Archel's hand to the table, making me grin and offer my hand to Henry who groans and hands over a dagger. "What the fuck? Aren't you some kind of assassin? You let a doc beat you!"

I throw the dagger in the air, grinning. "Nice blade. Here." I pass it to Evan. "Keep it, you earned it." Then I turn to the assassin. "Evan's going to steal your girl," I tease Archel who narrows his eyes on me.

"Me and you, let's go unless you're scared of being shown up in front of your warriors?" he taunts.

"Move over Evan, I'm about to make this assassin my bitch." Evan laughs and slides over, so I scoot until I face Archel. "Let's make it fair. Ever played Russian Roulette?" I nearly suggest the knife game from The Rim, but honestly, I'm running out of room for scars and I might need my arm to fight with.

"You're on. First to give up?" he asks.

"Yes, Bern, find me a gun and load it with only one bullet," I order.

Evan groans. "Fuck, I'm going to be patching people up again, aren't I?"

"Better get used to it, Doc," I reply, winking at him before staring down Archel. "I'll let your girl know you died trying to be a hero, I'm sure Evan will help her through her grief."

He narrows his eyes, looking like he wants to kill me. "I'll be sure to let Dray get a hit in once you're dead, make him feel better."

"She dies, you die," Dray warns, but he doesn't seem bothered, instead relaxing into his chair, trusting me to win this.

"Why does everything have to be to the death?" Evan grumbles again, making us all laugh.

"Aww, Doc, don't ruin our fun," I tease, just as Bern comes up and places a gun on the table between Archel and me. "Ladies first," I gibe, gesturing at him.

Archel picks up the gun without hesitation, places it to his forehead, and pulls the trigger. He grins at me and offers me the gun. I grab it and like him, don't hesitate to hold it to my head and pull the trigger. It's an old style gun, one Berserkers only use for this game, and I know the chamber holds six bullets. Four more chances.

I hold it out to him and he licks his lips before taking it and pulling the trigger, he lets out a sigh as I grin.

Three more chances, one with a bullet.

My heart is racing, my thoughts whirling, but I won't stand down now. Pressing the cool metal to the middle of my head, I meet his eyes and pull the trigger. My heart skips and my eyes want to close, but nothing happens except an empty click, so I blow out a low breath and pass it over.

Two chances. One of us will get the bullet.

"Scared, assassin?" I taunt. "I've faced worse odds, have you?" "Every day," he confesses and pulls the trigger. I see his eyes

wince, but nothing happens so he grins. "Your turn, queen, do you pull or give up?"

"I never give up." I grab the gun.

"Then you die. It's not about winning every fight, it's about always getting back up," Archel counters, leaning back, knowing he has me.

"And sometimes, it's about being the smartest in the room," I reply, aiming the weapon at my forehead, and just as I squeeze the trigger, I point the gun away and the bullet connects with the wall. "We only had to pull the trigger, we didn't specify it had to be aimed at us."

He bursts into laughter and I join in. Bern slaps the table as everyone else adds their mirth. Dray kisses my shoulder before whispering in my ear, "I fucking love you."

I grin wider and then feel guilty for it. I shouldn't be having a good time when God knows what is happening to my men. My smile fades, but they don't notice, thank God. "I'll grab some food," I say and stand up, stretching out my back.

Sands below, let them be okay.

I head to the biggest fire where they are roasting meat, some cooling to the side. When they spot me coming, they quickly grab a lot and add it to a tray they must have brought with them. "Thank you," I tell them before turning away and bringing it back to the table. I spot water and what looks like moonshine already on the table when I get back, and plonk the meat in the middle. Bern grabs some, immediately ripping into it. Henry is a more delicate eater, and Archel just nibbles. Evan grimaces, but eats a bit anyway. Dray rips into it like an animal, his other hand landing on my thigh under the table.

I eat and listen to their banter, but my mind is on my men again, wondering what they are going through right now. We are under the same sky with miles between us, yet I can still feel the connection there. I miss them.

An explosion rocks under my feet and I grab the table to steady myself. When the shifting stops, I hop up and I see everyone else doing the same, staring towards the bunker. I'm guessing they set off another explosive or it was triggered manually. We haven't heard one in a while. When nothing else happens, I slowly sit down, knowing there is nothing I can do. They have sealed the doors, this is their fight.

The silence eventually lessens as people start talking again, but everyone is on high alert, throwing glances at the wall, wondering what is happening down there. Something is bugging me about the bomb...they aren't really Berserker style. I'm not saying we haven't used them in the past and some warriors know how to handle them, but they aren't our preferred method. Too impersonal. Did Berserkers really set the bombs? We saw no proof, just had the word of the captain. Biting my lower lip, I stand again, needing some answers only my father can provide.

"Stay here," I tell them, before striding away to the dweller section of the camp.

The dwellers duck out of my way as I pass. I snort when I spot five of them trying to start a fire, they really are helpless up here. I find my father talking to a group of people in hushed whispers. He doesn't stop as I approach and I catch the tail ends of, "Trust them," and "It will be okay," so I guess it's reassurance. The people nod and wander away, leaving me with my father. I don't have time to mess around, I need to figure out why it's bugging me.

"Do you have explosives down there?" I question.

He frowns. "Yes, of course, they are locked up in the armoury."

It was mentioned the Berserkers must have breached the armoury. Could it be that simple and I'm looking at this too hard? "How many explosions can the bunker withstand?"

"It depends where the blasts are located, each section was built with their own blast doors to contain radiation and explosions, so in theory, if sections are compromised, they automatically seal. It will be liveable, if not all sections are ruined and the blast doors work," he answers.

"That's a lot of ifs," I grumble, rubbing at my head.

I feel responsible for these people. They are helpless if the doors don't open tomorrow. What do I do? I have to choose between looking after the defenceless or moving on to find my men...

Sitting around the campfire with our warriors, I let their talking and laughter wash over me, and they eventually pull me into the conversation and out of my own mind where I am obsessing over the bombs and my men.

"What about you, Worth?" someone asks.

I raise my eyebrows, looking around to see the gathered warriors, including Dray, Henry, and Erik watching me. "Me what?"

"We are showing old war and battle stories, show us your best scar." He grins, the fire lighting his face comically as he leans forward. I smirk, I can't help it. Most would be disgusted by scars, but Berserkers collect them like toys to show off and play with.

I think about it before flashing my shoulder scar, tracing my finger across it. "Got kidnapped by a Worshiper and locked up in his basement. He stabbed me with a blade when I pissed him off. I pulled it out and killed him with it," I tell them, and laughter sounds around me as I carry on, pointing out one on my elbow next. "Feral tried to bite off my damn arm, I let him chew on it while I hacked at him. I was drunk as hell." I pull my shirt up and point at one across my side. "I got this one fucking a girl at The Rim. She got a bit wild and we were both drunk. She tried to play with my knives and ended up stabbing me," I admit around a laugh.

"What about you, Henry?" I inquire, and he launches into a showcase of battle scars.

We laugh until late into the night, sharing war stories and our escapes, and just bonding. We all know each day could be our last, our stories carved into our skin through our scars, so for one night we let go and enjoy the camaraderie. The peace before the storm. A yawn escapes me, so Dray and I head to my tent after saying good-night and making sure the patrols are in place. I'm exhausted, and as soon as my head hits the sleeping bag, I am out.

Another explosion wakes me much later into the night, and I can't seem to get back to sleep. Dray is wrapped around me, snoring softly, his face harsh even in his slumber. Watching him and stroking his chest, I let my mind wander.

My back is cold and I wish one of my other men were curled up around it—probably Maxen, since he always has my back, my rock. Thorn would be playing with my hair, while Drax would be cheeky with his head in my lap, with Jax curled at my feet, always protecting me. If I close my eyes, I can almost see them, smell them, feel their touch along my skin, and their whispers in my ear. I fall asleep thinking of them.

Noise has me sitting up and I slip out of the bag, already dressed. I grab my sword as Dray hops up, going from deep sleep to awake instantly. I throw him a worried look and hurry outside. Shielding my eyes from the early morning rays, I spot the watcher on one of the next building's roof pointing into the distance just as a patrol comes skidding to a stop right in front of me.

"Someone's coming," he tells me.

Chapter Thirteen

Clash of the Queens

I fasten my holsters as he speaks. "How many, how far out, anything we can recognize them by?"

"Friend or foe?" Dray snarls from behind me.

"Couldn't see anything to distinguish them, two people at max, one bike, about ten minutes out, but they are heading right here," the man rushes out.

I frown. "Which means they know where here is. Maybe a dweller, a patrol?" I growl. "Get me Evan and my father, they might know who, and when they pull up, we will be ready. Two people against us is nothing. Let's see what they want, don't attack on sight, let them through," I order, and people scramble to do as they are told. I march through the camp. Bern and Henry fall in on either side, while Dray walks behind me, and I spot Archel already beyond the row of bikes, almost blending into the shadows of the building. Unless I was looking, I wouldn't have seen him.

I weave through the bikes and wait, my hands loose at my sides, ready to grab a blade if I need to. The rest of my people spread out behind me, waiting for them to arrive. It doesn't take ten minutes, so I guess they are speeding to get here. "Are there any patrols out there?" I ask my father when he rushes up to me, looking over my shoulder.

"No, no, they were due to go out when it all happened." He frowns.

"Well, someone knows where you are and they are coming right here. No one attacks unless I do," I call louder, and I hear the agreement just as the rumble of an engine reaches my ears. The bike slows, and I spot them in the distance zigzagging through the buildings and gates. They know exactly where to go. The riders head straight for the bunker doors so I whistle. They stop then, leaving the engine running and scan the horizon. I raise a hand, letting them decide. I can't make out much apart from the person at the front is a guy and there is a passenger behind him.

They seem to be debating their options, but slowly pull around the building towards us. I spot the Berserker guards from the bunker door closing in behind them as they come to a halt. They don't shut off the engine, obviously sensing trouble. I take in the guy in the front. He is huge, a beast of a man, and he looks like he belongs out here, not down there. That's what throws me off.

Then I blink incredulously as a brown-haired woman jumps off the back and steps next to him, facing me. I scan her, noting the bow on her back and swords at her sides. She's wearing a leather jacket, a crop top, and black jeans and boots. Her hair is wavy and tied partially back in small plaits. She is beautiful. She looks sweet and innocent and ever so young compared to me with all my scars, but it's the fire, the resolve, and anger in her eyes that has me almost smiling. She might look nice, but this woman is a fighter through and through.

"Piper," comes a strangled whisper.

"Pip?" a voice yells, and I turn to see Evan gaping. He lunges forward, but I nod and Dray holds him back. I look to Archel to see he has stepped from the shadows and is staring at Piper, his face not expressionless for once. He is staring at her in wonder and horror, but I can't help but note the happiness in her eyes when she sees him.

"Brawler?" the big man asks, but she ignores him, her eyes swinging from Evan to Archel then to me.

"Okay, someone better tell me what the fuck is going on before I start kicking ass and taking names...or Jago does and I cheer from the side." She props her hands on her hips and looks at Archel first. "Should have figured you would be here if there was trouble," she scoffs and then breaks into a smile. "Missed you, Shadow. Wait until you see what I can do with a dagger now." Then she seems to collect herself and looks at Evan.

He is sagging in Dray's arms, looking like he has seen a ghost. I feel for him. I felt the love he had for her, and now he's found her and he has to see her so clearly enamoured with two other men. "Hi Evvie, long time no see, loving the whole hobo chic look you are going for."

He gasps, sounding like he's in pain. "Pip, fucking hell. Pip, they told me you were dead!" he screams, tears gathering in his eyes and she winces.

I look around, noting the audience, and sigh, drawing everyone's gaze. "Let's take this inside, we have a lot to discuss." I whistle, waving my fingers in a circle at the Berserkers guarding the rolling door, and they go back to it. Then I look at Dray. "Let him go. Bern, get the patrol back on it. Henry, work with the dwellers. I want to know what the fuck is going on down there. Everyone else, I want no fucking bodies, fight, fuck, I don't care, but no deaths!" Then I turn to Jago and Piper. "Follow me."

I start to walk back to my tent while people break into movement, but Piper's whisper floats to me on the air, making me smile. "Who is she? She is badass as hell, total girl crush material. Think she would let me touch her swords? What? Don't look at me like that, I meant an actual sword, not cocks, jeez."

"Brawler..." The guy with her groans, sounding pained and amused all at the same time.

"What? Not saying I would swing that way—ha—but damn that

is one scary fine woman, like I bet she even fucks scary hot, you know?"

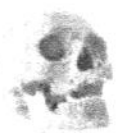

My tent is crowded with everyone, but we make it work. I stand rather than sit. Just because they know these people doesn't mean I should automatically trust them, and by the way the big guy, Jago, watches everything, I know he is a fighter, so I keep my eyes out and my body ready just in case. Dray has no such qualms. He sprawls back on the sleeping bag, watching the newcomers with half shut eyes like a big cat. Bern and Henry are in the back near the door. Evan still is staring at Piper, standing near me. Archel is close to Piper and I almost smirk at him.

"Feeling needy, assassin? Why don't I let your girl know how you lost to me last night?" I tease.

Piper looks between us, even as Archel laughs. "I'm calling a rematch once you know the whole war thing is out of the way." He waves his hand, dismissing the 'war thing,' as he calls it.

"Okay, seriously, what the hell is going on?" Piper asks, looking at me. Smart girl.

"I'm Worth," I reply. "Berserker Queen," Bern adds.

"The Champion of the Wastes," Henry inserts.

"Soulmate!" Dray interjects with a smirk, and I roll my eyes.

"Or just Worth, ignore them."

"More like pain in the ass," Evan mumbles, and when Piper looks at him he swallows and can't seem to look away. She appears to have the same difficulty, but manages it when I start talking.

"Why don't you tell us why you are here?" I query.

"Why don't you?" Jago fires back, almost seeming to prowl next to Piper, towering over her petite form, yet he doesn't leave her side.

"I'm not your enemy. My father used to run Paradise, I met him this last year, but I didn't even know he was alive. I was headed back here after...a pit stop, shall we say, to get some information. While we were here, however, they were attacked." Rubbing my head, I cross my arms and put them next to my blades. "We helped protect it. Now, the guards and captain are locked down there, sweeping the place for explosives and survivors. Why are you here?" I demand.

Piper looks to Archel and he nods at her. "A messenger came, told me Paradise was attacked, it was gone, so we came straight away. I wanted to make sure...you were okay," she finishes, looking at Evan.

"Came to where?" I question.

She doesn't answer and I sigh. "We are going to have to trust each other. Like it or not, there are bigger threats out here than me right now. I trust Archel and even Evan and they are vouching for you, so you should extend the same courtesy. We are not enemies. In fact, I think we might just be allies right now."

"What clan?" Jago inquires, and I look at him and let my face go cold.

"Was a slave for a while to Berserkers, then a fighter at The Ring, then a bounty hunter. I recently killed Ivar the Mad and took his throne, I now rule the Berserkers and have peace ties with all clans. Which clan?" I counter.

"None, not yet," he answers.

"This is getting us nowhere. I have information, you have information, we need to work together." I shrug. "Otherwise, feel free to leave, we have shit to deal with and a war to win."

"I've heard that twice now. What war?" Piper asks, and the excitement in her eyes has me smiling and looking at Archel.

"Huh, picked a fighter, did you? Can she kick your ass or do I need to teach her?"

He groans. "Fuck no, don't teach her your dirty tricks."

"What donkey dick war?" Piper questions louder, and Jago groans.

"Really, Brawler, donkey dick?"

"The Cities came north, took some of our people, and they want

Paradise. I plan to stop them, want to join?" I inquire, figuring I might as well be direct.

"Shit yeah," Piper calls, and Jago actually drops his head and pinches his nose as if in pain while Archel laughs.

"Why don't we discuss exactly what is happening?" I say. Deciding to make the first move, I go and lean back against Dray who's still sitting on the bed. The tension seems to dim and Piper plops herself on the floor crossed-legged, staring at me.

"I was from Paradise," she starts, and then seems to shudder, her eyes closing in pain, one I know too well.

"Piper," I call, and she looks up at me, her eyes swimming with demons. "Everything you have been through, I can tell you I have been through the same. You aren't a slave for years without seeing the worst of the world. My body is covered in scars, brands, their torture, and pain. Ivar, the king I killed, was my master. I was his favourite, and he tried for years to break me again and again. He raped me, his men raped me." Dray flinches then and Jago growls, even Archel steps closer to her. "They tortured me, they killed the boy I loved, they killed the man I loved, and they took me from my family. I don't say this to diminish your pain, I say it to be frank. Whatever happened, here, there is no judgement. How could there be when most of us have been through the same? You were from Paradise, correct? Evan told me you disappeared, that he was told you were dead, but he searched anyway. What happened? You do not have to share everything," I add, knowing personally how difficult it is to talk about.

She holds her head higher with each word, sitting straighter, that fire in her eyes burning brighter. "I was usually on patrol with Jago, they changed that, and on patrol that night they attacked, raped, and tried to kill me. Ferals got to them and Archel saved me. He took me to a place of people, The Forgotten, they were once from Paradise as well. They learned of the corruption and left."

"Who, what corruption?" I ask, sitting forward.

"The captain, he ordered it, he warned me. The people, my

people, told me this was done often, nearly all the time, and anyone digging too deep was killed. Paradise is corrupt, you say the captain is here? Let me be the one to kill him," she begs.

"He's yours," I agree instantly, knowing she needs that. "Sands below, I knew something was off here." Dray rubs my back. "Okay, you know anything about the Cities?"

She shakes her head but Jago looks at me. "I do."

I narrow my eyes. "Tell me," I demand and he growls, but Piper lays a hand on his arm.

"I trust her, Jago, and I trust Archel and Evan," she assures him softly. He curls into her touch and sighs.

"I've been there once, was sent to map it," he admits, and I almost flinch in shock.

Fuck, did we just find our leverage?

"Let us start from the beginning. Bern, grab some water and food and get Erik and my father," I order, and the big guy lumbers away to do just that.

Piper looks from him to me. "Will you marry me?" she blurts out of the blue, and I blink at her, unsure of what to say. "Sorry, but damn, that whole power, in control thing is hot as hell." She shrugs, not the least bit embarrassed.

"When she's marrying anyone it's me," Dray comments, and I turn to him with a glare and he smirks at me. "What? I said when."

"Does that mean I get to be best man?" Archel asks.

I look at Piper and she winces. "Sorry, awkward, so, I gotta know.

Girl to girl, you slept with him?" She jerks her head at Archel.

I can't help it, I laugh. "I like my heart in my chest, not on his knife, thank you."

"Plus, I'd kill him," Dray adds.

She nods, accepting this. "Okay, what about Evan?" She doesn't look at him as she talks.

"Nope, sorry, not my type."

"Huh, figured, you like the big warrior kind, right? I bet they throw you around and you get all kinky—sorry, I'll stop now."

I blink hard, really unsure what to say now, so we sit in awkward silence while waiting for Bern to return.

"I like what you've done with the place, very minimalist," she comments, looking around at the tent.

Just then the others push into the tent. My father doesn't seem to recognize her, but that's okay.

"Let's get started, shall we?" I suggest. "Jago, tell us everything." "I was born out here, came to Paradise as a kid, and when I made

guard they wanted maps of everything. I prefer it out here, so I volunteered. One day they said they knew of a city down south, they wanted it mapped just in case, so I snuck in..." He holds Pipers hand and starts explaining what he knows of the Cities.

The discussion takes hours, and after it my head feels like it's about to burst with information, but we have grudging peace, so even Jago started to relax. I leave them to talk between them and go over everything. I have enough drama in my life without adding hers. Plus, she seems like she can handle herself, even if she is a bit crazy. Probably from being with Archel too long, or dealing with Evan's moods.

While I leave the love birds to it, I try to focus on making contact with the captain and his men down in Paradise. They should have opened up by now. That, coupled with what Piper said about the captain, I have a bad feeling. I grab Jason on the way because although he's kind of annoying, he seems to know a lot about the mechanics of things up here. "Okay, is there a way to contact them down there? They can see us, so I'm betting they can hear us, yet we are blind. I want in or I want visual and audio. Tell me how."

His eyes fly wide. "Err—what?" he asks and I sigh.

"I want visual and audio or I want in, can you do that?" I repeat.

He nods, looking around, seeming to think before he actually jumps and claps. "Yes, yes, I think I can. If we access the control panel at the bunker door, I might be able to gain access, but I'll need help. Be right back!" he calls and jogs away.

I wait with Dray, both of us watching the camp, until Jason comes back followed by a skinny guy who looks away as soon as we make eye contact. "This is Lupin, he can help, come on." Jason starts towards the bunker door and I follow after him, with a nervous, pale Lupin close behind.

He's a tall kid, skinny as hell though—lanky, I would call him. He has on black glasses framing dark eyes and a long, pointy nose and high cheekbones. Even the way he is holding himself looks awkward.

Jason ignores the Berserker guards who stare at me questioningly and heads straight for a darker grey patch hidden to the right. He pulls out a screwdriver and pops open a small hatch, showing screens and wires he and Lupin bend together while whispering and working. So I turn to Dray and step closer, making sure to lower my voice.

"I don't want to leave them defenceless with whatever is going on down there..." I start.

He grips my chin. "But you have shit to do, I get it. These aren't your people, soulmate. Your people are hundreds of miles away and need your help."

I nod, leaning into his touch. "I'm being pulled in two directions," I admit, telling him my worries.

"Family always comes first, soulmate, no matter the cost. You have fought too hard to lose this now, so we stay today and help them as much as we can, then they need to learn to fend for them fucking selves like we had to. You can't save everyone, soulmate, you know that," he growls.

I nod, knowing he's right. Blowing out a breath, I straighten my spine. "We stay today, I will figure out a plan for them, then tonight we head to The Ring."

"That's my girl," he whispers, and then leans down and kisses me.

He sucks on my tongue and I lean into him, losing myself in his touch until a throat clears next to me. Instantly, both Dray and I are pointing weapons at the person and pulling away from each other to see a pale, shaking Lupin stumbling back from us, warding us off with his hands.

"Sorry, sorry, we, erm, fuck," he stutters, still backing away.

Rolling my eyes, I sheathe my sword before he pisses himself, and turn to fully face him. "What's wrong?" I ask impatiently.

"I have double-checked, but it looks like someone inside has disabled the cameras and audio on purpose. We can't see in at all. I'm trying to remotely open the blast doors, but the likelihood is low, they weren't made to be opened from the outside," he rushes to explain, not even taking a breath between sentences.

"So only those down there know what's going on, and we can't speak to them or know if they are alive?" I summarise and he nods.

"Keep working on it," I order and he nods again, stumbling over his own feet in his haste to get away from me. I look at Dray then. "It's time to come up with a plan."

We are all gathered around the makeshift table outside. My father and a few of his dwellers, surrounded by Seekers, Berserkers, and, well... Piper. She is sitting between Jago and Archel, swinging her legs back and forth. She looks happy and relaxed, but I spot the tightness around her eyes, and when someone comes up from behind she jumps and grabs a knife from her side, ready to attack.

"I'm going to make this fast and simple. We don't know if they are dead and we don't have time to stay and find out. If they are alive, they aren't opening that door and you could all die waiting for it, if they aren't, then they aren't opening it for a reason. My people and I are leaving this afternoon, we still have a war to win, so before then we need to come up with a plan for you." I look around then and stop on my father. "I say you leave Paradise for good."

He jumps to his feet, his eyes wide. "B-But this is our home! We don't know how to live out here!" he yells, drawing everyone's eyes while my men stroke their weapons. I stop them from attacking by raising my hand.

"I feel like I need popcorn," Piper whispers.

"Then you fucking adapt. Everyone else had to. It's time you stopped hiding in the bunker." With that, I dismiss him and look at Piper. "You offered your help, does that still stand?"

She sits up taller in her chair and for once doesn't babble. "Yes." "Good, I need you to stay here for two days, that is all. Help them

pack up and move out. There is an empty town near The Rim. It's called Spring, and it's probably the safest place even if it's not as habitable as everywhere else."

"Can I offer another suggestion?" she inquires, raising her hand and making me smile—this fucking girl.

"Sure." I nod.

"We wait for two days, if they don't open the door, we abandon Paradise like you suggested. Then we take them with us," she looks at Archel then, "to The Forgotten. There is enough room and they will be better protected. They will need to earn their place, but the people are friendly and will help them."

"They will accept them all?" I query.

She hesitates then, her face hardening. "Not any who harmed those there. I speak for my people, and they will face punishment for that. The others, yes."

I take in her tone and stance. She's a leader, that much is for fucking sure. Leader, survivor, and fighter, she will be good to have on my side.

"Then do that, your punishment and vengeance is yours to have, and Piper?" I lean forward. "Make them pay for what they did, make it fucking hurt."

The men around the table cheer as we share a smile. "Too fucking right, hotness." She holds out her hand in a fist and I raise my eyebrows, making her sigh. "You're too hot to be dumb, you fist bump it," she explains. She grabs my hand, and only years of practice stop me from killing her as she bumps my fist into hers, then pulls it back and makes an explosion with hers.

I know Jago spotted how close I was to attacking out of instinct, and he doesn't seem happy, but offers me a nod when I straighten up. "It is sorted then," I declare.

"I bet she has a bigger penis than even you. You should have a measuring contest," she whispers to Jago, distracting him from glaring at me.

"It's not sorted! My people should have a choice!" my dad shouts, and my patience snaps.

I get in his face, mine cold and my tone deadly. "Listen up and listen hard. I will say this only once. My men, the people I love most in this world are being tortured as we speak so I can babysit your fucking pompous ass. I don't give a fuck if you are scared out here, or that the last time you came out was when you lost my brother and me. You will do as you are fucking told for once or so help me God, we will leave you here to die. You are being given a better choice than most—protection and a new home. Everyone here had to earn that, had to fight for that, and you want to complain it's not fair? Life isn't fucking fair, sweetheart, but you keep on going, keep fighting because it's the only life you get. So you are going to go back there and tell your people what is happening, then you will pack up. You will listen to Piper, you will do as she tells you or you die, but I am not wasting another moment of my life on a man who left his own daughter to die at the hands of a madman, not when the men who saved me and brought me back to life are suffering. Do we understand each other?" I finish.

Everyone else is silent, all eyes on us. I watch my father swallow as tears gather in his eyes. "I understand," he replies.

I step away then, turning my back on him to face my men. "Pack up! We are rolling out soon!" I yell and then stride away, trying to hide how much I need to hurt something right now. My hands are in fists and my body is wired up.

I push into my tent and grab my bag, starting to pack to distract myself. I hear footsteps and know it isn't Dray, he wouldn't be that loud.

"Worth, can I have a minute?" Piper calls from behind me, as I shove things into my bags. I turn and sigh.

"Sure."

"I want to help with the war, I think I can."

I raise my eyebrow, crossing my arms. "Piper—"

"No, I was always saying I want an adventure and, well, this is it. I can fight, I can lead my people. If you fail, you said it yourself, the Wasteland is theirs and they will probably kill us all. If I can stop that, I will. When I take the Paradise people back to my people, I will speak to them and gather our fighters." She stands tall then without any give in her expression. She isn't asking for permission.

I smirk then. "Good, then help us, fuck knows we will need every man we can get."

The tent pushes open again and Evan, Archel, and Jago stand there, making me groan. "This isn't a fucking counselling chamber, take your lovers spat elsewhere," I warn.

"Worth, I'm going with her," Archel informs me. I nod. "I know."

He grins then and I wink back. "I wouldn't expect anything less. Look after her, will you, and meet us at the front line."

"I'm going too, if she will have me?" Evan asks, looking at Piper.

She swallows but nods without looking at him, and a giant smile curves his lips. "Shit, who's going to patch me up now, Doc?" I tease.

He laughs then narrows his eyes on me. "Stop getting fucking hurt. Don't let anyone else patch you up or do it yourself. I've seen your needlework on your skin already and it fucking sucks. No getting shot, stabbed, burned, tortured, or captured. I will see you after the Cities." He nods.

"Thanks, Doc," I reply. I'm going to miss the bastard. "I'm glad you found her," I add lower and he freezes, looking at me, his expression softening.

"You'll find yours again, Worth. They wouldn't dare die on you.

You aren't saying goodbye again, not this time, and I won't sing you a fucking song like Vas," he teases and I laugh.

"No goodbyes, not anymore." Then despite myself, I stride over and hug him, and he returns the embrace. Just two people with shared pain. We bonded in those cells and Vas's death only solidified our friendship. It's strange, I'm crude and rough, and he's sophisticated and posh, but it's ours. "Look after yourself, keep practicing what I showed you," I tell him, and then lower my voice again. "Don't let her get away this time," I whisper, then let go and step back.

"I'll see you at the front," I tell them all.

"What? I don't get a hug?" Piper pouts and everyone groans, making her smile. "I'm just saying, thought we were going to all hug it out? No? Guess not." Jago huffs, grabs her, and throws her over his shoulder, then nods at me and walks out as she carries on talking. Evan looks after them, smiles at me, and follows, leaving Archel and me.

"Take care of him," he murmurs. "I will," I reply.

Then he smirks. "Long live our fucking queen." He salutes and marches out of the tent after Piper.

Who fucking would have guessed it?

Now, it's time to get my men back. I've had enough distractions.

Chapter Fourteen

THE AGREEMENT

We pack up fast. All of our people are used to moving at a moment's notice, and the bikes are already lined up and ready to ride out. I don't say goodbye to my father, I have nothing else to say to him. Instead, I heave my pack onto my bike, stick my leather jacket on, and wrap my bandana around my neck. I spot Piper linger- ing, watching from the camp, and head her way. For all her bravado and strength, she is still so young, and despite all the pain and suffering she has been through, she has come out stronger and manages to keep her sense of humour. I hope that will still be the same next time we meet, because I like her.

"Hey." I nod, turning to stand by her side as I watch my people load up and swing onto their bikes.

"I gotta say, you don't seem weirded out by the three men thing," she observes casually.

I snort. "Three? That's nothing, come back when you have five." She turns to me and grins. "Five? Fuck, that's a lot of cock. Like, I guess I have three holes, you know, but do you take turns, is there a schedule? Do they play pick a hole?"

I laugh, I can't help it. "If we make it through this, I'll tell you."

"I mean like, three, I get it, I have three holes, you know..." She trails off.

"Evan never stopped looking for you, and even when he thought he was going to die, all he thought about was you—that he never said sorry, that he never told you how he felt. Just thought you should know."

I can feel her looking at me then. "I loved him for such a long time, but I don't know if I'm that same person anymore," she admits.

"So? Be the new you and see if the love is still there. He's different too, I'm betting. Maybe this time you can both love each other and get it right. Sometimes the person is right, but the timing is off."

"Fuck, you're smart. Brains and beauty, no wonder the six cocks," she teases.

"Stay safe, Piper." I nod, starting to walk away, but I freeze and grab the goggles off my head. Turning back, I offer them to her. "You're going to need these out there."

"But they're yours," she replies, not reaching for them, so I throw them at her and she automatically catches them.

"Then I'll get them back next time we see each other. Keep them safe for me." I wink and then leave her there as I head to my bike.

Dray is waiting with his bike next to mine as I swing onto it. Bern, Erik, and Henry are behind us. "Ride hard," I call out, then I pull up my bandanna and kick my bike to life. I don't look back as I pull away. Life's too short for that. Instead, I focus on the road ahead, knowing it leads to my men.

I'm coming for you.

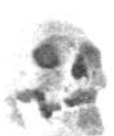

The ride to The Ring is long, and every passing minute and hour only makes me grip the handles tighter and try to go faster. Now that I know I am getting closer to getting them back, it's all I can think about, but I need to relax. I still have preparations to put in place to ensure that once they are free of the Cities, they are free of them forever. I won't ever let them go back and they will pay for taking my men.

We ride through the night and into the next day. It's almost dark again before I see the telltale signs of The Ring. It feels like so much has changed since I have last been here. I don't even know what to expect when I arrive with Major being gone. Will his men have let it fall into ruins? Will there be anyone left there?

Did they bury him?

The thought hits me and my heart clenches. Fuck, I didn't even get to say goodbye to him. I never thanked him for everything he did for me, I never told him how I felt, and now he's just gone and I know the place will be filled with his ghost.

When they die, some people go peacefully, and one or two people remember them, usually loved ones, but Major…Major was loved. His memory will live on in the Wastes for years to come, and I will make sure of that. He was powerful, loving, and someone everyone looked up to. In a world filled with pain, hate, and chaos, he turned The Ring into a place of safety, something the world desperately needed. He took in the strays and slaves no one wanted, and gave them a home and a purpose.

When we pull up outside the gate, cars upon cars are parked here and so are bikes. Slipping from mine, I unsheathe my weapon just in case someone has tried to take over The Ring, and stride up to the gate without waiting for everyone else. I know he's gone, I saw it happen, but it won't feel real until I am inside. I have this clawing need to see it for myself.

To see the space where he should be.

There are guards at the gates, some familiar, some not, and when they see me coming a call goes up, with a man hurrying inside and the others watching me with wide eyes. I stop before them, and a man with a purple mohawk on his head and rings covering his bottom lip steps forward.

"Champion, they are all waiting inside for you. We have kept the gates closed and eradicated any of Ivar's men left behind. We have not touched the office." He nods and I frown.

"Okay..." I respond, unsure, and he fidgets then.

"Was there something else we were supposed to do? That's all the order said." He looks panicked.

"Order from who?" I ask, narrowing my eyes as I hear my people catching up with me.

"Major."

One word, a name, and I am staggered. "He ordered you to keep...this place safe...for me?"

He nods, looking confused. "He left it in his final orders, a passing to you. You control The Ring now. Oh, he also said to check the top drawer in his desk. We all had to learn these orders when we took the job...you didn't know?"

"No, I didn't," I reply coolly, my mind whirling...how long had Major planned this for? He had put me in charge in case of his death and didn't fucking tell me? That rat bastard. A smile curls my lips then as I realise he probably knew I would run the other way if he did. Now look at me. How the fuck can I be a queen and a leader?

"Thank you, keep the gate closed. Are Priest, Reeves, and Nan here?" I question and he nods.

I start to walk through the gate and he calls out, "And more! People heard about what happened first with Ivar then the Cities, and they are pissed as hell and coming here. They want to fight, they want to help."

I stop, his words making me blink...they are coming here, waiting for me?

"Major was a good man, a good leader, but he shied away from the hard decisions. They know you won't," the man adds, and when I look back he is staring back out into the Wastelands.

Dray comes to my side, smiling at me as if to say I told you so, and my people gather behind me. "Get everyone inside, figure out sleeping arrangements if you can. We rest here while I talk to the other leaders, and then I will tell you the entire plan," I instruct.

Erik steps forward. "Take a minute and read the letter. They can wait," he advises, then he turns to my people and starts shouting orders.

I wish I could, but I have a feeling the letter will destroy me, so instead I head for the room we had The Summit in...the room Major died in. It's time to brief the other leaders. This time, there is no peace treaty or Summit. They will either join us or leave, the time for peace and discussions is over.

The doors to the building that holds the meeting room are thrown open. On my way here I spotted the increase of people—there are more than ever. The place is filled to the brim and they all stop what they are doing as I pass. Murmurs start up, and before I know it, they are chanting my name. I hold my head high and stride into the building, heading for the doors at the back. I hear them before I see them and a smile of longing curls my lips at Nan's voice.

"Shut ye fuckin' trap ya old bastard!" she yells.

Sniggering, I open the doors and slide in. "Any way to greet me, you old bitch?" I call.

"Who ya callin' bitch, girly?" she shouts, turning to see me at the door, but a smile twists her old lips before they flatten and she points at me. "'Bout fuckin' time ya got here, where tha fuck ya been?"

"Sit down before you fall down," I tease, walking around the table, purposely not looking over the other side of the room so I don't have to remember how he died here.

"I'll fuckin' teach ya some manners," she grumbles, but sits down anyway. "Bloody kids, thinkin' they are all that!"

I hesitate at the seat before sliding into it, not looking at the one to my right where Major sat. Dray takes the chair to my left again, and everyone else is in the same exact seats. It makes it obvious he is missing, and my heart pangs again, but I clear my throat and sit back.

"Fill me in, what's happened?" I order.

"Heard you are a queen now?" Priest asks, his eyes gleaming.

"You hear a lot," I counter.

Nan snorts. "Fuckin' whoop-de-doo, a fuckin' queen."

"I will shoot you, I don't care that you are old." I grin at her and she laughs, making Reeves laugh.

"Just checkin ya still got that fire, ya gonna need it," she says sadly.

"Ivar is dead," I confirm.

Reeves whoops, Nan grins, and Priest just nods like he expected this. "Now, tell me what has been happening."

"They started arriving soon after the Cities left. We tracked your men and the Cities' men all the way past The Rim, back to where they fucking came from. We have spies outside, waiting to inform us in case they send out any more raiding parties," Reeves tells me, and I nod.

"Then you know why I'm here." I look at the table then sigh. "Dray, get the booze, we are going to need it."

He grabs a bottle and some glasses and passes them around. I pour a shot and throw it back before pouring a bigger amount and handing the bottle around. "We don't stop them now, they will keep coming. They want the North, and they want Paradise and whatever hides there. We have to stop them. They will kill us all to get it. Apart we are weak, together we are stronger. I have a plan, but you all play a part. I need to know if you will?" I inquire, sipping at the amber drink, watching them.

"Sounds like we are going to war. The deaths shall be magnificent, and the angels and demons will walk among us," Priest muses.

"Well fuck," Reeves groans, and throws back his shot.

"I'll get me shotgun," Nan calls, stealing the bottle from Reeves and sipping from it. "Tell us the plan then, girlie."

Nodding, I throw back the rest of my drink, and start to outline what is going to happen and what I need from them. No one interrupts me, and when I am done, Nan throws back half the bottle and looks at me with respect on her face. "Ya got some big ole balls, girlie. Let's hope ya make it through this."

"I'll drink to that." I grin. Now that I am implementing the plan, a cool calmness is filling me. Either it works or it doesn't, and my worry won't change it, so why bother?

"We are with you," Reeves states, nodding.

"As are we, so bright is the cry of war," Priest agrees.

"What tha loons said," Nan declares and laughs. "Take ya a few days to get to The Rim, we will stop at the old man's on the way so he can grab his men, then stop at The Rim. I have some things that might help ya, girlie. To us, let's fuck some shit up!" she toasts, holding up the bottle.

After ironing out a few more details, the others file out, all intent on drinking and enjoying their last night here. I stay behind, and once the door slams shut, my eyes automatically go to the other corner of the room. Gripping the edge of the table hard, I fight back the memo- ries—the feel of Major's warm blood pumping into my hands, watching the light die from his eyes. There is still a bloodstain on the carpet, but it feels right, it shouldn't be clean after. It should be painted on every floor and wall in this place, his memory, his death.

This was his world, his house, and now he's gone.

I miss him.

"I'm sorry," he gasps, blood bubbling on his lips as his breathing turns erratic and his face pales.

Slumping back into my chair, I try to drag my eyes away from the bloodstain, but I can't as more and more memories swim through my mind and pain fractures my heart, aching for the man I loved. For the man who taught me to save myself.

"Again, or do you want to die in that pit?" he yells, watching me from the side.

Shouting, I get back to my feet, shaking and stumbling from all the pain and tiredness ricocheting through my body.

"You can do it, pain is temporary. Fucking fight!"

Wheezing, I choke on a sob, my mind crushing under the weight.

Gritting my teeth, I stare at his upturned face as he stitches the gash on my stomach closed. When he is done, he looks up at me with a soft smile curling his lips, his suit jacket tossed behind him and covered in blood from where he picked me up and carried me in here.

"There, all done, good as new," he says.

"I'm not, I'm so fucking broken," I whisper, looking down at the floor.

He presses my chin up. "Never lower your head for anyone, kid, you are worth double of everybody in this world. You aren't broken, you're a survivor, a warrior, and that is what this world needs. They just don't know it yet."

My chest is cut to ribbons from my breaking heart, and my body is weak and shaking with pain.

"Soulmate," Dray growls, and my eyes drag away to see him by my side, crouching next to my chair and looking up at me. I didn't even hear him move, I feel like I am trapped in the past with my body still in the present.

"Make it stop, make the pain stop," I beg, looking at Dray with pain and tears swimming in my eyes.

He grabs my face, filling my vision, not allowing me to look anywhere but into his artic cold eyes. "Look at me, just me," he demands, his voice harsh and jolting. The memories stop, calming in my head as if they wouldn't dare defy him. "You're here, only here."

Though I can hear his voice, I'm still stuck between as the pain tears me apart. A gasp leaves my mouth as I pulled back to the present. Pain, real pain, stems from a cut he just made on my arm. I blink down at it as blood wells, his knife waiting there like he wasn't sure if he would have to do it again. My eyes rise slowly, locking back on his. My whole world becomes him and the sanctuary he offers.

"Feel that pain, let it wash the other away," he orders, pressing his thumb on the cut. Everything else fades, my focus solely on his hand against my skin. "Are you with me, soulmate?"

I nod, but his eyes narrow. "Words," he snaps.

"I'm here." My voice is weak and cracked, but there. "Name, what's my name?" he demands.

"Dray," I say, stronger this time.

Blinking, I calm my breathing, and my heart slows as well as I stare into his eyes. He nods, lets go of the cut, and leans down and kisses it gently before looking up at me. "You're okay, you just got lost for a moment, but you're back now."

Swallowing, I blink back tears. "You brought me back."

"Always, when you can't bring yourself back, I always will," he promises softly, wiping the blood on my arm away. The cut is tiny in comparison to the others on my arm, but it did the trick.

Leaning forward, I frame his face and flicker my eyes to each of his eyes. "I'm so fucking lucky. I love you, you crazy bastard."

Before he can reply and melt my heart even further, I seal my lips to his, showing him how much it means to me that he is here right now, facing down my demons with me and keeping me from that edge. He deepens the kiss, but keeps it slow and sweet, neither of us in a hurry to break away. I have other demons to face, so for now I lose myself in the taste of him. Pulling back, I rest my forehead on his.

"I couldn't save him," I confess.

"I know. If you could, he would have been here," he whispers, looking into my eyes. "But he loved you, sacrificing his life for you is the best way he could have gone."

"How do you know he loved me?" I whisper.

He smirks then. "We recognised one another. That, and he pointed a gun at me when you weren't looking and told me if I ever hurt you, he would string me from his gates in warning."

A sob mixed with a laugh bursts from me. "He didn't!"

"Oh, he did. That's what made me like him, he was willing to risk the wrath of a king to protect you," he replies seriously, and I close my eyes.

"I loved him, I didn't tell him enough or hardly ever. I spent so long being mad at him, avoiding him, and all that time he was protecting me." I shake my head, keeping my eyes closed to try and stop the tears from falling, but it's no use, one falls anyway.

Dray kisses it away, pressing his lips to my cheek. "He knew, but I think you won't settle until you read that letter. So come on, soulmate, put your brave face on for two more minutes."

Nodding again, I keep my eyes closed as I rebuild myself. It takes longer than usual, but when I pull back and give him a small smile, I feel more like myself again and ready to face everyone outside. Dray is right, I need to read that letter, it's like a cloud hovering over me and I can't properly grieve with it still waiting for me.

I know whatever I find between those pages will break me, but sometimes you have to break to rebuild stronger than before.

CHAPTER FIFTEEN

MAJOR'S GHOST

I get lucky. No one is waiting by the room. I can hear them all outside, someone is singing, and there are cheers, which means someone is fighting, yet I have no intent on joining them. No, instead I head to Major's office, but I hesitate outside the doorway. This was our place, our sanctuary, and although I love Dray, some things

shouldn't be changed just because of love.

"I need to do this myself," I tell Dray, turning to him with a weak smile.

He nods before winking at me. "Figured as much, I'll wait outside and make sure no one disturbs you. I'll wait all night if I have to, so take your time, soulmate. Say your goodbyes." He kisses me on the forehead then, sweet and soft.

I watch him go before turning to face the office again. Throwing back my shoulders, I push open the doors and let them close behind me. I put the lock in place, not wanting anyone to see me break down. I'm their leader now, they are looking to me for guidance, and they can't see me weak. Dray is right. This is my goodbye to Major. I won't forget him and it won't stop hurting, but maybe I can start to accept his death and his ghost will stop haunting my every waking and sleeping minute with regret and pain. Maybe I can let him go.

The office looks exactly the same. It shouldn't, it should look different. Yet it's the same, even when I am not. I feel like I have grown so much since the last time I have been here, when Major told me about Ivar. I had been so tormented, so worried about him, and he had still held power over me as much as I didn't want to admit it. Now, I'm free of him, free to finally be me and to grow without his shadow chasing me across the Wastes.

In this place, I first became Worth. It feels fitting it's the place I come to when I have finally become more...me. The me Major always knew I could be.

Running my fingers along the books in the wall, I smile sadly. I remember all the hours we spent in here, talking and reading. Him teaching me as much as he could about everything and anything, regaling me with stories from pre-scorch. Even in a world like this, he still believed in the power of words, and it's evidenced by his collection here. Turning away, I face the desk where his chair sits empty behind it, while the one I always sat in faces it like it's ready for another of our meetings. But they will never happen again. He won't ever tell me another story, he won't teach me another skill or push me to be better than I was. We won't ever share a drink as we both lose ourselves in the books.

This room is filled to the brim with memories of him and I, and it's only now, in the end, that I realise how lucky I was to have him. He wasn't perfect, but neither am I, but in this place we found something we had both been searching for—family.

Swallowing hard, I step around to his chair and sit in it, looking out at his office. It feels wrong sitting here, but I don't change places. He wouldn't mind, and I guess now this is my office too, if what the guard said is true. Did he really leave The Ring to me? Why didn't he ever tell me? Who am I kidding, this is Major, the man had more secrets than even me. Always a plan working in the background, always a scheme ready to go into play without anyone knowing.

The Cities

Forcing myself to stop stalling, I open the top drawer on the left. Inside are some papers and a book but no letter, so I shut it and open the bottom drawer. This one is a lot deeper and inside is a full, unopened bottle of whiskey, two glasses, and a folded letter with my name on the front. Taking a deep breath, I pull out the whiskey and the glasses, placing them on the desk before carefully picking up the letter and unfolding it. It's a couple of sheets thick, and when I spot Major's neat, fancy handwriting, I drop it to the desk and cover my face.

Fuck, I don't think I'm strong enough.

Scrubbing at my face, I reach out with shaking hands, uncork the whiskey, and pour myself a glass. I throw it back and then reach for the letter again. Not focusing on the words, I smooth out the cream sheets against the desk, stalling once mods. *Come on, man the fuck up,* I tell myself, and force my eyes to the top line.

Hi, kid, this is going to be a long one, so open that bottle and pour yourself a drink.

If you are reading this, then I'm gone. I'm sorry. I wish I could have stayed with you forever. I would have liked to have gotten to know this new you and the men at your side.

There are some things I need to tell you and you need to listen. Don't stop reading just because it hurts, I know you will pretend like it doesn't, but it will. That's what the whiskey is for. Pour me a glass, won't you?

You told me once I wasn't your father or your friend, I didn't let you see, but that broke my heart. I know you were angry, you have every right to be, because I did let you down. I hope I get a chance to make that right before I die, I hope that I have a chance to win back your trust. You told me today I put my business first, my life first. I wish I could have explained how wrong that is. You were always my first priority and nothing else mattered but you. This place? I built it from the ground up to protect you, made it a safe haven for you. It was the least I could offer while I worked to try and free you.

I need you to know that in case I don't get to tell you in person.

You were the daughter I lost, you were my destiny.

She always believed I was made for more, she believed in that spiritual crap but she was right. I survived it all so I could save you, so I could help you. If it's the only good thing I do in this world, I can live with that.

I never told you about her, I should have. You would have loved her, she was so beautiful and fierce, and when she needed me the most, I wasn't there. I lost her, kid, I lost her and it broke me. I was never a good man. I did things, things others would shy away from, but after I lost her, I ceased to care. I did whatever I wanted and then you came along and it was like being hit by lightning. In your eyes, I saw that same fierceness, that same fragile beauty, and I knew. I knew why I had carried on fighting—for you.

By now, you will have heard you are in charge. That was always my plan, I built this place not knowing why, but now I do. It's for you, it's your haven. I squandered the peace you found here, but you can make it more. You can make it better. You are the only person I trust in this world, kid.

It's yours now. Do with it as you wish, keep it a safe haven for the lost and damned like us, or burn it to the ground, whatever you need to do. I'm sorry I can't be there to help, leading is hard, I know. The pres- sure, the responsibility, the having people's lives in your hands. It's a job I wish on no one, but I know you can do it. Let me give you some advice to help you on the way.

I know you're grown, I know you can make your own choices, but I hope you will at least think about what I have to offer.

Not every choice you make will be right, I learned that early on, but it's how you handle the consequences and outcomes that make you a leader.

You can't save every life, you just can't, and some- times you have to sacrifice a few to save the many. It hurts and you will never forget their names and faces, but it has to be done.

You make the hard choices, trust in those around you to help, but when it comes down to it, trust yourself.

Have a safe place, one to retreat to when the ques- tions, the choices, and the pressure get to be too much. Mine? In here with you.

You thought I was just bringing you here to teach you, to offer you a safe place to hide. but it worked for me as well. Your presence always helped calm me. Helped me realise what really mattered and what I was fighting for. You always asked the best questions and often, in teaching you, I taught myself as well, and found the answers I needed. You were my safe place, kid, still are. I hope this can be yours as well.

Most of all, life is short. Don't waste it keeping people away. I shouldn't have questioned your judgement about these men, I can see how much you care for them and how much they care for you. I just want you to be happy. You deserve it, kid, you deserve to be loved.

So let them. It doesn't make you weak or any less of a fighter to rely on them. Love them hard and love them fully, and don't ever let them go. This world can suck that from you in a moment, and life is so fragile, Tazanna. Don't have regrets like I do.

Oh, and that mad bastard Seeker, he's alright. I had a little talk with him when you left and we are on the same page now.

He loves you, just like I do. He might be rough around the edges and...well, bat shit crazy, but he really loves you. I'm glad, because it means as I'm writing this, planning for when I'm not here, I know you aren't alone.

I drop the letter, tears spilling down my cheeks as my heart rips open again. Hands shaking, I pour myself a drink before hesitating with the bottle in the air, then I pour him one as well. Fuck, I knew this would be hard, but I wasn't ready for all this. Taking a deep breath, I pick up the letter again, forcing myself to read on.

Back to The Ring, my men are yours as is everything here. They will follow you, they will fight with you. Keep them close.

By now I'm betting you are working your way through that bottle, save some for me, won't you?

I snort then, that bastard, how did he know?

I'm so proud of you, kid, I need you to know that. I watched a terrified girl grow into a warrior, and no one in this world will ever be worthy of your loyalty, least of all me, but I couldn't turn it away. I'm calling on that loyalty now, because I have one last thing I need you to do for me. I have no right to ask, but I have to.

In the bottom drawer is a key, and behind my copy of War and Peace is a safe. Inside is a picture of my little girl, Cara, and her neck- lace. I want you to have the necklace, I was waiting for the right moment to give it to you, but it never came.

Did you know butterflies are strong? They have beauty and are covered in marks from life, but they still keep flying.

Anyway, the picture. Bury it with me, let me keep her close for all time along with the drawing you find in there. I want both of my daughters with me in the end. The one I lost and the one I gained.

I have nothing else really to say, except goodbye.

This is my final goodbye. I hope I get to say all this to your face, but if not I had to ensure you knew everything I knew. I trust you, Tazanna, and only you. I knew from the moment I saw you what you would become. You are so strong and this world has a purpose for you. That I firmly believe, I don't know what that will be, kid, but I hope it brings you happiness.

Don't be sad for me, don't cry, even though you will and say you never did. I finally get to see her again, my little girl, the only regret I leave is not being by your side as you face the future and I'm sorry for that. Forgive me?

I love you, Tazanna Worth. Thank you for giving me back my life and purpose. Never stop fighting, Champion.

Major.

It's obvious he wrote this letter after the last time I left for The Summit. Did he know his death was coming? Wiping the tears pouring down my face, I gently fold the letter, and trace his words one last time before I grab the drink and throw it back. I leave his on the desk for him as I reach down and grab the golden key hidden in the bottom of the drawer. Sliding off the chair, I hunt through the books until I find the one I want, then I slide it out and gently place it on the desk, before spotting the black safe waiting for me.

Sneaky bastard, I never even knew this was here. I wonder what else he kept in here? Obviously valuables he was worried about losing. Using the key, I open the old-fashioned safe and reach inside. I'm careful as I pull it all out and lay it on the desk. I expected money, maybe weapons, maybe even information, but what I find...it breaks my heart.

He loved me, truly loved me.

Inside is a beautiful necklace on a long chain with a butterfly on the end. It's delicate looking, but when I feel, it I realise it's made of solid metal and won't break easily. I slip it over my head, playing with the charm before tucking it into my shirt next to my tree necklace. Next, I find an old photograph. It's tattered around the edges and I'm pretty sure it has a bloody thumbprint on one corner, but I can still make out the little girl in it.

She is pretty, with Major's eyes and lips. Hell, she even stands the way he used to. That same intelligence shines in her eyes, as does an inner strength so fierce I can't help but smile. I get what he means now. I smooth out the photograph and place it to the side. I will have to ask where he was buried, but I will do as he asked. There's a folded piece of parchment next, and when I unfold it, a gasp falls from my lips.

It's a drawing...of me.

I am half turned away with a smile curling my lips as I face someone. My hair is short and ragged, my brand crude on my skin, but I look so...fierce. My head is back, my spine straight, and I spot a knife in my hand. The drawing itself is beautiful. It is rendered in charcoal and looks exactly like me. Whoever drew it was very talented. I look at the corners, hoping for a signature, but don't spot one, so I flip it over to see the writing on the back.

"Tazanna 'Champion' Worth," is scrawled across it, and then in the bottom corner is "Major."

Major drew this? When? Why didn't he ever show or tell me he knew how to draw?

I find the chair behind me and slump back, staring at the drawing. I can feel the love coming from the page, and knowing he saw me this way, so fierce even when I was broken, kills me. When I can finally drag my eyes away from the drawing, I place it on top of the picture of Cara. Silent tears fall down my face as I realise what he meant in his letter now. He meant he wanted the picture and the drawing of me—both of his daughters, as he called us—buried with him.

What's left are scraps of paper, some drawings—obviously from Major—and some are my handwritten notes. They look like the stories I used to write when I got bored here, or the doodles I did when I was pretending to listen to him as he blabbered on about things. He kept them all. Not just kept them, but locked them away in his safe to keep them forever.

Major, you fucking asshole, not even here so I can hug you.

I grab the bottle and take a long swig, swiping across my face with the back of my arm as I try to steady my breathing. I flick through the drawings, some are of The Ring, some are of people, but it's the symbol that catches my eye. It's a thick circle on the outside, and on the inside is a smaller circle with an olive branch in it. It astounds me, because it instantly makes me think of The Ring, since I know he chose to focus on the fact this place is one of peace rather than pain.

For all his talk of being a bad man, of seeking the dark and never the light, he chose to design the symbol that showed the good in such a place of pain. I fold that up and press it into my pocket, not sure what I want to do with it yet, but I want to keep it with me forever— keep a piece of Major forever.

Grabbing my glass, I pour another drink. "Goodbye, Dad," I whisper, as I toast his glass and throw back the shot.

I wipe my face, build myself up, and throw open the office doors. I have Cara's picture and the drawing in my back pocket, which I'll need to bury with him tonight, so I head outside in search of someone who will know. I find Dray leaning against the doors, not letting anyone in the building, and in front of him is a glaring Nan. They look like they are having some kind of stand off, so I step up next to them, cross my arms, and wait.

"Whatcha doing?" I tease.

"Girlie, tell this fuckin' crazy killer ta get out ma way!" Nan shouts, poking Dray in the chest. He freezes, looks down at her finger, and then lifts his eyes to hers. They are ice-cold and deadly, his face blank like when he kills.

"Step back, crone, before I rip out your spine and wear it like a belt," he warns, his voice deadly as he watches her. Anyone else would be wetting themselves and running away, and I'm used to him, but even I can see how serious he is right now and he looks scary as hell.

"Fuckin' try it, ya tall ass cock sucker," she yells, poking him again. I can see he is about to snap, so I squeeze between them, and press my back to his chest to keep him pinned to the doorway.

"Nan, first of all, I can attest he does not suck cock. Second, why are you trying to get him to attack you?" I grin.

She huffs, hunching over like she is some weak old lady, and glares at Dray behind me who rumbles in warning like an animal. "A just wanted ta talk ta ya, girlie," she croaks.

"Uh-uh, cut the shit, what's up?" I ask, pressing farther back into Dray. He wraps his arms around me and drops his chin on my shoulder, probably still glaring at Nan.

She shuffles then, looking everywhere but me. "Nan," I snap and she huffs again.

"Okay, okay, keep ya panties on. A just wanted te say sorry," she mumbles, looking into my eyes.

"Sorry?" I repeat.

"Aye, for yer old man, Major. It's a damn shame what happened te him, he was a good man, did ya right. Am sorry it wasn't me that rat bastard shot," she finishes and I sigh.

"Neither option would have been good, I love you both," I admit, cringing when she starts to smile. "Don't let it go to your head, you old bitch. Ivar was never going to let a man like Major live, not after everything Major did to help me get away from him. It's not your fault, but if you feel bad, could you show me where he is buried?"

She nods. "Aye, a can do that, girlie. Follow me, bring yer pet if ye want." She spits at Dray's feet before spinning and marching away, not even pretending to shuffle. That old biddy, I shake my head with a smile and grin over my shoulder at Dray.

"You heard her, come on pet," I tease, but before I can move away he slams me back into the door, his hand wrapping around my throat as he leans in, still looking deadly as hell.

"Call me that once more, soulmate," he purrs.

"Pet," I gasp with the little air I can suck in, but I'm not afraid, no, my body relaxes into his, my pussy instantly getting wet, and my nipples hardening. He smirks, reaching down and flicking one through my shirt.

"Dirty little, soulmate," he murmurs, his voice deadly as he leans in and whispers against my mouth. "You will pay for that later," he threatens and I shiver.

"Fuck, I hope so," I reply, as he lets go of my throat and steps back. He winks at me, turns, and starts prowling after Nan, so I quickly jump into action and follow him to make sure he doesn't rip her apart for the pet comment and the whole poking thing.

I catch up with his big strides and he slows to match my pace as we follow Nan, who is weaving her way through scavs and roadies. Every eye turns to us when they realise who is walking in their midst, but I ignore them for now. Tonight is about Major and the last promise I will keep to him. They can have my attention later.

We move around the back of the main building, losing the crowd. I spot a couple of scavs fucking against the wall, but I leave them to their privacy as Nan keeps walking. Fuck, she walks fast for an old woman. I have to fast walk to keep up. She leads us to the very edge of The Ring, away from the noise and pit, to a private, quiet spot at the back near the fence.

There is a trunk of a tree there, the branches blackened slightly, and it looks half dead, but it's still standing. Under it, I spot disturbed earth. "Here?" I ask.

She nods, looking around. "This is his land, but I didnee wanna bury him near the fighters and slaves, ya know? This seemed right, they all helped me. I knew he meant a lot to ya, girlie." Then she turns and marches away, leaving Dray and me with Major's grave.

Crouching down, I move the top layer of earth so that the picture and drawing will be protected. I rip the bottom of my shirt and wrap them in that before placing them in the soil. "Goodbye, Major, thank you for loving me," I whisper, and then cover the pictures with the soil and sand until they are entombed with him in his grave. I get up and dust off my hands, my eyes goes back to the trunk, and suddenly I know what I want to do.

To keep his memory alive, to keep him with me forever.

Pulling a knife from my side, I step up to the tree, and then pull the parchment from my pocket. I trace the design with my eyes and start to carve it into the bark, leaving Major's symbol for all to see. Here was a man chased by his demons, craving peace, may it find him in his next life. Once I'm done, I step back and eye my handiwork, the first part of the plan finished. Now, I need to find someone for the second part.

"I have something I need to do, can I meet you later?" I address Dray.

He nods, looking from the symbol to me, and then smirks. "Me too. Be good, soulmate, don't kill too many people." He kisses me hard then strides away, leaving me to my thoughts.

"Goodbye," I whisper one last time, and then turn away, leaving Major's ghost with his grave and drawings. The tree offers him a new hope. While its canopy is damaged, its roots will carry on growing, spreading across this land like his memory, keeping him alive for all that knew him and those who never got the chance to. Just a man who fought for what he believed in.

Now, I will do the same.

Chapter Sixteen

ONE WHOLE SOUL

I find the person I need after asking around. I shouldn't be surprised The Ring has one. After all, I got my Berserker slave brand here. I explain what I want and we head to The Summit room where he sets up and I sit backwards on a chair, resting my head on the wood and losing myself in the comforting pain and buzz of the needle in my skin. With each stroke, I relax further, the feeling of rightness settling in my chest, and I know this was the correct decision. It takes at least two hours, and by the time we are done my back is sore, feeling heavy with ink, but I am smiling.

I thank the man who introduced himself as Hill and leave him to clean his equipment. My shirt sits heavy on the new tattoos, but I don't mind as I head out in search of Dray. I find my men have already set up camp, and they are working through the booze and girls here at The Ring. I nod at them as I pass, letting them know it's okay to relax tonight. There is no point riding out until the morning anyway. I catch a Seeker as he is strolling past, buckling his pants as he goes.

"Have you seen Dray?" I ask.

He looks over, his mouth flapping open and closed as he looks at me, and I arch my eyebrow at him, waiting. "Have you?" I ask again.

"Eer, yeah—I saw him going into the training pit about ten minutes ago. He was with that Nan chick before then." He nods.

"Thanks," I call and rush away as I head over to the pit, wanting to show him what I had done.

Ignoring the slave entrance to the training sands, I hop over the fence and land on the packed earth below.

Stepping onto the sand, I see him sprawled out on his back with his arms under his head, staring at the stars. I get hit with déjà vu for a moment, remembering when we were like this last time, but we fought then, pushing at each other as I ignored what was right in front of me—him.

Not this time. I head straight for him, and instead of lying next to him like last time, I kneel over him, pressing my knees to the sand on either side. I sit on his lap and look down at his grinning face.

He grabs my hips, keeping me there, pressed to the hard bulge growing in his pants as his eyes pull from the sky and settle on me. "Miss me, soulmate?" he teases.

"Maybe, what trouble did you get up to?" I grin down at him, rocking slightly just to tantalise him. His eyes flash as his hands tighten on my hips, stilling the movement.

He sits up suddenly, quickly kissing me before whispering against my lips, "I'll show you."

I slide off his lap and kneel in the sand facing him. He gets to both knees in front of me, his face blank and his eyes almost laughing. That alone makes mine narrow, knowing whatever he has done it's probably crazy. He pulls something from his pocket, keeping it locked in the palm of his hand as he smirks at me.

"Hold out your hand, soulmate," he orders.

I do as I am told, palm up, but he reaches out and turns it the other way so my palm is facing the sand. He holds his hand over mine, as he slowly curls open his palm to show me something glittering. I don't look away as he picks it up and shows it to me, my mouth drops open.

"Where did you find that?" I inquire softly, staring at the ring held between his fingers, dwarfing it.

It's not too big, consisting of a black band with a skull in the middle, and then what looks like diamonds and rubies on either side. I love it and I can't seem to look away.

"I've had it for a while, found it just before I found you. It's yours, has been for a long time. Here." He holds it out and I show him my hand. I expect him to slip it on my finger so I don't pay attention until I feel him staring as I admire it sparkling on my hand. I look up to see him smiling at me smugly.

"What?" I ask, confused. "Looks good on you, wife."

I blink, staring at him with my mouth open as my eyes slowly drop to the ring—which is on my ring finger. "What the fuck are you talking about?" I snap, going to pull it off and put it on another finger, but he covers my hand, stilling the movement.

"Taking it off won't make a difference, soulmate," he declares. "What the fuck are you talking about, Dray? Tell me!" I snarl, as

a bad feeling starts building in my stomach.

"Shh, behave, wife," he teases, and I glare at him as he laughs. "I married us." He shrugs.

I stare at him for a moment, my mind stuck on that. "How the fuck did you marry us?" I yell and throw my hands in the air. "Don't I have to be there for something like that?"

"I don't know, but I married us, you accepted the ring." He shrugs and I sputter at him.

I yell, tackling him to the sand and holding a knife to his throat. "Tell me," I grit out, almost snarling at him.

He just smirks up at me, cupping my arse in his hands. "So demanding, my wife."

"Dray," I warn, deadly serious. Again, not that he cares.

"Me and Nan worked out our issues, I asked her to marry us, and she did. You're wearing the ring, we are husband and wife," he says, like it is that simple.

"You. Married. Us?" I ask slowly, making sure I heard him right. "Yes, soulmate." He grins up at me. "Isn't it great?"

Fury wells up in me at him taking my choice away, the need to make him hurt rising with it, and he must see it in my eyes, because his darkens and he grips my ass harder. Throwing the knife to the side before I kill the crazy bastard, I do the only thing I can think of to hurt him—I lean down and bite his neck, hard. He thrusts up against me even as he yells, and I am ripped away, sent tumbling over the sands. I roll with it and land in a crouch, glaring at him as he gets to his feet and prowls towards me, blood running down his neck from my bite, surrounded by clear teeth imprints.

I move back, circling each other. "That's not a very nice way to treat your husband," he teases and I scream as I jump at him.

He catches me mid-air as I smack into his chest and then he throws me to the ground, following me down and pinning me. He yanks open my thighs and presses between them, letting me feel his hard cock as he rubs it across my pussy. "That's better," he whispers, leaning down to kiss me. I let him, relaxing like he's won, and when he slips his tongue between my lips I bite down. I can taste his blood as he groans into mouth, deepening the kiss, forcing me to taste him and the copper tang of his blood. Jerking my mouth away, I turn my head to the side.

"Dray!" I shout, pissed.

He grabs my breast through my shirt, making me gasp as my anger melts with my lust until I need to move, I need to get it out of me. I thrash, thrusting at him to get him off me as I wiggle away. Flipping to my front, I crawl away, dragging myself until I can jump to my feet and turn to face him. He watches me with a smirk, crouched on the ground, but gets to his feet again.

"Fine, get it all out, then I'll fuck the rest out, but you are mine, soulmate. Always have been, always will be. This changes nothing except I wanted everyone to see, everyone to know." He shrugs then, holding his arms open. "Give it your best shot, Champion."

I hold up my hand and go to take the ring off but he snarls, his eyes flashing in warning. "Take that ring off and I will tie you to a bed in this place and fuck you senseless. I don't give a shit about your plan or needing to get your other men. Try me, soulmate, I dare you," he growls, his voice deadly, so I drop my hands and instead grab my whip.

Uncoiling the whip, I launch it through the air, and it wraps around his wrist. He laughs so I tighten it, and it cuts into his skin, but he just smirks. Winding it tighter around his wrist, he uses it to reel me in until I stumble into his chest and have to let go of the whip as I pummel my fists into his chest.

"It's my fucking choice! You don't ever get to take my choice away!" I scream.

He growls then, grabbing my chin hard. "I would never take your choice away, I'm not one of those bastards who hurt you. But you were never getting away from me, soulmate. This? This marriage was for me, because I love you more than anything in this world. I wanted you to know that I always have your back, and even now when you have lost your family, I will be it," he snaps, forcing my eyes to his. "Don't you ever compare me to those bastards," he growls, and I can tell he's pissed as hell now.

He sweeps his leg out, knocking me to the sand, and pinning me with his body again. I don't even know why I'm fighting anymore, I'm not even pissed, I just needed to tell him he couldn't take my choices from me. Now? Now I want the fight that comes with an angry Dray, I want to take it out on his skin, so I keep fighting even when I shouldn't. Because I never know when to stop.

He restrains me there, while I kick and buck as he kisses down my neck. "We were two fractured souls, just waiting and searching for each other, but now we are whole like we were meant to be."

I still then, panting into the sand. He thinks I have stopped fighting, so he relaxes, his grip loosening, but he should know by now I never stop fighting. I flip us and I am on him in a second. The fighting turns to lust as I bite at his lips, smashing his hands to the sand on either side of his head. He throws me off him, growling as he jumps after me. He grabs my arms and spin me into his chest, pinning my arms behind me back, and I stop fighting, looking into his eyes as he keeps me there, on the edge of pain as he hoists my arms up farther, forcing a gasp from my lips.

"Are you really that bothered or do you just like fighting me?" He smirks.

I narrow my eyes on him, struggling a little, but the pain forces me to stop and he leans down, biting on my bottom lip before sucking it into his mouth and then letting go with a pop. "I think you just like fighting, I think you secretly love the idea of being married to me, you just want to fight and fuck."

"Then fuck me and find out," I taunt. He's right, but shit.

He narrows his eyes on me and smashes his lips to mine again, sweeping his tongue in and tangling it with mine. Groaning into his mouth, I press my chest further against his, my pussy already wet from our fight. Kicking my leg out, I knock him over. He stumbles, falling into me, and we tumble to the sand behind me. I grunt into his mouth as he knocks my breath away by landing on top of me, but it got me where I wanted to be, so I can't complain.

He rips my shirt over my head, leaving me in just my bra, before he flicks open my jeans and pulls them from my legs, tossing them behind him as he takes me in from head to toe, licking his lips as he does so. I want to get back at him, I want him as pissed and wild as I am, so I grin and slowly sit up. He frowns, but I just laugh as I flip to show him my back. It's silent for a moment and I hold my breath, wondering how he will react. I shouldn't have worried, not for a moment. After all, this is the man who just married me without even telling me.

"Soulmate," he snarls, his fingers tracing around the tattoos I got. "I-Is that a Seeker symbol?" His voice is raspy and sends a shiver of need through me as he presses his whole body against my back, fitting himself behind me like a glove and whispering into my ear, his warm breath hitting the shell. "Did you mark me on your body? So everyone would know?"

"Don't get too big headed, I just liked the symbol," I tease, and his hand wraps around my throat from behind, just a warning with no real pressure, but it makes my heart race and my nipples pebble as I push back into him. "Yes, it's your symbol, and Major's above it."

"You marked me on your body," he repeats.

"You marked me on yours," I fire back, almost rubbing against him now from the way he is holding me still without even thinking. His strength astounds me and sends lust pouring through my veins, making my pussy drip.

"Do you know what this means, soulmate?" he purrs, his voice low as he licks at my ear, his hand tightening slightly.

"What?" I almost groan, needing him inside me.

"I can see my mark on you as I fuck you from behind. Fuck, just thinking about it has me nearly exploding. Thinking of you writhing beneath me, fighting me as I take you, my brand standing out against your skin."

Sands below, what a fucking image.

"Then why don't you?" I dare, pushing into his hand, cutting off my breathing as he nibbles at my ear. He roughly pulls me back against him, my ass slamming into his hard bulge, which he rubs there.

His hand releases my throat and I almost whine out loud as he laughs into my ear. "Bastard," I mutter.

He slips his fingers down my belly before slipping into my panties and cupping my wet pussy. I bite my lip to stop myself from groaning, then press down into his hands, spreading my thighs for him. He strokes me, murmuring dirty nothings in my ear before he pulls his hand away, leaving me panting and on the edge of just throwing him to the ground and fucking his brains out.

"Dray," I warn and he laughs into my ear again, and I go to turn but he presses his hand into the middle of my back, pushing me to the sand. I fall to my hands and knees, and he kicks my legs open farther, yanking off my panties in one move, letting warm air caress my exposed pussy and ass as I feel him shift behind me. Leaning on my forearms, I wiggle my ass backwards, needing him inside of me.

A swat lands on my ass, making me moan at the fire that races through my cheek, I push back and he does it again and again, his hits getting harder and harder. I know this will hurt tomorrow, in a good way, and I can't stop the moans leaving my lips as I rock against thin air, the pain climbing higher and higher, and then he grabs my hips, slams me back, and slides into me in one thrust, forcing a scream from my throat.

He is the only man I have ever screamed for and it takes me by surprise.

He doesn't give me time to adjust, causing a bite of pain as I am forced to stretch around him as he pulls out and slams back in, again and again. His hips hit my ass, chafing the already red cheeks, only adding to it as the pain meshes with pleasure. "Dray," I demand, pushing back into him as his hips slam into me, his balls slapping against my skin with each thrust.

"Mine," he growls, his hands biting into my hips as he bends over me and licks up my spine, circling the tattoo of his symbol before nipping at the skin there.

My breasts drag against the rough ground with each thrust, and everything blurs together. It's too much, my body is overwhelmed, and all I can do is hold on as he claims me here where we first met— our blood mixing into the sand below, his ring on my finger, and his mark on my back. How far we have come.

I push back to meet each thrust, and when he twists his hips and smacks my ass again, an orgasm rips through me, pulling another scream from my throat as I fight him just like he said I would. My hands claw at the sand, and my body twists and turns beneath him with the power of the release blackening my eyes for a moment as I try to relearn how to breathe while he continues to fuck me ruthlessly through it, my pussy milking him.

The Cities

He grabs my hair, winding it around his fist, and yanks me up on my knees, my back slamming into his chest as he deepens the angle. Pain flows through me from my ass and I groan, not able to move much in this position, just taking his fucking as he builds me back up again. "Please," I groan, needing to come again. He tilts my head to the side using his fist, pulling on the strands, and claims my mouth, his tongue tangling with mine as he dominates me.

He lets go of my hair before reaching between us and playing with my clit for a moment, making me moan into his mouth. He drags his finger down my wet center and then presses it to my other hole, slipping just the tip in. It sends me careening over the edge and I scream into his mouth, clawing at his arm and side, everything I can get my hands on as I shudder against him.

He roars into my mouth, yanking away from me as his hips stutter and he fills me with his come, then stilling behind me as we lean into each other, both sweaty messes and weak as hell. I tumble to the sand and he follows me down, softening inside me before he slips free. We both groan as he collapses on my back, panting as he shifts slightly to the side so he doesn't crush me, and neither of us speaking.

Holy fucking sands below, that was incredible.

He lays an open-mouthed kiss over the tattoo, making me smile into the sand at the gentle way he does it. It's so opposite from the rough way he just fucked me. He really is a contradiction, and I guess now my husband? The thought doesn't bother me as much anymore, and I know he wasn't trying to control me, claim me, or make me any less. He just wanted to show everyone that he loves me and that we belong to each other, and make the most out of whatever time we have left in his blood soaked world.

"I love you," I say softly, and he wraps his arm around me, pulling me to my side and cuddling in behind me.

Fuck, I'm going to have sand in all sorts of places later.

"I love you always, wife," he whispers against my skin, kissing my shoulder again, right over a scar.

"Crazy fucking husband," I joke, and he groans behind me. "Fuck, that's hot on your lips. Say it again."

"You are insatiable." I laugh as he presses against my sore red ass.

It goes quiet for a moment, as both of us become lost in each other's arms, the joking and laughing of our men drifting to us on the night air. Last time I got up and left, but now I regret that, so I promise to never regret a moment again. "So, soulmate, want to fight or fuck?" he teases, repeating those same words he said to me last time.

"Both, always both."

CHAPTER SEVENTEEN

THE LAST SUPPER

After we have dressed, we head back to the celebration. I need to speak to some of the guards here, and put people in charge for when I leave and just in case I don't come back. I also need to speak to my generals. Dray and I are leaving tomorrow, and they need to be made aware of exactly what needs to happen. I leave the ring on, the stones catching the firelight and shining as we make our way through The Ring. It seems so strange here now, like the weight of Ivar's reign has lifted. There's more laughter, I don't spot any slaves, and everyone is drinking and enjoying themselves.

I stand for a moment on the edge of the crowd, just looking out at them all. Who knew a slave girl like me would end up here? Dray reaches for my hand, twining our fingers as he looks out with me, and I feel nearly complete. There is a hole at my back and other side where my other men should be, but hopefully next time we are here, they will be with me and I will be complete again.

"Let's get something to eat before you start giving orders, I'm hungry," Dray says, tugging me along with him.

I roll my eyes but follow him over to the building that holds the cafeteria. People are spill out of the doors, drinking and eating, and spread out outside because there obviously isn't enough room inside. I nod at some and greet them as we pass, but it's like the mention of food has reminded me how hungry I am, and my stomach growls and I grin. I'm used to going without eating, but I've been spoiled recently, and it's clear my stomach is used to it now.

When we step through the door, the chaos hits me square in the face. It's really loud in here with men drinking, fighting, and eating over ever surface. Women sit on laps, joking and teasing men, and I grin at the sight. This feels like a home no bike on the road ever could. I head to the bar in the corner, grab a bottle, and head to the table where Erik, Henry, and Bern are sitting with a few others. Dray goes and gets us some food as I hover over the table. A Seeker gets up instantly, nods at me, and moves to a different table. I sit in his spot and they all grin over at me, and Bern hollers in laughter when he spots the ring on my finger. I flip him the bird and down some of the alcohol as they all whoop and howl. Word must spread, because soon everyone is looking over at me and changing our names.

Sands below.

I turn to see Dray grinning as he hops up on a table and holds out his arms. "It's true, I have been tamed!" he yells, and everyone stomps and cheers. "The Seeker King now has a queen!" he finishes, and toasts everyone with a stolen drink. He tosses it back, grabs two trays, and saunters over to me, plonking one in front of me as he straddles the end of the bench by my side.

"Really?" I mutter, but he winks at me and I can't help but smile.

Eventually, everyone quiets down and goes back to their own conversations, and I work my way through the meat on my plate as I listen to them all.

"So, tomorrow we leave?" Erik inquires, watching me as he sips from his metal goblet.

I nod around a mouthful of meat before washing it down with some booze. "We'll eat and then I'll go over everything, but yes."

Bern butts in then, slamming his fist onto the table. "I cannie wait to get back at those Cities fuckers," he declares loudly.

"We will win." Henry nods.

That makes me feel better. I'm not leading them to slaughter, but I know I'm right. This is about more than just my men, they wont stop there. They will keep coming and the Wastes will fall into chaos, becoming easy for them to snatch and rule, and from what I've heard, they don't rule fairly. The North has suffered enough, they need to be stopped, and if it means we have to lose lives to do it, then so be it.

You can't save every life, you just can't, and sometimes you have to sacrifice to save the many.

Major's words ring in my head. Did he know what he was preparing me for, or did he just know the burden of leadership? I will sacrifice before this war is through, I know it, but I won't be asking for that without giving myself. I will be right there alongside them, fighting until the bitter end.

I finish eating and sip my booze as I join the conversations, laughing and joking with my men, and forgetting everything for a while. We play drinking games, watch a Seeker get knocked out, and Dray only kills one person. Overall, it's a good night, but I can feel time passing and I know I need to have our discussions before we leave and get some sleep. Who knows when we will get to sleep again? It won't do to fight tired.

Erik must notice, because he tosses back his drink and stands. "Come on, generals, our queen needs us."

"That sounds filthy," I mutter, and Dray laughs next to me and leans in.

"It better not be, I still have twenty blades on me," he threatens, and I look him over, wondering where they are hidden before I shake my head and stand, drinking the rest of the bottle. Bern and Henry follow, while Dray grabs more meat on his way out, munching as we head over to the meeting room. I would bring them to Major's office, but I remember his letter, and honestly I don't want strangers in that space. I look over at Bern. "Will you grab me the head guard of The Ring please?"

"Aye, Ma Queen." He plods off, and he's so big, people dodge away from him, clearing his path. I grin as I carry on walking.

There is a dead body on the steps of the building, and I don't even blink as I step over it and head inside. I spot Nan turning a corner, obviously heading for one of the rooms with a pissed looking Reeves behind her. I hide my smirk. Seems the dirty old bitch likes to ride the scavs, I can't wait to use it against the old broad. The Summit room is empty when we get there, and I take my seat at the head of the table as we wait for Bern to get back.

He trudges back in with the man I met at the gate behind him. Bern takes a seat, the wood creaking under his weight, and the guard hovers at the end of the table, clearly unsure.

"What's your name?" I ask. "Ace," he replies instantly.

"Good, sit." I nod and he grabs a seat, spinning it and sitting backwards as he looks around at us.

"I've read Major's letter, I know I'm in charge. Now, I'm not going to change many of his rules, they mostly still stand. This is a safe place, so no fighting on the grounds or they are killed. The only thing I'm changing is this—no more slaves here. It isn't welcome. I know I can't stop everyone from having them in the Wastes, but they aren't welcome here. Anyone, man or woman, caught with a slave will be killed, and the slave given his possessions and freedom."

He whistles then but doesn't seem angry. "That's a hella big rule change, might piss some people off."

"Good, can you handle it?" I inquire, grinning at him. He smirks back. "Fuck yes I can! Ya leaving?"

I nod. "Hopefully I'll be back, but if I'm not, I want you to leave a woman named Piper in charge with you helping her."

It seems like the best option. Archel won't let her die and she is strong enough to hold it. I would leave it to Dray, but if I don't make it back then neither will he or my men, so it needs to be someone outside of my circle. "I will leave her instructions in case it comes to it."

"It won't," Dray interjects and I roll my eyes.

"Just in case. Anything else you need? I'll be leaving in the morning," I inform him.

"Nope, we will keep it running in your absence, just make sure you come back. This Piper woman might have your trust, but she doesn't have ours, you do. You've fought with us, drank with us, and lived here, this is your home as much as anywhere." He nods then stands and leaves, and I gape after him. Well shit.

The door shuts after him and I lean back in my chair. "Down to business. We are leaving first thing in the morning, and stopping at Reeves' and The Rim on our way. I expect you to be waiting in position in three days." I pull out the maps then and show them everything I know. "If I don't come back, build a fucking check point to give your selves a warning when they come for you, and haul ass to kill those bastards. If we do come back, we will lead them right to you. I want people waiting at The Rim, here and here, then they close in behind the Cities' people as we lead them to you."

"We box tha fuckers in." Bern nods in respect.

"We do, and we decimate them, send a message that you never fuck with us again. It will be awhile before they try that again." I look at Dray. "As for our part, I want you to sneak in using this open system here like Jago explained. I want you to rile up the locals. Thorn said poverty was rife, so I'm betting we drop a match in that and boom. Attack them from all sides, cause riots and chaos, enough that we can escape if my part of the plan doesn't work. Then meet me back at the gates, but only wait one day. If I'm not back, you leave," I order, but he narrows his eyes and I laugh. "Joking, I know you won't. You burn that place to the ground and come save my ass, but only if I can't save it first."

"Sounds like a plan, soulmate." He nods his agreement, reaching over and kissing the ring before leaning back and smirking at the others in the room, making me roll my eyes.

"Piper, The Forgotten, and rogues will meet you there, Archel will work with them and get them in position. Erik, you have the rebels, Bern and Henry, you have the Seekers and Berserkers. Reeves has the scavs and roadies, Nan will have...her shotgun," I tease and they laugh. "We can do this. The next time I see you will be on the battlefield."

"We will win this with you leading us," Erik affirms. "Fight well, Ma Queen," Bern states.

"Long live our fucking queen!" Henry calls, and I laugh as they all repeat it.

Long live our fucking clans.

They leave after that, and Dray and I head to my room, needing to get some rest after the long day we had. I open the door and stop in the threshold as memories of my men filling the space bombard me. If I strain hard enough, I can almost still smell them here.

Dray presses to my back and I lean into him before forcing myself inside. I lay my bag and jacket on the table before stripping down to my bra and panties, and head to the shower. I wait for the water to warm up as I wash my bra and panties, and then hang them to dry before looking up into the mirror. I don't look as happy as I did last time. I look harder, more confident. Maybe what Dray said was true, I was worried about what people think and now I'm not. Though a weight was lifted from my shoulders, a ton more was added, and you can tell by the jaded and calculated look in my eyes.

I appear hard, but when Dray stops behind me, framing me in the mirror, he makes me look soft. He's taller than me, and his muscles upon muscles accentuate my soft curves, showing off my own muscular arms and stomach. We look fierce and like we shouldn't be messed with, and that makes me smile. I meet his eyes in the mirror and see the icy blue watching me with all the crazy love he has to offer. He wraps his arm around my stomach and pulls me back against him, propping his chin on my shoulder. I reach up and hold his arm, the ring he gave me shining in the light.

"King and queen," he murmurs, the steam curling through the bathroom.

"How about this king shows his queen how much he wants her by helping her relax before it all gets crazy?" I suggest and he grins.

"As you order, My Queen," he croons and then spins me, picking me up under my ass and stepping into the shower. He presses me back against the tiles as he covers my mouth with his.

I tangle my hands in his hair, licking at his mouth as the water hits us from the side. He grunts, pressing between my legs as his chest rubs against my hardened nipples. My body reacts to his instantly like always, craving his brand of crazy, even though I only had him hours ago. What happens next is looming over us, which could explain why I'm so sentimental and needing him so often. I want to be alive, to not miss a thing like Major said, and that includes tonight. He holds me against the wall as he moves down my body, biting and licking my nipples. I rest my head back on the tiles, closing my eyes in bliss as I wrap my legs around his waist to hold him to me, then I remember what I haven't done yet and what I have been wanting to do. An evil smirk crosses my face as I grab his hair and yank his head back. I kiss him hard before pushing him away. He stumbles into the spray, letting me drop to my feet, and I close the distance between us. He watches me, licking at his lower lip, but they widen when I drop to my knees in front of him, his body shielding the spray of water as I grab his hips and tug him to me.

He grabs my hair to stop from falling as I blow my breath over the tip of his cock, his piercing shining under the light. I bet I can't swallow him down because of that, but I still want to taste him, to see him weaken for me like Drax did.

"Soul—" He cuts off with a growl, tangling his hands in my hair as I lick the head of his cock, stroking his hard, velvety length with one hand as I gaze up at him.

He looks startled, his mouth open in need, and a fire burning away that ice in his eyes as he watches me. Has he never done this either? I ask as much, pulling back slightly so each breath teases his cock.

He smirks down at me. "Which woman would I let near my cock? They would either try to kill me or I would kill them."

The idea of him with other women has me narrowing my eyes in jealousy, but I can't really talk, so instead I dart my tongue out and taste the precum on his tip before hollowing my cheeks, and sucking him down slightly. He groans, thrusting deeper as I pull back and then swallow him again, curling my hand around his base for the length I can't take. He soon finds his pace, his stance widening as he fucks my mouth ruthlessly. I catch my teeth on his length and he groans loudly, almost making me grin around his girth.

"Soulmate," he rasps, and I roll my eyes up to meet his as I pull back and suck on his tip, before licking and tugging on his piercing.

He roars, exploding in my mouth, and I swallow quickly before licking him clean and sitting back, satisfied with myself. His thighs are shaking and he falls to his knees in front of me, cupping my cheeks as he watches me. "How did a bastard like me ever get so lucky?"

"Why, 'cause I suck your cock?" I tease, but he turns serious. "Because you are incredible, sexy, smart, and so fucking good

with knives and swords it makes me almost bust in my jeans when I watch you," he replies, rubbing his thumb over my bottom lip. "All of this fucked up, burnt world and I found you."

I don't know what to say, so I kiss his thumb before laying a kiss on his lips. "Let's wash, we don't want to use all the water."

We clean up, and he helps wash my hair and get the tangles out before bathing me. I help wash him, it's become our routine of sorts, and it does relax me. By the time we dry off, I don't bother slipping back into my wet things. I just pad through the room naked and slip into bed, with Dray following behind me. I recline back onto his chest and stare at the darkened room, lost in my thoughts.

"Dray, do you think we will get them back?" I ask, voicing my fears out loud— fear that I will never see them again, never hold them, never kiss them, or hear them talk.

He pulls me back tighter, kissing my hair. "I think you can do whatever you set your mind to. You love them, they love you, so nothing will stop you from getting to them."

"But what if I'm too late?" I inquire softly, the night grabbing my fears and holding them secret for me.

"Then we kill them all," he offers straight away, but I tense, the idea of them no longer being in this world hurting my heart. "Worth, look at me."

I turn and he cups my face, staring into my eyes, his face in shadow. "They wouldn't dare die on you. You said it yourself, the Cities want something, they have been up here, and they wouldn't risk killing them. Plus, they haven't come back for Paradise yet, so I bet they are trying to break your men to get them to lead them to it. That means they are alive, in pain, yes, I won't sugarcoat it, but alive. Pain can be forgotten, but death is final."

I nod, leaning into his touch. "They are strong and smart, they will be okay."

"They will, and you will make sure anyone who hurts them pays for it. You will be with them soon enough," he says, and then I feel bad.

"Dray—" I start but he covers my mouth.

"I'm not mad or jealous, I know you need them too. I can't deny I've enjoyed having you to myself this time, but you can't be fully happy or relaxed without them. Don't worry, I know you still love me and I still love you. Love is big enough to love more than one person, Tazanna, and you have the biggest heart of all. Now get some sleep, I promise you before the week is through, you will see your men again."

I let his words soothe me as I close my eyes and fall asleep in his arms. In that moment, before sleep and wake, I hear Maxen's voice.

We are waiting for you, Mi Alma.

Chapter Eighteen

Mad Max, Baby

The next morning I am up, dressed, and covered in weapons before the sun even rises. Dray and I fucked early this morning. I took all my worries and frustrations out on him so I could lock it back up after and pretend to be as confident as I act. It works, and when I reach my bike, I feel more like myself. Nan and Reeves stumble after us, and I smirk at the messed up quality of her hair but she narrows her eyes, warning me to fuck off with just a look. She gets into a car with a scav driving, while Reeves climbs onto his bike. Dray and I mount up and I cover my mouth with my bandana, looking out at the Wastes stretched before me.

It's like Mad Max, baby, and I'm the fucking hero in this book riding off to get my men. Does that make them damsels? I smirk then, reminding myself to tell them that when I see them.

I lead the ride, setting a breakneck speed through the sand and dust as the sun crawls through the sky, lighting our way. We should reach Reeves' by nightfall, where we will stop for a few hours before carrying on to The Rim, then we should be at the Cities in under two days if we time it right.

Two days until I see them again.

I speed up, wanting to see them sooner as Dray chases after me. I told them no stops, so I don't bother slowing at all, just pushing my bike to its limit as we race through the rapidly heating dust. Ferals chase us for a while before giving up, and I spot some bodies at the side of the road, but I don't check for life. I do stop when I see a blockade of cars across the main road we were taking up head. Reeves stops next to me and looks at me in confusion.

"Wasn't here when we came up," he informs me.

"They don't look like scavs or roadies," I mutter, squinting hard to see what and who they are. The trucks are too clean, too well looked after. They don't look like anything I've seen in the Wastes before. "I think they are from the Cities."

"Fuck."

"Let's go see, shall we? Maybe they can help...introduce us." I grin and Dray smirks as I pull up my bandana and crank my engine.

I hear them laugh as we ride up on the trucks, I circle my finger and I know Dray is headed around the other side to angle them between us. If they are from the Cities, they aren't prepared for being out here. Just like I thought, their words drift to me, music covering our approach.

"It's too fucking hot out here," a man complains from somewhere in the truck, and I spot two men lounging in the back, their eyes closed and the music blaring. Fucking morons. I search for anyone else, but don't see them as I cut my bike and stroll up to the truck, the bass almost vibrating the clean metal. One of them has a hat over his sweaty face, his body encased in black trousers, and a white tank top, showing through an open grey shirt. The man next to him has the trousers but no shirt, and he's covered in sweat and clean. It's obvious they don't belong here. Their clothes are brand new looking and way too dirt free, and their boots nearly have me salivating. They are shiny and big lace up ones. Shit, I wonder if I could get my feet in them? I look down at mine, realising they are wearing out. Fuck, I love these boots.

Pulling my sword from my back, I lean it against the bare chested one's neck. "Sorry, boys, didn't mean to interrupt your afternoon nap," I tease as I spot Dray leaning against the other open door, playing with his knife as he watches the hat covered man.

They react, but slowly. The bare chested man's eyes fly wide open and he freezes when he spots the lustre of my blade—smart man. The other isn't as smart. He sits upright, dropping his hat into his lap as he tries for the gun at his side. "Fuck!" he yells, as Dray leaps forward and smashes a knife into the man's scrambling hand. He screams, the sound loud and pain filled as he falls back to his seat, clutching his bleeding hand as he darts a look between us.

"Now that I see we have your attention, how about we have a little talk, hmm?" I grin slowly as the man at the end of my sword narrows his eyes.

"We don't fucking talk to savages," he spits, his eyes glaring at me defiantly as his sweat covered chest heaves.

I laugh, I can't help it, and Dray joins in. "Then this is going to be a painful time for you. You see, your people took something of mine and I want it back, and you are going to help me. Aren't you?" I purr, pressing the sword harder against his flesh, drawing blood, and he grits his teeth, his eyes wide in pain. What a pussy.

"Fuck you," he snarls.

Why is that always their response? You would think they would wise up. I sigh, pull back the sword, and sheathe it. "I was really hoping to do this quickly. Oh well, your choice." I shrug and my arm darts out before he can spit another insult at me, smashing into his face and sending him sprawling back into the seat. Dray is hauling his man—still screaming—from the car, so I tap mine. "Out," I order.

"Fuck you!" he yells, turning to face me to show me his split lip. "I thought we just discussed this?" I reply with a grin.

"Would do as she says boyo, she has an awful temper on her, ya know?" Nan calls, and I wink over at her where she is standing with Reeves, watching us.

I look back at the man and shrug. "She's right, I also have a tendency to kill first and ask later. I only need one of you so...your choice."

Stepping back, I wave over to the sand next to us. "Come on, sleeping beauty,"

His gaze darts to everyone behind us, his mind spinning so fast I can nearly see it. "I wouldn't try it. In fact, I would, so please fucking try it. I have a terrible temper recently and it needs to come out, otherwise that guy is going to get the brunt of it later," I say, jerking my head at Dray.

"I fucking love it, soulmate," Dray retorts.

"He's not joking, he's crazy," I comment like the man asked. "Fuck," he mutters, and he slides from the car, keeping his

distance from me as he steps up next to his friend. Dray kicks out his legs and they both kneel in the sand, watching us as I prowl around them.

Crouching in front of them, I let my face go blank and cold, and my eyes go dead. "Now, to business. You answer every question or I will let crazy here have his fun."

"What do you want?" the man Dray stabbed whines. I spot sewn on name tags declaring him as "Yates."

"Information, of course." Everyone but them laugh then. I look to the man I cut to see him glaring at me again.

"Why are you here?" I begin easily.

They look at each other and I sigh. "Am I going to have to kill one of you to prove how serious I am?"

Yates instantly shakes his head and I zero in on him, knowing he is the weak link. "We were sent to report back anyone heading south."

"Why?" I snap.

"I don't know, they don't tell us," he replies. I pull out a knife and he shakes, falling back, his eyes wide. "I think they are planning something, they are mobilizing troops, sending us farther than ever past the Dead Sea into the dead lands up here, they are stretching us thin."

"Dead lands, huh?" I grin at Dray then. "I prefer Wastes."

Yates nods, obviously encouraged that I haven't stabbed him. "They don't want us to know, but I heard rumours they are running out of food and water, more and more outer ringers are dying, starving."

"Shut up," the other man hisses, but Yates throws him a glare.

"I don't plan on dying for them," he snaps, finally showing some backbone, and looks at me. "There is unrest in the Cities, people wanting to know the truth, unhappy with the dividing of supplies and the labour they pull compared to the inners."

Blowing out a breath, I still the blade. "Inners?"

He nods then. "The Cities are split into three rings—outer ring, middle ring, and inner ring. Outer is for labour force, they are the last to get supplies, middle is for the...well, middle, like engineers and that, and inner is for the government, doctors, and the rich," he explains and I scoff, what a way to run a place. "The government is getting paranoid, claiming riots as an act from the outers and sending troops in to 'cleanse' them. I think they are just trying to reduce the population."

"You think a lot," I point out.

He turns red and slams his mouth shut.

"Are there more check points along the way?" I inquire, and he shakes his head.

"Not on this route, further west and east there are, but we are the last check point before that shanty city and then the Cities," he offers helpfully, kind of making me sad. I wanted an excuse to vent my frustrations on the spoiled pricks.

"The Cities, tell me everything. Everything I need to know to get in, who's in charge, the people, don't leave anything out," I order, sitting in front of them and waiting.

"The Cities used to be a city back in the day, cut off from bombs, and separated into three, but the rulers built bridges to connect them all. The one in the middle, which is heavily protected, is in the inner. The one to the right is middle, and the one to the left, the most destroyed, is the outer. Each have their own guards and jobs, none interact unless called for. Each have separate entrances and exits, one gate at the front of each. It's filled with broken buildings and the reminder of the world before, the inner is the least destroyed, and if it wasn't for the walls and crumbling architecture, you might believe it was from a time before..."

He blabbers and I listen as he tells me everything and anything, letting me decide what is relevant and not, and with each word I get a stronger sense of confidence. They have hidden behind their walls since this all started, and they don't know what it means to have to fight for survival. They might have weapons, trucks, and a fucking city, but we have something they will never have.

Stubbornness, and the fighting strength to keep on going, even in the face of death. Each time we go into the Wastes, we gamble with the reaper, and yet we do it again and again. We fight for fun, and we live with cannibals and ferals. They have no idea what they have unleashed upon themselves

After he finishes talking, I sit back and stare from Yates to the other silent man who looks so pissed at the Cities' guard for spilling.

"I like those boots," I say with a grin, and Yates looks at his boots and blanches. "What size are you?"

I don't let them go, that would be a stupid fucking move, and I know they would report back. No, instead, I let Nan drive their truck with them tied up in the back as we head to Reeves', they can stay there for now. I have all the information I need and it makes me feel better. I think the plan might work. If I know anything, it's that people like the outers, as the Cities call them, will never be happy under someone's boots. They want freedom. I can use that. If there is one thing I know, it's that when there is an iron ruler, there is rebel- lion, those who fight back.

The Cities

It makes sense to us out here, those who can fight, those who work hard and have skills to survive. The people like the ones who run their government died out a long time ago, or like the people of Paradise, they don't last long. They don't know what hard work means, depending on others to do everything for them while they sit back and claim they are creating a new world, a better world. The question always is—for who?

The Cities are trying to be like the countries of the past, but what they don't realise is the world has changed. Diplomacy and governments aren't needed anymore and they sure as shit aren't wanted up here in the Wastes. We have our own leadership, our own rough and ready justice, and it works just fine. They are going to have the shock of their lives when they meet us.

They thought they were ready for us, they thought we were just savages, and I can't wait to show them how wrong they are.

The ride to Reeves' is boring after that, with no other surprises, and we pull up outside the compound late in the day. In the middle of nowhere with sand and Wastes stretching on all sides, stands what looks like a scav's wet dream. Made of wood, it resembles a rundown bar, complete with a metal sign declaring it "Dive" with an arrow pointing downwards. It has two stories with a wrap- around, wooden porch filled with scavs and roadies drinking and playing. To the left of the bar is what looks like a well with a pump leading out of it. Stationed near us, facing into the Wastes, are the remains of a crane with two scavs on tops, obviously using it as a lookout. Rows upon rows of bikes and cars fill the right-hand side. I whistle when I see it all. It has a certain road charm to it, if you can ignore the stench of booze, blood, sex, and sweat seeming to hover over it.

"I stay upstairs in my quarters, the rest of my men stay around back, so you can stay there for the night," Reeves tells us, before grabbing the nearest scav. "Show them to the plane, will you?" he orders, and then strolls over to two guards that come and wait for their leader's instructions. "I need a fucking drink and a wet pussy to sink into," he mumbles, groaning and cracking his back.

"Ya can fuck right off, ya fat bastard, if ya are talking about me!" Nan calls, before striding up the steps and inside with a laughing Reeves following after her.

"Come on, Delouris, don't be like that!" he hollers after her, and my mouth drops open.

Delouris?

Laughter bursts from my throat and I look at Dray to see him laughing as well. "Fucking Delouris, no wonder she never told anyone," I gasp out between laughs.

"Oh, I can't wait to throw that in her face." He smirks and I shake my head.

"One of these days, she will shoot you," I warn, but he smiles widely at that.

"She could try."

"Er, this way," the scav says, looking between us before turning and rushing away. He's in nothing but shorts and boots. He leads us around the bar and I spot makeshift tents, sleeping quarters, and poorly constructed huts and trailers. Behind it all is what I'm guessing is the plane—fuck, I didn't think he meant an actual plane.

What looks like the broken parts of a crashed plane are hidden behind the worse for wear building, with some metal steps leading up to the open plane door and material shielding it from the sun. The scav looks back at us and must see our surprise. "Reeves said it crashed here a couple days after the floods. It's safe, though, that old tin is never moving. It can get hot during the day, but they've set up some fans in there."

"Fans? Fucking la-di-da," I tease, and he turns red before turning back around and moving over to the plane.

"Outhouses are to the right, and drinks and food are inside Dive," he explains, before he stops at the steps. "You stay here for the night, no one will disturb you." Then he rushes away, a roadie knocks into him from the side, and they go down snarling and fighting.

Stepping onto the ladder, my new boots ring out on the metal as I head up to the plane. I stop on the threshold of the open door and look around. Shit, okay, this is cool as hell. Some of the seats are still there, while others have been ripped away and a mattress lies in their place. All sorts of junk litters the space—fans, music, bottles, and clothes. It looks like a storage area, but I like that it's away from the others with privacy, and we are up high so I can have a good lookout. Stepping inside, I drop my bag and jacket on the mattress, and then stalk around, lifting up items and putting them down as Dray prowls after me like always.

"You want a drink?" he asks.

"Yes, but honestly I'm drained. I don't want to socialise or have to be the Champion right now. I don't want to be that tonight. I just want to sit and relax and come up with a better plan after all the information we got today." I turn to him, leaning onto a chair behind me and he nods.

"Then I'll go get us a bottle and some food," he offers, before dropping a hard kiss on my mouth and heading outside, leaving me alone with my thoughts. Looking around again, I sigh and lean back against the chair.

All this information, all these plans and worries, are rattling around in my brain, but the resounding question is—will it work?

Stripping off my stained shirt, I sort through the pile of clothes on one of the chairs in the back, and I find a black, sleeveless shirt with an A in graffiti type lettering on it. I try it on and decide to keep it. I kick off my new boots, placing them at the end of my mattress, wiping away the dust on them before I lean back and just let my mind wander.

Causing chaos is still our best bet, making dissension in the ranks and splitting their focus, but with the way the Cities are laid out, I don't know how to do that. I want to face them, knock on their gate, maybe I still can? Just then, Dray comes in with a bottle dangling from one hand and a bowl in the other. He passes both to me as he strips out of his boots and unbuttons the top of his jeans, and then sits back on the floor in front of me.

"I need your advice," I start and he nods, leaning farther back, reaching out to touch me with his leg like he can't bear not to touch me, even for a moment. "What would you do?"

He tilts his head, those icy eyes locked on me. "Probably storm the place and kill them all, but that won't work, so why don't we hash this out together?"

I nod, setting the bowl between us, before flicking off the lid of the bottle and placing it next to it. He sits up, crossing his legs, and I explain the ideas I have and what I want to achieve, as well as the parts where I don't know what do. He listens intently, only taking a swig after I have finished, his eyes turning distant as he thinks.

"Let's simplify it. What do you want?"

"My men," I reply instantly, and he smirks. "Get them distracted on two fronts while I enter the other."

"Then let's do that. You planned for me to sneak in anyway, so who's to say we both can't rile them up, and then sneak back out and knock on the front door like we planned?"

It's so fucking simple that I curse as I grab the bottle and down some before looking at him. "Fuck," is all I say.

"There is a reason a leader has generals and advisers. Sometimes you are too close, too involved to figure out a solution. Humans work better together," he remarks, then grabs some of the food and starts eating it with his fingers. I do the same, watching him the entire time. "What happened to your mother?" I inquire out of the blue. I know what happened to the rest of his family, but I never heard about his mother.

"She died when I was very young, infection, she was a vile woman. Mean right hook." He shrugs, still eating and sipping the booze.

"I would ask how you turned out so normal, but…" I trail off and he laughs, throwing his head back, and when he looks at me his eyes are sparkling.

"You can't talk, Champion."

"Bastard." I grin and throw back my drink. The sun is setting and the orange rays shine through the plane, reflecting on his beautiful face and body in front of me. I hear Reeves' men get louder the later it gets, but we are in our own little hideaway up here, and that allows me to relax a little. Once I have finished eating, I lean back on the bed, staring at the curved, plane ceiling.

It goes quiet, the silence comfortable as he strokes my feet, massaging them while I relax, and when night finally comes and the plane darkens, he gets up and lights the candles dotted around the space, before hovering over me. He takes in my face and then wanders off again. I can't be bothered to move, so I let him, only turning my head when music fills the air.

The woman's husky voice sings of meeting someone again. I spot him standing in front of what looks like a portable, wind-up record player before he turns back to me, prowling towards me then offering his hand. "Dance with me, wife."

I glance from those ice-blue eyes to his hand, and I place my palm in his. He pulls me up effortlessly and then spins me away before pulling me back, my spinal hitting his chest. A startled laugh erupts from me when he wraps his arms around me and rocks us to the music, humming along as her voice fills the air, winding around us.

"She's singing for us," he murmurs into my ear, before spinning me and pulling me back to his chest. Leaning my head against him, I let him guide as he moves us from side to side, his arms wrapped around me and holding me against him. His heart beats under my head, echoing in time with mine.

I let her sorrow filled voice croon to me as my husband holds me. What a strange thought, for sure, but it feels so perfect to be here right now in his arms. Dray often claims he's lucky he found me, but in reality, it was the other way around. I was a familyless, broken slave before, and now I have this—an incredible man who loves me and would follow me across this world and into the next. I know that's what he's saying.

No matter what happens, we will meet again, not even death itself could keep us from each other.

CHAPTER NINETEEN

BACK HOME

I spend the night curled in Dray's arms, half asleep and relaxed, while the other half of me that can never fully switch off thinks about everything that is to come in the next few days. When the pre- dawn light filters through the small airplane windows, I sneak out of Dray's arms and head down to the outhouse, doing my business before strolling over to the Dive.

The shack looks worse in the daylight with bullet holes and blood covering the wood, but it makes me feel at home. Anything too clean out here, I wouldn't trust it. Strange but true. There's a back door facing the sleeping scavs and roadies that's propped open, so I slip through the half broken screen door and it shuts behind me, the silence echoing around me. Is everyone still asleep?

The back door leads to a corridor where broken frames hang from the walls, and writing decorates both sides like every scav and roadie has carved their road name here, and maybe they have. Running my fingers across the etchings, I follow the dim hallway. There is a door to the left and I open it, peering in to see restrooms, but the smell has my nose wrinkling and I shut the door as I carry on down the hall.

There is one picture still in its frame and it stops me as I trace the image with my eyes.

There's a large, black bearded man with a bandanna covering his head and shades over his eyes. He has a leather cut in place with a white shirt underneath and blue jeans tucked into big boots. Next to him is a tiny female with bright blue hair and she is grinning. She looks so happy while he looks stern, but the way he is holding her is loving, and the bar is behind them looking better than it does now. The sky is blue and shining in the picture. I spot his hand hovering over her stomach and suck in a breath. Her hand covers his with a ring shining there. On the bottom of the corner in neat, scrawling handwriting is just two names, Tag and Lera, with a little heart drawn after.

For some reason, it makes me unbearably sad. I've seen this world, I know it's filled with death, but seeing the beauty that was once here in this place where now only destruction stands saddens me. At least they had each other. I trace their faces when shuffling and muttering reaches me from somewhere farther down the corridor, so I cast the picture one last glance before carrying on walking, searching for the reason for the sound. The hallway has one more door to the right before it opens up into what I'm guessing is the front of the bar.

I peek into the room, noting the tables, poles, and bar curving around the whole room. Wooden stairs are tucked into one corner, leading upstairs. The walls are wooden and covered in posters, dart boards, a broken TV, and other games. A pool table stands at the back with a scav asleep on top, and a naked girl curled up on his chest, which makes me smirk.

More men and women are passed out around the room, so I leave them be and turn to the other door which opens and leads into a kitchen. The place is surprisingly tidy, with a silver grill, cooker, microwave, and other appliances, as well as a stainless steel counter in the middle of the room. Spoons, ladles, and cutlery hang from hooks in the ceiling. A skinny woman is bustling around, muttering to herself about men being pigs. Her hair is short and swept to the side, a greyish colour tinged with blonde. She turns to me and I freeze, she is beautiful, truly beautiful, but that's not what stops me…it's the face. It's the woman from the picture.

"Hello there. Sorry, I didn't know anyone was awake. Are you hungry?" she asks, moving over to the stove, but I stop her by stepping into the room.

"Lera?" I inquire.

She grins then, stopping and wiping her hands on an apron tied around her skinny waist. "Saw the picture, did you?"

I nod and she sighs. "Least no fuckers broke it again, I had to stop him from chopping someone's balls off last time they did." She waves it away, coming towards me with her hand outstretched. "Nice to meet you…"

"Tazanna, but everyone calls me Worth." I don't know why I tell her my real name. "I'm sorry, I'm confused. Is this your bar?" I query, looking around at the kitchen again and she laughs.

"How about a drink and I'll explain, huh? No one else will be up for a while, they partied hard last night. No one told me why, but I can tell by the looks of it that something bad is coming, isn't it?" I don't answer and she sighs. "I thought as much. Please sit." She nods at the counter and I hop up as she moves a pan onto the cooker and watches it boil.

She grabs two black mugs embossed with wings and places them on the counter, grabbing what looks like leaves and dunking them into the mugs as she talks. "Tag, my husband, bought this place for me when we were younger. He was part of a club, a motorcycle gang, and once the world went to shit, we just stayed here. Reeves turned up and, well, the rest is history."

"And you let them put you in the kitchen? Want me to kill them?" I growl and she laughs.

"I like cooking. He bought this place for me to cook, so it was my life before and now after, it's where I'm happy. Not everyone wants to be a she-warrior." She winks then. "Truly, I love it down here, helping them, providing for them." She shrugs. "It's always been who I am from a young age. I raised my four little brothers when my parents passed before they were taken away by social services, and then the scorch came and, well, I just stuck to what I know. I was lucky Tag found Reeves, and we invited his men to stay in offer that they protect our bar, our home."

She must catch my wince and laughs. "I know it's a bit rough, but honestly, it was before all this, bit like my husband. Guess I like the bad boys."

I laugh, I can't help it. "Uh-huh, that why you are carrying a knife in your boot?"

Her mouth flops open before she roars with such deep sounding laughter that my eyes fly wide. "See that, did you? Oh my, Tag would love you."

"Likes dangerous women, does he?" I tease and she leans closer. "Sort of, but he likes the kind that knows when to fight and when

to submit." She shivers then, her eyes heating. "Did you know the sub actually has all the power?" She winks at me then before grabbing the mugs and passing me one, while keeping one for herself as she leans back against the counter opposite me. I sip the concoction, my eyes closing for a second at the earthy, reassuring taste.

"Sands below, this is good," I mutter.

She smiles at that. "Thank you. I loved a good brew before the world went to shit, so I've been searching for years to re-create it."

"Tag is one of Reeves' men?" I ask, balancing the mug on my knee and she nods, sipping at her drink.

"His right-hand man, or his enforcer, whichever you prefer." She waves her hand then. "Means a lot of worry on my part, but that man can take care of himself, don't tell him I told you that though. His ego is big enough."

Just then boots round the corner. "Sweetness, where did you go? I was going to kiss—" The voice cuts off and I look over my shoulder to see an older version of the man in the picture standing there. His eyes narrow on me and go to his wife before he rushes into the room. "Who the fuck are you?" he booms.

Lera places a hand on his chest. "Hush, dear, she's a friend." She pats his chest and turns away from him, leaving the big man staring at her like a love-struck puppy, even though he throws me a narrow-eyed look.

He wraps his arms around her and dips her into a passionate kiss. I don't bother looking away, if they didn't want an audience then they shouldn't have done it in front of me. Instead, I sip my tea and wait for them to come up for air. Lera laughs and pulls away, her face flaming, but happiness shines brightly in her eyes. "Psh, you really getting territorial over her? Want me to bend over and let you fuck me to prove the point?" she teases and pulls away. "As usual, you are an overzealous fool." But she says it with a gentle smile, making the insult like an endearment.

"I remember your college years." He narrows his eyes.

"Oh my God, you have a girlfriend once and you never live it down. She isn't interested," she scoffs and I laugh.

"I don't know, you're a hot piece of ass," I taunt and he snarls, moving closer as Lera's mouth drops open. "There was a time I would have hit that. Sorry, big guy, don't worry, I have six of my own very protective males..." I trail off then feeling Dray enter. "And here's one now. Tip, I would stop looking at me like that, he's a little bit crazy and might kill you," I offer, sipping the tea as Dray slips in front of me, his spine straight and vibrating with the need for blood.

I drape my arms around him and lay my head on his shoulder, stopping him from killing them. There is no doubt he is stroking the blades across his chest. "Be nice," I warn.

"When am I ever nice?" he grumbles.

"Now or I will stab you with every one of these blades," I threaten and he shivers, leaning farther back into me, and I know it's from lust not fear.

"Please do, soulmate," he groans, tilting his head back.

"Psycho," I mutter, and look at the couple to see them openly watching me. Tag has relaxed now. "Tag, Lera, this is Dray."

He doesn't say anything, just watches them as Tag nods and Lera smiles. "Want tea?" she offers sweetly, but I see the bit of fear she tries to hide. Not that I can blame her, he is an intimidating sight, sometimes I just forget.

"I need to get you a collar and leash so you stop scaring people," I tease, and he winks at me over his shoulder.

"Kinky. Will you choke me with it while you fuck me?" he inquires, completely straight-faced.

Lera makes a noise like a gasp as Tag booms out a laugh and I just roll my eyes. "Depends, will you get it bedazzled with my name?"

"Oh my gosh!" Lera laughs and I wink up at her. "Sorry, cutie, I'm no sub, I like it to hurt and fight back."

"She does," Dray agrees, and Lera's face turns beet red as she smacks a still laughing Tag's arm.

"I like her," he declares, and Dray growls as he tenses, ready to pounce on the man, making me snigger.

Men.

We have breakfast with the couple before I head back to the plane and grab our bags and load up, I get everything on my bike and go in search of Nan, who is coming to The Rim with us. I ask Lera where Nan is and she grins knowingly, telling me to head upstairs and knock on the big double doors. Uh-uh, knock? I don't think so, payback is a bitch and she is old and called Nan. This will get her back for that time she interfered with me and my men.

I sneak upstairs and then kick open the doors Lera told me about, grinning at the sight. "Morning sunshines!" I holler.

Nan swears, trying to get up, but it's no use. Her and Reeves are tangled in the sheets in his bed, her hair mussed and his chest covered in bite marks. "Damn, didn't take you for a kinky bitch, should have guessed," I tease, leaning against the door.

"Ya fuckin' little pervert!" She shouts and I snigger.

"Uh-uh, remember how you pushed me and those guys together..." I trail off and she quits fighting to get up. Instead, she just glares at me as I wink. "Payback." I blow her a kiss then and shut the doors. "Get up though and no fucking, we are leaving in five!" I yell, hitting the door once and then sauntering downstairs.

Dray is waiting at the bottom and he raises his eyebrow, but I just grin and move past him as I hear them swearing and stumbling around upstairs to get ready. While we wait, I grab our canteens and fill them at the well outside, and then add them back to our packs. Dray is on his bike, so I go and lean against him, and his arm winds around me straight away, pulling me closer to his side.

"Good morning," he mumbles, kissing me hard, and I grin against his mouth.

"Don't think I'm fucking you on your bike," I tease, and he laughs.

"No? I've heard the vibration can be...bliss." He bites my lip then and I groan.

"Break it up, ya cunts," Nan calls, grumbling as she trots to her new car.

"Cock blocker!" I holler back, and she laughs as she flips me off. "Come on, let's get going before she shoots me." I kiss him again

before backing away and swinging on my bike. I pull up my bandana and peel out of Dive's car park, heading towards The Rim, with Nan and Dray hot on my heels.

The ride to The Rim doesn't take long and we are there by midday. The sun beating down on us is nearly blinding, but when we roll over the horizon and they spot the truck, guards begin converging on the front gate. I park and slip from my bike, before lowering my bandana, and spotting the guy who usually pays me. He is standing by the gate, and when he spots me, his eyes go wide and then he looks at Dray. "Shit, you here to cause trouble?"

"Tha fucking better not be," Nan grumbles, climbing from the car and the guards instantly go on alert, moving closer to her to protect her. "Tha staying for tha day." She looks at me then. "Rest, eat, get ya weapons, and leave for the Cities in tha morning."

"Don't worry, cupcake, no trouble." I wink and his lips twist into a smile as I nod at Nan. We do need a full day, but we won't wait for morning to leave. We will leave when it is still dark, but I don't tell her that. Instead, I follow her to the gate.

I grin at the guard and he returns it as it cranks open, admitting us to the shanty city I used to call home. Just stepping inside and seeing the hustle and bustle, the houses, the swaying bridges, and the paths leading to the bazaar has me relaxing. I know this city like the back of my hand. Out there, I'm a queen, but in here I am just Worth. Nan breaks off going God knows where, but I leave her to it. I slip through the alleys of the buildings and head straight for Corky's shack, I have some bartering to do. Dray follows behind me.

Whores call out as we pass and a twinge goes through me when I spot Cherry's usual working corner, reminding me so much life has been lost recently. Will it ever calm down, will there ever be an end? Shaking away the morbid thoughts, I bang on the cracked wood as Corky turns in his chair and eyes me. "Figured you were dead," is how he greets me and I smirk.

"You fucking wish. I have a list and I need it quick. If you don't have it, have your men find it by nightfall," I order.

"What's in it for me? Where's ya payment?" he questions, picking at his teeth.

I grin then, knowing this will piss of Nan. "The truck outside these walls, brand new from the Cities, it's yours."

He grins, nodding at a man to the left who breaks away, heading for the gate, obviously to confirm it's there before we start our deal. "Whatcha need?"

"Bombs, as many as you can get your hands on. Dark clothes to hide me and him." I jerk my head at Dray.

He whistles, eyeing me again. "That truck better be worth it.

That will cost you, bombs aren't easy to come by."

"Don't fuck with me," I growl, getting in his face. "I know what stores you have, I brought most of it to you, get me my goods. I will be by later," I snap, before turning on my heel and leaving him stewing.

I make my way around the shops, not looking for anything in particular, just killing time and enjoying my last moments of peace. Dray sticks close but says nothing, allowing me my silence, and even though it feels like before when I was all alone, I know I never will be again. His body heat behind me reminds me of that every time I forget.

Something catches my eye, glinting in the sunlight from a table facing the bazaar at the stall I am at. I drop the shirt I was fingering and head over, moving the other junk out of the way to reveal what caught my eye.

There, nestled in the cast-offs and unwanted junk, is a ring, but not just any ring. Grasping it between my fingers, I lift it up to the light, unable to pull my eyes away from it. The band itself is simple, just silver and covered in scratches, but the stones nestled along the thick band blow me away. Four stones, all different colours, divide in the middle with a heart stone. The heart is red, the colour dark and shining in the light. To the left are blue and green stones, and to the right are yellow and orange gems. Four stones and a heart. It seems like fate, if I believed in that kind of shit.

"Thinking what I am, soulmate?" Dray murmurs.

"What's that?" I ask distractedly, still turning the ring in the light. "You just found your ring for your other men," he whispers. I scoff but don't drag my gaze away until I hear him talking to someone else. I spin quickly, realising he has left my back and is handing something over to the shopkeeper who nods and then turns away. Dray strolls over. "It's yours," is all he says.

I can't help it, I grin, and he holds out my hand and slips the ring onto my other hand before kissing both of them. "One for your darkness, for your past, one for you light and your future," he whispers as he kisses them. Is he right?

"You're my future too," I reply.

He winks at me and straightens. "Damn right I am, but I'm also your past."

"Let's get a drink," I blurt, lost on anything else to say, and he laughs as I turn around and head into the bazaar. It's busy even at this time of day, with scavs and roadies spread out, but they seem more sombre, more on edge than last time I was here, and I remember Nan saying Cities boys came through here. It shows, they are ready for a fight, they are ready to protect. Some even sit with untouched bottles in front of them, their eyes scanning their surroundings.

I choose a table towards the outskirts, shielded by the bright coverings hanging over the bazaar. Dray sits with me, kicking his legs out on another chair and closes his eyes, leaning his chin on his chest. His body is relaxed, but I can tell he is awake and ready to react if any trouble heads our way. I relax back in my chair, scanning the bazaar, never allowing my eyes to linger on one person for too long, but that doesn't stop them. Like always, a big man feels the need to challenge me. Maybe it's because I'm not hiding my tattoos and scars, or maybe it's because of my weapons or the Seeker at my side. Either way, he stands up and heads over.

I expect him to start something, so I grin up at him, my face cold, ready to tell him where to shove it, but he surprises me by nodding respectfully. "Champion, I heard rumours you are going to war."

I say nothing and he grabs the seat opposite me, swinging it around and sitting on it backwards as he watches me. "You're one of us, a bounty, a Rim fighter."

I blink in shock, but he forges ahead, his eyes angry. "We might not look like much, we might kill each other on the daily, but we stick together. If you are heading to war, so are we. We protect our home, we protect the North." He slams his hand over his chest and stands then.

I get up slowly and turn, hearing others doing the same. Every man, woman, and fighter in here is on their feet, with all eyes on us and their hands fisted over their chests, ready to face down death. I thought I was alone for so long. Even here I was always on edge, always having to protect myself. Running from my past and forgetting it at the bottom of a bottle, but now I see I was wrong.

We might fight, we might kill, we might even hate each other at some point, but we all stick together, and they are showing me that. They are showing me that I am home no matter where I go, that they haven't forgotten I am one of them despite the fancy new titles. They are showing me they will stand by my side and fight.

The bazaar is silent for the first time ever as they all wait for me to make a move, and then, as one, they drop to their knees, waiting. "Don't kneel for me, ever, I don't deserve it," I call, and then clear my throat. "It's true, there's a war. Fight if you want to fight, I won't force anyone, but know if you do we are doing it to protect our home, to save our people from the Cities' rule. You might die, you might not," I stutter then, unsure what to say, and a voice catches my attention.

"We face those odds every day. This is our home, we fight with you!" a scav yells, and some agree, getting to their feet as cheers go through the crowd, their voices blending in anger. Their words are different, but the meaning is the same—they will fight, they will stand with me, and die at my side. I force myself to remember their faces, each and every one, because before this is through, some will die, and I want to remember them, even if no one else does.

"In three days, meet where the sand turns to stone before the Cities, and be prepared for war!" I shout.

They cheer, popping bottles open now as excitement races through the crowd. They were waiting for someone to make a move, for something to happen, and now that they have a plan, a battle, they are ready to live again. Bottles are passed out, and the big man from before drops one on my table with a small smile before heading over to his friends. I sit down and my eyes go to a grinning Dray.

"Do you just collect people wherever you go, soulmate?" he teases.

"No, I usually kill them, this is a first," I admit, grabbing the bottle and taking a gulp, warmth spreading through my chest from the liquid.

"You prefer the killing, the loyalty makes you unsure." He nods and I flip him off.

"Know-it-all." I grin.

He laughs and toasts me with the bottle. "To the woman who will lead us to war, may we find beauty in their death!"

A cheer goes up at his words, and music starts up as the bazaar gets into full swing. Another group of people added to my army, making our odds better, yet it's also more men who will die because of me, more bloodshed, but with my men's lives on the line, I can't seem to care.

So I grab the bottle and drink with them, as my past, present, and future clash in the place I started.

Chapter Twenty

Nan's Rules

I'm conscious we are leaving in the morning, so I don't drink too much, and once the crowd is distracted by the women and fight- ing, we slip away, heading to Nan's place to get our room ready. The doors are open and a crowd of men peek into the hotel with scared expressions. I push through their midst, ignoring their warnings as I

step through the door to see Nan wielding her shotgun, scream- ing. "Ya fucking bastards! Fucking stains! Fucking bodies everywhere,

ya animals!" she hollers, waving her shotgun around. I spot one scav who has clearly been shot, so I'm betting she put some of the bodies here herself. Stepping over it, I move through the lobby of the old hotel, leap up on the counter, and swing my legs, watching the show. The men are cringing away, terrified of the little old lady. Grin- ning, I look down at Dray who leans next to me, neither of us moving to interrupt the show.

"Ya clean it up! Ya hear me? Or ya all fuckin dead, useless fuckin' men!" she screams, and men rush in, grabbing the bodies and tossing them outside.

She turns away then, looking furious, but stops when she sees me, her eyes narrowing with a huff. "Ya here to put more bodies on ma floor?"

"Wouldn't dream of it," I offer, swinging my legs back and forth.

She shakes her head, muttering to herself as she hunches back over and shuffles behind her desk, stowing away her gun as the men clean up the mess obviously left while she was at The Rim. I mean, really, they should have known better. I'm surprised she didn't kill more. "You checked your rooms?" I ask.

She huffs, cleaning up her desk before looking at me, so I hop down and lean on the counter, watching her. "Aye, they wouldn't dare leave them a mess, least they got some sense. Come with me, will ya? I have something for ya."

I tilt my head in question, but she just turns and shuffles away. I grab the key to my usual room and pass it to Dray with my bag. "Take this, last room, I'll meet you there." I kiss him quickly before hopping over the counter and following Nan to the open door, which leads to the office—not that I've ever been back here. The men aren't the only people scared of the old grouch.

I shut the door behind me, closing out the sounds of grumbling scavs as they clean. The office is a mess. A desk with an old, small TV with an antenna on top sits in the corner, while a radio stands on top of silver drawers, and then a shelf unit covered in keys, maps, and newspapers is pushed against one of the walls. The floor is carpeted, and one window is situated at the back with the blinds drawn, throwing the room into darkness.

"Nan?" I call out. I hear her shuffling to the left, so I move around the drawers and spot the door hidden there. It's open with Nan's grumbling coming from within, so I follow after her.

"I swear, old bitch, if you are trying to kill me, I will come back and haunt your old wrinkly ass every time you are fucking Reeves," I mutter.

"If a wanted ya dead, ya would be dead, now stop your whining," she hollers.

Whining? Narrowing my eyes, I stop at the threshold of the room and raise my eyebrows. The room is darker than the others and I wince when she lights a match, the flame flaring in the dark room as she moves around lighting candles. I let my eyes adjust and take in the little back room. It's clearly her bedroom. A table with two rickety chairs stands in the middle of the room, and on the back wall runs a counter with a sink and what looks like a coffee machine. Cupboards hang on the wall above it, the doors missing to show boxes of food in one, clothes in another, and one filled with books.

A small, single bed with a metal frame is pushed up against the wall opposite the door with a shelf above it, holding a half melted candle and a trunk at the end, which is closed and locked. There are no windows here, just another door, which I'm guessing leads to her bathroom. Is this where Nan lives? It's in better shape than the rooms, but it's small and kind of constricting. She doesn't seem to mind as she shuffles around the room, no longer bent over as the wood under her feet creaks with each step. She yanks off her cardigan, throws it on the bed, and shakes her hair before looking at me.

"Ya want a drink?"

"I just had one," I admit. Before, I wouldn't have hesitated, but I no longer need to numb myself with alcohol.

She scoffs then moves over to the counter. "Not tha piss swallow out there, the good stuff," she explains, laughing as she pulls away boxes to reveal a bottle. She brings it to the table and sets it between us, grabbing two mugs with a hotel name on them before putting them next to the bottle, and sitting down with a sigh as she looks at me.

I sit down opposite her, leaning back in my chair and throwing my arm over the wooden back, and watch as she pours a mug and pushes it across the table to me. I reach for it and take a sip. She's right, it's not the cheap kind or home brewed. It's smooth with a pleasant aftertaste, more fruity than the whiskey and booze I'm used to.

She sips at hers and leans back, studying me. I watch the years melt away then as her facade falls. "Ya reminded me a lot of myself when a was younger and I could see past ma tits, my back was broken like a hooker, and ma fanny was tight as a virgin."

I snort the booze through my nose then, my eyes watering from the sting. "Fuck, that hurts like a bitch," I complain, and she laughs.

"That's why I took a shining to ya, that and I saw the pain in your eyes, tha ghosts there and how lost you were. You were looking for a purpose, so I gave ya one and a roof over ya head. I saw that shielded look get stronger and tha ghosts start to recede, and then those men came." She smiles then, her eyes sparkling. "Damn fine men, tell ma ya fucked em, or I will when ya get them back."

"Hands off, you dirty old bitch." I grin and she chuckles again. "You don't have anyone? I've always wondered."

She shakes her head, playing with her mug. "I liked men too much, never wanted to settle down and limit myself to just one cock, ya know? There were so many out there to try, so why waste myself by tying down to one man? Nah, that was never ma style, girlie. Probably a good thing, 'cause when tha end came, I had no one ta lose. The Rim became ma home and ma family."

"Is that what Reeves is to you then?" I wriggle my eyebrows, unable to help myself.

"I met him when he was a lot younger." She grins then. "He was fine. I was a bit older than him, but he didn't care. He passed through here every now and again and we entertained ourselves, nothing serious, we both knew we couldn't with tha position we were in. Then he stopped coming." She shrugs. "I always thought he found someone or died, that's life."

"Then you met him again at The Summit."

"Aye, he wanted to pick up where we left off. I fucked him of course, he's gotten fat, but he's still a good lay," she comments, and I snort again. Jesus, that's an image I don't need in my mind. "Life is too short, girlie, so enjoy it while ya can, take it from an old hag. I never had love, never thought I wanted it and tha chains that came with it, but at tha end I will be alone and that's my fault."

"You won't be alone," I say, reaching across the table and covering her hands.

She smiles softly. "Don't get all touchy feely on me now, girlie. Ya a hard bitch and that's what ya good for. I ain't afraid of dying, a had a good life."

"I'm not afraid either. It was always living that scared me," I confess, sipping the booze as I lean back again.

"Aye, I could see that, good that those men forced ya, otherwise ya probably would have stayed here forever. You were meant for more, I don't believe in that density crap or go spouting weird religious shit, but even I could see that," she offers.

"Let's hope it's not to lead us to destruction," I scoff.

"Nah, ya got a good head on ya shoulders, Major knew that. Ya can do this, girlie."

I blink, feeling confidence spill through me at her belief in me. Nan tells the truth, brutally so, so if she thinks I can, then I believe her. It makes me feel better, but we have our relationship to maintain so I don't get all emotional. Instead, I smirk. "Is that why you invited me here? To get emotional and talk about your wrinkly cunt?" I ask.

She glares at me, a grin tugging at her lips. "Nah, I wanted to know if ya needed any of this," she answers, climbing to her feet.

She heads to the chest at the end of the bed, pulls a key from under her shirt, and unlocks it. I stand up, curious about what she has locked up when she lets everyone get an eyeful off everything else. Peering over her shoulder and into the chest, my eyebrows rise and I whistle.

"Shit, you are one lethal motherfucker," I say proudly and we share a grin.

"Can you use them?" she inquires, and I nod. "Fuck yes I can."

Carrying my new bag of goodies, I head to the room I always use while I'm here. The door is unlocked, and I drop the bag inside before kicking it shut behind me. Dray isn't in the room, but he leans out of the bathroom, sees it's me, and winks before ducking back inside. Stripping off my jacket, I place it with my bag and flop back onto the bed, staring at the ruined ceiling, and just letting myself breathe and relax. Tomorrow will be a busy day, and hopefully before nightfall, I will see my men. Worry courses through me, but I push it away. Now is not the time to sink into it. I have a job to do and I can't afford to be distracted.

I hear Dray step into the room and then his face appears upside down above me, smirking. "What did she want?"

"To compare dick sizes," I tease and he laughs, throwing himself on the bed, and making me bounce as we end up rolling together.

He lays his head on my chest and I stroke his hair, letting my mind be peaceful.

"We leave early. We will go back to Corky before dark, and then try and get some sleep," I whisper.

"It's time to get your family back," he murmurs and I nod, feeling a smile curling my lips. Yes it is.

When we get back to Corky's, he is just getting ready to close up. He sees us coming and passes over two bags without a word before slamming the door shut. What an ass. I grab the bags though, and weave back to Nan's. In the room, I get everything ready and lay out my outfit for tomorrow. Dray does the same, and then we curl up in each other's arms, the sound of the city coming alive lulling us to sleep.

When I sleep again after this night, I will have them in my arms.

It's my last thought before darkness claims me, and when I wake again, I can feel time has passed so I get up, use the bathroom, and get washed quickly before sneaking back into the room, but I shouldn't have bothered, Dray is awake and getting ready.

I get dressed silently, both of us aware of the magnitude of today. Either it goes well, and my plan works out and by the end of the week we will be fighting in a war, or we will die on sight. He helps me strap on my weapons, his fingers lingering against my skin, and I do the same. Stroking him, loving him, showing him I'm here and no matter what happens we face it together. When we are ready, he leans down, settling his forehead against mine, his icy eyes staring into my dark ones.

"We can do this, soulmate. No other two people could. We won't fail, no matter what happens, we keep going," he demands, grabbing my chin and keeping me there. "Together. We live and die together, no matter what."

"Together," I whisper, closing my eyes and as I do, he kisses me.

Not soft and gentle, not comforting, no, it's hard.

He's giving me a reason to keep fighting. He pushes his tongue into my mouth and lays claim to me as I lay claim to him. Our hearts race in sync, and when we break away, we both smile at each other.

"Let's go," I demand, stepping back, and letting all softness go as I turn into the woman who wins the fights and destroyed a mad king.

The Champion is back and she's mad as hell. I let it fill me up as I head out of the room and into the lobby where scavs and roadies are sleeping. Nan has her orders, everything is in place, and now it's our move. I don't spot Nan, so I turn to leave, but just as I reach the front door, I hear her telltale shuffling coming from behind me.

"Goodbye, girlie, don't get dead before I get a chance to shoot some fuckers!" she calls and I wave as I head out into the night.

We stay silent as we wind through the city. The gate opens as we approach and our bikes are there waiting. I heave my bag onto it and then swing on.

Straightening, I give The Rim one last look—it could be the last time I see it—then I turn and face my future, my men. Pulling up my bandana, I fire up my bike.

I'm coming for you.

I look at Dray and he nods, so I race into the night, away from the city lights, and towards the Cities.

Chapter Twenty-One

One Bad Motherfucker

We reach the Cities early morning when the sky is still dark like I wanted. I follow the map that Jago and the guards explained. We are waiting in the dust, looking up at the towering walls that connect and contain the three Cities. I can see the bridges the guard explained from here. The wall is grey and covered in deep grooves, cracked edges, and crumbling stone, but despite that, it looks strong and I can see where people have attacked and failed over the years. Lights shine on top of the wall, illuminating the sand below around the perimeter. I can see skyscrapers lit up inside, and it looks so different from the North. Like a city from before, the lights, the buildings...in the destruction, they managed to save this and that makes me wonder what they sacrificed to keep it... or who they sacrificed.

After I finish gawking, I pull around to the left and head down the sand dunes. There are no roads here, but we spot the dried up river, which is now a dump site for their rubbish and toilets. We leave our bikes, throw our bags on our backs, and continue around it, holding our breath at the stench before we reach the water tunnel we were told about. Metal bars cover it, letting the water pass through but allowing no one in. A rusted lock seals the bars—waiting to be destroyed, in my opinion. I pull out the pliers and cut it off, letting it clank to the ground before pushing open the gate.

It takes both of us to open, stuck from ages of disuse, and we are both sweating when it finally moves, screeching as it does. We wait to see if anyone has heard, but no one comes to investigate so we slip inside, shutting the gate after us so if anyone takes a cursory look, it will all appear the same and they won't be suspicious. We have to duck to fit inside the tunnel and I flick on the torch, Dray's lighting up the dark behind me. I point it at the ground just in case and trudge through the sludge. It's hot down here and stinks, but it's part of the plan so I man the fuck up and keep walking. The tunnel seems to run for ages. There are three stops, one for each city, and as much as I want to rush into the inner, I don't, since that would get them killed. The thought that they might be suffering right now does have me hesitating, but I stick to the plan and keep on walking, only stopping when we reach the last sealed entrance.

The outers.

The door is like a giant vault door with a wheel to turn, and I leave Dray to it as I shine my torch around the tunnel behind us, keeping watch. I hear him grunting, and then finally, the loud turn of the wheel interrupts the quiet of the tunnel, the only other sounds the squeaking of rats and dripping water. I turn around as he swings it open and I go first, peeking out. Like we hoped, it leads out into an empty section of the city. We slip out, keeping the door opened only slightly.

Dropping the torch and flicking it off, not wanting to draw attention, I flip up my dark hood, which conceals most of my face, and Dray does the same. We don't know if they know what we look like, but we aren't risking it, and from the information we got from the guard, a lot of the outers wear cloaks.

Crumbling, half destroyed buildings line the road we are on near the wall of the third city, which is where the poor are. The road is cracked with holes in it, the yellow paint worn off in some places.

Rubbish blows in the breeze, the windows whistling from the buildings on either side of us. It doesn't smell much better here than in the tunnel, but it's not unbearable.

Rushing along the road, we keep our footsteps as quiet as we can and head down the street to the corner. A road sign lays on the ground, abandoned and covered in graffiti. A dog howls and races across the road, chasing something, and we wait for it to pass before heading down the next street. We make turns and weave through the buildings, and the closer we get to the city center, the more looked after the houses become, and we start to see people inhabiting some of them.

Down one of the roads, I spot a graveyard. Some of the graves have crosses on top of the turned soil, but towards the front I spot mounds of skulls and bones, tossed there and forgotten. What the fuck is wrong with these people? Do they not even bury their dead? Or do too many people die here to bury them all? The thought is unsettling, and I move past it and down the next street, the apartment buildings on either side protecting us from the stinging sand in the wind.

When we reach the center, we stop and orient ourselves. A casino is right up in the center where people seem to be flocking to it. To the left, where there once used to be a park, is what looks like a camp filled with tents, shacks, and people. That's their homes, while the inners live in skyscrapers. This is going to be easier than I thought. The buildings here housing people are a mixture of red brick structures and apartment buildings. They don't look much better than the ones we have passed before, but there are lights inside some of them. Except the amount of people I glimpse crammed inside makes my stomach clench. They are living right on top of each other in awful conditions. I find myself just staring around. The Wastes might be brutal, but at least there is plenty of room, this...this feels like slums. People have been mistreated and abused and just left here. On the floor in a shadow I spot an unmoving body, and to the right I spot dirty faced children chasing a dog.

Shaking my head, I walk towards the casino like the guard told us. He explained if we wanted to find someone in charge then that's where they would be. Apparently there has been more and more pressure from a man in there when it comes to policing this city. They aren't officially in charge, but it looks like they have claimed this section of the city, and from the muscled men guarding the entrance, they have firepower and followers, which is what we need.

There are women loitering outside in skimpy clothing, luring men and women into the casino. I spot one woman heading into an alley followed by a hurried looking man and I smirk. Some things never change. They can rebrand it, but everyone in this world is the same. We all deal in blood and flesh.

Two men block the glass doors to the casino, so I throw back my hood. "We are here to speak to Vert," I say strongly.

They exchanged glances, the one on the left in nothing but a waistcoat and trousers, with a machete strapped to his leg. The man on the right is only wearing trousers, leaving his tattooed, barrel chest on display. "Who's asking?" the one on the left demands with a thick accent.

"A friend, a friend who is about to offer him a sweet deal, so I suggest you stop pulling my dick and let me in," I snap, growing bored of this. Each lost moment is like a countdown clock in my head, reminding me that we are wasting time. I'm so close to getting them back and no one will stand in my way.

They look at each other again but shrug. "I'll take her in. If the boss don't wanna see her, we can kick them out," the one on the left mutters, rubbing at his bald head. He throws me another look.

"Follow me," he orders, and then pushes through the door, not holding it for me.

I follow after him with Dray on my heels. The fucking fools didn't even pat us down for weapons. The noise hits me straight away, as does the cool air...is that air con? Sands below, I want to strip down and race through this place to feel that cold air on my skin, but I don't. The sound of wheels turning, music, laughter, and screaming all blends together. The smell of booze, unwashed bodies, and...food hits me. It's a lot to absorb. The lights are bright and I stumble to a stop for a moment just taking it all in.

Tables with roulette wheels, pool tables, and other types of gambling line the bottom floor with slot machines at the back. This place is busy as hell as well. I spot a bar to the left filled to the brim and what looks like a buffet to the right. The bottom floor is huge with a metal barrier with people leaning on it up top. Two big, winding staircases lead up to it from the middle of the floor. Chandeliers hang from the ceiling, and I just blink around before following after the guard, not wanting to be caught gawking.

He leads us through the glitz and glamour, and to an open door to the side, which leads into a bar unlike any I've ever been in. The lights are dimmed with candles spread around, and two seater tables are spread around the red carpeted room, with a bar to the right and a man in a hat serving spirits from the shelves, which reach to the ceiling with a ladder leaning against them. A stage is set at the front with red velvet curtains, and a woman in a short black dress sings in a low, purring voice. It looks like something from a fifties sitcom or mobster movie, and there is only one man in here, sitting in the middle of the room, sipping from a tumbler, as he watches the woman. We are forced to wait until she finishes and he claps before we are led over to who I am guessing is Vert.

We are brought to his table and before we can be introduced, I pull out the chair and sit opposite him. His guard grunts, going to grab me as Vert's eyebrow rises as he takes me in, and he waves off his guard. "Well, hello there." He grins, showing perfectly straight white teeth. He's traditionally handsome with bright blue eyes that have a piercing quality. Stubble covers his chin and cheeks, and he has short brown hair. Overall, he's well put together for the Wastes and it all screams power, but I can see the imperfections. His skin is burned from the sun and his clothes are worse for wear. He craves power and riches, but he can't quite reach them yet. He has goals and I'm betting the Cities are keeping them down.

"What can I do for you?" he asks, crossing his legs and regarding me.

If there is one thing I know, it's people and what they want. I can see it in him and in this place. He wants power and followers. I'm betting on that because I am going to have to trust him with information that could get my men killed.

"It's more what we can do for each other." I grin and his eyes light up. Bingo.

"Call me intrigued..." He trails off, looking me over. "I'm Vert, but my friends call me Strand, and you are?"

"Your new best friend." I grin. "Worth."

He tilts his head slightly. "Worth, that name sounds familiar." He is obviously digging for information. He doesn't like not being in the know.

"You might know me as the Champion, I'm not from around here though," I hint and he grins.

"I can see that, so, Worth, what is the deal that will blow me away?" he questions, holding his hand up, and two drinks are brought over and placed in front of me.

"First of all, do the people of the outers listen to you?" I inquire, needing to know. I've heard my own rumours, but I want to see how honest he is with me.

"Yes, or they are scared of me. I help these people. I might not look like it, but I protect them as much as I can." I can tell it grates on him how little he can protect them.

"And you don't like the current leadership," I surmise.

His eyes narrow. "Perceptive, not smart to point out though," he adds.

"It is for what I have planned. I don't give a fuck about their rules or wrath, they have never met someone like me before." I take a sip of my drink as he considers me.

"I can see that. The government plays political games, but you don't, do you?" he asks, seeming pleased with that.

"I prefer a more...physical approach." I nod.

"And will that approach be soon?" he probes, both of us talking in riddles.

"Yes, let's cut the shit, Strand. I'm here for two reasons—I can't do this without you, and you can't do this without me. You have been waiting to make your move and now is the time. I will be heading into the inners and forcing them to confront me while I retrieve something, then I will be leading them outside the city limits where I will kill them."

His eyes go wide and I continue, "To ensure this happens, you need to cause distractions here. I'm betting there are a lot of angry workers, rile them up, do what you need to. Use the fact the inners are 'cleansing' them to get them involved. I brought some toys for you to play with, and when I kill them, the Cities will be yours to take. We attack them on two fronts, confuse them, and spread their masses." I wait for his response as he seems to think it through.

"How do I know you will kill them? If you fail and lots of others have, I will be executed with anyone who helped me," he points out, and I let my face go cold.

"I don't fail, I'm not just anyone," I reply coldly, deadly. "Plus, I have three armies waiting in the North for them," I inform him and he whistles, impressed.

"Shit, what did they do to you?" he asks. "Took what is mine," I answer and he laughs.

"Remind me not to piss you off. Okay, let's plan. We had a plan in motion anyway, but this is better if we can agree on terms of course. I will order us a bottle." He grins and I smirk, knowing I have him.

The bottle is almost empty when we shake hands. I hand over the bag of goodies and he smiles when he spots what is inside. "Oh, this will work." He hands the bag over to his guard. "I will make preparations tonight. Do you need a place to spend the night?" he asks.

"No, we are heading back out before they catch us. Be ready tomorrow night," I instruct him as I stand.

He stands as well and grins at me. "Can't say I expected this when you walked in." He laughs and I smirk as I pull my hood back up.

"No one ever expects me until it's too late. The next time we see each other, you will be in charge." I nod and turn to leave as he starts issuing commands. Dray follows after me as we weave through the casino and back outside into the Cities.

I spot some guards patrolling, but they give the place a wide berth and we turn, pretending to talk as we wait for them to pass, and then we quickly head back to the tunnel. Once there, I give the outers another look, noting the hard faced men and women here. Hopefully I can free them. This has become more than just freeing my men, and is now about freeing a city. What is it with me and toppling empires? Maybe I should be called King-killer not queen, I muse as I slip into the dark tunnel and shut the door behind me.

Dray lights up the torch and we share a look, wordlessly communicating before we head back through the dirty water to get ready to knock on the front gates tomorrow morning. We are more confident on the way back, sure in our steps, and soon we reach the metal grate. I wait for a moment, listening in case anyone is passing by, but it's silent so I slip the grate away and head into the dark with Dray following. I watch his back as he moves the gate into place like we were never here. We head back over the sand to where we left our bikes and set up camp beyond a dune, with no fire or tent tonight, and one of us awake at all times to be safe. Dray takes first watch and I curl up with my jacket under my head, my eyes closing and seeing my other men waiting there for me.

One day, I tell myself, that's all there is until I see them again, but I fear what state I will find them in. Fear will get me nowhere, so I force it away and go to sleep. Who knows when I will sleep again, and with a war coming, I need to be as rested as possible, because we will win.

When Dray wakes me for his turn to sleep, I quickly find myself bored. His snores are quiet and the only noise around, and I wish something would happen, even though it's a good sign nothing has, but all this silence, this empty time, only lets me linger on my men and how much I miss them. Thoughts plague me of what could be happening to them right now as I sit outside these walls. Grabbing my swords, I decide to clean all of my weapons to occupy my mind. The rhythmic and familiar feel helps, and I find myself going into a trance between keeping watch and cleaning, wishing the time away until I can see them again.

I want Maxen's arms, Thorn's smile, and Drax's teasing. I want my Jax's dark eyes telling me he trusts me. I want them all.

When the sun starts to rise, I have cleaned and sheathed all my weapons, and I am already on my feet ready to move. I wake Dray and he stretches, awake instantly, and nods at me. "Come here, soulmate." He opens his arms and I slip into his waiting grasp.

"Stay strong, remember who you are," he whispers, and then tilts my chin up and kisses me hard, having me gasping into his mouth in no time, but I reluctantly step back, my focus split between him and getting the Cities. "Let's go. The sooner this is done, the sooner I can slaughter them all for you," he offers, and I laugh like he knew I would. We decided Dray would head back today and help the outers. We doubted they would let us both through the front gate and I need to show them I don't fear them. He didn't like the plan, but agreed to it eventually.

We climb on our bikes and I head straight to the Cities' gates, not hiding now that we want them to know we are coming. Dray breaks off to go back through the tunnel and my heart slams at seeing him go, but this is my plan after all. If it gets us all killed, only I am to blame, but it's too late to turn back now. I just hope I'm right and that we all make it through this.

The sand batters me from both sides as I ride up. There is no protection from buildings out here, the walls towering into the sky like a mecca for those lost and damned in the Wastes. For me, it represents a challenge, and I always did love a challenge.

As expected, there are guards waiting for me there when I stop and climb off, and they don't look happy. Like the ones we met before, they have guns strapped across their chests and they don't hesitate to aim them at me now. More are aimed my way from the top of the walls. All in all, there are about twenty rifles pointed my way.

What a welcoming party.

Holding my hands up in surrender, I smirk at them. "Hello, boys. You have something of mine and I want it back."

Chapter Twenty-Two

Show No Fear

I wait patiently at gunpoint at the front gate as they radio in. One of the guards drops his gun, eyeing me worriedly, and snatches a black radio clipped to his shoulder while holding the button down as he speaks. "Boss, we have a woman at the gate." A beep sounds and we wait for the response.

"So? Kill her," comes the crackled response. The guards all move closer then, but I don't react apart from letting my smile disappear.

"I wouldn't do that if I were you. You see I'm the queen of the fucking North and you came into my lands, took my people, and left yours behind. I have them, of course, but there are a lot of angry people there waiting. So unless you want to start a war you can't win, I suggest you let me in." I shrug, smiling and nodding as they gape at me. "Did you get all that, or would you like me to repeat it?" I taunt when they just stand there staring at me.

The same guard grabs his radio again, swallowing as sweat dampens his temple. "Erm, boss, I think you are going to want to see her. She said she's the...erm, queen of the North and that we took her men and she will declare war? Is that right?" The guard looks at me and I nod.

"Good boy," I mock, and he narrows his eyes. "Oh, and I'm not a patient woman, so don't fuck me around or I will get my armies just to be a spiteful bitch," I warn with glee.

He relays the message and I pretend to look around as I wait for the response. "Nice walls. Bet they won't withstand bombs though, or rocket launchers," I point out idly, and they just gape at me again, clearly having no idea what to say.

The radio crackles to life and he juggles it in his hand. "Bring her in," the voice commands, and I lower my hands.

"There, that wasn't so hard, now was it? Lead the way," I offer. The two guards out front bang on the gate house to the side.

"Open her up!" he yells, and the gate starts to crank open, revealing the city beyond. I step up behind them and wait, standing uncomfortably close just to annoy them. I know they sense me, because their shoulders tighten and their grips on their guns get harder. "Don't do that boys, wouldn't want to start a war because you had premature shooting problems, would you?" I tease, then move around them and stride into the inner city like I own the joint. I spot the cameras on me instantly, and know the guards we captured were right, they are tracking my every move. I wave at one then blow them a kiss, waiting for the guards who are supposed to escort me to catch up.

The buildings here are bigger, shinier, and looked after. Smaller apartment style buildings line the main road with bigger ones towering behind them. There are shops, even a shopping center, to the left, and a fucking supermarket with trolleys outside. All are open and filled with people. The road leads to the huge skyscrapers you can see from beyond the wall. I'm guessing that's where the government stays in the center in the richest part.

I spot people walking the sidewalk in dresses and suits, one even has a dog on a leash. It looks like a before advert for pre-scorch, whereas I look like the after picture. People stop and stare as we pass some even gasp so I make sure to play it up, flashing weapons at them and grinning at their shocked and disgusted faces. I'm marched down the center of the city into a giant square. In the middle stands what I can only guess is an art piece of two men on a bridge, surrounded by gardens on either side with people eating lunch or just relaxing. Skyscrapers box in each side, looking down on you, putting you on display. Trying to intimidate you of course. I'm not given a tour or even spoken to, merely led to the biggest building, the one with a spire on top and glass windows looking down on everything.

The doors are even glass and rotate as we enter into a lobby with a guard stationed behind the desk and a turnstile. It looks like an old office building that they have converted. The lobby has those low settees and chairs, but there is no one there waiting, and I am led straight to the turnstiles and the man lingering there.

"They are expecting her," is all the guard says, then throws me a dirty look before they step back, obviously going back to their gate duty.

"Nice to meet you, boys," I tease, and turn back as the gate is opened, and I am ushered through it to an elevator that works. Fuck, these bastards must have unlimited power. How did they get it? Or are they simply showing off? It would make sense they would send all the power to their building and not spread it everywhere, especially considering what I have learned from them.

The doors open to reveal another guard, and now I know they are doing it on purpose in an attempt to intimidate me—all this show of force against one woman. But I've been in worse situations, so I just smile and get on board, again standing close to the guard to unnerve him. The other man climbs on and I am bracketed between them, so I lean back against the wall and let my cape fully open, and then drop it to the floor since it's no longer needed. I know they see my weapons in the shiny, silver reflections before them when they stiffen. Did they really think I would come unprotected?

The ride is filled with strained silence, their bodies wound tight, expecting me to attack at any minute. Music fills the space as we rise quickly, only adding to the tension until the screen above the doors finally announces "12" and a mechanic voice informs us the doors are opening.

When we reach the twelfth floor the doors open, and they step out to show, yep, you guessed it, more guards. This time the big man turns to me. "We need your weapons."

I expected this, so I hand all the visible ones over, expecting they wouldn't think I would hide any with the arsenal I was carrying. As the pile at his feet grows, I feel them getting tenser and tenser. "That's it, boys. Oh, and lose any of that and I will kill you. They were gifts." I wink then and big guys points at me.

"I need to pat you down," he snaps.

"Do it, but don't let my men find out, they are the jealous sort." I shrug, holding out my arms. He falters at my words and quickly pats me down, not finding any of the weapons I have hidden. What an idiot. As usual, they are underestimating me because I'm a woman and alone. I'm guided down the hallway to what looks like a conference room. A big, silver table with glasses of water wait there. Windows on one side look out onto the Cities, and glass separates it from the rest of the hallway. I'm gestured inside, and then they shut the door and press their backs to the glass and wait.

Feeling like a bitch, I knock on the glass. "You know I can see you, right?" I harass.

They ignore me, so I snoop around the room, getting bored. Feeling vindictive, I choose the big leather chair at the head of the table and place my boots on the pristine table, knocking dirt and sand everywhere as I wait for them, then I close my eyes and lean my head back against the leather and wait. They keep me waiting just long enough to be considered rude until I hear the clacking of their heels down the hallway. They are so loud, I could hear them coming from miles away. I keep my eyes closed as they enter the room, not giving them what they want—an audience to their show. This is all part of the plan to try and intimidate me, and I'm going to flip that on their fucking heads.

They have never met anyone like me.

The Cities

The room goes silent. I can hear their brains whirling, they are clearly stumped on what to do. Did they think I would be nervously waiting in here? Bitch, please, I've faced down Nan after fucking all night. Nothing is scarier than that. Only when they start to shuffle do I crack my eyes open while leaning back casually in their chair. "Hello, boys, have we finished with the dick measuring contest? Let's get down to business now, shall we?" I suggest, getting comfier as I scan them. The fools aren't even carrying any weapons, depending only on their guards to keep them safe.

Just like pale faces.

The group gathered is made up of nearly all men, apart from one woman, who's' stern face, cold eyes, and tangible power make her the obvious pick for being a leader. Her hair is an auburn colour and pulled back so tightly in a bun that it stretches her eyebrows, making her look angry at all times. No hair dares to escape that grip. Her perfectly pink painted lips are thin and turned down. Her cheeks are also painted pink, and her tight skirt and white shirt look brand new. Fuck, she's even wearing heels. To her right are two men who look similar—brothers, I would guess. They must be in their late forties, with grey, receding hair and bellies poking through their shirts. The only difference is one is taller with brown eyes and one is shorter with blue eyes. To the left of the woman is an older man, hunched over a cane. His head is bald on top with grey, thin hair on the side, his skin tanned and wrinkled with an angry looking scowl, and he is wearing a perfect suit. It all screams money and protection. These people have never suffered or worked a day in their lives. I'm betting they took advantage after the scorch and took charge, getting others to do the dirty work.

The old man steps forward. "Who are you?" he asks, positioning himself as leader, but I ignore him and look at the woman, recognizing a true leader when I see one. I don't know what they were thinking trying to hide her from me. When I simply watch her, she huffs, throwing away the pretence.

The woman steps forward, her eyes running down me and

ending on my dirty boots. Her lips purse and her eyes tighten, the only sign of her displeasure. "I was pulled from a meeting discussing the potential land grab...for her?" she snaps, looking at the men behind her. The old man steps forward and throws her a narrow-eyed look.

"Yes, she came with terms of war, she's from the North," he announces, and the woman throws her hands in the air.

"Most of these fucking savages are from the North! Do we just open the fucking doors to them whenever we feel like it? She's one fucking woman!" she shrieks, her eyes twitching before she huffs and straightens her suit, and I start laughing.

"That's what they all say, until I kill them." I shrug then and pull out a knife, making them stumble back and their guards swear, but I simply start to clean my nails. "One woman, with three, wait, is it four armies? I can't keep track, anyway, they are all waiting for you. If I don't come back, they will storm your little Cities here, and they will get in and then you will all be dead. So, I suggest you sit the fuck down and listen for once in your life. I'm betting you are used to giving orders, but if you want to be alive at the end of the day, you are going to start taking them," I finish, wagging my knife at them. None of them seem to know what to do, looking between each other instead, and I get bored. "Sit the fuck down," I bark loudly.

They share looks, but slowly pull out chairs and sit down, all apart from the woman. "You're in my seat," she snarls, and I grin at her.

"So find a different fucking chair," I reply, my blade glinting in the light.

When they are all seated, I pull down my feet and slip off my jacket, enjoying their gasps of shock at my extensive tattoos and scars. Twisting in my chair, I drape my legs over the end of the table and look them over, making them shift with my intense gaze as I let them sweat it out like they tried to do to me. "Right then. First things first, you have my men. I want them back or I am going to blow up this city building by building until I find them," I say sweetly.

The two older brothers share looks. "Men?"

I ignore them, focusing on the woman. "Don't play fucking dumb with me, sweetheart. You sent them North and when they didn't return you took them back. They are mine. I want them, so go get them, or these negotiations go nowhere."

"We don't negotiate with savages," she spits.

"Oh, you're going to negotiate with me," I purr. "Do I need to prove to you how serious I am? Which city do you like less?" I taunt, my face calm and cool.

"She's bluffing," the old man interjects.

"Maybe I am, but how will you know until it's too late?" I reply, letting my face go cold. "Now get me my fucking men. The longer you wait, the angrier I get, and you don't want me angry. I could kill you all without even breaking a sweat. You have ten minutes," I order, and then with that, I close my eyes again, showing them exactly how unconcerned with them I am.

They are silent before I hear them start to whisper among themselves, without looking, I interrupt them. "Nine minutes. Which one of you will die first?" I wonder out loud, and they start to argue then.

"Eight minutes. I bet at least one of you will faint at the sight of blood, maybe even piss yourself in fear. You ever seen that? I have, real stink, not as much as when you shit yourself when you are dying," I tell them, my eyes still closed, and I hear one of them get up and whisper to the guards at the door before they come back.

"We are bringing them up," she snaps and I hum out loud. "Seven minutes. There was this one guy. I hunted him for two

weeks, really slippery bastard, but when I found him...damn, that boy knew how to beg. Never seen anything like it, and as I was cutting strips of his skin away, he screamed, I still remember that sound. Then he lost control of his bladder. You see, everyone breaks eventu- ally. I wonder what your breaking point will be?"

I let them ponder that, while I feel their assessing gazes. "What's your name?" the old man asks.

"I have many, The Champion, Berserker Queen, but feel free to call me Worth. Easier to beg with such a shorter word," I taunt then open my eyes. "Who will I be killing? I do like to have a name to a face."

"I am Phineese, this is William and Derkin," the old man introduces.

"And I am Regina Locost, appointed prime minister of our government and Cities." She sniffs, looking down her nose at me.

"Woopity fucking doo, queen beats prime minister, bitch. Five minutes," I respond, and then shut my eyes again to the outrage on her face.

"You vulgar idiot. Did you really think coming here and demanding was going to work? We will wipe you savages from the map!" she snarls.

"Four minutes," is all I say, and then I hear the door open and shuffled footsteps. I prepare myself, telling myself not to react if they are hurt or worse. I can't let this woman see how much they mean to me, or she will use them against me ruthlessly. I compose myself and open my eyes, my heart racing and lungs wheezing for air, but my face is cold and calm, and when I look at my hand it isn't shaking.

Sands below, thank fuck.

Only then do I raise my eyes and time seems to slow down. It has only been two weeks, two weeks without them, yet it felt like a lifetime. Every day dragging on, moving from one mess to another, fighting every minute not to race to their sides, and now I can see them again and all I want—

Where the fuck is Jax?

Rage surges through me, but so does terror. I count them again. They are blindfolded, but I know the difference between Drax and Jax and the way they stand. Their clothes are the same as when I was with them, but they are filthy and ripped, with blood covering some of it, and I note every cut and wound. Maxen starts to struggle against his bindings, and only then do I realise they are gagged.

"These men?" she asks, and I look over at her, noting the way she is focused on me, so I lean back. "I think you will find they were my men before they were yours." She sniffs and I grin.

"You wouldn't know what to do with them, lose the gags and blindfolds," I order, and she narrows her gaze. I feel my men react to my voice, but I focus on her.

"Do not push your luck, savage," she snaps, but nods at the guards and I turn back in time to see them pushed to their knees as the gags and blindfolds are removed, their hands still bound behind their backs.

I meet everyone one of their eyes. Maxen's widen in fear, but then settle on smouldering as he runs them over me. Thorn's are filled with relief and happiness, and my Drax's gaze glints with amusement, but I see the flicker of fear there as well. I spot cuts, bruises, and dried blood everywhere I look. I can't tell what is from injuries or worse, which will have to wait until I can inspect them later, but none of them look like they are about to die. Once I am sure they have nothing life threatening, I look back at Regina.

"Where is Jax?" I growl.

"Jax?" she replies, pretending to look confused, even though her lips are curling into a smirk. "I don't know who that is."

I hear them start to struggle. "You fucking—" Drax starts, but one of the guards smacks him with his gun across the face, and I am across the room in an instant, slitting the guard's throat and stepping back. He falls to the floor, spurting blood everywhere as I grip the knife, ignoring the other guards who move towards me with guns out and shouts leaving their throats. Stepping to the table, I stab the bloody knife in the middle and lean closer, letting Regina look in my eyes and see how close I am to killing them all.

"Where is he?" I enunciate every word slowly, leaning into her space until I am looking deep in her eyes.

"*Mi Alma*," Maxen rumbles from behind me, making me almost shiver. Fuck, I've missed him. I want to turn around and jump him, fuck these stuck up rich people. I want them in my arms, but I'm the leader now, and that comes with responsibilities, so I keep my gaze on her.

She shivers, fear tinting her expression as she leans back from me. "We don't know, he escaped the second night they were here once we were...investigating where they had been," she admits, and oh how it hurts her pride to share she lost him, but if he's not here, he must be safe. I just wish I knew where, but at least I know he is alive.

I lean back slightly. "Investigate?" I drawl slowly. "Is that rich people's way of saying you tortured them for information?"

I go cold all over as she just smiles at me, this fucking bitch. I grab the knife, ready to gut the bitch, but a soft touch lands on my shoulder, a touch I would know anywhere. "*Mi Alma*, it is not worth it, we are okay," he murmurs quietly, just for me. I lean back into his touch before turning to face them.

Drax winks at me, although blood drips down his hairline from the gun, but he still has a smirk on his lips, and Thorn gives me that smile that makes my knees weak, while Maxen takes me in front head to toe, not missing a single thing. "You sure you are okay? 'Cause I will kill them for you if you want?" I offer and Drax laughs.

"Fuck, I've missed you, babe." "Baby girl," Thorn says fondly.

Maxen's lips turn up as he cups my face. "Not yet, we knew you would come for us." And despite the seriousness of the situation, he kisses me in front of them, kissing me hard, and I lose myself in him almost crying from how much I've missed him, but he pulls back, his eyes filled with amusement and love as he nods and then steps back. "You can fill us in later, for now, I'm betting if you are here instead of killing them all there is a reason."

My fucking men, always ready to trust me and have my back despite being tortured for two weeks. Later, later I will check them over from head to toe and they will pay for hurting them, but Maxen is right. *Stick to the plan*, I remind myself, and straighten again as I flip off the guards who are still hesitating, looking from the dead man to me.

I slip back around the table and into my seat. "It's not a real meeting without at least one death." I smirk and Drax laughs.

"Or more, if you are here," he teases, and I wink at him and turn my attention back to Regina. Then I lose all emotion, going into the mode I kill in, and let her see how much she has messed up. She swallows, but tilts her head back. Defiant until the end. Good, it will be more fun to break her. Maybe Ivar did pass on more than I thought, but right now, I couldn't give two fucks.

"You came into my lands, you stole my men, killed my people, and then you tortured my men," I say, and hold up my hand when she opens her mouth to speak. "Those are acts of war, *prime minister*," I tell her, saying the title sarcastically.

"They were from our Cities, our people—" She starts.

"Which you sent up north to steal our land and secrets and report back." I slowly start to wipe the blood on my knife away on the napkins on the table. "Now, prime minister, tell me why I shouldn't kill you all?"

Chapter Twenty-Three

Fake It Till You Make It

"You speak of war, child, and you don't know war," the older man, Phineese, spits at me. I turn my head slowly to meet his eyes.

"I know more than you do, old man, sitting up here in your fucking glass towers with your workers to wipe your fucking ass, protect your walls, and feed you. I fought, every fucking day, to survive. I've killed more men and women than you can imagine. I have faced the devil himself and walked out of the flames with his scars on my skin. I have conquered clans and kingdoms, won fights and lost them. So, tell me, you old cunt, tell me again how I don't know anything?"

He goes silent and I nod. "That's what I thought. Where I stand, it is you who knows nothing. You're here, secluded with your riches and slaves, and you know nothing of this world anymore. Nothing of what lies north, the land you tried to take from us so-called savages. You kicked the fucking hornet's nest and now you have to pay the price. We will go to war and we will win, and I will take your cities and burn them to the ground...unless you give me one good reason why I shouldn't."

Just then, an explosion rocks the building, and the government gets to their feet, turning their eyes to their windows in shock. A smoke cloud billows in the distance, and over the shouts of the guards and the squabbling of the idiots in the room, I start to laugh. "Looks like you are running out of time, prime minister," I sneer, and she turns to me in anger.

"This is you?" she screams, pointing at the window.

"No, I wish it was. Looks like you have more than me to worry about," I reply and laugh.

I see Maxen's calculating eyes flick to the windows and then back to me, and he smiles slowly, knowing I have a plan. "Calm down, that was a tiny bomb. Send your guards to investigate, but I won't have you delaying anymore. We have business to discuss, and I will make that look like a cut on the fabric of your Cities if you ignore me once more," I warn, deadly serious.

They look back at me, and Regina's face flares in indignation before she sits stiffly on the edge of her seat before looking to the guards. "Send out Team A, find out who that was," she orders, her voice hard, and one of them ducks out of the room, talking into the radio as she turns back to me, sniffing.

"We don't want war with the North," one of the brothers, the one with blue eyes, says and the brown eyed nods.

"We don't," he defends when she sends them a glare.

"It would be silly. So tell us, how do we make peace?" the old man asks and she interrupts.

"That it not your choice to make." She turns back to me. "It is mine, I was voted in by my people to lead."

"Voted in by the rich people," I correct, and then wave for her to carry on.

"That decision is mine, so tell me...Worth. What do you want?"

"A nice beach somewhere and these guys naked, but that isn't happening," I snark, and my men laugh before I get serious. "It's what you want. My armies are waiting to attack, you want peace. You want to ensure you haven't angered the one person in the North capable of pardoning you, so why don't you offer me something, prime minister?"

"We will allow you and your men here to leave, you may have them." She waves her hand and I wait...is she serious? That's it?

I laugh, I can't help it. "You suck at negotiations." Her eyes narrow then. "It is what I am offering."

"Not acceptable. Here are my terms." I grin then, I'm not expecting her to keep them of course, but it's good to lay them down. Fuck, if she does, it solves one issue. "My men leave with me, and I get whoever tortured them and I can do whatever I want to them. We leave the city with a treaty, which states you won't come north we won't come south."

"You cannot!" the old man roars, rising to his feet.

"Sit down!" Regina screams before looking at me. "Do we have time to discuss this, as a government?"

More like time to prepare or think of a way around it. "Of course." I nod, rising and sheathing my weapon.

She rises as well. "Until then, we will of course provide you with a suite to rest in, and your men can bathe. I will send some more clothes for them," she offers, and I almost snarl. I don't want to stay here, but if I say no, I'm the one breaking the truce, so I nod and allow her guards to escort us from the room to the elevator. I notice my swords over one guard's elbow and narrow my eyes.

"Don't get comfy, they are mine," I warn and he gulps, nodding as the elevator pings and we step inside.

A guard steps in with us as I stand in the middle of my men, with Maxen pressed to my back, and Thorn and Drax on either side. Sexual tension fills the air, my skin turning electric from every touch of theirs until I'm almost panting as we rise slowly. It's slow going until the elevator finally pings and we are led down what looks like a hotel hallway to a room at the end, which is unlocked with a key card.

The guard holds the door and I go in first, my men following, and then the door is shut behind us, the light turning red. So they locked us in, not to worry, I could kick down the door.

I turn to face them, but I gasp when lips smash into mine and a body presses to my front, and soon one is pressing against my back as lips explore my shoulders. Hands cup my face, hard, as he stabs his tongue into my mouth, and I melt into his grip, my hands resting on his chest. It's Drax, but this kiss isn't teasing like my usual, flirty love. No, it's hard and desperate and filled with unspoken words. Thorn's cock presses against my ass as he leans over me, covering us both while he kisses my neck and shoulders, and I wrap one of my arms behind his head, holding him to me as my eyes open and lock on Maxen, who is watching us all. His eyes are on fire and his mouth is firm.

Groaning, my eyes flutter closed again as I am picked up and held between them. Neither show signs of slowing, so I rip my mouth away and Drax stumbles as I slip from their hold. They look wild and make moves as if to advance on me again, so I hold out my hand. "Shit, we need to talk first." My voice is rough and my eyes are darting down their bodies, wanting what they are offering.

"Fuck talking," Drax spits, and my eyebrows raise at that as he grabs me around the waist and tosses me in the air.

I sail through it and land on something soft, a bed, and then he is on me again. He grips my hair and turns me to face him, locking his lips to mine as he pushes between my thighs and I let them fall open, moaning at the feel of his hardness pressed against my pussy. He swallows my moan, pulling at my shirt with his other hand like he can't get enough.

"Drax," Maxen orders and Drax moans, burying his face in my shoulder and hair, breathing heavily. I wrap my arms around him and hold him close. My mouth opens, but Maxen shakes his head, holding his finger to his lips and turns and nods at Thorn. I watch as they start at opposite sides of the room and start searching for something.

I want to ask what they're doing, but I trust them, so I relax back into the bed with Drax like a blanket on my body as his breathing returns to normal, but he still rests there as if he can't stop touching me. I know the feeling. My eyes narrow when they pull what look like tiny microphones from inside lamps, walls, and light switches, and start a pile on the table. Soon, the pile is huge with little cameras mixed in. Fucking bastards. Only when they sweep the adjoined bathroom do they nod, then they gather the pile and toss them out of the window and go for another sweep, just to be sure. I relax, letting them do their thing as I look around the room.

The door leads into what looks like a living area, with two cream settees near the windows and a brown table between them. A small kitchenette is on the back wall, which closes into the hallway and the door. The floor is covered in a white rug, which carries on past the partially closed opening and leads into the bedroom we are in.

This room is comprised of one huge bed with matching wooden bedside tables, a chair sitting in the corner near the windows, and a door leading to the bathroom. It's filled with riches, yet bare at the same time. Paintings cover the walls, adding a touch of colour or to hide the devices, I'm not sure. It's so...clean and tidy, and not something I thought I would see in this world. It only showcases our differences.

When Maxen and Thorn nod and relax, I crane my head to see them over Drax's prone form.

"Now can we talk?" I ask. I drop a kiss on his head and roll from under him, rising from the bed as I step towards them, Drax lies back, watching me with predatory gaze, and I don't doubt if I show any hesitation, he will be on me in a second. My eyes go to Thorn and they widen when he rushes at me, twirls me, presses my face against the wall that divides the room, and kicks open my legs while ripping at my trousers.

"Thorn," I start, but he ignores me. "We need to talk, to plan," I press, but he ignores me as he wiggles my trousers down, impatiently growling when they get caught, and then he rips my shirt over my head, kissing down my spine and making me shiver. My eyes go to Maxen and Drax who are just lying on the bed staring, their bodies tense and hard, with heat in their eyes but grins on their lips. My eyes narrow on them, but I gasp when Thorn finally gets my trousers down, and without hesitation, slips his hand in my panties and thrusts a finger inside me.

Fuck.

"Thorn, I need to check you over. We have a lot we need to—" But my fight is diminishing as he starts to move, and despite my words, I'm wet as hell and moving against him. I almost whine when he pulls his finger free, and before I know it, his cock has replaced it, slamming inside me. Fuck, I forgot how big he was. It's pure pain for a second as I grip onto the wall. He pulls my hips back, holding still for a moment as I catch my breath, and then he reaches around me and starts to circle my clit, all the while groaning in my ear.

"Missed you so fucking much," he snarls, and my pussy clenches around him at his words, the pain receding to burning pleasure and I push back, giving up fighting. It's not like I didn't want this. I always want them. "Never thought I'd see you again," he gasps into my ear, before sucking my earlobe into his mouth.

I push back, meeting his thrusts with desperate ones of my own, my body crying out for his. Missing his rough touch and thick cock.

"Had to get rid of them, couldn't let them hear you scream," he rumbles, and I press my face to the plaster, my eyes on my other men as pleasure rockets through me, drawn by his thrusts and hands as he sweeps them down my body. He keeps up that maddening circling on my clit, my nipples scraping against the wall as he touches that spot deep inside me and drags his thick cock over my nerves inside with each hard, brutal thrust.

It's not soft and slow or even fucking, this is goddamn feral. A reassurance, a way to check the other one is really here, and before I know it, I'm screaming as I clench around him and he roars in my ear as he fills my pussy with come.

We both slump into the wall then, with him still inside me, and Maxen beckons me over with a curl of his fingers. Groaning, Thorn slips from inside me and I have to kick off my jeans and panties, not caring about being naked with them as I head over to my other men, almost stumbling on weak legs after the fucking Thorn just gave me.

Their eyes drink me in. Drax grunts as he cups his cock, while Maxen's fists clench as he takes in my body.

I stumble to the bed and Maxen holds his arms open, so I flop onto his chest and lay my head there, listening to the pounding of his heart. It's so fast, like mine. "I missed you," I whisper brokenly.

"We missed you so much, *Mi Alma,*" he rumbles, clutching me to him, but Drax gets tired of waiting and grabs me again, twisting me so my back is to Maxen and I am peering up at his grinning face, which darkens and fades when he looks into my eyes. He moves some hair away from my face, his gaze bouncing between my eyes and over my features like he is tracing them.

"You don't get to leave us again," he whispers darkly, sounding like his brother.

"You left me," I counter, and his eyes narrow.

"If you start getting smart, I will fill that mouth," he warns. "Promise?" I tease.

Maxen grabs my hands, drags them above my head, and holds them to his chest there as Drax yanks me down Maxen's body until my head is resting on his stomach. Maxen's legs spread wide, allowing both Drax and me between them, and I lick my lips as I crane my neck back and stare at Drax, who is running his eyes over my naked body, before meeting my eyes, and I freeze at the dark- ness still there. "I missed you so much, every day and every night I thought of you. Hoping you were safe, imagining what was happening to you..." His fingers trail between my breasts as he talks, and I bite down on my lip, trying to concentrate on his words when fire is trailing in his fingers' wake. "It drove us crazy. You're the strongest person we know, but being without you. Not being able to check that you were okay and with that fucking—" He cuts off, his hand stilling on my thigh before he shakes his head and goes back to trailing it across my body. "Later, you will tell us what happened.

Now, I need to feel you around me. Prove to me you are really here."

His fingers trail across my nipples, back and forth, back and forth, featherlight. Arching up, I try to chase him, but he just pulls away again and goes back to teasing me. I struggle in Maxen's grip and he tightens his hold on my hands, keeping them above me and kissing my wrists over the pulse point. He wraps his ankles over mine and drags my legs wider, pinning me to him for Drax's teasing. Narrowing my eyes on Drax, I snap, "Are you going to fuck me or what?"

"Feeling impatient, babe?" he purrs, twisting my nipple before tracing his fingers across my stomach and down over my pussy and back up again, driving me wild as I buck between them.

"Either fuck me or move and let someone else," I growl, trying to raise my hips as he skates over my pussy again and back up.

He leans down, getting in my face as he cups my neck, again reminding me so much like of his brother it almost hurts, wishing he was here as well. "Behave, I've only had my memories of you for two weeks. I will fuck you when and how I want, and you will lie there and take it. Let them hear your screams," he murmurs before kissing me hard, and swallowing my protests.

I nip at his lip in punishment, and he laughs as he pulls away, his eyes lightening slightly to reveal my usual, teasing Drax. I didn't like the seriousness there, the anger and pain, so if I have to lie here and give up control, the thing I crave, I will. For him, I would do everything. Relaxing back into Maxen, I let him do whatever he wants and he rewards me by trailing his fingers back to my pussy, dipping them inside my wet heat, before stopping to circle my clit and trace around my nipples with my cream. Biting down on my bottom lip, I watch as he dips his head and sucks them clean, rolling his eyes up to me and smirking when he lets go and moves away again, making me groan in frustration.

Maxen laughs underneath me, and I roll my eyes back to glare at him. He smiles down at me, his face filled with love. "So funny watching you trying to be good, *Mi Alma*." His voice rumbles through me. Fuck, is it bad I missed that sound? I could sit and hear him talk all night, just so I know he is here with me. He narrows his eyes on me, obviously seeing the thoughts in my gaze, and turns his head and kisses my arms again in a promise, licking my pulse point as Drax draws my eyes again when he dips his fingers back into my pussy and traces a circle around my belly button, and then licks the path clean before looking at me.

"Fuck, I missed how you taste," he groans, licking his fingers clean before dipping them back inside of me.

"Then why don't you eat me?" I demand, and he licks his lips, watching his fingers as he slowly fucks me with them. "Drax."

He looks up, a grin curling his lips. "Say please."

I narrow my eyes on his, fighting it, and he twists his fingers, speeding up and making me want to rock into them, but I can't because of Maxen. All I can do is lie here and take it. "Please," I snap. "Say, 'please, Drax, eat my sweet little pussy,'" he teases, his

thumb rubbing at my clit now.

Panting hard, sweat dripping between my breasts, I writhe against Maxen's touch, needing to move, and finally give in. "Please, Drax, eat my pussy," I beg.

He doesn't waste time then, he lies between my legs, his tongue lapping at me and making me groan, and arch my head back, unable to move as he eats me. His fingers dip back inside me, teasing me with their slow movements as he sucks my clit into his mouth, humming around it before letting go and dipping his tongue inside of me. Maxen trails kisses down my arms, and before I know it, both of their touches have me coming so hard, I do scream, silently of course, but I writhe between their bodies, needing to move.

I'm still coming down from the high when Drax rears up, grabs my legs from Maxen, tosses them over his thighs, and rams inside of me. My pussy is still sore from Thorn, but I love the bite of pain. It makes it feel, lets me know we are really here together, and if I feel it tomorrow, it's just another bonus. I'll have them with me still.

Crossing my ankles across his back, I urge him to fuck me harder, arching my neglected chest into the air. Maxen switches his grip, holding my hands with one of his own, and cups my breast with the other, feeling the heavy weight and squeezing before playing with my nipples.

Drax watches him and me, his eyes burning as he pulls out and slams back in, before grabbing my hips and lifting me into the air, tilting me so when he slams inside again and pulls out, he drags over that bundle of nerves. He's determined to make me come again, not asking, just yanking it out of me. He keeps up his hard and fast pace, his balls slapping against my skin, while Maxen plays with my nipples. I want to feel him though, I want him to come, so I clench my pussy and his thrusts stutter before he just lets go.

Fucking me, owning me, forcing my body to accept his, he slams inside of me again and again. I realise I am chanting his name as sweat covers every inch of my body, while I move against him and Maxen, rising to meet his thrusts. When he reaches between us and flicks my oversensitive clit, my release takes me by surprise, roaring through me until my eyes blacken and my hearing goes for a minute.

"Eyes on me!" he grits out, and when I flutter them open, he slams home one more time, groaning, his neck straining as he comes.

He collapses on top of me, both of us panting and I wrap my legs around him tighter, keeping him here with me as I try to catch my breath. Sands below, I missed them. Eventually I can breathe properly, but my body is like jelly after being fucked by two men, and I just recline back against Maxen's chest. He pulls me farther up and Thorn joins us on the bed.

Maxen doesn't seem to want to stop touching me either, running gentle, loving strokes all over my body. He draws circles in the palm of my hand, strokes my thigh, and cups my belly, all without even noticing as his hands move over me again and again. *He's reassuring himself I am really here*, I think, but I don't say anything. I love his rough touch, so I lean back and close my eyes, just listening to their breathing.

"So, what happened?" he rumbles from behind me. "Is Ivar..."

"Dead," I admit, and he sighs behind me.

"That mustn't have been easy, I'm sorry, *Mi Alma*, sorry we weren't there." He wraps his arms around me, dropping his chin on my head. A touch on my ankle has me opening my eyes to see Drax flip over onto his front and circle my ankle with his hand, just holding me as Thorn moves closer and presses his head to my thigh.

"Vasilisy is dead," I tell them, my voice empty, and I see Drax wince. I look away then. "Oh, and I'm a queen."

Drax laughs and Thorn smiles, and I feel Maxen grinning against my skin. "You always were," he whispers.

I sigh and lean into them, and tell them everything that has happened, getting them up to date. They listen, asking questions, and wincing when I explain Paradise. When I'm done, I'm exhausted, so I lapse into silence as Drax picks up my hand and starts playing with my fingers, only to freeze at Dray's ring there. Shit, I didn't tell them that. He looks up at me with questions in his eyes, and I swallow. How will they react?

"Tazanna," he warns, narrowing his eyes on me, as Maxen and Thorn still at his tone. "Why the fuck are you wearing a ring?"

Licking my lips, I try to look away, only to meet Thorn's shocked gaze, so I let out a groan. "Dray gave it to me, the crazy bastard married us without asking."

The room is silent for a moment and my heart flips, but then they erupt in laughter and my mouth drops open. "It's not funny!" I mutter, and they only laugh harder, but then Drax stops and looks at Thorn.

"Hey, we need to get her a ring, if this was all it took, I would have done it before now," he whines, and Thorn nods.

"Do I not get a say in this?" I snap, and they both look at me guiltily, so I grin and hold up my other hand.

"I guess I'm as crazy as him, 'cause I got this ring for me from you guys. I didn't do the ceremony like Dray, but I figured that means we are married now to," I offer.

"Is that your way of asking us to be your husbands, *Mi Alma?*" Maxen rumbles behind me.

"If you'll have me?" I ask, suddenly nervous.

"Like you could get away from us," Drax replies with a snort.

"You have me forever," Thorn adds, and I wait for Maxen's reaction.

"We were yours the moment you told us to fuck off, I've told you that before," is what he says, but it wasn't exactly an agreement and he must know that, because he kisses my shoulder. "I'm yours, *Mi Alma*, never doubt that. I don't need a ring to tell me that, my heart has been married to yours for a long time."

Tears fill my eyes as a radiant smile splits my lips.

"Awww, I change my answer to that, let me change my answer!" Drax whines, making me laugh.

"Looks like you are stuck with me," I quip, wishing Jax was here. They seem to know that as well, because they share a look and Drax turns serious for a moment.

"He will be okay, and when we find him, you can ask him to marry you all sweet like you just did us," he teases, and I kick my leg out, making him laugh.

"Asshole," I murmur, although it did settle my nerves.

I relax back, letting their teasing soothe me. I must close my eyes because when the bed moves, they snap open. Thorn is still curled up around me and Drax is snoring at my feet. I catch Maxen's retreating back as he heads into the bathroom and shuts the door. I'm disappointed and a little hurt. Drax and Thorn ravished me the moment I saw them, they missed me that much...but Maxen didn't. Maybe he's holding back. He seemed to be even when he was holding me—afraid to hurt me, possibly? But I want my Maxen, the rough man, I don't want his protection, I want his body. I want him to show me how much he's missed me, so I leave the others asleep and pad after him, intending to confront him.

The door is closed, so I push it open and step inside, closing it softly behind me, and then look around. Steam is billowing through the room already, what the fuck? My eyes widen when Maxen emerges from within it, his face hard, his fists clenched, and his eyes wild. I barely get my mouth open before he is on me. He grabs me under my ass, hoists me into the air, and slams my back into the door, notching his cock at my pussy entrance as he stares into my eyes.

His fingers dig into my ass and I gasp, rubbing against him, and he takes that as permission, burying himself inside of me in one stroke before stilling, his eyes never leaving my face. "Maxen," I whisper, breathing heavily already.

His hair is tied back, so I reach up and undo it, letting it fall around his face in a mass of brown waves, his piercing eyes standing out. He looks fucking brutal, like the savages they claim we are, and it has me clenching around his cock. He flashes pearly white teeth in a predatory grin as he leans closer, his lips almost touching mine. "I wanted you all for myself. I don't mind sharing with my brothers, but sometimes I want to lock you and me away, and fuck you until you can barely walk."

"Is that your plan?"

His lips turn up against mine. "I wish, but I don't think they would let you out of their sight for that long. They have missed you too much."

I swallow hard at that. "And you? Did you miss me?"

He pecks at my lips before answering and I hold my breath. "Every minute of every fucking day we were apart. Do you know how many that was? Fourteen days, three hundred and thirty-six hours. Too many. Too many without that devious smile, without you killing someone, without you stealing my heart without even meaning to. They asked us for information, *Mi Alma*, and all that came to mind when I thought of the North was you. Your fucking face, every time. I couldn't have told them anything even if I wanted to, which I didn't. Jax never doubted you would come for us, he wanted to make sure it was safe when you did. Drax was terrified of what was happening to you, Thorn was worried you would think we just left you, that we wanted to go," he whispers.

"And you?" I repeat.

"Me? I knew you would be safe, no one kills you. I never doubted you, I was worried, worried I would never see you again because they would kill us when we proved useless to them. Worried I would never get to hold you like this, taste your lips, feel you in my arms, watch you close your eyes and curl into my chest. You never needed us to protect you, yet you let us...I was worried I would never get to again. Then you walked into this place like you owned it and demanded us back, and all I could think about was..." He rubs his lips against mine then. "How fucking lucky we are."

He kisses me then before pulling back. "How lucky that in this fucked up, scorched world where people deal in death, we could find you. The other half of our soul, our lost family. It's brutal, it's hard, and each day is a fight out there, but you make it worthwhile, you fight alongside us and make me want to keep going. Keep fighting, for you, always for you. *Mi Alma*, I called you that because I knew when I saw you for the first time, you would either love us or kill us. Either way, I would do it for you. Don't you ever doubt how I feel, because words aren't enough to describe it. It's like trying to describe the intensity of the sun or the beauty of the night sky...but I can show you. Every day for the rest of my life, however long that might be, I can show you. Starting here and now."

Then he swallows my whisper by kissing me hard and starts to move between my legs, showing me with his body just like he said. He stares deep into my eyes, loving me, not fucking me. Each thrust is slow and gentle, cognizant of my aching pussy and body, each a deliberate movement ending with him hitting my clit.

"Maxen," I gasp, pulling his head to me and kissing him.

He holds me there, keeping up those slow thrusts and swallowing my moans, his other hand playing with my breasts or stroking my thigh. It's so fucking sweet, and each time he buries himself in me, bumping my cervix, I feel my next release building up, stronger than ever before, teased out of me, pulled from my very soul.

"I love you," he whispers against my lips, twisting his hips as he tweaks my nipples, and my release roars through me, seemingly pulled from my toes. My throat clamps shut, my legs turning weak as he holds me against him, my pussy clamping around him, and I throw my head back, unable to take it as it seems to keep rolling through me. He waits until I open my eyes again and meet his gaze before he stills, groaning as he comes, filling me so I know I will feel him there tomorrow. He leans his head onto my shoulder, both of us panting. What the fuck just happened? I swear he was controlling my body,

making me feel things I'd never felt...soft things.

Shit, am I going soft?

When he lifts his head from mine, he kisses me so softly that my heart seems to explode in my chest, before turning with me still in his arms and hopping into the shower. He lets me slide down his body and spins me to face the spray, then washes my body for me with gentle, insistent strokes of his hands, cleaning every inch of me. He inspects me, noting any new scars and marks, and asks about them before kissing them better and moving on, and when we step out and he dries me, refusing to let me do it myself, I feel like he just won my heart all over again.

Sometimes, I want hard and rough in my men, but behind closed doors, I can admit that once in a while I need to be held and treasured.

A knock from the hallway door has us freezing, and I quickly grab my clothes and slip into them as Maxen does the same. Have they come to a decision? Or are they about to declare war? Either way, I'm doing it with pants on.

Chapter Twenty-Four

MY SILENT DEMON

When we reach the other room, Thorn is already opening the door. I palm a knife and keep it hidden behind my thigh just in case, and then wait next to Drax and Maxen who have spread across the living room entrance with enough room to fight between us. One of the guards who was stationed outside of the door comes in, and brings in an armful of clothing, then places it on the sofa as we put our backs to the door. He takes that moment to sweep the room, an angry spark in his eyes, probably from the fact they can't spy on us anymore, so I step forward.

"You can leave now, oh, and please tell Regina to send some food up if she plans on dicking us around much longer." Then with that, I turn my back on him and head into the bedroom.

I hear my men escorting him out before the door is shut and locked again, then a disgusted snarl comes from the living room, so after plaiting my hair, I head back out and lean against the doorway, seeing my men hold up the clothing they brought for us. Drax is holding up what looks like suit trousers and a shirt, his mouth twisted in horror and he looks at me. "I'm not fucking wearing that."

I laugh, I can't help it, until I take in the dress Thorn is dangling from his finger and then it snaps my mouth shut as I stand up and step towards it. "What the fuck is that?" I ask, eyeing the skimpy bit of clothing they provided. It looks like something a common whore would wear. Gold material—okay, so maybe more like a high-class whore—low cut, and skin-tight. "How the fuck do you fight or hide weapons in that?"

"I think that's the point, *Mi Alma.*" Maxen smirks and I shake my head.

"Still, I'm not wearing that." An evil idea comes to mind then and I grin, holding out my hands. "Give it to me though."

Thorn laughs, throwing the material to me. "Oh, and search the pile and where he went to make sure he didn't plant any more listening devices," I murmur as I turn and head to the bed.

"Shit, I didn't even think of that," Drax groans.

Laying the dress down on the bed, I grab my knife and start cutting, almost laughing as I imagine Regina's face when she sees what I did to her fancy fuck you dress, one clearly meant as an insult to me. She doesn't know who she is playing with. Once I'm finished, I look down and almost smirk as I twine the edges together, making an impromptu weapons holster and also a strong bit of doubled up fabric into a choker—just another handy weapon. I should be thanking her really. I strap on the holster and slip one of my knives in it, openly wearing it as I head back to see the other clothes tossed in a pile on the floor and my guys sat around waiting for me.

When they spot me, they start laughing, their eyes lighting up. "Oh, she is going to lose her shit," Thorn comments, and I nod.

"I can't wait. Now, what do we do while we wait for her reply?" I inquire, tilting my head and looking around.

"I can think of something," Drax purrs, wiggling his eyebrows at me.

"This was not what I had in mind when you said you thought of something." I laugh, he's like an excited kid, and yes, I guess so am I. His enthusiasm is contagious, and although my mind had gone to dirty places, I have to admit this is better. My body is still sore and I could do with a bit of a laugh, which he knew, like always, and took it upon himself to help us all lighten up despite the looming war.

I might be a queen now, but here, with my men, I'm still Worth and apparently...a child right now. Sands below, if my armies could see me now.

We are having a fashion show. My men readily dress up and parade in front of me. Every time I laugh or smile their eyes light up, and they seem to try extra hard, competing to see who can make me laugh the most. I have to admit, they look good in the suits, but then the outfits get more and more ridiculous. Drax makes one of the shirts into a crop top and walks around with his hand bend out and his head thrown back. Maxen cuts his into shorts and pulls the socks up to his knees, looking like a bloody schoolboy, but Thorn. Oh God, when he steps out of the bedroom, I swear I pee a little.

He has the rest of the gold material that I had cut up and fashioned it into a top and what looks like a skirt. He winks at me, sashaying across the room and striking a pose in the middle of the living room. I can't take my eyes off him, even as I laugh so hard tears track down my face. Drax actually falls to the floor laughing and

Maxen is holding his stomach, all the while Thorn winks and shimmies between us in the golden number.

"Stop, make it stop," Drax cries, and rolls over and looks up before cringing when he looks up Thorn's skirt. "Shit, I didn't need to see that," he grumbles, setting us off again. When we finally catch our breath, Thorn comes and sits next to me, smirking at his obvious win of making us laugh the most.

"Your turn!" Drax calls, still spread on the floor from where he fell laughing. All eyes go to me then, ready and waiting, so I stand up, make sure they can all see me, and strip. When I'm in nothing but my boots and knives, I wink at them and head into the bedroom, hearing them groan.

"Oh, she fucking wins!" Drax calls as he races after me, making me laugh once again as I hear Maxen and Thorn fighting each other to be the second to reach me.

Food gets delivered not much later, and we all sit on the floor around the coffee table in the middle of the sofas and eat while they fill me in on what happened. They don't gloss over what happened to them, and for that I'm grateful. They know I am strong enough to handle it. They were tortured for at least three days, while I was out there. I make them tell me exactly how and afterwards, I am filled with rage, but I keep it in check until they have finished telling me.

After the government realised they couldn't torture the information out of them, they left them alone to look for a different approach, and then when Jax escaped they turned their attention to him, sending patrols to the North to check if we were advancing on them. Apparently, they sent patrols near where Piper is as well, but I know she can handle it, so I don't stress. Once I'm full and know what happened, I sit back and look over each and every one of them.

"They will pay for hurting you," I declare, and Maxen reaches across and twines our hands.

"Let it go, Worth, we are together again. That's all that matters. Now, how about we talk about this plan? You getting revenge will have to wait, I think," he says softly, and as pissed as I am, I know he's right. I can't go up there and kill them all, no matter how much I want to, so instead I focus on the plan we have in place. Too many people are depending on this plan for it to go wrong. Then, while they are cleaning up, I head to the door. I have to knock and when the light turns green I stick my head out, glaring at the guards there.

"I need to speak with Regina," I snap, and they share a look.

"She is indisposed. She will be meeting you in the morning. You are not to leave your suite," he orders, and I step out to face him.

"I just left it, what are you going to do?" I ask, tilting my head at him.

He freezes and I laugh. "Just what I thought. Don't make idle threats, boy. I will gut you for breakfast." Then I slam the door in their incredulous faces.

Morning, we have to wait until morning. I know my armies will be moving into place soon, so let's hope I can pull off my end of the plan.

Staring out of the living room window on the city below, I am lost in my own thoughts when arms wrap around me and pull me back into a hard chest. I inhale deeply and smell Thorn, even as he lays a gentle kiss on my shoulder, not talking, just holding me as I stare. I've spotted at least two more explosions, so it seems Strand and Dray are doing their jobs, keeping them distracted and running around the city. One was even close to this building—Dray's idea, I am betting. A way of telling me he is close.

"Do you think it will work? What if they just decide to kill us?" Thorn asks.

"Then they face the army I told them was waiting outside their walls, and when I don't come back, they attack. I've looked at this from every direction, and I don't see how they could refuse, not to my face anyway, and now that I have met them, I'm only more certain. They prefer to work in the shadows, make sly moves, so they won't turn down a peace, but they won't uphold it either," I explain, turning in his arms to face him.

"We will stand with you, no matter what," he replies, cupping my face. I lean into his touch, resting my cheek in his huge palm.

"I know. Whatever happens, we face it together," I say, closing my eyes and just soaking in his warmth. I hate this waiting around and political manoeuvres, I would rather just fight and get it over with, but I rein myself in, knowing this is the best way. Patience, that's what I need, something that has never been my strong suit.

I turn back to the window and we silently watch the sun setting over the sands in the distance. Somewhere out there my armies are mobilizing, waiting for me to lead them to war.

"*Mi Alma*, come on, you need to rest. I have a feeling we won't be getting much of that after today," Maxen calls, and I look over my shoulder to see him already stripped down to his briefs, waiting for me at the bedroom door. I nod and twine my hand with Thorn's heading to the bedroom. He's right, of course, and in there I can relax and let down my guard. Soaking in their protection, just for a little bit.

Drax is already sprawled on the bed, waiting for me, so I climb up next to him, placing my back to his, and open my arms for Thorn who slips in next to me. Maxen lies on the other side, turned to face the door. With their heat around me, I close my eyes and force myself to sleep, their scents mixing, their bodies touching mine somewhere, and when Maxen reaches over resting his fingers on my stomach, I finally go to sleep.

I wake up suddenly, my heart racing, and sit up. Thorn's arm falls to my lap from where it was draped across me, his body curled around me from the side. Drax is on my other side, face down in the bed, and his legs are entwined with mine. Something is off. I search the room, my eyes landing on a figure in the chair. From the bulk, I know it's Maxen, but I don't know why he's over there.

He's leaning forward, his arms dangling between his legs as he watches me, his face cast in shadows. I slip from between my men, rising slowly, and head over to him. He leans back as I approach him and I climb on the chair, straddling his lap with my legs either side. "What's wrong?" I whisper, so I don't wake the others.

"Just watching you," he rumbles, his arms coming around me and pulling me further down until my chest meets his. "I never thought I would get to see you again, so I am memorising your face. I don't want to look away in case this is all a dream. I want to watch you all day every day, so you don't disappear again."

Sighing, I lean into him, loving his touch. Thorn's and Drax's deep snores are our lullaby as we hold each other. "I don't know what will happen out there, they might be stuck up, but their guards are fighters and have guns. I need you to promise me something," I whisper, and then look into his eyes, grabbing his cheeks and holding him still. "Promise me you will fight like a Berserker. You don't get to die on me, any of you. This isn't fucking Romeo and Juliet, I plan on us living a long time together, so no fucking tragic endings for us. Promise me you will live," I demand, knowing what I am asking is harsh and steep, but I need to hear it. I couldn't bear to lose any of them, which I know is stupid in times of war. Life is so fragile and easily extinguished, but I'm asking him to fight the grim reaper for me and stay. Stay with me, give me that life I dream of and we talked about.

He smiles, a sweet fucking one that wrecks my heart. "I won't promise that, *Mi Alma*. If it comes to saving you and dying, you know what I will pick. I will promise you to live or die by your side though." Cutting my eyes away, I want to smack his fucking handsome face, to scream at him, but he pulls me closer, forcing my gaze back to his. "I know it's not what you want to hear, and I know you can protect yourself, but everyone needs someone to put their back to. Everyone can be hurt or worse, killed, and I will not lose you. This world needs you, *they* need you." He nods at the men sleeping behind us. "If I have to die to keep you alive, I will, I don't fear death, I fear living in a world without you. I know it's hard for you to accept, you are so fucking strong and stubborn, but you can't stop me, Tazanna Worth. You are irreplaceable, I am not. You have four other men to

love you and give you that life, I will make sure you stay alive for it."

I rip myself away from him and stomp into the living room. I hear him silently following me and spin to see him, outraged. "You think you are replaceable? You aren't to me!" I almost yell. "I can't do this without you! Don't you see losing any one of you, losing you, would kill me? You would die to protect me? Well, it goes both ways!" I do shout this time, I hear the others' snoring cut off, awake now, but I don't care. Let them hear.

"*Mi Alma*," Maxen says, but I turn away from him, pacing the room, staying away from his grabbing hands.

"You all say I'm this big fucking deal, that I'm the one the world needs, but I'm nothing without all of you. I was fucking surviving, that's it, kept fucking moving, and you-you came in and made me live again. Forced me to feel, made me love you, and now you are saying you will die." I stop then, my fists clenched at my sides and my chest heaving. "You can't, you can't die on me, Maxen, I won't allow it."

He walks towards me, watching me closely like I'm a wild animal, then he cups my fists. "Okay."

"Okay?" I repeat.

"Okay, how about we promise each other something else instead. We promise each other to fight, to love each other always. Promise that no matter what, we never give up on each other, even when we don't see eye to eye," he says softly, staring into my eyes as I search his for the answers to this. "Promise me, *Mi Alma*, promise me you will always love me."

"I promise," I reply raggedly.

"I promise too, I'll never leave your back, that's where I belong. Protecting it for the rest of our days," he vows, placing his forehead to mine, and I close my eyes, the fear of losing him subsiding.

"I love you," I whisper. That's where this all stems from. Love, I love him, and it would be so easy to walk away right now, to stop the pain that would come if I lost him, but that would be the weak woman's way out, and I have never been weak or a coward. It takes a strong person to love someone, and an even stronger one to stay when it gets hard and the future is uncertain.

Arms wrap around us both then, silently promising us too, and we stay in our huddle. All our fears are on display, yet we choose to stay together through them all until a knock at the door interrupts us. I grab a shirt, slip it on, and palm a knife as Maxen opens the door, peeking out before it's pushed open and a guard strides in. He ignores the men who are now surrounding him, ready to attack, and looks at me.

"I have a present from Strand," is all he says and then steps back, revealing a man in a cape waiting there. I can't make out much of his face or body because of the frumpy material so I frown, looking between him and the guard, until the man throws back the cape and I gasp.

"I thought he was lying to me, Angel, but you're here. You are really here."

I can't seem to move, and my breath is caught in my throat as I stare into those grey eyes. Ones I missed so much it hurts. It feels like I'm whole again, my heart exploding in my chest, and before I know it, we are both moving towards each other. We clash hard, his hands fisting in my hair and yanking me to him as I smash my lips to his. I bite hard on his lower lip in punishment and he groans, our kiss turning harsh as I wrench him to me, but he comes willingly. His hands traces down my back and cups my ass, bringing me flush against him as our teeth clash.

He groans into my mouth and I swallow it down, yanking on his hair, pulling his head back, and breaking our kiss. I stretch his neck at an awkward angle, making it hurt and his eyes dilate as his lips part. He does not fighting me as I hold him there. Jax's demons come out in his eyes as he watches me, waiting for whatever else I want to do to him. "Angel," he begs, wanting more, but I jerk his head back more and he hisses.

"What the fuck were you thinking?" I snap.

"Babe—" Drax starts, but I snap my eyes up to him, glaring at him and he shuts up, miming zipping his mouth.

I look back at Jax to see him smiling at me, loving the pain I give him like always. "Had to make sure it was safe for you," he offers, and I narrow my eyes on him, twisting my hand in his hair, tugging on the strands and he licks at his lip, panting. "I knew you would come, I wanted to make sure you could get to us."

Bending my head to his, I whisper against his lips, "You do shit like that again and I will strap you to my bed and leave you there, then I will make you watch as I fuck everyone but you, and still I will leave you there, not even touching you," I purr, ensuring he hears the fucking warning, because I had been terrified when I didn't see my damaged man waiting for me. My poor, silent demon.

He lets out a moan, pulling against my hand to tug on his hair, always ready for more from me, taking whatever I give out. Whereas me and Dray fight a constant battle, Jax takes it all without reservation or judgement and begs for me. I could cut him open and pull out his heart, and he would let me with a smile on his face and my name on his lips. "I'd do it for you," he replies, begging me with his eyes for more, for me to touch him.

"I know you would," I murmur, kissing him softly, making him chase after my lips. Jax is all mine, his body yearning for me, for my touch. I love teaching him new things and being in charge with him, so I let go of his hair and step back and he frowns, moving closer again, not knowing how to tell me what he wants. He doesn't speak much, always silent from his upbringing. I love to hear him speak so I wait, not letting him get away with not speaking now.

"How are you here?" I question eventually and he sighs.

"Dray and some man named Strand found me. I had been working some of our contacts from back when we lived here and getting them riled up. They heard and found me. Dray explained everything and they snuck me back in to help piss off the government and prove your power. Dray and Strand will carry on with the rest of the plan, I'll be by your side," he explains, stepping closer again, his eyes not moving from mine.

"They are okay?" I ask, and he nods.

"The leaders have started raids on some of the lower houses and camps, but they are turning up empty, they don't know who is behind the bombs." He smiles then. "Least of all that she is under their roof."

"Good, let's keep it like that. We are meeting with Regina in the morning. We will pretend like nothing has happened and not give an explanation for why you are here. It will annoy her that it happened right under her nose." I smirk then, winking back at Drax as he laughs. When he catches my eye, he winks and looks to his brother with a pleading look, and I nod.

"Right, let's leave the love birds to catch up," he suggests, grabbing Maxen and Thorn.

Thorn frowns, looking to me and Drax nudges him. "We let you fuck her into a wall within two minutes of seeing her," he reminds him, and laughs as Thorn grins at the memory. They all head into the bedroom, presumably going back to bed and sleep, leaving Jaz and me alone in the living room. He watches me from meters away, not even blinking, waiting for me to make the first move. Stepping around him, I walk into the kitchenette and hop up on the counter, parting my legs and beckoning him closer.

He's in front of me in a minute, pressing between them, with his hands resting on the counter next to me. Not touching, but so close I can feel his heat. I wonder how far I can push him, making that other side I know of Jax come out. The one who knows exactly what he wants and takes it. "On your knees," I order, and he drops to them instantly, his head level with my crotch and my bare pussy—I did only slip on a shirt, after all. His eyes light up with hunger as he licks his lips, his fingers digging into the counter to hold himself still.

"Angel, please," he begs, rolling his eyes up to mine.

"Please what?" I ask, leaning back casually, spreading my legs wider.

"I need to taste you, I need you," he rushes out, his hands grabbing my thighs and digging in as he looks at my pussy.

I'm just as needy as him, wanting to feel him inside of me, missing my Jax, but this is our dance. Each of us pushes the other to the breaking point and then further, losing ourselves in each other. "Then taste me," I purr.

He grabs my thighs, yanking me to the edge of the counter, and covers my pussy with his mouth. He's a quick learner. The first time he did this was under the stars, and I still remember his talented fucking tongue and he reminds me of it now, flicking it across my clit in harsh little taps before dipping it into my pussy and spreading my wetness everywhere. Tasting me, leaving no spot untouched as he declares battle on me. His fingers dig deeper into my legs, no doubt leaving bruises, always leaving his mark. Tilting back on my arms, I press my pussy to his face, wordlessly begging him for more as I stare at the darkened ceiling, thinking of his brother and my other men feet away, able to hear us.

Without me telling him, he presses a finger to my opening, just teasing me as he nips at my clit, making me gasp and raise my hips to rock against his face. Reaching between my legs, I grab his hair, twining my hands in the short strands and yank him closer, making him hum against my pussy and dip that finger inside, but it's not enough. I rock against him, frustrated as he teases me, until I nearly rip his hair out and he adds another finger, his thumb pressing on my other hole, just holding there.

Sands below.

Closing my eyes, I ride his face and fingers, pushing them deeper, and his thumb slips inside of me, making me moan. He twists his fingers inside me, lashing me again and again with his tongue, and I come apart on that clever tongue, shaking with the force of it, biting on my lip to keep quiet as I clamp down on his fingers. He doesn't stop licking me though, instead pushing me through it and straight into another, and a squeak escapes as I thrash against his face. He pulls back, panting, his chin sparkling with my cream and his eyes alight with satisfaction. He pulls his fingers from my pussy and flicks open his jeans, palming his cock and stroking himself as I watch.

"Jax," I snap, and he grins at me as he carries on stroking, thrusting into his own hand as he takes in my prone body, my pussy still on display for him.

"You told me you wouldn't touch me. I'm making sure you don't." He grins and I narrow my eyes, that little bastard I never—fuck.

I almost groan as he stands up and leans back against the island and spread his legs, watching me as he fucks his own fist. He looks at my pussy again and then back to me. "Touch yourself."

I raise my eyebrow and yank off my top, baring my breasts and he groans, staring at them as I twist and flick my nipples, playing him at his own game, wanting him to break and fuck me. I run hands across my body, slipping one over my pussy and the other at my breasts, fucking myself for him as he stares.

Watching his hand, his cock, my eyes drag over his body as I imagine my hands are his. Bringing up a leg, I bend my knee and place my foot on the counter so I can get a better angle and show him everything. He moans, his eyes wide and desperate, and when I see him trying to hold back, I smirk. He steps closer, almost touching me.

"Come," I demand, and he does like a good boy.

He comes with a groan, his head falling back as he shoots across my flushed chest, and I come on my own fingers. He stumbles into me, leaning next to me on the counter as we both catch our breaths. He didn't fuck me. I narrow my eyes and he smiles softly at me, before standing enough to give me a soft kiss. "The way I see it, you punished me now," he whispers, before throwing me over his shoulder and striding into the bathroom. I would fight him, but honestly, I can't be bothered to. I've been well used today, and my pussy is sore and aching, and my brain is almost mush from the whiplash, so I let him clean me up and then he tucks me into bed, next to a snoring Drax.

Thorn and Maxen are behind him, both asleep. Jax slips in next to me, even though it's a tight squeeze. He basically lies on top of me with his head on my chest, no doubt hearing my still racing heart, and we just hold each other, both of our eyes locked, communicating silently. We don't need words to tell each other how much we love each other, how much we missed each other, and in this moment, everything is how it should be.

Even in the middle of enemy territory, I found happiness.

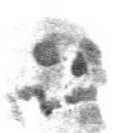

I wake up hot, really hot, with a body against my back and lying on top of me. Blinking, I turn my head into the pillow to see Thorn and Drax still asleep, now cuddling each other, and I can hear the shower running in the other room—must be Maxen. I'm just about to go back to sleep when fingers push my legs apart, wiggling between them and stroking my still sore pussy, so softly that it doesn't hurt.

Shit, now I'm wide awake. I crane my head and spot Jax draped across my back, watching me. "I figured my punishment was over."

I find myself rocking against his hand, needing to come again even after all the releases I had yesterday. These guys have made me insatiable, and when he pulls his hand away, I groan, but he replaces it with his cock. The angle isn't right, so he grabs my hips and yanks my ass into the air, pressing my face farther into the pillow, and slips inside of me slowly, being gentle. He drapes himself back over me, kissing my shoulders as he fucks me slowly, lovingly...until I start pushing back on him, begging him for more as noises leave my lips when he picks up speed.

He bites my shoulder and I let out a breathy moan. He moves behind me, kneeling, and starts to fuck me in earnest, his balls slapping against my skin as I twist the sheets in my hands, needing more.

"Will you two keep it down?" Drax mumbles, turning over and cracking open an eye, but when he sees me, he opens them fully and a smirk covers his face. "Well, fucking good morning to you too."

My face is pressed to the bedspread as Jax hammers between my legs, pain and pleasure mixing together. I need more and Drax eyes my mouth, no doubt thinking about his words yesterday. He moves up, pressing his back to the headboard, and Jax pushes me over to him, where his cock is already hard and waiting. I don't wait, I suck him down deep and he yells, thrusting deeper into my mouth, waking Thorn who I can see watching us out of the corner of my eye. I don't know why the thought of him watching makes me moan, but it does, around Drax's cock who gasps and pushes deeper, forcing me to take his length. I pull back and suck him down again, catching my teeth on his length. Him and his brother find a rhythm, when Jax pulls out, Drax thrusts in, until they are holding me between them, fucking me, but I know I have all the power here. I clench my pussy on Jax who roars, and then suck all of Dax down who yells, spilling in my throat, and when I lick him clean and look over at Thorn, I see he has his hand wrapped around his cock, his chest covered in his release.

We all slump back to the bed, spent. "Shit, I missed all the fun," Maxen complains from the door and we all laugh. I didn't even hear the door open, but it doesn't matter. I'm just glad they are all here.

What a way to start a day, especially when I will find out today if we have to fight our way out of the Cities. The thought sobers me, and I kiss them all good morning before heading to the bathroom to clean up. Group sex is fun, but afterwards there is one hell of a mess.

CHAPTER TWENTY-FIVE

THE DEAD MAN

Once we are all dressed, we sit in the living room, waiting for them to come and collect us to meet with Regina again. Two explosions went off during the night and another one sounds now. It comforts me, letting me know Dray is still out there, and by now I'm betting Regina is plenty annoyed. She keeps us waiting and I am starting to get annoyed also when the door finally opens.

"She is waiting for you," the guard announces, and I stand up slowly, checking over my golden holster before stretching, taking my time. She kept us waiting, so I will keep her waiting as well.

The guys fall in behind me as we are led to the elevator and back up to the meeting room we started in yesterday. Regina is there when we arrive. She takes me in, frowning when she realises I'm not in the dress, and when she sees the golden holster with a knife, her eyes flash in displeasure. I grin and then almost laugh when I step in, revealing Jax behind me. Her eyes go wide, looking from me to him, but she doesn't call us out, since that would make her look weak and it's not just her in here today. All the other men are back, and there are a few more who she introduces as parliament as I head to the seat at the head of the table and sit again, watching while she glares as I take her chair once more.

"Have you come to an agreement?" I inquire straight away, cutting through the bullshit.

"No yet, we are meeting to discuss that today. We had other matters which occupied us yesterday. Ones I thought you might like to be part of." She stands then, smoothing out her skirt. "We were investigating the bombs, if you would follow me," she calls, and I stand as we all file out of the room. She falls in next to me as she leads us to an open area of the office space.

"We found someone inciting the outers and brought him here. He was tortured for information and then killed of course." She dabs her mouth then, like the thought is distasteful, but my heart freezes.

Strand? No, she would have known he was one of hers...Dray?

No, it can't be.

"You wouldn't happen to know anything about it, would you?" she asks.

"Me? Don't blame your mess on me," I snap. Playing cool and calm when I am anything but, with my heart clawing at my insides and banging against my ribs to get out as my head screams at me, is the hardest thing I have ever done.

No, it can't be him. He's indestructible.

No one can kill the Seeker King.

The ten steps it takes to get down to where her guards are blocking someone on the floor, only his feet visible, are the longest of my life. My heart is in my throat and bile claws at me as I repeat his name in my head like a mantra, trying to tell myself I'm wrong, but I have a bad feeling. A really bad fucking feeling.

When we stand in front of the guards, I nearly throw up, but I hold it down as they step aside to show me the man face down on the floor in a puddle of his own blood, my own icy and frozen in my veins.

It's not him.

I have never been so happy to see a dead body before, but I don't let that relief show knowing she is scrutinising my face for any hints of recognition. When she doesn't find what she wants, she almost snarls but holds it in. "We thought he might be one of yours."

"Sorry to disappoint." I shrug.

She steps closer then. "And how did you find your other man?" she questions, her voice low and not carrying.

"Secrets, Regina, are what the Cities runs on. You should know that. If you haven't decided yet, maybe we should let you. The clock is ticking after all. If I'm not back with my armies tomorrow, they will attack. Tick tock," I call, before turning and leaving, heading for the elevator. She wanted time, she wanted to wound me, and she was getting too close to the truth. Hopefully reminding her of what is waiting just outside her gates, and being left with no other options, she will agree to my terms.

"You will have your answer in the morning," she retorts, and I ignore her as I step onto the elevator. When the doors close, a relieved breath hisses through my teeth. Fucking hell, I just saw ten years taken of my life right there.

Shit, another night in this snake's den. At least I have my men to pass the time with.

We are escorted back to our rooms, and just when the door shuts an explosion rocks the building. I rush to the window to see the plume of smoke not two buildings down. Strand and Dray are getting daring. Hopefully, it will put more pressure on Regina and her government.

We are brought dinner and then locked up again. I start to get really frustrated. I'm not one to be locked away with nothing to do. Usually, I'm on the move all the time. Out on the open road of the Wastes, not locked in this gilded prison.

When they get bored with watching me pace, Thorn snags me around the waist and pulls me down on top of him on the sofa, forcing me to cuddle into him as the guys and him talk about every-thing and anything, including their life before they met me here in the Cities. Having been to the outers, I can understand why they were getting out now.

"Do you have any family here?" I ask out of the blue, and they stop talking to look at me.

"Nope, they are all dead." Drax shrugs. "Nothing left for us here. We have some old friends, but no one that would risk the wrath of Regina and her lackies."

That makes me feel better, petty, but true. I guess all we have is each other now. I force myself to relax into Thorn and join in their conversation. My body is still sore from our reunion and Drax must notice me shifting with a wince, because he hops up and disappears. I watch him go with a frown until I hear water running in the bathroom. He comes back a couple of minutes later and offers me his hand. "A hot bath will help," he says sweetly.

I place my hand in his and let him lead me from the room. Maxen kisses me on the way past and carries on talking to Jax about what he found out there. I know they will let me know anything important, so I leave them to it and let Drax tug me into the bathroom where a bath is nearly half full. I slip out of my clothes, leaving my remaining daggers on the sink, and slip into the warm water as it is still running. He shuts the toilet lid and perches there, swirling his finger in the bathwater before adding some pearlescent liquid. My eyes widen when the bath begins to froth up and he laughs. I grin and lean back, unashamed to be naked. He looks his fill, but keeps his hands to himself and lets us lapse into silence as I float in warm water. He was right, it relaxes my muscles and I do feel better, but it also makes me think of Dray.

It was a close call today. I never knew I could feel fear like that, but Dray has always seemed so indestructible, yet faced with his death, I was a fucking mess and now sitting in the bath, the thing we always do together, I find myself aching for his arms just to know he is okay. Drax must sense that, because he kneels next to the bath and grabs my leg, starting to massage in the soap all the way from toe to hip before doing the other, his arms getting wet as he leans over me. The caring and soft way he is looking after me brings tears to my eyes, which I blink away and let him work me until I'm putty. He even washes my hair and shaves my legs for me. And when he's done, I do feel better, refreshed and ready to take them on again. He pulls me from the tub and drains it. While I dry off, he heads out into the room. I finger comb my hair before throwing it back wet, and I'm just about to leave when he comes in with a shirt for me to wear.

"I'll wash your clothes. Go and sit with my brother, won't you?" He kisses me on the cheek and I grin as I slip into his shirt, noting he's now shirtless. Cheeky bastard. I check out his muscles, but leave the bathroom when he spanks me with my jeans, making me laugh and go in search of his brother, who is sitting alone on the sofa, watching Thorn and Maxen arm wrestle over the coffee table. When he sees me coming, his eyes light up and he moves over.

I recline next to him, cuddling into his side, and he draws me closer, so I throw my legs over his and curl into his side, leaning my head there as I watch Maxen and Thorn. Jax leans down and kisses my head softly, sighing in happiness, content to lapse into silence as long as I am with him.

Eventually, Drax joins us, cuddling into my other side and we take turns arm wrestling, they all beat me, not bothering to let me win. We laugh, we talk, and I feel happy again. Like a weight has been lifted with them by my side, but what I told Regina is true, the clock is ticking, and I can feel each move of the hand.

With the countdown on, it splits my attention and I realise that it's always like this. We are always waiting for something to happen or we are on the move, fighting something, making our snatched moments meaning so much more...but I can't wait to not have to snatch moments one day. For the rest of my life to be like this, filled with my men, happiness, and family, but I can't help but feel it would be better out in the sands instead of this pretty prison...I never believed in fairy tales, but these guys have me believing. Too bad the fairy tales always turned sad before the characters live happy ever after.

We are brought more food for tea. I've never been fed so well. Regina is clearly taking the time to show off if the spread of the buffet is to suggest anything. There is enough here to feed an army. As a person who has felt hunger before, who had to watch like a dog at a man's feet, waiting for scraps, it annoys me. Especially when I think about all those mouths who need feeding in the outers. I try not to waste any, but after eating a whole roast pig, some form of potatoes and veg, and yes, even chocolate, I am beyond full and end up sprawled across the bed. If her plan was to feed us so much and then kill us while we were in a food coma, it would certainly work.

With nothing else to do, we all just lay about on the bed, a tangle of limbs and full stomachs, and eventually I go to sleep. When I wake up, it's dark out and the room is pitch-black, snores filling the air and limbs holding me down from all angles. I'm a sweaty mess from all the bodies. I groan and roll, slipping from the bed and padding into the kitchenette to grab a glass of water. I'm sipping from it when the floor shakes, and I look out of the window, seeing two more explosions spread across the Cities. At this rate, they will have nothing left. "You have to give it to that crazy man. He sure knows how to have a party," Drax mumbles tiredly, and I grin over at him as he yawns and stretches, coming over to peer out of the window with me. He grabs my water and takes a swallow as we see another explosion go off, followed by what looks like blue lights flashing afterwards, heading that way. We watch the lights of the Cities as they respond to the explosions and the darkened sands beyond the wall, calling us home.

"I always thought it was too bright in this place. Watching the stars on the sands with you only hit that home. We came back and saw everything for what it was. Even camping with sand in places there shouldn't be, sweating our tits off and usually covered in blood, I was happier out there than I ever was in here," he admits and we share a smile.

"I feel the same, this feels so foreign to me, a world that doesn't belong anymore. Like people are clinging on to the past. That might make me a savage, but I won't deny I feel so much more at home out there than I ever could here," I agree, and he leans against me, both of us looking over the sprawling city below. For some, this would be paradise, people are even fighting over leading it. They can have it for all I care, this isn't home, just a stepping stone on the way to securing our home.

"Let's go back to bed, baby." He kisses my shoulder, grabbing the glass and putting it on the window ledge before leading me be back to the bedroom.

I climb up onto the bed, spotting Thorn awake and watching us in the dark, his skin glistening in the moonlight. Crawling towards him, I stop and lay a kiss on his stomach and then on his lips. He smiles sweetly up at me, cupping my cheek.

"Need help sleeping?" he whispers and I nod, kissing his hand.

He looks behind me then and shares a grin with Drax, who I feel crouched behind us. "You heard her, we need to help her sleep."

"As she commands," he teases, his voice loud in the dark room, but Jax and Maxen are still sleeping. It's just Drax, Thorn, and I.

Thorn pulls me down to him, kissing me sweetly, and sucking on my tongue before pulling back and pecking my lips. Keeping me chasing after him, he massages my lower back which has me groaning in bliss. How did he know it was sore?

"Drax is going to play with that pretty ass, I'm too big to," he whispers, and I shiver from his words, pressing down harder on his cock, which is rapidly hardening against me. He goes back to kissing me, just massaging my back, neither of them in any hurry. Drax kisses across my shoulders and down my spine as he strokes my legs.

When Drax's hands finally go to my pussy, I'm wet from all their touching, and the glide of their rough hands on my skin. He kisses above my new tattoos so sweetly that I shiver again and press back into his hands, telling him without words I want him to touch me. He runs a finger down my pussy, while Thorn swallows my encourage-ments and skim his hands upwards, massaging until he brings them between our bodies and uses that same soft skill on my breasts.

Drax dips two fingers into me, scissoring them before slowly pulling them out and pushing them back in, stretching my pussy as his other hand plays with my clit. Thorn covers my nipples, his hands hard on my breasts as I rock against Drax, my body humming with need again, and I yank my mouth away from Thorn, kissing down his throat.

He twists my nipples, flicking them before moving his hands to my back, running them down until he cups my arse and then he parts my cheeks. "Make sure she is nice and wet," he whispers to Drax who groans, matching the noise that escapes me when he pulls his wet fingers from my pussy, and slips one in. I push out to let him, the ring of muscles giving way and letting him in, and he slowly fucks me with it before adding another, stretching out my ass for him. He adds a third and I bite down against Thorn's neck to muffle my yell, pushing back onto his fingers as he plays with my ass.

Thorn holds my cheeks for Drax, his cock still hard between us, and I moan, needing someone in my pussy. Drax must hear my unspoken plea, because he lines his cock up and slips inside, stilling once he is balls deep, letting me stretch around his width before fucking me in time with his fingers in my ass. We find our rhythm, with me pushing back as I nip and suck at Thorn's skin who is patiently waiting, and when Drax pulls out of my pussy, I bite down hard, punishing Thorn. I need to be filled, and when he pulls his fingers from my ass, I nearly scream in frustration.

"Fuck me," I demand harshly, and I feel his cock prodding at my ass.

"Let me in babe," he whispers and I push back, letting him slip into me. He stills before pulling out and slipping in deeper, working through my tight muscles with patience, each thrust getting him further until he is balls deep in my ass, and then he drops a soft kiss on the middle of my back in thanks as Thorn lifts me slightly. Drax helps him until he is at my pussy, his cock thrusting inside roughly, his length and width stretching me to the point of pain, and I writhe between them.

They wait until I stop and then Drax pulls out before thrusting back in, and Thorn copies him. They settle into a maddening rhythm, filling me again and again. I feel full with them, my pussy and ass stretching in the most delicious way, and I have to bite down on Thorn again to muffle my moans.

"Fuck, this is hot, watching you take both of us," Drax whispers against my sweaty back, his hands gripping my hips and slamming me back into him. Thorn thrusts up, arching off the bed with the power of his movements, and I break my hold on his skin, a moan slipping free when he bumps my cervix.

Together they fuck me hard, each thrust harder than the last, moving faster until I am just held between them, unable to move or speak until finally, it all gets to be too much and I explode. My nails scratch into Thorn's chest as I bite down to muffle my scream.

Drax follows, biting down on my side to stifle his yell as he stiffens against my ass and comes. Thorn isn't far behind, thrusting twice more before he stills and grunts, filling me too. I flop back onto Thorn's chest, completely boneless, and Drax kisses my back again before pulling from my ass. I feel his weight lift from the bed, but don't bother to look until he comes back and cleans me up before heading back to the bathroom and then joining us on the bed a couple of minutes later. I lift from Thorn, letting his cock slip free, and snuggle into his side, as Drax curls around my back.

"See? Bet you're tired now," Thorn teases, and I smack his stomach lightly.

He's right though, I can already feel my eyes closing. With a smile on my face, I go back to the waiting darkness, ready for whatever tomorrow might bring.

Chapter Twenty-Six

A Politician's Game

The table is filled with men and Regina when we are brought into the room. It's so early, sunlight barely streams through the glass windows, however, I had been awake early, ready to leave this place with an answer one way or another. I had been dressed, washed, and ready by sunup.

When we get there, I spot her sitting in my seat at the head of the table, so I grab another chair and pull it to the other end and sit. She narrows her eyes on me, but forces a smile as my men spread out around me and her guards behind her. The divide is clear in the room, the tension high as we all wait for the other to make a move and shatter the silence.

"We have discussed your terms," she begins, sipping from a mug as she watches me across the table.

I wait, not bothering to speak, and her eyes twitch in displeasure. "As you might have seen, we have been undergoing an attack from inside our own walls, this, plus the fact that I have been persuaded we were in the wrong to come into your lands...we have agreed to your terms," she states.

"Good, took you long enough," I taunt, but inside I sigh, thank fuck. I was starting to get worried, maybe this plan will work after all. "You will bring the men responsible for my men's torture?" I confirm, and she inclines her head, but I spot the harsh grip she has on the mug. I'm betting she was outvoted by this because she doesn't seem like the type to want to give in, even when faced with odds she couldn't win against. "They are being brought down to the lobby as we speak. We thought you might want an audience, to show what the people outside these walls are capable of."

Fuck, she has managed to twist it. It will make us look like the ones who are in the wrong. She smiles, knowing I have come to that conclusion, and it's my turn to grind my teeth. Shit, I need to think fast.

"Of course, shall we?" I inquire, bluffing, and she scowls but stands.

"Let's," she snaps, thinking she has won this round. We all follow her to the elevator, having to split in two to fit as I rack my brain, trying to think of what to do to make this better. If the people of the Cities see me executing men with no explanation, they will rally with Regina and never follow Strand. No, I have to make this look like they are the bad guys, or all of this is for nothing.

The ride down is over quickly, too quickly, and I don't have a plan. We are led across the lobby like a firing squad and out onto the steps of the building where six men are waiting on their knees, with fear in their eyes and a crowd gathered there waiting for what will happen. I spot our faces being broadcasted and the screens held across the square. Shit, I bet this was her plan and why she was waiting to tell us, she needed time to put this in place.

She steps forward, silencing the crowd with her hand in the air. I search the ranks distractedly, tuning out her speech. Major would know how to twist this, but me? I don't, who the fuck did I think I was coming here and demanding things? I'm not smart enough and now I've been played. This will cause a riot and we will be lucky to escape with our lives, and when we attack with the army and kill them, we will look like the savages she accused us of being. We got played.

"As you can see, we have come to a peace treaty with the Northern people, they have demanded these men in sacrifice, and we have agreed to save our great city—" Motherfucker.

I look to Maxen for help, but he is frowning, his eyes filled with the same conclusion I have come to. Just then, during Regina's speech, I spot movement in the crowd. People are being pushed out of the way as a man races towards us. I scan his face for hints of familiarity but find none. Who is he? I watch him come, looking towards the guards, but they are distracted trying to contain the outcry from the amassed people with the announcement of the executions to take place, and don't see him coming.

He changes direction now, his eyes hard and face determined, heading straight for a still speaking Regina. Fuck, it's an assassin. I move without thinking, leaping at him as he breaks from the crowd. People scream, seeing the bomb strapped to his chest as he points at Regina, his voice booming, "You will pay for—"

I tackle him to the ground and squeeze my eyes shut, expecting an explosion at any minute to blow me sky high. When nothing happens, I open my eyes and look down to see him knocked out, his hand holding what looks like a trigger for the device. I kick it away and search him for weapons as my men surround me, checking for injuries before helping me up. Guards are surrounding Regina, aiming into the crowd, it's a mess. They are turning on her own people.

That's when it hits me.

Standing up, I scan the dazed and scared Cities people, all fighting to get away, some not understanding why they are panicking, but fighting them all the same.

I grab the discarded mic and step into the camera. "People of the Cities!" I yell, and the crowd looks my way, slowly stilling, their scream tapering off as they realise the threat is neutralized. "I have saved your leader from death as she hid behind her people, leaving you to certain death. I feel you can accept this is bad leadership, as is the speech she just gave. It was not the truth. These men kneeling on these steps aren't good men, they hurt my family. They tortured those I love, tortured them for information about me and my people beyond these walls. They stole them from me and hurt them, yet I showed no violence when I came here with an extended hand of peace. Not ten minutes ago, your leaders and I agreed on peace, but now I see that was all for show. Another manipulation. Yes, I asked for these men's death, I won't lie, but look at the men on the steps by my side."

I search the crowd, seeing them start to listen to me, and I fucking hope this is working, because I am bullshitting out of my ears at this point. "You know them, they are one of you, they grew up here, on these streets, and fought to protect you. They were sent north, into my lands to spy on us, and report back so your guards could march on the North, because the truth is your Cities will not last. Your food is running out, you know this, you've seen the cullings, yet your rich stand here on these steps well-fed and rested. How can this be right?" I stop then, looking around at the faces before me. "Our peace still stands, we will leave the Cities today and go home with no inten- tion of attacking these walls. What comes after is up to you. It is not too late to save your people—all your people, not just those gathered in this square, but all three Cities. Look inside and look deep, are massacres to save the few the way to go? Or is there a leader more suited here? I will leave you with that and these men on the steps, men I am betting have hurt more than just the ones I love. Today, these savages leave you with options to save your future. We leave you with a decision to make, now, it is up to you." With that, I drop the mic, looking over at Regina.

"I accept your terms, we are leaving now. Don't ever come north or you will die." I look at my men and they step closer as we leave the steps. Madness is breaking out in the square, public outcry, but over it I hear Regina's voice.

"You made a mistake here!" she yells, but I ignore her, not looking back. No, I didn't make a mistake, I lit the match that will burn this whole place down. I fanned the flames of war.

We slip through the crowd, my men staying behind me as we break out into the streets, which are filled with confused people. No one knows what is happening, but I can almost feel the change in the air. Even if they don't ever change, this confusion gives us enough time to escape the Cities and get a head start on them. No doubt Regina is amassing her guards now to send them after us, probably has been for days, but with that final insult in front of her people, she will have to. I know she will.

When we reach almost empty streets leading to the gate, a man slips from the shadows, slow clapping with a grin, and I laugh when I see him—Dray. "Good going, soulmate," he purrs, and I wink. "Seems you have found your lost boys. I think that's our cue to exit?" he inquires, nodding when we hear horns blaring near the city center and an announcement declaring citywide martial law.

"Seems like you had fun with your bombs," I comment, and laugh as he falls into step next to me as we head to the gate up ahead, our steps light and quick.

"Oh, it was magnificent, you should have been there. We should conquer cities more often, wife." I snort and look around, checking for guards, but it's quiet here, and when we reach the gate the guards there open it with no issue. We leave before they change their minds, the gears cranking as it slams shut with a resounding bang behind us, holding in the chaos we created there. My bike is still waiting there, but so are five others. I don't ask, but I know Dray is responsible when he heads over.

"Time to lead the lambs to slaughter. Are they ready?" he asks, swinging on one and looking at me, his eyes blazing with the heat of battle.

"Let's do it," I declare, striding to my bike and slipping on, grinning when I spot my weapons there.

He winks at me. "Broke in and got them for you."

"Crazy bastard," I mutter, and he laughs as we start up our bikes. I meet the eyes of all my other men and they nod, we are ready. It's time.

CHAPTER TWENTY-SEVEN

LONG LIVE OUR FUCKING QUEEN

We wait on the sand dunes just across from the Cities, my heart pounding. What if I'm wrong? What if she stays to calm the Cities? What if she doesn't come—

Just then, the gate opens, and rows upon rows of cars and trucks face us, some mounted with guns. Okay, I was right, the sight of that much artillery sends shivers of fear down my spine. The loss of life will be huge, but I can't think about that now. It's too late, all I can do is to fight with everything in me. Turning back to face the stretch of road, I rev my bike as I hear the trucks starting and heading towards us. Pulling up my bandanna, I gun it, riding hard and fast across the dunes, letting them chase us. Maxen already rode ahead to let them know we are coming and have them ready. So much is relying on timing.

Not every choice you make will be right, I learned that early on, but it's how you handle the consequences and outcomes that make you a leader.

Major's words from his letter float in my mind as I ride. I might not have made the right decision. Was there ever one, or do we always just make a choice and deal with the aftermath as best as we can? Who's to say fate plays a part? Humans have choice and I made mine. Now, all I can do is deal with the consequences, like the leader he told me to be.

Nerves race through me as I think through everything that led up to this point, and I question whether the people I am depending on will be there waiting.

Trust in those around you to help, but when it comes down to it, trust yourself.

I trust them, I hope they trust me, because it's time to put it to the test. I hear the roar of engines shredding sand, coming closer as I twist and turn down the roads, heading to the long stretch of sand between The Rim and the Cities where my armies await. I see the flash of metal before I spot them all.

Bikes, trucks, and even a fucking tanker wait in the distance. My army, ready to face down the Cities with me leading. I crank the engine, pushing it to the limit as the trucks behind us start firing, the bullets hitting the sand. I make sure to zigzag, feeling adrenaline firing through me and pushing all my worries aside. I eat up the distance, my bike faster than their trucks, and when I reach my front line I spin around and face the oncoming trucks on the horizon. Bern, Henry, and Erik ride to my side.

"Everything is ready, Ma Queen. We are all here," my giant of a general calls.

"Ready to kill them," Henry agrees.

"On your command, Queen." Erik nods, his face covered in a grin.

I search my armies, spotting Nan on the front line with Reeves. Nan is in a side car of his bike holding her shotgun, swearing at the oncoming trucks. Priest and his men are to the left, all armed and silent, waiting to meet their God. To my right are the Seekers, wearing all dark clothing and weapons, and behind me are chanting and stomping Berserkers, all giving a war cry as they wait for me. The sands vibrate with the sounds of the engines and shooting bullets, but my army only roars louder as fear does not even enter their minds. As I look back once more, I meet Pipers gaze, she is next to Archel who looks fierce and ready to face down death itself. She nods at me with a grin on her face, and I spot the words "fuck you" painted on her chest and stomach, almost making me laugh. Behind her is a group of people I have never seen. They don't look like warriors, but each one is ready and waiting to fight. More than I could imagine.

Bullets tear through the air as the trucks bear down. "Worth."

My name makes me turn to face the front, sit back down on my bike, and steady my breathing.

"With you until the end, *Mi Alma*," floats to me. "Let's kick some ass!" Drax yells.

"I wonder who will scream first, soulmate."

Sucking in a breath, I find my center, Major's words ringing through my head. His ghost haunts me now, not Ivar's.

I know you aren't alone.

He's right, I'm not, I never have been, even in my darkest times, and now those people are gathered here to fight and die for me. Never alone, thanks to Major.

"It's time to fight!" I scream. "For the North!" I yell, and fire up my engine.

"Long live our fucking queen!" they shout back, their engines starting behind me.

As guns fire, cars crash, and bikes explode, the war begins. I scream into the face of destruction. We will win or die trying. Kicking up sand behind me, I race towards the threat. Who knew a slave would end up leading the war cry to save our lands? Major is my guess. Maybe he was right, maybe I always did have a destiny, and maybe this is it. Or just fucking maybe we make our own way in life —no destiny or fate, just stumbling along the way, and eventually we find some people to ride it out with. These are my people, it's time we showed the world you don't mess with us.

The end is here for all of us. Long live our fucking queen. Long live the North.

Acknowledgments

I couldn't have done this book without the continued support of my beta readers, so for those of you who put up with my teasing, questions about sex scenes and all the other times I bombarded you, thank you from the bottom of my heart.

To my girls, without you I would be a mess rocking back and forth in the corner, thank you for keeping me sane.

To Sue, yes I wrote that scene for you.

To Jess's husband, I added in as much bloodshed as I could, feel free to skip the sex scenes.

About K.A. Knight

K.A Knight is an USA Today bestselling indie author trying to get all of the stories and characters out of her head, writing the monsters that you love to hate. She loves reading and devours every book she can get her hands on, and she also has a worrying caffeine addiction.

She leads her double life in a sleepy English town, where she spends her days writing like a crazy person.

Read more at K.A Knight's website or join her Facebook Reader Group.
Sign up for exclusive content and my newsletter here
http://eepurl.com/drLLoj

Also by K.A. Knight

THEIR CHAMPION SERIES *Dystopian RH*

The Wasteland

The Summit

The Cities

The Nations

Their Champion Coloring Book

Their Champion - the omnibus

The Forgotten

The Lost

The Damned

Their Champion Companion - the omnibus

DAWNBREAKER SERIES *SCI FI RH*

Voyage to Ayama

Dreaming of Ayama

THE LOST COVEN SERIES *PNR RH*

Aurora's Coven

Aurora's Betrayal

HER MONSTERS SERIES *PNR RH*

Rage

Hate

Book 3 *coming soon..*

Monstrous Lies

Monstrous Truths

Monstrous Ends

DEN OF VIPERS UNIVERSE STANDALONES

Scarlett Limerence *CONTEMPORARY*

Nadia's Salvation *CONTEMPORARY*

Alena's Revenge *CONTEMPORARY*

Den of Vipers *CONTEMPORARY RH*

Gangsters and Guns (Co-Write with Loxley Savage) *CONTEMPORARY RH*

STANDALONES

The Standby *CONTEMPORARY*

Diver's Heart *CONTEMPORARY RH*

Crown of Stars *SCI FI RH*

AUDIOBOOKS

The Wasteland

The Summit

Rage

Hate

Den of Vipers (*From Podium Audio*)

Gangsters and Guns (*From Podium Audio*)

Daddy's Angel (*From Podium Audio*)

Stepbrothers' Darling (*From Podium Audio*)

Blade of Iris (*From Podium Audio*)

Deadly Affair (*From Podium Audio*)

Deadly Match (*From Podium Audio*)

Deadly Encounter (*From Podium Audio*)

Stolen Trophy (*From Podium Audio*)

Crown of Stars (*From Podium Audio*)

Monstrous Lies (*From Podium Audio*)

Monstrous Truth (*From Podium Audio*)

Monstrous Ends (*From Podium Audio*)

Court of Nightmares (*From Podium Audio*)

Unstoppable (*From Podium Audio*)

Unbreakable (*From Podium Audio*)

Fractured Shadows (*From Podium Audio*)

SHARED WORLD PROJECTS

Blade of Iris - Mafia Wars *CONTEMPORARY RH*

CO-AUTHOR PROJECTS - *Erin O'Kane*

HER FREAKS SERIES *PNR Dystopian RH*

Circus Save Me

Taming The Ringmaster

Walking the Tightrope

Her Freaks Series - the omnibus

STANDALONES

The Hero Complex *PNR RH*

Dark Temptations *Collection of Short Stories, ft. One Night Only & Circus Saves Christmas*

THE WILD BOYS SERIES *CONTEMPORARY RH*

The Wild Interview

The Wild Tour

The Wild Finale

The Wild Boys - the omnibus

CO-AUTHOR PROJECTS - *Ivy Fox*

Deadly Love Series *CONTEMPORARY*

Deadly Affair

Deadly Match

Deadly Encounter

CO-AUTHOR PROJECTS - *Kendra Moreno*

STANDALONES

Stolen Trophy *CONTEMPORARY RH*

Fractured Shadows *PNR RH*

Burn Me *PNR*

CO-AUTHOR PROJECTS - *Loxley Savage*

THE FORSAKEN SERIES *SCI FI RH*

Capturing Carmen

Stealing Shiloh

Harboring Harlow

STANDALONES

Gangsters and Guns *CONTEMPORARY*, IN DEN OF VIPERS' UNIVERSE

OTHER CO-WRITES

Shipwreck Souls (*with Kendra Moreno & Poppy Woods*)

The Horror Emporium (*with Kendra Moreno & Poppy Woods*)

Find an error?

Please email this information to thenuttyformatter1@gmail.com:

- *the author name*
- *title of the book*
- *screenshot of the error*
- *suggested correction*